Father of the Rain

Also by Lily King

The Pleasing Hour
The English Teacher

Father of the Rain

Lily King

ATLANTIC MONTHLY PRESS
New York

My deepest gratitude to my husband and very first reader, Tyler Clements, and to Susan
Conley, Sara Corbett, Caitlin Gutheil, Anja Hanson, Debra Spark, Liza Bakewell, Wendy Weil,
Deb Seager, Morgan Entrekin, Eric Price, Jessica Monahan, Lisa King, Apple King,
and my mother; and to my beloved daughters, who put up with all this.
A special, devotional thank you to my extraordinary editor, Elisabeth Schmitz.

Published simultaneously in Canada
Printed in the United States of America

FIRST EDITION

ISBN-13: 978-0-8021-1949-0

Atlantic Monthly Press
an imprint of Grove/Atlantic, Inc.
841 Broadway
New York, NY 10003

Distributed by Publishers Group West

www.groveatlantic.com

10 11 12 13   10 9 8 7 6 5 4 3 2 1

For Lisa and Apple

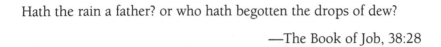

Hath the rain a father? or who hath begotten the drops of dew?

—The Book of Job, 38:28

Father of the Rain

I

1

My father is singing.

High above Cayuga's waters, there's an awful smell.
Some say it's Cayuga's waters, some say it's Cornell.

He always sings in the car. He has a low voice scraped out by cigarettes and all the yelling he does. His big pointy Adam's apple bobs up and down, turning the tanned skin white wherever it moves.

He reaches over to the puppy in my lap. "You's a good little rascal. Yes you is," he says in his dog voice, a happy, hopeful voice he doesn't use much on people.

The puppy was a surprise for my eleventh birthday, which was yesterday. I chose the ugliest one in the shop. My father and the owner tried to tempt me with the full-breed Newfoundlands, scooping up the silky black sacks of fur and pressing their big heavy heads against my cheek. But I held fast. A dog like that would make leaving even harder. I pushed them away and pointed to the twenty-five dollar wire-haired mutt that had been in the corner cage since winter.

My father dropped the last Newfoundland back in its bed of shavings. "Well, it's her birthday," he said slowly, with all the bitterness of a boy whose birthday it was not.

He didn't speak to me again until we got into the car. Then, before he started the engine, he touched the dog for the first time, pressing its ungainly ears flat to its head. "I'm not saying you's not ugly because you *is* ugly. But you's a keeper.

"From the halls of Montezuma," he sings out to the granite boulders that line the highway home, "to the shores of Tripoli!"

We have both forgotten about Project Genesis. The blue van is in our driveway, blocking my father's path into the garage.

"Jesus, Mary, and Joseph," he says in his fake crying voice, banging his forehead on the steering wheel. "Why me?" He turns slightly to make sure I'm laughing, then moans again. "Why me?"

We hear them before we see them, shrieks and thuds and slaps, a girl hollering "William! William!" over and over, nearly all of them screaming, "Watch me! Watch this!"

"I's you new neighba," my father says to me, but not in his happy dog voice.

I carry the puppy and my father follows with the bed, bowls, and food. My pool is unrecognizable. There are choppy waves, like way out on the ocean, with whitecaps. The cement squares along its edge, which are usually hot and dry and sizzle when you lay your wet stomach on them, are soaked from all the water washing over the sides.

It's my pool because my father had it built for me. On the morning of my fifth birthday he took me to our club to go swimming. Just as I put my feet on the first wide step of the shallow end and looked out toward the dark deep end and the thick blue and red lines painted on the bottom, the lifeguard hollered from his perch that there were still fifteen minutes left of adult swim. My father, who'd belonged to the club for twenty years, who ran and won all the tennis tournaments, explained that it was his daughter's birthday.

The boy, Thomas Novak, shook his head. "I'm sorry, Mr. Amory," he called down. "She'll have to wait fifteen minutes like everyone else."

My father laughed his you're a moron laugh. "But there's no one in the pool!"

"I'm sorry. It's the rules."

"You know what?" my father said, his neck blotching purple, "I'm going home and building my own pool."

He spent that afternoon on the telephone, yellow pages and a pad of paper on his lap, talking to contractors and writing down numbers. As I lay in bed that night, I could hear him in the den with my mother. "It's the rules," he mimicked in a baby voice, saying over and over that a kid like that would never be allowed through the club's gates if he didn't work there, imitating his mother's "Hiya" down at the drugstore where she worked. In the next few weeks, trees were sawed down and a huge hole dug, cemented, painted, and filled with water. A little house went up beside it with changing rooms, a machine room, and a bathroom with a sign my father hung on the door that read WE DON'T SWIM IN YOUR TOILET—PLEASE DON'T PEE IN OUR POOL.

My mother, in a pink shift and big sunglasses, waves me over to where she's sitting on the grass with her friend Bob Wuzzy, who runs Project Genesis. But I hold up the puppy and keep moving toward the house. I'm angry at her. Because of her I can't have a Newfoundland.

"Fuzzy Wuzzy was a bear," my father says as he sets down his load on the kitchen counter. "Fuzzy Wuzzy had no hair." He looks out the window at the pool. "Fuzzy Wuzzy wasn't fuzzy, was he?"

My father hates all my mother's friends.

Charlie, Ajax, and Elsie smell the new dog immediately. They circle around us, tails thwapping, and my father shoos them out into the dining room and shuts the door. Then he hurries across the kitchen in a playful goose step to the living room door and shuts that just before the dogs have made the loop around. They scratch and whine, then settle against the other side of the door. I put the puppy down on the linoleum. He scrabbles then bolts to a small place between the refrigerator and the wall. It's a warm spot. I used to hide there and play Harriet the Spy when I could fit. His fur sticks out like quills and his skin is rippling in fear.

"Poor little fellow." My father squats beside the fridge, his long legs rising up on either side of him like a frog's, his knees sharp and bony through his khakis. "It's okay, little guy. It's okay." He turns to me. "What should we call him?"

The shaking dog in the corner makes what I agreed to with my mother real in a way nothing else has. Gone, I think. Call him Gone.

Three days ago my mother told me she was going to go live with my grandparents in New Hampshire for the summer. We were standing in our nightgowns in her bathroom. My father had just left for work. Her face was shiny from Moondrops, the lotion she put on every morning and night. "I'd like you to come with me," she said.

"But what about sailing classes and art camp?" I was signed up for all sorts of things that began next week.

"You can take sailing lessons there. They live on a lake."

"But not with Mallory and Patrick."

She pressed her lips together, and her eyes, which were brown and round and nothing like my father's yellow-green slits, brimmed with tears, and I said yes, I'd go with her.

My father reaches in and pulls the puppy out. "We'll wait and see what you's like before we gives you a name. How's that?" The puppy burrows between his neck and shoulder, licking and sniffing, and my father laughs his high-pitched being-tickled laugh and I wish he knew everything that was going to happen.

I set up the bed by the door and the two bowls beside it. I fill one bowl with water and leave the other empty because my father feeds all the dogs at the same time, five o'clock, just before his first drink.

I go upstairs and get on a bathing suit. From my brother's window I see my mother and Bob Wuzzy, in chairs now, sipping iced tea with fat lemon rounds and stalks of mint shoved in the glasses, and the kids splashing, pushing, dunking—the kind of play my mother doesn't normally allow in the pool. Some are doing crazy jumps off the diving board, not cannonballs or jackknives but wild spazzy poses and then freezing midair just before they fall, like in the cartoons when someone runs off a cliff and keeps moving until he looks down. The older kids do this over and over, tell these jokes with their bodies to the others down below, who are laughing so hard it looks like they're drowning. When they get out of the pool and run back to the diving board, the water shimmers on their skin, which looks so smooth, like it's been polished with lemon Pledge. None of them are close to being "black." They are all different shades of brown. I wonder if they hate being called the wrong color. I noticed this last year, too. "They like being called black," my father told me in a Fat Albert accent. "Don't you start callin' 'em brown. Brown's down. Black's where it's at."

The grass feels good on my feet, thick and scratchy. I put my towel on the chair beside my mother.

"You heard Sonia's group lost its funding," Bob was saying. I don't know if Bob Wuzzy is white or black. He has no hair, not a single strand, and caramel-colored skin. When I asked my mother she asked me why it mattered, and when I asked my father he said if he wasn't black he should be.

"No," my mother says gravely, "I didn't."

"Kevin must have pulled the plug."

"Jackass," my mother says; then, brightening up, "How's Maria Tendillo?" She pronounces the name with a good accent that my father makes fun of sometimes.

"Released last Friday. No charges."

"Gary's the best." My mother smiles. Then she lifts her face to mine.

"Hello, Mr. Wuzzy," I say, and put out my hand.

He stands and shakes it. His hand is cold and damp from the iced tea. "How are you, Daley?"

"Fine, thank you."

They exchange a look about my manners and my mother is pleased. "Hop in, honey," she says.

This morning she told me I was old enough now to host Project Genesis with her, that all the kids would be roughly my age and I could be an envoy to new lands and begin to heal the wounds. I had no idea what she was talking about. Finally she said I should just be nice and make them feel welcome and included.

"How can I make them feel included when there is only one of me and so many of them?"

I knew she didn't like that answer, but because she was worried I'd tell my father we were leaving, she asked me softly if I could just promise to swim with them.

I stand on the first step, my feet pale and magnified by the water. I feel my mother willing me to behave differently, but I can't. I can't leap into the fray like that. It isn't in my nature to assume people want me around. All I can do is watch with a pleasant expression on my face. The older kids are still twisting off the diving board. The younger ones are here in the shallow end, treading water more than swimming, their faces flush to the surface like lily pads. In the corner two girls are having underwater conversations. A boy in a maroon bathing suit slithers through them and they both come up screaming at him, even though he is underwater again and can't hear. There are four boys and three girls, all different sizes, and I wonder if some of them are siblings. They seem like it, the way they yell at each other. But no one gets mad or ends up crying like I always do.

I move slowly from one step to the next, then walk out on tippy toes. They aren't looking at me, but they all pull away as I approach. At the slope to the deep end, my feet slip and I go under. It's cool and quiet below until a body drops in, a sack of bubbles. Normally when I look up from the bottom of the pool, the surface is only slightly buckled, like the windowpanes in the attic, but now it's a white froth. The boy in the maroon bathing suit passes right above me. His toes brush through my hair and he screams.

When I surface, the littlest boy pushes himself toward me. The others watch him.

"This your pool?" he asks. The water lies in crystals in his hair.

"Yes."

"You swim in it every day?"

"When it's warm out."

"But it's heated, right?" He swings his arms around fast, making his fingers hop along the surface.

"Right."

"I'd swim in it every day," he says. "Even if it was twenty below. I'd get in in the morning and not get out till night."

"You'd have to eat or you'd die."

"Then I'd die in this pool. It's the perfect place to die."

I decide not to tell him about Mrs. Walsh, who did. She had a heart attack. "Is that Mrs. Walsh floating in the pool?" my father likes to say sometimes when I've left a raft in the water. My mother doesn't think it's funny.

This leaves a pause in the conversation and the boy paddles away. I feel bad and relieved at the same time.

My mother's smile fades as she realizes I'm getting out. Bob is telling her about some fundraiser and she can't interrupt to prod me back in. After I dry off a little, I cross the lawn and run up the steps.

My father is in the den, watching the Red Sox and smoking a cigarette. I sit next to him in my wet bathing suit. He doesn't care about the possibility of the slipcover colors bleeding. At the commercial he says, "You didn't enjoy your swim?"

"I got cold."

He snorts. "The pool's probably over ninety with all the pee they're putting into it."

"They're not peeing in it."

I wait for him to say I sound just like my mother, but instead he puts his warm hand on my leg. "I promise this will never happen again, little elf. I'm going to put a stop to it."

It will stop without you having to do a thing, I think.

They only come a few times a summer. On other weekends they go to other people's pools or private beaches in other towns. "Project Genesis," my brother said at the beginning of the summer, on one of the few days he was home between boarding school and his summer plans, whatever they are, making his voice deep and serious like a TV announcer. "In the beginning there was blue chlorinated water in backyards. There were trampolines and Mercedes and generous housewives in Lilly Pulitzer dresses willing to share a little, just a little." My mother giggled. My father scowled. He can't amuse her with his teasing the way my brother can.

They swim for hours, until Bob calls them all out and makes them dry off and change in the poolhouse. He and my mother get the charcoal lit in the bottom of the grill and, once the coals are hot enough, put fifteen patties on the rack. The kids explore the yard, back and front, running from the space trolley to the swing set to the low-limbed apple tree. They dare to do things I don't, like hang upside down on the trolley as it whizzes from one tree to the other, crawl on hands and knees across the single narrow tube on the top of the swing set, and flip off the stone wall around my mother's rose garden.

I watch them from the kitchen window.

"Bunch of monkeys," my father says, mixing a drink at the bar.

They have so much energy. They make me feel like I've been living on one lung. The littlest girl skins her knee on one of the huge rocks that heaves up through the grass in our yard and the two oldest take turns jogging her in their arms, planting kisses in her hair and stroking away her tears. She clings to them for a long time and they let her.

"Daley." My mother stands at the screen door. "Please come out and eat with the rest of us."

"Oh, yes," my father says. "Do go eat with the fairy and his little friends."

My mother acts like no one has spoken. On the steps, away from him, she puts her arm around me. She always smells like flowers. "I know it's hard, but try not to be so remote. This is important, honey," she whispers.

Normally I eat dinner with Nora, but she's in Ireland for two weeks visiting cousins. She goes every summer and I never like it. The rest of the year she lives with us except on Sundays when, after church, she drives over to Lynn, where her sister lives, and spends the night with her. "Lynn, Lynn, the city of sin. You never come out the way you went in," my father often says when she drives away, but never to her face. She is a serious Catholic and she wouldn't like it. I've gone with her many times to see her sister in Lynn on Sunday nights. They eat cutlets and play hearts and go to bed early. There's no sinning for them in Lynn. There's a picture on Nora's bureau in our house of her and my father on some rocks near the ocean. She's eighteen and my father is one. He's holding onto her hand with both of his. His mother hired Nora for a summer in Maine, but she ended up going to Boston with them and staying for nine years, until my father went to boarding school. When my brother, Garvey, was born, she was working for another family somewhere in Pennsylvania, but she was free when I came along. After dinner Nora and I watch TV on her bed, *Mannix* and *Hawaii Five-0*, both of us in our bathrobes. She puts me to bed and we always say "Now I Lay Me" and the Lord's Prayer, though at her church it has a different ending. My mother says that after we leave, Nora will stay on to take care of my father, who can't boil an egg.

My parents didn't name my brother Garvey. They named him Gardiner, after my father, and he was Gardiner all my life until he went to boarding school and came back Garvey. My mother tried to stop it, but he is Garvey now. At his graduation a few weeks ago even the headmaster called him Garvey.

We sit in a jagged circle in the grass. My mother's dress is too short for her to sit Indian-style so she folds her legs off to one side, which tilts her toward Bob Wuzzy. I'm aware of how it will look to my father in the kitchen window, sipping his drink.

Bob makes us all go around and say our names, but after that we're silent. Even the two grown-ups seem unable to keep up a conversation. We eat our burgers, then Bob says, "Who wants to play sardines?" and all of them cry out, "Me!" I know my father would rather I come in and sit with him, but my mother's eyes are locked on mine.

Bob tells us we can only hide in the yard as defined by the back and front driveways, and not inside any of the buildings on the property. He makes it sound like a small college campus. Then he chooses a girl named Devon to hide first. The rest of us count aloud as fast as we can to fifty, omitting vowels and syllables, like racing down stairs three at a time. Then we scatter, to find Devon without anyone else seeing. I'm sure I'll get to her first, since I know the terrain and all the good hiding places. I go first to the rhododendrons in front, then to the small empty fountain in the rose garden. After that I check behind the granite outcropping near the street. Soon everyone else is missing, too, except the little boy named Joe, my friend from the pool.

"Let's check over there," I call to him, pointing toward the small pines beyond the pool, but Joe runs off in the opposite direction.

As I pass the back porch, I hear a crinkling sound. They're all in a tight cluster beneath the back steps, in a small, dark, spidery space that has always scared me. As I draw closer, the buzz of their chatter is so loud I wonder how I could have passed by twice without having heard them. I bend over and squeeze in. To fit all the way, I have to press up against several bodies. We're all hot and our skin sticks. All their buzzing stops. No one says a thing. It seems to me that they've all stopped breathing. I try to think of something to say, something goofy the way Patrick can, that will make us all giggle. Out in the twilight of the yard little Joe begins to cry, and Bob Wuzzy tells us to come out.

The boy who found Devon first goes off to hide, and the rest run off to count. I slip back up the porch steps.

My father is eating a minute steak with A-1 sauce slathered all over it. His forehead and his nose are covered in sweat, the way they always are when he eats dinner. He's staring straight ahead and I can't tell if he knows I'm there.

"You's a good kid, you know that, elf?" His words are skating slightly sideways.

When he's done with dinner, he makes another drink. He gives me two tiny, vinegary onions from the bottle. In four days I won't live here with him. When we come back to Ashing in the fall, my mother says, she and I will live in an apartment and I'll only come up here on weekends.

The game outside has ended and no sounds come through the screen door. Then the pool lights go on, the little mushroom-shaped lamps in the grass and the big underwater bulb beneath the diving board. Bodies stream out of the poolhouse and crash into the water. My father's body goes rigid at the sound.

He finishes his martini, jiggles the ice as he drinks to drain it of every drop. Then he sets the glass down on the counter. "I've got an idea," he says.

I don't say no to my father's ideas, just as I don't say no to my mother's. If my father had asked me to go away with him, I would have. My brother says no all the time when he's home, and that just gets everyone all riled up.

We take off our clothes on the back porch. The puppy is with us, jumping around our ankles, sensing something different.

"*Un, deux, trois,*" my father says. He knows French from fishing in Quebec. "Go!"

He heads straight for the pool, his long tennis legs springing across the grass he keeps shorn and stiff, a bulb of muscle at the back of each calf, his thighs thin and taut, his bum high and flat and stark white in the dark, and his long arms flashing fast as he moves, the right stronger than the left, with an Ace bandage at the wrist. He moves in a way no one else in my family does, graceful as water. When he reaches the pool, he begins to grunt. He veers right, away from the corner where my mother and Bob Wuzzy sit with their sodas, and runs along the patch of grass between the length of the pool and the garden's stone wall.

A boy floating on my red raft sees us first.

"Streakers!" he yells.

My father leaps over the short toadstool lights, one at a time, his grunts getting louder, his arms beginning to buckle toward his body, his spine bending forward. He takes the turn around the deep end, his body all sinew and strength, flecked with silver veins and tendons, glowing in the pale green pool reflection.

All the kids are yelling now, hooting and slapping the water, laughing so hard they have to swim over to the edge and hang on.

He saves my mother's spot in the corner for last. He comes at her now head-on, past the poolhouse, right toward her seat in the chaise longue, his balls whipping from side to side, the penis boylike, small as a mouse. He curls his arms up all the way now, scratches at his armpits, and says, "*Ooooo-ooooo-ooooo*" right in her face, and then is gone.

My mother, for a moment, looks like she's been tossed out of a plane. Then she reassembles a smile for Bob, who, for the children's sake, is pretending it's an odd but innocent prank. But when she sees me, something snaps. She lunges out of her chair to grab me, but I'm fast and slippery without clothes. I feel the thick, tough grass between my toes and the wet summer night air moving through the hair on my arms and through my hairless crotch. I'm boylike, too, with tight buds on my chest, and this night I'm nearly as lithe and quick and nimble as my father. Both my lungs are pumping hard. I don't want to stop running, stop the burning of my stomach muscles and the ache in my throat, stop the stars from seeing my bare, newly eleven-year-old body in the grass, fast and graceful as a deer through the woods.

On the porch we stand laughing and panting together with our clothes at our feet and our puppy spinning in joyful circles and my father grinning his biggest grin and looking at me like he loves me, truly loves me, more than anyone else he's ever loved in his life.

2

The day before my mother and I leave Ashing, I ride my bike down to Baker's Cove. There isn't much of a beach, and it's smelly at low tide, so we usually have the place to ourselves. If you climb way out around on the rocks, no one can see you from the road.

Mallory's got her mother's Larks and I've got my father's L&Ms and Gina's got her father's Marlboros. Patrick says his mother ran out, and Neal says neither of his parents smoke. No one believes him. This is the first time Neal Caffrey's come to the cove with us. I'm not sure who called him.

"You're just scared to steal," Teddy says, pulling out a silver box full of menthols.

"My father has asthma," Neal says. He takes one of the Salems and shuts the box. "Who's G.E.R.?"

We all look at the swirled initials cut into the silver. Teddy's last name is Shipley.

He shrugs. "Who cares?" He takes off his shoe. "Are we going to play or what?"

"I want to finish my cig," Mallory says. She looks exactly like her mother when she smokes, her free hand tucked under the other arm which is bent up in a V, the cigarette never more than a few inches from her mouth.

The boys only ever want to kiss her, so they wait.

The air is thick and hot, but every now and then a cool gust comes off the water. You can see it coming, wrinkling the surface from far away as if it were a huge dark wing. Afterwards everything goes light and flat again. Neal's curls have been blown around. He's the closest thing I've ever had to a crush and my heart is thrumming a little faster than normal. I can't look at Patrick because I know he knows. He's like that.

"Who wants to go first?" Teddy asks.

"Me." Mallory scrapes her cigarette out against the rock and pulls her hair into a ponytail, all business.

She spins Teddy's topsider. When it stops, the toe points at me and everyone laughs. She spins again. It points to the space between Patrick and Gina.

"If it's between people then you can choose anyone," Teddy says.

"Patrick," she says, and Patrick rolls his eyes. He always pretends he hates to be kissed.

They lean in toward each other and their lips meet for a quick peck. Mallory says she likes to pick Patrick because his lips are nice and dry.

It goes clockwise from Mallory. Neal is next. He spins the old crusted topsider with two hands. It wobbles to a stop, the toe pointing undeniably at me.

He stands all the way up, walks around the outside of the circle to me, takes my hand, pulls me up, and kisses me. It's a warm kiss, not quite as quick as Mallory and Patrick's. He lets go of my hand last. I know my face has flamed up and I keep my head down until the burning stops.

Gina kisses Teddy. Teddy kisses Mallory. Then it's my turn. Neal, Neal, Neal, I beg but the shoe points at Teddy.

"Hat trick," he says, meaning he's gotten to kiss all three of us.

I get it over with fast. His lips are wet and flaky, like soggy bread.

When it's Neal's turn again, it lands between Gina and Teddy.

"Your choice," Gina says, hopeful.

"Daley."

And this time he leads me even farther away from them, nearly to the trees.

"You got a bed in the bushes?" Teddy says.

"I don't like an audience," Neal says. And to me, quietly, "You mind that I chose you again?"

I shake my head. I want to say I was hoping for it, but I can't get the words out before he kisses me, longer, opening his mouth the slightest bit.

"That was nice," he says.

"It was." Everything feels so strange, like I'm walking into someone else's life.

"Teddy says you meet here every week."

"This is only our third time."

"You coming next week?"

"I'm not sure."

"Hey, stop yacking. It's my turn," Gina says. "And Patrick has to meet his grandmother at the beach club for lunch."

They're all turned toward us now. "Try," Neal says quietly.

The game breaks up soon after that. We smoke a few more cigarettes and watch the seagulls drop mussels against the rocks and then fight over the smashed pieces.

"Can you imagine that being your life?" Patrick says.

"I'd throw myself off a cliff," Teddy says.

"But you're a seagull so it wouldn't work," Gina says. "Your wings would just start flapping. Are you taking sailing this year?"

"Yeah," Teddy says. "You?"

"All three of us." She points her thumbs to me and Mallory.

"Do you think any animal in the history of animals has ever committed suicide?" Neal asks.

"No. Their brains aren't big enough to realize how stupid their lives are," Teddy says.

I don't know if it's the cigarettes making me feel funny, but they all seem far away. If I spoke I would have to scream for them to hear me.

When we go, I let the others ride ahead, the five of them weaving around each other, taking up the whole road. I look back at the cove.

I thought I had the whole summer for cigarettes and spin the shoe. A seagull lands where Teddy left a plum pit, pecks at it twice, then lifts back up into the air. The water is higher now, creeping up the barnacled sides of the rocks. Neal looks back for me through the opening between his right arm and the handlebar of his ten-speed, casually, as if he's just looking down at his leg.

In the driveway my mother takes a wrench to my bike. I've never seen her use a tool from the garage before. She removes the two wheels easily and loads them along with the frame on top of our suitcases in the back of her convertible. She's wearing a kerchief around her hair, the way she does when she gardens. Her movements are sure and studied, like a performance. She presses down on the trunk several times, and when it finally clicks a laugh bursts out of her, though nothing is funny.

Sometimes, when no one else can come get me, a teacher drives me home from school. It feels like that now, like a teacher, a stranger, is taking me somewhere.

"Hop in, sugar," she says.

The ugly puppy is scratching at the screen door. My father will come home to his bright yellow urine and soft shit all over the newspaper I just spread across the whole kitchen. An hour ago I promised him I'd keep the puppy outside most of the day.

"You have to give him a lot of attention every time he goes to the bathroom outside," he said. He was dressed in his summer work clothes—a tan suit and a light blue tie—his hair still wet from his shower, cleanly parted on the right. "You've got to go like this: good boy, good boy, good boy"—and he rubbed my belly and back at the same time, hard and fast, practically lifting me off the ground.

I laughed and said, "Okay, okay." I held onto his arms after he stopped, dangling from him.

"You sure you can do that?"

"Yes."

His hands were wide, tanned and bony, the nails bitten down, the veins sticking out blue-green and lumpy. He said goodbye, and I kissed his hands and let go.

In my mother's car, the radio is always tuned to the news, WEEI. "Only five days after completing a tour of the Middle East," a reporter is saying, "President Nixon arrived in Brussels, Belgium, today to confer with Western European leaders before going on to Moscow on Thursday."

My mother speaks directly to the radio. "Oh, you can run, Dick. You can run, but you cannot hide."

At the four-way stop, I look down Bay Street. Mallory's house is the big white one on the corner, and Patrick's is the last driveway on the left, across from the beach club. They will both call my house today, and no one will answer.

"As the president flew across the Atlantic today, his physician told reporters that he was still suffering from an inflammation of veins in his left leg. The president has known about this ailment, known as phlebitis, for some weeks now, but ordered that the condition be kept secret, his physician said."

My mother snorts at the dashboard.

We drive through town. In the park, trailers have arrived with rides for the carnival that comes for a week every summer. Men are taking off enormous painted pieces of metal and setting them in the grass. The big round cars for the Tilt-a-Whirl, with their high backs and red leather seats, lie splayed out near what is normally first base. But once the rides, the stalls, and the vans with pizza and fried dough are set up, you can't find the old park anymore. A few little kids look on, from the bleachers, like we used to.

Downtown is small, just one street with shops on it. Neal's mother sometimes works at the yarn shop. Her car is outside it now, an orange Pinto with a small dent on the driver's door. Traffic is slow coming from the opposite direction, tourists heading toward Ruby Beach. People wave to us—Mrs. Callahan and Mrs. Buck—but my mother is gnawing on her lip and listening to the news and doesn't pay attention to them. When we reach the highway she takes my hand and guns it to seventy-five.

We stop at the Howard Johnson's for lunch. I like their fried clams because they're just the necks, no bellies. The bellies make me throw up. But there is a mountain of them. They look like fat fried worms. I eat three. My mother can't eat much of her club sandwich either. The waitress asks if we'd like to take the food home with us, and we both shake our heads no.

"We are going to be okay, you and I," my mother says, rubbing my arm.

"I know," I say, and my mother looks relieved.

Back in the car, she lets me put in an eight-track for a little while. I play John Denver singing about his grandma's feather bed. I play it over and over until she asks me to stop. It makes me happy, that song, all the kids and the dogs and the piggy in the bed together.

We cross into New Hampshire. Until she got married when she was nineteen, my mother spent every summer of her life on Lake Chigham. She says I've been there before, but I can't remember it. I can only remember my grandparents in our house for Thanksgiving or Christmas, sitting in chairs. I have no memory of them standing up.

After a while we get off the highway onto narrow then narrower roads. The trees seem to get taller. We turn onto a dirt road with a small white sign with blue paint: CHIGHAM POINT ROAD. Below it, in much smaller letters: *Private Way*.

My mother sucks in a deep breath and says, letting it out, "Here we go."

I look down the road. There are no houses, just trees—pines and maples—blocking out every drop of sun.

"Remember it now?" my mother asks.

"No."

We drive in. It's a very long road with other roads leading off it, long driveways with last names painted on wooden boards nailed to trees. Occasionally, through all the trees and bushes and undergrowth, you can see the dark shape of a house or the glint of water. We turn down one of the last driveways and park beside a brown sedan. The house, made of dark brown wood, is only a few feet from the lake, which is still and too bright to look at after the dark road.

"Home again, home again," she says in a sigh.

My grandfather comes out. His mouth is all bunched up like he's angry and he moves quickly down the porch steps and my mother practically runs to meet him and they hug hard. My mother lets out a noise and Grindy says, "Shhhh, shhhhh now," and strokes her hair until the kerchief falls on the grass. She says something quietly and he says, "I know. I know you did. Twenty-three years is enough trying."

He motions to me with an arm and when I get close enough he pulls me into their hug and kisses me on the forehead.

Nonnie is in the doorway when we come in with all our bags. She kisses us both on the cheek. Her skin is fuzzy and she smells like one of those tiny pillows you put in your drawer to scent your clothes. She isn't really my grandmother, my mother tells me that night, when we are lying in our twin beds in the room we share. I have never known this. It turns out I've never met my real grand-mother. She lives in Arizona, and my mother hasn't seen her since Garvey was a baby.

Nonnie still has a young face but old hair, completely white. She keeps it pinned up, but if you go down into the kitchen early enough you can catch her in a blue plaid robe and her hair, brushed to a shine, spilling down past her waist. The rest of the day it's gone, braided and coiled behind her head.

At dinner that night, Grindy argues with my mother about Nixon. "All these testimonies and hearings are just putting a stopper on everything else. These ridiculous tapes! The country doesn't need to listen to all that nonsense. We are in a serious recession. Let the man deal with things that matter."

"Nothing matters more than this, Da. People need to be held accountable. Otherwise we're paving the way for another Hitler."

Grindy shakes his head. "Little girl," he says, and then his voice grows very sharp. "You mustn't ever speak of Richard Nixon and Adolf Hitler in the same breath. Ever. Richard Nixon did not know about Watergate." My mother tries to interrupt but he holds up his hand. "He did not know about it, and all he is guilty of is trying to protect his own men from going to prison. You are naive, little girl. There is *always* internal spying. *Always*. These people got caught. But the president needs to be able to get back to the business of running the country."

My mother looks like she's looking at my father. Nonnie asks if anyone would like more beans.

After dinner my grandfather watches the Red Sox. I stand behind his chair and polish his bald head with my sleeve. I'm fascinated by the sheen of his scalp, the white age spots, the brown age spots. My mother tells me to leave him alone but he tells her it feels nice. The thin layer of brown shiny skin smells like mushrooms before they're cooked. When I go to bed, he puts his hands over my ears and gives me a hard kiss of bristles on my forehead.

My mother insists that my father knows where we are, but I can't understand why he hasn't called or driven up. I pick up the phone every now and then, to see if it really does work, then hang it back up. He must be so mad at me.

On the map of the lakes region in my grandparents' dining room, where we are is circled in red. Our point looks like a little tonsil hanging off the north side of the lake.

"It's like being in a bunker," my mother says to someone on the phone, probably her friend Sylvie. "No light comes in the windows. You have to go out into the middle of the lake to see the sun."

In the upstairs hallway there is a photograph of my mother standing on the dock in a white two-piece bathing suit, scratching her leg. Her skin is brown against the white and she is smiling. In the background a few girlfriends are waiting for her in the water. Those friends still come back here, with their own families, and my mother wonders aloud to me in our slope-ceilinged room how they can do it, return each summer, year after year, to the same people, the same cocktail parties, the Fourth of July picnic, the August square dance, the endless memorial services for all the old people who died over the winter.

Eventually my mother drags over a girl named Gail to meet me. She's going into sixth grade too, but looks much older. I take her up to my room to show her my albums.

"You're tiny," she says, wrapping her fingers around my wrist. She pulls out a pack of cigarettes and we smoke a few on the third floor next to an old seamstress's mannequin. The taste reminds me of kissing Neal.

She comes over nearly every day after that. I'm the only other girl her age nearby. When it rains we play Spit and War in our living rooms and on sunny days we swim out to the float that is for all the families on the point or play tennis on the disheveled court in the woods. She introduces me to the other kids. Most of them are my second cousins, though they don't really believe that. Or maybe they don't care. Even though we aren't in school I can tell Gail is the popular type. She has that thrust of personality that matters so much more than looks. I follow her around, the tail to her kite, grateful to be mysteriously attached.

*   *   *

After two weeks my father calls during dinner. Nonnie answers and returns quickly.

"It's Gardiner." She stands in the doorway, waiting to see if my mother will take the call.

"I'm not sure you should," my grandfather says, but my mother gets up and goes to the phone, which is below the stairs in the living room. She speaks so low we can't hear much, but I can see her straight stiff back and the way she holds the receiver several inches from her ear. When she calls me in and passes the heavy black receiver to me, my father asks me to come home.

"That's what I want. I want you and your mother to come home." His voice is high, like he's making fun of something, but he isn't. He's almost crying. I smell him, smell the steak and the A-1 sauce and the little onions in his drink.

I'm not sure what to say. After a long silence, he tells me he's named the puppy Scratch, that he's a good boy, and that Mallory and Patrick came over to the pool to swim yesterday. His voice becomes regular and he says he took Scratch to the vet that afternoon. He got four shots and he was so brave.

"He's right here," he says, "right next to me, and he says hello to you and wants you to come home soon, little elf."

"I'll try, Dad."

After I hang up I can see his hands and the sweat on his nose, and I miss him so much it feels like my skin is coming off.

In the dining room, my mother is complaining about him and the martinis and how he obviously talked to a lawyer who advised him to act like he wanted her back. "You watch," my mother says, "he'll write a letter. He'll put it in writing."

My grandmother sees me listening and asks if anyone wants more chicken.

I write to Mallory, Patrick, and Neal Caffrey. Mallory writes back first. She typed her letter in the shape of a giraffe.

                    Dear
                        Daley,
                  How are ya? I
              miss
              you
              a ton.
              I can't
              believe
              you left
              without
              telling me.
              What else
              haven't you
              told me?? Just
              joshing. Are you
            having a really good
          time there with your grand-
        parents? Do you have a new best
      friend yet? Don't worry about missing sail-
ing. The teacher has a hairlip and is really queer.
He came in my boat yesterday and gave us all
the creeps. We're going to a dude ranch in
    Wyoming in   August.
    It's a sur-   prise
    for my   mother's
    birthday   (but my
    father   told
    me—   he's
    not   as
    good   as
    you   are
    with   sec-
    rets!)   Wish
    me   luck
    rid-   ing
    West-   ern
    style!   Can't
wait till you come back. Love ya loads—M.P.G.

Patrick writes next, on a turquoise card with his name embossed at the top.

> **Dear Daley,**
> **I got this stationery for Christmas and this is the first time I've used it. It's kind of dumb. We've been using your pool a lot. Hope you don't mind. It's hot here. Mr. Amory and me went to the supply place for more chlorine and a new DPD kit. We also went to Payson's for an extension cord and thumbtacks. When are you coming back? The carnival is over. Elyse threw up on the Scrambler. It was gross. We capsized three times yesterday.**
> **Love,**
> **Patrick**

I was the one who used to go with my father on all his weekend errands. The last time we were at Payson's, he bought me a round key chain, one of the big silver ones like the kind the janitors at our school have that clip on a belt and have a little hard button in the middle you push to reel the keys back in. I forgot to bring it with me, and after I read Patrick's letter I cry hard for that stupid key chain.

Then my father writes, like my mother said he would, a joint letter to both of us, asking us to come back. He used the white stationery from the desk in the living room that has our name and address on it in red letters. He wrote in blue ballpoint, pressing down hard against the blotter beneath so it feels like Braille on the other side. He says he misses us and loves us and wants us to come home and live with him. My mother lets me keep the letter in the pocket of my suitcase. She doesn't write back. I do, but I don't want to sound like I'm having a good time and I don't want him to worry that I'm unhappy, so it's a bad, boring letter. He never writes again.

After my father's letter, Nora begins to send me cards with flowers or bluebirds on them and little poems on the inside. One says,

Before this little bird flies away
He wants to wish you a happy day.

She signs them *Love Always, Nora.*

I wait for a letter from Neal. I go with my grandfather nearly every morning to the Chigham General Store, where he buys a *Boston Globe* and a pack of Hot Tamales for me. Then we cross the street to the little post office. A woman named Mavis sits behind the counter. She blushes no matter what my grandfather says to her. I stand in a different spot in the small room each time, thinking if I can just stand in the right place a letter from Neal will be in my grandfather's box. It can be as long as five or ten minutes that my grandfather talks to Mavis, never seeming to notice the hot flush of her flabby, downy cheeks. And then he reaches into his pocket for the key and steps over to box No. 5 and I stare down at the wooden planks of the floor until I hear the box click shut, my heart leaping in my body until I see that there's nothing from Neal, and then it slows slowly down.

At the end of July, my brother comes to Lake Chigham with his new girlfriend, Heidi.

"Hermey!" he says, and picks me up in a big squeeze. He's a little smelly and unshaven. "Hermey's gotten so tall and even more fluffy-haired." He calls me Hermey because I remind him of the little toymaker who wants to be a dentist on *Rudolph the Red-nosed Reindeer.*

"It's the humidity," I say, trying to mush down my frizz.

He introduces Heidi. She has long smooth hair and clear green eyes. He met her at the end of June at a party in Somerville, where he's living for the summer.

"What day in June?" I ask him later, after dinner.

"I don't know. It was a Monday night."

"The twenty-fourth." She hits my brother softly.

"Ow," he says, not meaning it.

"The night before we left Myrtle Street," I say. Everything for me is divided there, the before and the after.

"I'm going to marry her, Daley," he says on the couch after dinner, when she goes to the bathroom. He puts his hands on his head and presses down. "Fuck. I'm going to marry her."

When she comes back he clutches her tight, paws her hair, whispers something, and laughs into her neck. I've never seen him with a girl. He always only came home with other boys. They'd stay in his room all weekend, playing their guitars and rolling what looked like dirt into little squares of tissue paper. They listened to records I'd never heard of, cleaned every scrap of food out of the fridge and pantry, and then disappeared in a car until next time. But with Heidi, Garvey is very different. He's soft and mild and always asking her what she thinks or what she wants.

"He's really fallen in love," my mother says.

We lie in our twin beds and listen to them murmuring in Heidi's room. My mother tells me about her first love. She met him here one summer. He was visiting her cousin Jeremy. I know Jeremy. He looks like an old man already with tough leathery skin. He always wants a few kids to go out sailing with him, but he barks at you if you pull the wrong line on his boat. Jeremy's friend was named Spaulding. He spied my mother from Jeremy's porch.

"'You're a pretty thang,' he said to me, just like that, *thang* because he was from Georgia and that made me curious. I was fourteen. I climbed right up onto the porch. The first night we went out I told him I felt like I was in a novel. That's the way he made me feel. It's the way I always feel when I fall in love."

Garvey and Heidi have stopped talking and are making other noises. I know what they're doing but it sounds like they're both jumping on the bed, which I'm never allowed to do.

"We're all lucky my father is losing his hearing," my mother says.

The next day we go to one of the islands in the middle of the lake with a bucket of fried chicken. On the picnic blanket my brother licks the grease off Heidi's fingers until my grandmother reminds them of their napkins. Then they go for a walk around the island. My grandparents walk in the other direction, shoes on, arms linked, leaning into each other as they speak. My mother, in her yellow bikini and enormous sunglasses, reads the newspaper, talking to it like she always does. "A five-minute-and-eighteen-second gap in the latest tape. How shocking."

For a split second I think it's my father on the front of the paper —the stoop, the heavy eyebrows, the small eyes—but it's Nixon, waving from the metal stairs of his airplane.

Late that night, Garvey, Heidi, and I go for a walk all the way to the main road where the sky opens up and there are so many stars it's hard to find the dippers or Cassiopeia. They seem to all be receding even as I watch them, but everything feels far away this summer; everything feels like it's backing away from me. Heidi explains to me that most of the stars we're seeing don't exist anymore. They've died. But because they're so far away and their light takes so long to get to us, we can still see them, even though they're not there anymore.

"Aren't there any new ones?" I ask.

"Yes, but we can't see them yet."

I crane my head up and stare at the dead stars. I don't like that we're seeing light from things that don't actually exist. I feel how flimsy a life is, how flimsy the universe is. I'm just going to die and not even leave a spit of light behind. I jerk my head down to the earth but it doesn't help. There are no streetlights. I can't seem to take a deep breath. My hands and then arms begin to tingle, like they have fallen asleep, like they can't get enough blood. In a split second, for no good reason, my heart starts racing, faster than it ever does in the post office, so fast it seems like there's nothing for it to do but explode. I'm dying. I feel suddenly sure of this. I keep walking but I feel like crouching, curling up in a small ball and begging someone to make the feeling pass. My brother and Heidi walk ahead and it seems like they are about to step off a huge cliff and I know that I'm dying but I can't call to them. My voice is gone. I'm disappearing. They turn back down the point road. I urge my legs to follow them.

"No they're not," I hear my brother say.

"Yes they are."

My brother laughs and for a second he sounds just like my father. He taps her head. "What do you have in there, marshmallow fluff?"

"It's true. My dad and I used to take walks at night, and he taught me about the stars."

"The french fry maker is a closet astronomer?"

She punches him. Hard. He laughs, then punches her back just as hard.

I can't get enough air. I can't get my heart to slow down. I can't even feel any space between the beats.

"Screw you," Heidi says, and takes off running.

"Garvey," I begin, wanting to tell him that I need to go to the hospital.

"She's not mad," he says. "She likes to play a little rough sometimes."

The sound of his talking to me is soothing. "She's nice," I say. My voice is strange, like from a tin can. But I hope he'll keep talking and he does. He tells me that she has this birthmark on her hip that drives him wild and that she kisses like a catfish in heat.

When we get back to the house she isn't there. Garvey calls for her and she answers from far away. We find her sitting on the grass outside Cousin Jeremy's house.

"All the driveways look the same," she says.

My brother leans down and she pulls him to her and I don't stay for the rest. I decide I'm not going to die and go back to my grandparents' house.

Every Friday morning, my mother drives down to Boston to see her lawyer. She stays in the city for dinner, and I fall asleep on the couch waiting up for her. She brings back a present each time: a jump rope, a deck of magic cards, a Watergate coloring book about people called the Plumbers and a hippie talking to a faceless man named Deep Throat in a parking garage. The rest of the days she stays on the point with me. She says I can take sailing lessons, but I don't want to. I like being with her. We listen to the music I brought—Helen Reddy, Cat Stevens, The Carpenters—in our room. We ride bikes to the ice cream shop on the main road. I teach her how to play Spit but she never beats me. She never leaves to go to a luncheon or set up a fundraiser or attend a rally. When she has to fill a prescription, buy a present, or get her hair done, I go with her, like I used to go everywhere with my father. She tells me stories about her relatives, about her childhood, about books she's read and plays she's seen. She has all sorts of stories she's never told me before.

One day in my grandfather's rowboat she points to a red boat-house across the lake. "That's where I met your father," she says.

"Where?"

"That's a tennis club in there. Your father was playing in a tour-nament. I saw him on the court and I walked slowly past the fence. He was warming up, practicing his serves. And when he went to pick up the balls, he asked me if I wanted to have an iced tea with him afterwards."

Was it really like that then? Did you just get picked like a flower by some guy? "And you said yes?"

"No. I said I had a hair appointment. So he asked me to the movies, which was much better than an iced tea."

"Did you like him?"

"I did. Of course I did." She stops rowing. I think she's looking right at me but it's hard to tell with her sunglasses. Her bottom lip scrunches into her top one, like she's only just realizing my full connection to the story. "He was very attractive, very funny. I can't remember the movie we saw, but in the middle of it a couple got into twin beds and your father leaned over and said, 'When we get married, we're going to have a double bed.' I was so charmed by that." She shakes her head. "All it really takes is a few words here and there. You can hang on to a few words for a long time. Fill in the rest with the fluff of your imagination."

She starts rowing again.

"But when did he ask you to marry him?"

"At the end of the summer. I don't know why it happened so fast but it did back then. We were all in such a hurry. And your father was an only child. He'd just graduated from Harvard and I think he was scared of being alone."

When Nixon resigns in August, we have to watch it up in our bedroom, on the little TV we brought from the kitchen on Myrtle Street, because my grandfather wants nothing to do with it.

"Good evening," Nixon says. He's wearing a black suit and black tie. "This is the thirty-seventh time I have spoken to you from this office where so many decisions have been made that shaped the history of this nation."

My mother usually berates Nixon whenever he appears on TV, but tonight she's silent. She listens intently on her bed, chewing her lip. Nixon holds his stack of papers, reading from the top one then setting it gently to the side and starting at the top of the next. His hands don't seem to be shaking. His words wash over me: political base, national security, American interests. It sounds like any other speech. He glances up only briefly to the camera, except at one point when he lowers his papers and without reading says, "I have never been a quitter."

After a long time his voice starts to slow down and I know he's getting to the end.

"To have served in this office is to have felt a very personal sense of kinship with each and every American. In leaving it, I do so with this prayer. May God's grace be with you in all the days ahead." And then he gathers his pages and they shut the cameras off.

"Goodbye to your sweet ass!" my mother hollers, then falls back on her pillows, exhausted, satisfied.

3

At the end of August we leave Lake Chigham. It's like our arrival played backwards, with Nonnie giving us kisses in the doorway and then Grindy pulling me and my mother into a hug in the grass beside our stuffed car. But we don't drive directly to Ashing. We go to Boston, where we meet Garvey at Park Street and I get out of the car and my mother drives away. She'll pick me up at Garvey's in three days. We go down a grimy set of steps below the street and take the T to Somerville.

Garvey's apartment is on the third floor of a house that has slipped off its foundation sideways. A corner of the porch is sunk into the ground. Everything is broken—the porch railing, the windows. Even the front door has a crack running up the middle.

"This is the best part, right here," he says, stopping in the dark stairwell to breathe in. "Smell that?"

I smell a lot of things and they're all disgusting. "Your BO?"

Garvey laughs. "No. It's Indian food. She makes it every day at lunchtime. She's gorgeous, too. She wears these"—he sweeps his arm along his leg to the floor—"wraps. And she has this smirk I can't interpret." He shakes his head and keeps climbing, saying nothing about the people through the door on the second floor and the music they're blasting. It gets hotter the higher we go. At the top of the stairs it's bright—the sun pours through two big windows—and broiling. He pushes open a door that doesn't seem to have a knob.

"Here we are. Home sweet home."

It smells like vinegar and wet dirty socks. There's linoleum, not just in the kitchen but covering the whole apartment, and my sneakers stick to it as if I have gum on both soles.

"Here. Bring your stuff to my room."

Off the short hallway are three rooms. "Deena," he says, pointing into a tidy blue room with a lime green bedspread and hundreds of earrings, the dangly kind my mother won't let me wear yet, hanging from ribbons on the wall. "Heidi"—her room is just a pile of clothes and no bed—"and me." Garvey's room is all bed—two queen-sized mattresses put together. "We like to sprawl," he says. "I'll put one back in Heidi's room and you can have your privacy in here."

"Do Mom and Dad know you live together?" I've heard my father rant about Garvey's generation enough to know he wouldn't like this at all.

Garvey's eyes widen and he covers his mouth with both hands, mocking me. "Ooooh, don't tell them. I'm so scared of what 'Mom and Dad' think."

"They're not dead. They're just getting a divorce."

"Oh, thanks for the clarification."

"They're still your parents."

"They're my progenitors, not my parents. The word *parent* suggests something a little more hands-on." He starts to drag one of the beds toward the door. "Besides, they're both getting more than I am now."

"Getting what?"

He drops the mattress and pats me on the head. "Little babe in the woods. So much to learn."

There's a fan in the corner of the room. I squat down to feel it on my face. My sweat turns cool, then disappears.

Garvey lies down on the bed by the door. "I'm surprised you let Mom escape for an assignation with her paramour."

I have a bad feeling about what he's just said. "Do you mind speaking English?"

"You let Mom go off with her boyfriend."

"She just went to Sylvie's. I've been there before."

"She went to Sylvie's. But Sylvie's in France. And so a guy named Martin is going to be there with Mom. You are definitely not the sharpest tack in the box."

Tears rise and the fan blows them toward my ears. *Say hi to Sylvie for me,* I just said to her in the car before she dropped me off. *I will,* she said.

"You really didn't know?"

I shake my head. When I find my voice, I say, "Is he from Ashing?"

My brother laughs, loud because he's on his back and because he loves it when I'm stupid. "Shit, no. God, Daley, do you think she'd ever have anything to do with the warmed-over corpses in that town?"

"But that's where we *live.* We're moving back there on Monday. I'm starting sixth grade. Mom found an apartment downtown on Water Street." I say all this to make sure it's still true.

"I know. And that's all for you. For your benefit. Mom outgrew that town a long time ago."

"So who is Martin?" I can barely move my lips. I forgot how bad my brother could make me feel when he wants to.

"I don't know. That's what I was trying to ask you."

If my mother lied about who she was with, she could have lied about where she was going, too. It makes me woozy to think of a whole weekend of not knowing.

At least I know where my father is. On a Friday night at five-thirty he'll be sitting in the den with his second martini. He'll be looking at the local news, thinking about the pool and how he'll clean it in the morning, test the chlorine balance. The dogs, just fed, will be moving swiftly around the yard, looking for the right place to pee and poop. Scratch will be trained by now, but if he lifts his leg in my mother's rosebushes, my father will leap up and holler at him.

"Have you seen Dad?"

"Yeah. I went up there last weekend. Stupid."

"What happened?"

My brother covered his eyes and groaned. "I don't think I should tell you."

"What's wrong with him? What's the matter with Daddy?" I picture him on the kitchen floor, for some reason, unable to stand. I can see it so vividly. I stand up myself, as if I can go to him.

"Nothing's the matter with him, Daley. Have a seat." He says this like a homeroom teacher. "He's hooked up with—" He looks at me, deciding whether I can handle it. But it turns out I already know.

"Patrick's mother."

"I knew you weren't as dumb as you look."

Mr. Amory and me went to Payson's. Mr. Amory and me cleaned out the shed. I've been reading about it all summer.

At six, we walk to the Brigham's where Heidi works. After my brother's roasting pan of an apartment, the street is cool; Brigham's is like walking into a fridge. Heidi is waiting on a boy and his grandmother. She gives us a small smile, then turns her back to us to make their frappes. A blue apron is tied loosely at her waist and her hair hangs in a frayed braid. She slides the tall drinks and two straws to her customers and takes their money without speaking to them. Her face is moist, despite the air conditioning. She looks different than I remember, faded somehow.

"Hi there," she says to me, but she is not glad to see me or Garvey. Her eyes are dull and olive, not the clear green I remember. "You made it."

Garvey and I share a raspberry rickey at a corner table until her shift is over. Outside it is hot again, and the sidewalk is crowded with people coming up from the subway stairs or racing to them. After a summer in the woods, the chaos makes me uneasy. I stick close to my brother, who leads us to a Greek sandwich shop.

"Haven't been here since yesterday," Heidi mutters.

"I can't really afford La Dolce Vita," Garvey says, pointing to a fancy place down the street.

"You wouldn't know *la dolce vita* if it hit you on the head." She smiles but my brother does not.

The restaurant is hot and smelly and it's no wonder Heidi doesn't like it. We sit crammed in a corner. My brother orders me a falafel sandwich that tastes like sawdust mixed with onions. He has a big plate of diced meat and Heidi tells me to watch how he chews like a cow chewing cud. My brother tells her she should have stuck it out with Graham, and Heidi's eyes get pink. She catches her tears with her thumb. They are drinking something called grappa and it seems to make them hate each other.

That night my brother's apartment is a cauldron, as if all the city's heat has risen and gathered here. I lie on the remaining bed in the dark, my feet and hands swelling, my skin stretching like a sausage being boiled. They took the fan into Heidi's room. No air is coming through the three open windows. I miss the water and its cool breezes. Neither Ashing nor Lake Chigham ever got this hot. Headlights and brakelights swim across the ceiling. The cars and people below begin to seem responsible for the heat. A siren blares, spewing hotter air. I dream that I am rebraiding Heidi's hair over and over. I can't get it tight enough. I wake up to the sound of a door shutting.

Out the window my brother and Heidi are walking away, down the sidewalk, not touching. Garvey told me last night that they had to run an errand in the early morning and they'd be back by ten. I stay in the room as long as I can, but my hunger and need to pee drive me out. The bathroom is filthier in broad daylight. I don't let my skin touch the toilet seat, the way my mother has taught me. I find cornflakes and milk in the kitchen, and just as I sit down with my big bowl on the couch, Deena's door opens and a man comes out, naked. He's very hairy.

"Hey," he says, reaching for his jeans and T-shirt, which are beside me on the couch. He leaves, still naked, out the swinging, knobless front door. I hear him dressing in the hallway, then his bare feet sticking on the stairs on the way down.

The heat has retreated slightly; a breeze, an actual breeze, comes through the windows.

Deena's door opens again. "Shit. Is he gone?"

"Yeah," I say.

"Shit." She looks down at a pair of glasses in her hand. "Shit."

She throws them out the window. Then she stretches her long arms up to the ceiling and side to side. She is naked too, and her breasts are enormous, three times the size of my mother's. She's thin so they don't even seem to fit properly on her chest, the nipples nearly facing each other. Her waist tapers in and then her hips flair out and her thighs are thick and strong. Her body is fascinating to me, womanly in a way my mother and my aunts in Chigham are not.

"I'll get something on and join you," she says, noticing my stare. She comes back in a short shiny robe that barely covers her bum.

"So your parents are splitting up," she says, sitting beside me where the man's clothes had been.

"Yeah."

"How does that feel?"

How does that feel? The question echoes. I shrug.

"Was it hard with them fighting all the time?"

"They never fought. They didn't really talk to each other all that much."

She laughs. "I guess you and Garvey had different parents."

"No," I say quickly, before I get what she means.

"He tell you where he was going this morning?"

"No," I say again.

She pushes her thick lips in and out, thinking. If I ask I know she'll tell me but she strikes me as dangerous, full of things I don't want to know.

"He is really fucked up. You know that, don't you?"

My heart starts beating really fast, the beginnings of the dead star feeling. I put my bowl in the sink and go back to Garvey's room. I lock the door. When I glance out the window, there they are in front of the house, not moving. The top of Heidi's head is pressed into my brother's chest and his arms are wrapped awkwardly around her. It looks like he's the only thing keeping her from collapsing to the ground.

A half hour later they come inside. I wait for Garvey to come back to his room to check on me but he doesn't. I hear them moving things around in Heidi's room, then a kettle whistles and my brother calls, "Milk and honey?" down the hallway and she says, "Yes, please," her voice low and ragged like she hasn't used it yet this morning, or maybe has used it too much.

They settle in there, on the other side of the wall from me. Their talk is quiet and intermittent, calm, like little waves lapping against a hull. Then I hear something awful, a sort of yelp, like the wail of an animal in the woods, impossible to tell if it is male or female, only that it is coming from the room next to mine. Then it's quiet.

I find a thin paperback on the floor called *The Breast*. "It began oddly," it begins. "But could it have begun otherwise, however it began?" I read a few chapters. A regular guy has turned into a big hundred-and-fifty-five-pound boob. His penis changes first, into a nipple. Only Garvey would own a book like this. When I get tired of reading, I try to snoop but there is nothing, no secret notebook

or hidden scraps of paper in his drawers. I'm angry at him for forgetting about me and I want to find something terrible about him
that I can shove in his face.

When he finally does come in, he drops down face first on the
bed and doesn't move or speak for a long time. His threadbare flannel shirt has risen up with his arms and I can see the pale skin on
his skinny lower back and a patch of dark hair at the bottom of his
spine. His bum is flat like my father's, the jeans covering it nearly
black with dirt. I can tell he isn't sleeping; his breathing is loud but
uneven, as if there are words attached that I can't hear. He looked
at me when he came in, but now I'm not sure if he saw me. Then he
flips over and fixes his restless eyes directly on mine, breathes another lungy loud breath, and says, "Please, Daley, whatever you do,
don't let any guy touch you. Ever. Not until you're thirty. Or forty."

I think of Neal, how I will see him in less than two weeks, how
he never wrote.

"Please. Please listen to me. They will only fuck you up. Don't
fall in love. Don't let 'em close until you know exactly who you are
and where you are going."

"All right," I say quietly so he'll take his eyes off me.

He does, and then he looks up at the ceiling and starts to cry.
I've never seen my brother cry before and he's bad at it, spastic, his
mouth contorted and his hands flailing around his face like they
don't know where to go. I don't really recognize him as my brother
anymore and I put my fingers on the inside of his arm to reassure
myself it's still him. He seizes me, pulls me into a hard, tight hug.
My head bobs on his chest as he sobs. Just as suddenly it's over and
he says fuck and shoves me off him and leaves the room.

In Heidi's room their voices start off quiet again but soon my
brother is screaming at her. And she's screaming back but then she's
doing something that's not screaming. There are no words anymore;
it's like the horrible yelp I heard earlier but it doesn't stop; it's a long
deep pitted howl that goes on and on and I feel in my own stomach

that need to howl, and for a few seconds I get scared that I am actually the one howling, so hollow and jangly is my stomach.

After that it is silent and I lie all the way down on the bed and fall asleep. When I open my eyes again, the sun is gone and the night outside is a pale green haze. I hear voices in the living room and follow them. My brother and Heidi are facing each other on the couch, eating noodles from blue bowls.

He says something and she giggles and then they both look at me.

"Grab some chow on the stove," Garvey says.

"Let me see if we have any milk left."

"Milk? She doesn't drink milk with dinner. She's not four."

"Kids need milk, for their bones."

"Yes, little mama."

"We don't have any," Heidi says, shutting the fridge hard, her voice suddenly flat. When she comes back to the couch with her bowl, she doesn't sit as close to my brother.

"Sorry," I hear him whisper behind me as I get my food. "I'm such an idiot."

I sit on a foam chair.

"So Heidi went with me last weekend."

"To Dad's?"

"She got the full monty. 'Patrick, where's that puppy?'" My brother can do the most amazing impressions of my father, making his voice just as tough and cracked and pissed off. "'Goddammit, did he run off again? You kids have got to keep an eye on him!'"

"'Did he pee in the pool?'" Heidi says, but her imitation is rotten.

"'No, I think he shat on my tennis whites! Goddammit, that's a golf ball coming out of his ass!'"

Heidi breaks into peals of high-pitched laughing. I can tell they've been doing this all week.

"Mom has a new name," Garvey says.

"What do you mean?"

"She's not Mom or Meredith. She's Your Fucking Mother. You better get used to it. 'Do you know what Your Fucking Mother did?'" It's amazing how he can just switch into my father's body. "'She literally stole the family jewels!' Did you know that, by the way?"

I don't know what he's talking about.

"I think I'm going to lie down," Heidi says.

"I'll come," my brother says, taking her bowl and putting it by the sink, then coming back to help her up.

"I'm fine," she says, but she lets him. Then she bends back down to me and gives me a kiss on my forehead like my grandfather did at bedtime. She smells nice and I hope my brother will marry her like he said. They call good night to me over their shoulders and disappear, arm in arm, into her room.

I do our dishes. There's a TV in the corner and I would turn it on but I'm scared Deena will reappear and want to talk to me again, so I go back to Garvey's room, read more about the man who is a breast, and go to sleep.

I forget to go to the bathroom, so I wake up in the middle of the night. As I quietly open the door and cross the sticky hallway, I keep hearing my brother imitating my father. *You kids have got to keep an eye on him!* I can see that twenty-five-dollar mutt and his prickly hair and long ugly face. *You kids. You kids.* And he isn't talking to me or my brother anymore.

I don't flush or wash my hands for fear of waking someone, but as I cross back I look down the hallway and see that someone else is up. Garvey. I can see the narrow outline of his back. He's moving, stretching or scratching, tilting his head to one side. I want to go back to bed, but I have a feeling he needs me, wants some company.

"Hey," I whisper as I move closer, but he doesn't hear.

A few more steps and the whole scene changes, from Garvey alone itching his back to something else altogether. The hand on his back is not his own and it's not a hand but a foot and a shin. There are two of them, locked together, moving together, kissing, twisting, all in complete silence. And then they turn, Garvey carrying her in a frontwards piggyback, his legs buckling slightly as he moves toward the couch, her legs wrapped around him, both of them naked, scraping against each other, and then falling into the cushions, her enormous breasts flopping to the sides and Garvey scooping them and shoving them into his mouth, all the while his bum moving up and down and her hands down between their legs, and her face, Deena's face, in a silent scream.

4

On Monday my mother picks me up and we drive straight to Ashing. It feels like I have been gone many years. We pass the Christmas tree farm, the inn at the corner of Baker Street, the Citgo station, and then my mother, instead of driving through the middle of town and up the hill to Myrtle Street, turns right onto Water Street and then left into a parking lot. It looks like a miniature motel, beige with white trim, with six apartments, three up and three down. My mother pats my leg. "We're home."

Our apartment is on the bottom in the middle. There's a large 2 on the door, which she opens with a key she's already hidden in the little lantern above the doorbell.

"I don't think either of us want to bother with carrying a key," she says. We never, as far as I know, had a key to our old house. I don't even remember there being locks on the doors.

All the furniture has been moved in, chairs and couches and beds that used to be on Myrtle Street. I sit on the sofa with yellow flowers that used to be in the den. Is my father sitting on the floor now?

"Come see your room."

I follow her down a long hallway. My room is small and dark. The one window looks out at our car in its spot. But my old beds are in there, with the same white bedspreads, and all my stuffed animals are on top. I forgot to pack any of my stuffed animals in June, and now they seem strange to me, stupid, with their puffed-up bellies and sewn-on smiles.

"Well?"

"I like it." I hate it. "Can I see yours?"

Hers is at the end of the hallway, as large as the living room, with French doors that go out to a deck, and the canopy bed she took from the guest room. All my life I've been asking to have that bed in my room.

"We need to hang things on the walls, buy some plants, but it has potential," she says. "And it's convenient, being downtown. You can meet your friends whenever you want."

I nod.

"Does Dad know we're back?"

"I have no idea," she says.

"Can I go up there?"

"Now?" She looks at her watch. It's only two-thirty.

I get my bike out of the car and put the wheels back on it.

It's Labor Day, and Ashing is clogged with cars and pedestrians streaming off the train from Boston, making the trek to the beach. Some kids my age are hanging out on the steps of Bruce's Variety. I recognize a couple of them, but I don't know anyone's name. I've gone to the same private school all my life and only know the kids from Ashing who go there too.

"Reggie," one of them says as I pedal by. I've heard this word before. I think it's a blend of rich and preppie. I don't know, when they say things like that, if they know me specifically, or just that I don't go to school with them.

I live in Water Street Apartments now, I want to call out. My mother doesn't have a job and she's worried my father won't pay the child support.

I pass the yarn shop. No orange Pinto. I look for Neal in every face I pass. When I get to Dad's I'll call Patrick and find out everything about the summer. Mallory's at her aunt's on the Cape until Wednesday.

I ride straight up the hill and then take a right at the blinking light to the stucco house on Myrtle Street with the halfmoon driveway. I stop there, like a tourist. The front of the house is a facade no one but the mailman uses, with pretty white stones instead of regular gravel, and slate steps that wind up through the rhododendrons to a wide terrace. Through the windows is my father's den but he wouldn't be in there during the day unless it was raining. Once, when I was in second grade, I was dropped off here after a birthday party by a parent who didn't know any better. I climbed up all the steps and was greeted at the top by a stray dog who was lapping up rainwater that had collected in the wide saucer of a planter. He attacked immediately, knocking me over, ripping open the skin on my arms and left ear. I screamed and screamed but no one heard. I remembered the goody bag full of jelly beans in my coat pocket and tossed it down the steps. The dog leaped after it and I got myself inside. I still have faint lines on my arms from that attack. The front of this house is fake; all the activity is in the back. I can hear shouting coming from the pool.

I keep going down Myrtle Street and ride up the back driveway, through the small patch of woods where sometimes in winter rain will gather and freeze and you can skate all around the trees, to the poolhouse and the hum of its machines. Home. Finally I am home.

Mrs. Tabor, water sluicing off the bottom of her bikini, is just stepping out of the shallow end of the pool.

Patrick's clipping the grass around the little toadstool lights. He's the first to see me. He drops the shears.

"Daley," he says.

"Daley?" His mother laughs, as if he's making an old joke. And then she sees me and says, "Oh my God."

It's a little bit like coming back from the dead, a little bit like Huck and Tom when they show up at their own funeral. Only Frank, Patrick's older brother, ignores me, launching himself off in a swan dive and gliding along the bottom of the pool like a stingray.

"Sweetie pie, when did you get back?" Mrs. Tabor says, quickly putting her head through a terry-cloth dress before coming over to me.

"Today."

She hugs me. She's cold from the pool and water from her hair drips down my neck. Her black hair is no straighter wet than dry and hits the small of her back in a straight line. She is normally pale but now her skin is like copper. She must have spent a lot of time beside my pool this summer.

"Well," she says, looking down the driveway, then at the house. I wait for her to start asking me questions—she was always so full of questions for me when I went over to Patrick's house. "Your dad will be sorry he missed you."

"Where is he?"

"Radio Shack. Isn't that where he went?" she asks Patrick, who nods. "Can you come back later?"

There's something strange about the way she's standing, I feel like if I try to take a step closer to the house, she will tackle me. I glance at the garage to see if my father's car is gone; it is.

"Hey." Patrick hits me on the arm. "I gotta show you what we got for the pool."

His mother starts to say something and stops herself. I follow Patrick into the poolhouse. It's mostly the same, except for some of the towels hanging on the hooks. Patrick leads me to a new little cabinet next to the bar and tells me to open it. Inside is a stereo with a turntable, an eight-track, and a radio. He pushes ON and music blasts inside and out. He points to some yellow speakers in the trees beside the pool. "They're waterproof," he says. "For rain. Oh, and I gotta show you something else, too. It's so cool."

"Stay out in the sunshine. Don't go indoors," Mrs. Tabor calls as we pass her chaise on the way to the house. "Patrick, are you listening to me?" But Patrick keeps on moving, and by the time we reach the back steps she's lain back down again.

The kitchen table is gone. The only furniture in the kitchen now is a red leather armchair I've never seen before. They've moved the table into the pantry and covered it with an orange and brown tablecloth that's not ours. In the living room there are two new lamps (my mother took the blue and white Chinese ones) that have shiny black bases and silver shades with a kind of veiny green mold design. In the den, where the yellow flowered couch and chairs used to be, are two baby blue recliners. On the mantelpiece is a photograph in Lucite of two old people I don't know.

Patrick heads up the stairs possessively and into my parents' room. Same bed, missing dresser, new chair with ottoman. Weird geometric sheets on the unmade bed. He sits on my father's side of the bed and opens the thin drawer of the bedside table. He lifts up a black plastic thing shaped like a small egg with the top cut off and a bright red button there instead. A cord runs out of the other end.

"If you push this, the police will come."

"What?"

"It's called a panic button. Gardiner—I mean, your dad—wired the whole house. Downstairs there's a box and when you go out you turn it on and if anyone crosses any threshhold anywhere in the house a signal goes off downtown at the police station and they have to come in two minutes or they get fired. Isn't that so cool?" He's sitting on a gold velour robe.

In the drawer with the panic button are several old watches, receipts, white golf tees, one cuff link, and a silver fountain pen my mother gave him for his fortieth birthday. I used to play in this drawer on weekend afternoons while my father napped and a ballgame flashed on the TV at the foot of the bed. He slept so deeply I could thread the golf tees through the circles of hair on his chest and he wouldn't wake up. Sometimes I fell asleep beside him. The drawer, this whole side of the room, holds the smell of him, which is humid and spicy.

In the drawer are two new things: a tube of something called KY Jelly and the note my mother left on the kitchen table on the morning of June 25th. It's crumpled and in the back but I know what it is. If I were alone I'd pull it out and read it, but I don't want Patrick to know it's there, though he probably already does.

I get up and go down the hallway to my room. The door is shut. Patrick whispers something to me, but he's too far away to hear and I really don't want to listen to him anymore. I open the door. My beds have been replaced by a double bed I don't recognize, and in the bed is a little girl. I'm not sure how I forgot that Patrick had a little sister, but I did. She lies on her side in a deep sleep, a short pigtail sticking up above her ear, two hands curled under her chin.

"Mom will kill me if she wakes up," Patrick says behind me, so I shut the door.

It is afternoon in somebody else's house. I don't know what to do now.

"We're not living here," he says. "I mean, not really."

We just stand there in the dark hallway.

"We thought you were coming back next week. School doesn't start until a week from Wednesday, you know. Why are you shaking?"

I hold my hand out flat. I'm shaking like I have a disease. "I don't know."

"Let's get out in the sun."

We go down the back stairs and out onto the porch.

"He's back," Patrick says, pointing.

My father is in his chair at the pool in his bathing trunks. He's sitting sideways to us, talking to Mrs. Tabor. She glances over but he doesn't. I walk all the way across the grass to the concrete squares around the pool before he looks up. He fakes surprise. "Well, hello there!" He fakes friendliness. I know it's fake because I've heard that voice when he talks to the neighbors he hates. He hates Mr. Seeley for building his garage so close to our property line, and he hates the Fitzpatricks for having so many children. He hates the old Vance sisters down the hill for feeding our dogs and Mr. Pratt across the street for playing taps at sunset. He grumbles about them, swears about them, and makes fun of the way they walk or talk or laugh. But whenever he sees one of them, at the post office or the gas station, he always says, "Well, hello there!" in that same fake friendly voice.

I hug him tight but his arms are loose around me.

"You come up for a swim? The pool's nice today." He reaches for his drink and I notice his hand is shaking like mine.

"No, I didn't bring a suit. I just—"

"Why not? The pool's nice today," he says again, just before sipping.

"I don't know. I haven't unpacked yet," I say, then regret mentioning anything about being away. At the same time I want him to know that I came up here first thing. "We just got back an hour ago." I realize this isn't true. It's been more like three hours by now.

"Oh, really? I thought I saw the convertible downtown this morning."

Now *he's* lying. We drove in well past noon. I shake my head, but I don't have it in me to fight.

He's glaring at Mrs. Tabor. I know that look, too. It means, *Can you believe this little shit?* Sweat has popped out on his nose.

"I missed you," I say.

"Oh yeah?"

"Gardiner," Mrs. Tabor says.

"I missed you, too."

Our eyes catch briefly. His are a yellowy green. My throat aches from not crying.

"Why don't you go help your dad finish unloading the car?" Mrs. Tabor says.

We walk across the stiff healthy grass together. He lights a cigarette with his lighter, a heavy silver rectangle that makes a wonderful *shlink* when he flips it closed. The familiarity of that sound, of everything about him, hurts. The driveway is hot, the way-back of the station wagon hotter. I have to get on my knees inside to reach the last two bags. The smell of the dogs reminds me that I haven't seen the puppy.

"Where's the puppy?"

"What?" my father says over his shoulder. I hurry to catch up.

"Scratch. Where is he?"

"Ran away."

"Ran away?"

"Summer for running away."

"Have you looked for him?"

"I know where he is."

"Where?"

"He's with the old biddies. They've been trying to steal my dogs for years. I decided to let them have this one. You didn't want it."

"I couldn't take him. I asked, but I couldn't."

He flicks a look of raw disgust at me. He's putting it together, my refusal of the Newfoundland, my secret with my mother. "Ugliest goddamned dog I ever saw."

I help him put away the batteries and the rest of his purchases. He leaves a pack of lightbulbs out, saying there are some that need replacing, and when he leaves the room to do that I follow him. I have the idea that if I stay with him long enough he'll remember me, like an amnesiac who needs time for the memories to filter back in. We change a bulb in the den, then one in the upstairs hallway. He doesn't comment on any of the missing furniture or the strange new items or the fact that Elyse Tabor is sleeping behind the closed door of my room. We move around the house in silence, with only the sound of his breath squeaking loudly through his hairy nostrils.

When we're done, he says, "Lemme show you something."

I figure he means the panic button or some other new gadget, but he takes me into the laundry room. He opens the cabinet that holds the safe, a heavy lead-colored box with a combination lock.

"Open it."

We all know the combination: 8-29-31, my father's birthday. As a special treat my mother will sometimes let me bring the silk bags of jewels to her room and lay out every piece on the bedspread. It feels strange to be opening the safe without her in the bedroom.

It is empty.

"Did you know?"

I shake my head

"She took it all. She just took it and ran." He slams the heavy safe door, but it bounces back and swings hard against the cabinet, making a dent in the wood. He points to the dark empty inside of the box. "She took it all, all of my mother's and grandmother's jewelry." His voice cracks and his face is purple. He pounds his fist on the top of the washing machine and shouts, "Bitch bitch bitch!" His voice is high, like a small boy's. Then he stoops over and little wordless gasps came out of his mouth.

He straightens up and looks at me. "Come here."

I do and he hugs me, hard this time, my ear pressed into the coarse hair on his chest, and says, "But you're mine. You're mine. Aren't you?"

"Yes," I whisper to his chest hair.

When we come downstairs, Mrs. Tabor is making dinner, and Patrick and Elyse are playing cards on the floor where the kitchen table used to be.

"Can Daley stay for dinner?" Patrick asks.

Mrs. Tabor looks at my father, who nods.

"I'll have to call."

"Stay the night," my father says.

"All right. I'll just go to the bathroom, then call." I don't want to use the kitchen phone—I don't want to be in the same room with both my parents' voices.

There is a little telephone room off the den, next to the bathroom. I sit down on the swivel stool. One of my mother's pads with the thick white paper and the words DON'T FORGET in red at the top is on the phone table. It makes me miss her and I'm glad to hear her voice when she picks up.

"I'm at Dad's still."

"Oh, good. It's going well then."

"Mostly. They want me to stay for dinner and the night."

"All right," my mother says, and as she is speaking I hear a little click. "I have to go into town in the morning. Bob's lined me up a few interviews, bless him."

The click is probably my father listening in on the extension in the sunroom. I wish she hadn't mentioned Bob Wuzzy.

"Okay. I'll see you in the afternoon then."

"We'll have to get you some back-to-school clothes. When do you want to do that, Thursday?"

I just want to get us all off the phone. "Sure. Sleep tight."

"Sleep tight, baby."

I wait. Mom hangs up loudly. Dad's is the tiniest *tic*.

We come into the kitchen at the same time. He goes to the bar to make a drink and drops the jar of onions. It doesn't shatter but he shouts, "Fuck! Fuck! Fuck!" in a kind of wild strangled voice as if the bottle had sliced him open. Elyse, holding out a fan of cards, scoots closer to her brother.

"Oh, knock it off, Gardiner," Mrs. Tabor says, spooning tuna noodle casserole onto three plates.

Frank comes in then, tossing a tennis racquet toward but not in the coat closet.

"Pick that goddamn thing up and put it where it belongs," his mother says, much more sharply than she'd spoken to my father.

"Hello, Frank. How are you, Frank?" Frank mutters from the closet. It's my brother's Davis Classic he's been playing with.

"Why hello, Master Frank," my father says, bowing. "How kind of you to grace us with your presence this fine evening."

Frank smirks, about the nicest response you can get from him.

"And what, pray tell, has become of your opponent?"

Surprising me, Frank plays along. "He has entered an insane asylum, so profound was the psychological blow of losing to me."

"You beat him?" my father says, no longer in character.

"Six–three, six–O." Frank looks like a little boy then, waiting for my father's reaction. Their father, Mr. Tabor, hasn't been around in a long time. He moved to Nevada even before Elyse was born.

My father's face lights up. I remember that face. I remember what it feels like to receive the full glow of that face. "Six–three, six–O. Jesus, Mary, and Joseph. You clocked him. You really got his number. He couldn't get a game off of you, could he, once you figured him out."

Frank shakes his head and then takes his enormous smile out of the room before too many people see it.

We are all handed our portions of the casserole and some sliced cucumbers on pink plastic plates. We eat in the pantry; the plates clash with the tablecloth. My father and Mrs. Tabor take their drinks into the sunroom. You can see the backs of their heads through a window in the kitchen. They're watching the news. It's weird to see my father and all the dogs in there. It was always my mother's room because there was no TV in it.

"So, Daley," Frank says. "Here you are, after—what—three months?"

"Two."

Frank and Patrick are over three years apart in age but, because they're nearly the same height and have the same straight brown hair, people always get them confused. I never do; Frank is mean, and his meanness is the only thing I ever see.

"And now you're here, back in your old house. Looks pretty different, doesn't it?"

"Never ate in this room before." I scrape another forkful of noodles together and hope he's done with me.

"You like my mother's taste?"

My heart begins to thud. "It's different."

"You think your mother is classier, don't you?"

"Leave her alone, Frank," Patrick says.

"Protecting your girlfriend, Weasel?"

"Shut up."

"Well, she can't be your girlfriend now, can she? Pretty soon she'll be your—"

"Shut the fuck fuck up!"

Frank laughs at the two fucks.

I've never heard Patrick swear before.

Elyse eats. She finishes her casserole and moves on to the cucumbers. Her mouth does not reach the table so all her food has to be brought down to it unsteadily. She's spilled all over the place. I ask her if she wants a cushion but she shakes her head without looking at me.

After dinner Frank goes outside to shoot things with a BB gun, and Patrick and I play the game Life in the living room. Elyse comes through every now and then, dragging a little beagle on wheels by a string. Sometimes she drags it right through our money piles to get our attention, but we don't give it to her. Through the swinging door I can hear Mrs. Tabor making her and my father's dinner, and Dad mixing more drinks at the bar on the other side of the door. Their voices rise, as if drinking made them deaf.

"Oh, that ass. I can't believe she said that to you!"

"I was just minding my own business. Standing in line at the drugstore, for chrissake." My father is enjoying himself. "But I set her straight."

"I bet you did, pet."

A while later his voice drops to a scratching sound, his attempt at a whisper. All I can hear is something like alcar over and over again.

"What's alcar?" I ask Patrick.

"You don't know who Al Carr is?"

"No, obviously."

"He's your mother's lawyer, and he's trying to take Gardiner to the cleaners." Patrick says this wearily, without accusation, as if he's tired of the sentence.

My father's voice scrapes on. It sounds like he's choking on his sirloin.

Mrs. Tabor doesn't bother to lower her voice. She just says mm-hmm and of course and you're right about that.

Outside you can hear BBs slicing through the leaves in the trees.

If you play all the way to retirement, Life is a long game. My car is full of babies. I've had two sets of twin girls and a boy I have to lay down the middle.

Mrs. Tabor comes into the living room and asks us where Elyse is. We don't know.

"What do you mean, you don't know? I thought she was in here playing with the two of you." She is speaking with her eyes shut, but when she starts to tip forward she opens them and catches hold of the back of a sofa.

"Nope," Patrick says.

"Nope," she mocks, badly. "Get off your ass and find her!"

Her words are so slurred I can't take her anger seriously. I want her to leave so Patrick and I can laugh about it, but he gets up and leaves the room.

"There are responsibilities, Daley, if you want to stay here." Her eyes are shut again. She pronounces my name Day-*lee*.

I almost say Fuck you. It almost flies out of my mouth.

"Catherine," my father calls. "He's got her."

I get up and follow her in. Patrick is holding Elyse, who is sound asleep.

"She was under the dining room table."

"Let me have her, pet," Mrs. Tabor says.

"No, I'll take her up."

"I'll take her."

"You'll just wake her up." Patrick moves quickly to the back stairs. "Or drop her," he mutters.

"C'mere," I hear my father say. I turn—I thought he was talking to me—just as he is wrapping his arms around Mrs. Tabor. He puts his face close to hers and waits for her to kiss him. Her lips separate and I watch her tongue go into my father's mouth. He grabs her by the butt with two hands and shoves her into him. "I love this ass," he says, not even trying to be quiet. "I love this fucking ass."

I go out the back door. I have the idea that I will walk home to Mom's, but then I hear a BB hit the side of the house and don't want to risk it. It's too dark to see where Frank is. I push out the little chest of drawers that has some gardening stuff in it from against the wall and sit behind it for protection.

My father is always in a good mood in the morning. He is up before anyone else, showered, shaved, and dressed in bright colors. He sings in the kitchen as he makes coffee and feeds the animals.

I can hear him humming below my window in the guest room, on his way to clean the pool. I slept in my clothes, so I catch up with him before he reaches the poolhouse.

He stops humming; then he says, "Does it look a little cloudy to you?"

The water is its usual rich clear turquoise, but I want to do the chlorine test with him afterward so I say, "A little."

He connects the pieces of the vacuum cleaner, the long silver shafts and the rectangular head, then sidesteps slowly along the edge of the pool, the long pole sinking as the vacuum travels toward the drain in the middle, then rising up over his head as he brings the vacuum closer, directly beneath his feet at the bottom of the pool. He gives me turns, helping me when I let it out too far and don't have the strength to pull it back, and for brief flashes I feel just like I used to feel when this was my only home and my mother was still asleep upstairs and nothing had changed. Even though it's going to be a hot day, it still feels like the beginning of fall. The leaves are brittle and loud when they shake in the breeze.

My father used to sing a back-to-school song he got from an old ad on TV. He changed the words and put our names in it. He always sang it when my mother and I came home with shopping bags in early September. The tune would linger in the house for weeks, someone breaking out singing it just when the others had nearly forgotten. The tune is in my head now, but I know if I sing it, it will be a betrayal. I know—I sense all the new rules, though I could never explain how— that I'm not allowed to refer in any way to the small particular details of our past life together, the details that made it uniquely ours. We had an array of refrains among us, my father, my mother, Garvey, and I, clusters of words repeated so many times I thought they were universal clichés until I slowly learned, one by one, that they belonged solely to us. *I don't like you, I don't like Pinky, and I'm not having a good time,* is one. It came from my parents' honeymoon in Italy. On their third day in Rome, my father returned to the hotel room with a puppy. My mother was not happy about this and the puppy sensed it. He bit her little finger, which is why my father named him Pinky. I was born twelve years after their honeymoon, but the expression was still very much alive, used by all of us in our sulky but self-mocking moments. But I know this expression and all the others have to be buried now. They are a dead language. If I ever said, *I don't like you, I don't like Pinky, and I'm not having a good time* to my father, something would perish between us, as if I had broken a blood oath.

And so I do not sing the back-to school song as I push the vacuum toward the middle of the pool and pull it back to where I stand at the edge. And I do not ask about Nora, whose bureau has been cleared off, her Jean Naté, silver pillbox, and photograph of her and my father in Maine gone, her drawers empty, and even her soft blue bathrobe no longer hanging in her bathroom.

"You missed a spot," my father says of a thin line of dirt I was just going back to get.

"Okay."

"How's Mr. Morgan doing?"

This surprises me, for I would have thought that speaking of my mother's father would be completely against the rules. "He's good," I say, then wish I'd just said okay, in case my father was hoping my grandfather missed him.

"Still playing a lot of golf?"

"Every morning. He won the tournament this year."

My father laughs. "You know, all his life he was a terrible golfer. Never got better. Year after year." I know this story well, but my chest swells at my father's telling of it, my father talking about my mother's father, those two smashed sides of me fusing briefly. "And then"—my father lets out a shrill wheeze of delight—"he had that stroke, remember, in 'sixty-seven, and suddenly he could hit that ball like nobody's business. He was hitting in the seventies."

I laugh as if I've never heard it before. I feel like I'm glowing. I don't want him to stop talking about Grindy. "He still has that smelly old spaniel."

"Oh yeah?" he says, but he hasn't heard me. His attention has moved on. "You missed another spot right there." He takes the vacuum from me and finishes the rest of the pool. We do the chemical tests but he won't let me hold the little vials or squeeze in the drops. Then Patrick comes out and he and my father start talking about grub control and some sort of seeder or feeder. My father wants to show Patrick something in the machine room. It's hot and electric-feeling in that room and they stay in there for a long time, my father wanting to know if Patrick thinks the pressure on the something-or-other is too low. I go to the minifridge and pull out a tiny can of V8 juice. Then I go into my mother's rose garden.

The regular flower beds—daffodils in early spring, then tulips and peonies, daisies and lilies—begin outside the living room's French doors, where they curl around a stone terrace, drop alongside a set of stone steps, spread along the edges of another, smaller terrace, then drop again to fan out along the stone walls that are the border of the main body of the garden, an English garden with a floor of grass and two long, squat hedges whose ends are scrolled toward each other. On either side of these sculpted center hedges, in long dense prickly rows, are the beds of roses. At the far end of the garden is a small fountain painted robin's-egg blue with a centerpiece of two pudgy children holding a large fish that spurts out water. Behind the fountain are two sets of moss-covered steps that lead to a black wrought-iron door, which opens onto that patch of woods on the inside of the curve of the back driveway. The garden and the door seem to belong to something much more ancient than the house and the driveway.

On a summer day, in full sun beneath a dark blue sky, this garden is magical. My mother is normally in it somewhere, crouched down beside a rosebush with her gardening basket, a kerchief holding back her hair, her gloved hands digging deep into the dirt. She has many varieties of roses and knows all their names: Southern

Belle, Black Magic, April in Paris, Mister Lincoln. If I don't understand the name, she'll explain it to me. A full pale pink rose with a tiny yellow center is called Christopher Marlowe, and she tells me all about his plays, the one about the doctor who exchanged his soul to the devil for twenty-four years of magical powers, and the one about the queen and the sailor who fall in love in a cave during a storm. Her roses are different colors and shapes, some thin and delicate like a teardrop, others thick and fluffy with a million petals. They are pale yellow, dark pink, deep red, salmon, lavender, and white. The white ones are the puffiest. They look like they're made of meringue. I used to play around the fountain, trying to catch the eyes of the smiling children wrestling their fish, running up one set of steps to the black door and down the other, around and around, until I got so hot I'd fling off my clothes and slip into the cold, ice cold, fountain water.

But now everything in the garden is dead or dying. The heads of the roses, if they have not already fallen off, are dry and drained of color, their leaves hole-punched by insects. Every plant is encircled by a wreath of its own debris. The grass is burnt, the shrubs white with aphids. The fountain water is olive green. A black sludge covers the bottom. Nothing trickles out of the fish's mouth. This whole spectacular place, the most spectacular thing about the property, is being punished for having been my mother's.

While my father and Patrick move from poolhouse to shed, drive off someplace and come back, and operate many machines all at once, I try to resuscitate the garden. I drain the fountain, scrape out the slimy leaves and dirt, and refill it. I spray the shrubs and rake up all the death. And then I water. I press my thumb down on the lip of the hose to create a spray like my mother always did. I can feel the leaves and roots of the plants thanking me as they gulp the water down.

"Well, you've been a busy little bee this morning," Mrs. Tabor says when she brings lunch out to the pool.

"It will perish if no one tends it." I've been reenacting scenes from *The Secret Garden* as I work and haven't completely stepped out of character.

My father puts the back of his hand to his forehead and tips his head to one side. He's taken my accent for southern and become Scarlett O'Hara instead. "Oh, my. It will simply perish. Whatever shall we do?"

"I could think of a thing or two," Mrs. Tabor says in her regular voice, smiling at my father as she sips her drink.

She drinks vodka like my father but mixes it with orange juice during the day. My father used to have a rule about waiting until five o'clock on the dot before having a drink (sometimes we'd watch the clock on the stove and count down the last minute together), but now I wonder if that had been my mother's rule. Today he drinks two martinis with lunch.

After he's finished his sandwich, he pushes his plate away, sits back, and sighs. "I wonder what the poor people are doing today."

Mrs. Tabor chortles.

Then he stands up. "Well, I think it's time for a swim." He pulls down his swimming trunks in one fast motion.

Patrick and Elyse erupt in laughter at the sight of his bare bum and floppy brown penis.

"Well," Mrs. Tabor says, and stands up unsteadily, "I guess I will too." Off comes the top and then the bottom to her bikini. Her breasts hang square and low, and her pubic hair is not black but salt and pepper, like Mallory's grandmother's old schnauzer.

Patrick and Elyse, howling, struggle to inch off their own wet bathing suits, the struggle only increasing their laughter.

The four of them splash around together at first, then Patrick and Elyse go to the diving board to do naked jumping and screaming, and my father and Mrs. Tabor hang onto each other in the shallow end.

"Look at the old prude in her chair," Mrs. Tabor cackles.

My father doesn't look. He's touching Mrs. Tabor's breasts.

"Watch out, Gardiner," Elyse says, looking down from the diving board, wearing only a life jacket because she can't swim yet. "You're gonna get a boner."

Everyone but me bursts out laughing.

"What's a boner?" I ask, and that puts them over the edge. Even if it's at my own expense, I like making my father laugh. He has a lot of pretend and halfhearted laughs, but his real one makes a clicking sound in the back of his throat that I love to hear.

I cannot seem to get on my bike and return to Water Street, even though it feels like I have come onstage too late to be anything but the straight man to their summer antics.

In the early evening, without my father knowing, I call my mother.

"Can I stay another night?"

"Of course. I'm glad it's going so well. All summer I worried."

"Worried about what?"

"I just worried, that's all."

"What do you mean?"

"You two were so close."

After a while she says, "Daley?"

"Yeah."

"Are you sure you want to stay?"

"Yeah," I say, but my throat is tight.

"Oh, honey. Maybe you should come back here. You'll see him on the weekend. You'll see him every weekend. And things will fall back into place with him."

"Mrs. Tabor is here a lot."

"Mmm," she says, which means she already knew that. "Patrick's one of your best friends."

"Uh-huh."

"Isn't he?" She's doing something, painting her nails maybe. The phone keeps slipping away from her mouth.

Patrick follows my father around like one of his dogs. It isn't the same. Nothing is the same. "How'd your interviews go?"

"Pretty well. One in particular."

"What?"

"This child advocacy lawyer needs an assistant. He's a good guy. He helps children."

"When will you know if you got the job?"

"Within a week, he said. But I've got two more interviews tomorrow. I'll be home by four. Come home for dinner, okay? I miss you."

"I miss you, too."

I hang up and nearly pick it up again to ask her to come get me. Then Patrick calls for me, saying we're going to Peking Garden for dinner.

I've come here a lot with my parents. We always got a booth along the wall and had a waiter named Roy, the owner's son. My father would order the moo goo gai pan just because he loved to say it to Roy in a funny voice. My mother would get a drink with a bright paper parasol so I could play with it. I liked to pretend it belonged to my spoon and that the fork was in love with her, though he could never see her face behind the parasol. I never suspected we all weren't having a good time.

There are six of us now—Frank showed up again right at dinnertime—so they put us at a round table in the middle. Mrs. Tabor is wearing a shimmery green dress that falls to her ankles and has wide sleeves that droop onto her plate and into the small bowls of sauces without her noticing. She and my father order a new drink every time Roy comes to the table. Roy winks at me but he acts like he doesn't know my father, who is quiet tonight, his head hung low over his plate, his eyes casting around, seeing little. I wonder if he misses sitting in our booth, the three of us on a Sunday night.

Patrick and I order spareribs. We slather on the sweet-and-sour sauce and compete to see who can gnaw down to a clear bone quicker.

"You two are revolting," Frank says.

My father looks at me hard. "You ever see your mother eat a piece of chicken?"

"No," I lie.

He breaks into a fake smile and chuckles. I can tell there is nothing funny about how my mother eats chicken. "She'd eat everything—tendons, cartilage, the works. Then she'd crack open the bone and suck it dry. I'm not kidding." He shakes his head. "She was a beauty."

"Now you're the chicken bone," Mrs. Tabor says, pleased with her analogy.

My father isn't pleased. He mutters something I can't hear and tries to gesture to Roy, who turns and goes into the kitchen without acknowledging him.

Elyse, reaching for a different crayon, knocks her water straight into my father's lap.

He leaps up and screams "Goddammit!" as loud as he's able, as if he's forgotten we're in a restaurant. "Goddammit! Goddammit!" His yellow eyes in his purple face flash from Elyse to Mrs. Tabor. The restaurant is silent. Roy stands stunned by the fish tank.

Mrs. Tabor starts laughing.

"Fuck you, you little bitch. Fuck you!" He picks up a chair like he's going to throw it at her, but it just shakes in his hands until

Roy's father comes and puts it back down and wipes up the spill. Mrs. Tabor never quite wipes the smirk off her face.

My father sometimes irritated my mother by complaining too much about Hugh Stewart, his boss at the brokerage firm. She'd tell him to hush and sometimes he might say *Hush yourself,* but that's about as heated as they ever got in front of me. He yelled, but it was never at her; it was always about someone else. And when she was mad at him, she squeezed her lips together and looked away. I wonder what Roy and his father think has happened to my father, who used to chat easily with them up at the counter while he was paying the bill.

Elyse continues to color in her place mat and Frank looks blankly at the wall ahead of him, but Patrick is crying. I take slow breaths and count backward from a thousand in my head. Roy slips a blue parasol beside my spoon. It has a thin band of paper around it, keeping it shut.

On the way home, Elyse asks my father to sing her favorite song. He seems to know what she means because he starts singing: "Mr. Rabbit, Mr. Rabbit, your ears are mighty . . ." He pauses and she fills in—*blue*—and he continues: "Yes, my Lord, I've been pooping in my shoe." Elyse tries to join in but she's laughing too hard, so my father sings the chorus alone:

> *"Every little creature's gotta shine shine shine.*
> *Every little creature's gotta shine."*

It's hard to leave the next afternoon. I want to go, but it feels awful, like I'm leaving my father all over again. I keep putting it off, letting Elyse talk me into a game of Candyland, making water balloons with Patrick.

They're in the sunroom when I go to say goodbye.

"I'm going to hit the road now."

"All right," my father says, looking at Mrs. Tabor. "See ya."

I go over and kiss him on the cheek. He keeps his eyes fixed on Mrs. Tabor and does not kiss back. "I'll be back Friday."

"When school starts, come with Patrick in the car pool. I think it's Mrs. Utley on Fridays," Mrs. Tabor says.

I don't know if I should kiss her. "Okay. Thanks for everything."

"You're welcome."

As soon as I cross the threshold, my father begins his hoarse whisper and Mrs. Tabor shushes him and then begins whispering, too.

At the end of the driveway I almost turn my bike around. I picture going back in the sunroom, asking if I can stay just one more night. But once I'm out on the main road, my legs start pumping the pedals hard and I don't even look at the front of the house as I whiz past.

I feel light and free as my bike drops down the long hill into town. I flip it into the hardest gear and pedal the whole way down, moving faster than I ever have on my bike, not bothering to look around for cars turning in or out of side streets and driveways. A few hippies hanging out on a bench in the park shout something to me but I'm going too fast to hear. I rise up from the seat going over the train tracks. The bike bucks and twists but I stay on. I pass the gas station and the sub shop, the kids on the steps of Bruce's (who make no comment today), the gift shop, the library, the Congregational church, and the chowder restaurant. This is still my town. I'm still home.

I remember Neal. I forgot to ask Patrick about him. How did I forget? It's like I had static in my ears up there on Myrtle Street and I couldn't think about the other parts of my life. I feel like calling him up when I get to the apartment, then remember where he is and that my father might answer and how weird that would be.

I turn left down Water Street. I pass our apartment building to see what's at the end of the street. It dead-ends at the harbor. There's a tiny patch of dirty sand and a bench. Two teenagers are sitting on it, making out. My bike makes a *tic-tic-tic* sound as I make a wide U-turn, but it doesn't bother them.

The apartment is nicer than I remember it. The carpet is clean and soft, the ceilings are high, and there's a picture window looking out onto the make-out bench and the harbor beyond that lets in two huge squares of light. My mother is in her bathrobe, straightening chairs at a new table.

She hugs me hard. She smells of lemon furniture polish. It seems at that moment like the best smell on earth. I remember I need to ask her a lot of questions about taking care of her garden.

"How was it?" She pulls away just far enough to see me clearly. She pushes hair from either side of my face. Her skin is shiny from lotion.

"Good."

I feel her eyes raking across my face, as if I've hidden something there really well.

It's the moment I could tell her about the whispering, the drinking, the word *boner,* but the moment passes.

"I'm so glad." She takes her eyes off me and points to the table and the high-backed chairs that surround it. "What do you think?"

"Nice." I stand next to a chair. It has a silky striped cushion sewn into it. "Fancy."

"And," she says, pointing to the walls. She's hung paintings from Myrtle Street. She took the ones of the sea, which are my favorites too. In her bedroom she hung the portrait of me and Garvey sitting on the lip of the fountain when we were much younger. In the painting I have no freckles, and my eyes are too far apart, and you can see where the artist had to paint in more background over Garvey's head when my mother brought it back, complaining his hair was too poufy.

Her room looks even bigger than I remember. I see the canopy bed and know that I'm not done feeling angry about her having it, along with the big beautiful room and the deck.

My mother has climbed up onto the bed and is dangling her legs off it and staring out the French doors. I'm aware of something different about her, something lighter. She is happy. Beneath her is a folded duvet, velvet on one side, satin on the other.

"Nora called, sweetie. She really wants to see you."

"Oh."

"You know your father let her go."

"Yeah, I guess I put that together."

She looks like she's going to say more but stops. Then she says, "You should call her."

"I will." But the idea of Nora is like my stuffed animals. It feels like there is suddenly no place for her. I stroke the velvet blanket. "Is this new?"

"Yes," she says. "Isn't it divine?"

"Did you get me one?"

"They only had them for a queen-sized bed."

"It's a good thing you have the bed then. Good thing you got that, too."

"Daley."

"I don't know where you're getting all this money. All you did all summer was worry about money, and now you're buying yourself all kinds of things. I guess you sold some of Granny's jewelry."

"What?"

"I know about how you emptied the safe."

"I didn't—I needed to have some—Jesus. He told you that?"

"He told me you cleaned it out. I saw it. It's empty."

"I didn't steal it. I just needed to get some protection, Daley. For you. For me to take care of you. But we've agreed now on a settlement."

"I wish you'd tell me things, Mom. I wish I knew what they were talking about when they say things like Al Carr. I wish you'd told me you weren't going to see Sylvie but to meet some guy so he could stick his boner into you."

My mother has gone pale. She is pointing a finger at the door. "Go. Go to your room right now."

"Go to your crappy shit-hole room, Daley." The anger is like vomit. I can't stop it from coming out. "I'm only here five nights a week and I'm not sleeping with anyone, so it makes perfect sense to give me the dark smelly room with the little shitty beds." I slam her door hard. Bitch, I think. Bitch bitch bitch.

5

School starts. Five new kids join our grade. It's always the same with new kids. They come on the first day in their public school clothes, their huge pointy collars, polyester blends, and all the wrong shoes, but by the next Monday they're in topsiders and Bean shoes, the boys with tiny buttons at the tips of their little collars and the girls in wraparound skirts. Then, once they look like the rest of us, they change everything around. No one is in my homeroom with Miss Perth. Mallory, Patrick, Gina, and Neal are all with Mr. Harding. I think on the first day that Neal will explain why he didn't write back. I stand right behind him in the lunch line, but he never says a word. By Thursday I hear he likes a new girl named Tillie Armstrong. I decide never to speak to him again.

On Friday I take a suitcase to school and in the afternoon I wait with Patrick and the other kids from his carpool for Mrs. Utley to pick us up. She's late because she had brownies in the oven. She brings them and we pass the warm pan from the front to the back to the way-back, cutting out huge squares. She's even brought napkins. The brownies are dense, undercooked, and delicious. Like many of the mothers I've seen since I've been back, she's curious about my summer "adventure" and wants me to be sure to say hello to my mother for her. I feel her watching me in the rearview mirror more than she watches the others.

All week Patrick has been saying there's going to be a surprise at Myrtle Street, but he won't tell me what it is. I think maybe my puppy is back, but when Mrs. Utley pulls in I see that the surprise involves construction of some kind. There's a bulldozer in the driveway and a huge truck piled high with dirt and brush. Embedded in the dirt are glints of pale blue. I grab my bookbag and suitcase, holler out a thank-you, and run. I stop at the stone wall. The rose garden is gone. There's still the terrace off the living room and the steps leading down, but the scrolled bushes and flower beds, the roses, the fountain, the stone steps, and the iron door leading nowhere are all gone.

"We're building a tennis court!" Patrick has big teeth with flecks of white and he flashes them at me until I punch him hard in the stomach.

"Goddamn," he gasps, bent over. "I thought you liked tennis."

My father comes home from work early on Fridays. He is sitting in that armchair in the kitchen, the dogs pooled at his feet.

"Well, what do you think?" He's proud of himself. He wants me to show my shock. He wants that satisfaction.

"Looks good," I push out. I go outside again so he won't see me cry. The bulldozer and the truck have driven away, but the smell clings to the air. The smell of my mother.

I have to get off the property. I head to the front, and once on the road I know where I'm going. I cross the street and follow a thin pretty driveway down to the little house at the bottom. They have geraniums in pots on either side of the front door. The bell is the old-fashioned kind, attached to the middle of the door, that you twist like a can opener. It makes a racket inside, but no dog barks.

The taller, gaunter one answers.

"Hello, Miss Vance." I rehearsed my speech on the driveway. "I was wondering if I could just say hello to your dog." I know I have to say *your dog,* so they won't think I'm coming to reclaim him. "I've been away all summer."

"Yes, you have." Her voice is low. "Step into the parlor."

We stand in the black-and-white entryway. She makes a funny sound with her teeth and tongue, as if she is cracking nuts, and the puppy races from a room, leaps down a few steps, and scrambles across the tiles to me. He's whining and pressing his nose hard into my hand, but when he jumps up Miss Vance says, "Major!" and he puts his paws back on the floor quickly. When I squat down he nuzzles his nose in my neck and his tail whaps so fast back and forth I think he's going to hurt himself. He's grown in height and girth and his hair is longer and soft. His eyes are a pale olive green. He is a much more beautiful dog than I remember.

"Well, I think someone was greatly missed." She sounds angry, but when I look up her narrow face has bunched into a smile. "He likes his tea in the garden at about this time. Would you like to join us?"

I follow her to a door at the back of the house. Before opening it, she calls up a thin set of wooden stairs, "Teatime, Mother."

I thought there was just a sister. The mother would be at least a hundred. How will she get down those stairs?

Major bolts through the door as soon as Miss Vance turns the knob, but then he tears back to lick my hand. He hears a squirrel rustling in some leaves and he's off again. The whole time I'm there he seems torn between his usual routine of chasing and sniffing and making sure I'm still there.

Miss Vance and I sit in white latticed iron chairs that press the bare skin of my legs into small cubes. A woman in a white dress and white shoes comes out with a tray and sets it on a glass table nearby. On the tray is a silver teapot, a small pitcher of hot water and an even smaller one of cream, half a lemon wrapped in cloth, three blue teacups, four saucers, and a plate of thin lace cookies.

"Thank you, Heloise," Miss Vance says, leaning toward the tray. She makes the nut-cracking noise again and Major comes to her side. Onto the extra saucer she pours tea up to the rim and sets a lace cookie to float on top. She nestles the saucer in the grass by her foot while Major sits watching. Another crack and Major bends down to eat and drink.

"There you are," she says, without looking at the woman approaching in the grass.

This is the shorter, rounder one, the one who always wears a blue wool coat in winter, the one I thought was her sister.

"You'll have to pull over a chair, Mother."

I jump out of my seat. "Please, sit here. I'm happy on the grass."

The woman waves me off, heading toward another cluster of chairs. I don't notice the garden until the old woman walks into it. It's a wilder, more chaotic garden than my mother's, the stone pathways overgrown, the flowers tall and frizzy. There are tufts of long tangled beach grasses, wildflowers, and even a few miniature trees in no particular design. She moves slowly; both her legs are wrapped in bandages. She pulls out a thin green chair from the chaos, and as she sets it down she knocks the tray slightly and mutters something that sounds awfully like, "Sorry, Father," under her breath.

I stare at her face. Its flesh is soft and powdery, but no more lined or weathered than the other Miss Vance's. They couldn't be more than a few years apart in age. They fuss about the tea together, asking me how I take it—strong, weak, or in between; milk, lemon, lump sugar, or sifted—and then argue pleasantly about the amounts put in and their effects on the hue of the tea. "It's too pale now!" "It's just right, just right for me," the plumper Miss Vance reassures her.

I feel like a character who has stumbled into another world where things are slightly creepy but also beautiful and soothing. The tall flowers in the garden cast long shadows on the grass and everything that is not shadow is gold in the low late-afternoon sun. If they asked me to stay the night, I would.

After he's finished a second saucer of tea and cookie, Major lays his head in tall Miss Vance's lap. She bends her head over the dog and strokes him for a long time, then she straightens up to look at me. "I understand if you want to take him back." She begins the sentence loudly but finishes in a tremble.

"Oh, no. Oh, no." I shake my head furiously. "I just wanted to visit, to make sure he was really here. I wasn't very attached to him."

"Oh," she says sadly.

"I'd only had him for a few days. I knew even when we got him that I was going to be leaving, but my father didn't."

"That sounds like an awfully big secret for one little girl to carry around."

I'm careful not to nod. I don't want them to think I feel sorry for myself or anything, which is what Garvey always teases me about. *Is widdew Daywie feewing oh so sowwy fo' hewsewf again?* My throat aches, and I wonder if I'm coming down with something.

A warm hand clutches mine. "Father, I think a game of Parcheesi would do us all a world of good."

On Saturday my father and Mrs. Tabor have friends over for lunch. Some of the guests are old friends of my father's, people I've seen in our living room for years, and some are Mrs. Tabor's friends, a few married couples and a lot of divorcées like her. The two groups don't mingle much. Mrs. Tabor is younger than my father; her male friends look like they come from Garvey's generation with their shoulder-length hair and thick sideburns, and the women wear looser clothes in bolder colors than the wives of my father's friends in their stiff pastel dresses.

Patrick and I mix the Bloody Marys at a table we've set up on the lawn. Elyse turned five this week and rides her new red bike with training wheels around the edge of the pool. By three, no one has had lunch and the adult faces are red and screaming at each other. At least that's what it sounds like to me.

"What do you mean you're giving up paddle! Gil, did you hear this?"

"Did I hear what?"

"Your wife. She's giving up paddle this winter to volunteer at the loony bin."

"Precisely where she belongs!"

Mr. Porters goes running into the poolhouse and comes out with an umbrella. Then he leaps off the diving board in his clothes, the umbrella open above him like Mary Poppins.

Everyone screams and hoots. A man I don't know jumps in with a set of golf clubs. More shouting. Wives towel off the clubs and the leather bag and spread everything on the grass to dry. The sun slips down farther and they switch to gin-and-tonics and martinis. Mrs. Tabor sends me inside to make up a platter of cheese and crackers, and Patrick is sent downtown on his bike for more ice. When I come out, I see Elyse ride her new bike straight into the pool. I drop the platter on the grass and run.

"Elyse went in the pool!" I scream, but my voice is swallowed by the boom of the adults' talk.

I dive in. She's still on the bike at the bottom, tilted toward the drain. I grab her, expecting her to come free easily. But she's clutching the handlebars, and though everything is lighter underwater I can't lift the two at once. I tug at her hard but she's so stubborn, even underwater, even when she doesn't know how to swim, and will not let go of her new bicycle. Then the water shudders with a muffled crash and the man who jumped in with the golf clubs is lifting me, Elyse, and her bike to the surface.

Elyse doesn't need CPR. Her lips are blue, but her face is bright red and she comes up hollering about her bike being wet and ruined.

"Let me take you to your mommy," the man says to her once we're all out and dripping on the cement. Mrs. Tabor has her back to the pool, waving an arm in the air, shouting out a story.

"I don't want my mommy. I want to dry off my goddamn bike!"

I can't catch my breath but I look at him gratefully and he touches the top of my head before he drips off and blends back in with the crowd.

Sunday is quieter. By noon it has begun to rain. Mallory comes over and we make prank calls in the kitchen. Patrick is really good at voices.

"Is John Wall there?" he asks, becoming a man calling on business. "Then is his wife Susie there?" He smiles at us, then takes the smile right out of his voice when he speaks again. "Well, aren't there any Walls there?" He tilts the phone away from his ear and we can hear the lady saying no. Patrick switches back to his regular kid voice. "Then what's holding up your house, lady?"

We always save the best for last. Patrick gets out his stop watch and we each pick a number in the phone book. The minute the person answers, the timing starts. The goal is to keep your person on the line as long as possible. My trick is to always go for the old-sounding names, Lillian or Evelyn or Elijah. Old people are much more trusting and have time to talk. My record is twenty-five minutes. No one has been able to touch it.

Today Mallory goes first. She pretends to be a little girl who burnt herself. "It hurts," she says. "Mommy isn't here. She ran away. With the garbageman." Patrick and I are dying. "They live at the dump now. I don't like to visit." And then she slams the phone down fast. "He said he was going to call the police."

The phone rings beneath her hand and we jump and crack up but don't dare answer it. It rings five, then six times. Finally I realize it could be about my mother: Car accident. Hospital. I pick it up. There is a long pause at the other end; then a woman asks for Mrs. Tabor. "I wouldn't have called here," she adds, "but it's important." I recognize the voice but can't place it.

"Who is it?" Patrick and Mallory whisper as I set down the receiver.

I shrug. "Where's your mom?"

He points to the den. But the rest of the downstairs is empty. I call up the stairs and think I hear something. I go up. My father's door is slightly ajar and I can hear the TV.

I knock and no one answers. "Mrs. Tabor?" I say as I poke my head through.

I can't make sense of what I see except their faces, which turn toward the door in shock and then fury.

"Get the fuck out!" my father hollers at me, and when I don't move instantly Mrs. Tabor echoes him: "Get the fuck out of this room, Day-*lee*!"

I'm down the stairs and back in the kitchen before I even know I've moved away from their door, before I even register what I saw: my father naked on his hands and knees on the bed, his shoulders between Mrs. Tabor's spread legs, licking her red vagina like a beast bent over its kill.

"She's busy right now," I hear myself say into the mouthpiece.

The woman lets out a sigh. "Will you just tell her to call me about the orange slices for the game on Wednesday?"

"Okay." My voice wobbles. Patrick and Mallory are staring at me. I don't want to get off the phone and have to explain.

"Daley, I'm so sorry about your parents. It must be very hard for you."

"Yeah." It's more a breath than a word.

"You can always come talk to me if you want. Anytime. My door is open."

I still have no idea who she is.

My father, bent over, head low between his shoulders, nothing more than an animal. I didn't know about that, I want to tell her. I never knew about that.

*   *   *

That night my father and I begin a ritual that will last until I get my driver's license. After Mrs. Tabor feeds us, I put my book bag and my suitcase by the back door. My father makes a drink. I wait. He makes another. He snaps at Patrick to turn down the radio. He tells Frank a joke about a black couple going to a costume ball. The punch line is the word fudgsicle. I've heard it before. He glances at the clock. I glance at the clock. I play solitaire on the kitchen floor. Elyse kicks all my cards and I tell her to put them back and Mrs. Tabor tells me to pick on someone my own size. Mr. Seeley calls to say the dogs are barking so loud he can't hear himself think. My father is polite on the phone, then slams it down and marches around the room swearing. My cards get kicked again. He makes another drink. I need to go home and start my homework. The cuckoo clock chirps eight times.

"I'm putting the steaks on now," Mrs. Tabor says to him, which is his cue.

He puts down his drink and moves slowly to the drawer across the room where he keeps his checkbook. It's a blue binder and he turns the pages slowly. With the ballpoint pen he keeps in it, he writes out the check for my mother. He folds it in half and hands it to me. He looks at me like I'm draining the blood from his veins.

He doesn't speak much on the short ride to Water Street. We pull into the farthest spot from my mother's car. He bought that car for her birthday last year. He doesn't cut the engine or walk me to the door. He will never once in seven years get out of the car, as if the pavement around my mother's apartment is radioactive. He keeps his fists clenched on the steering wheel as I kiss him. I get my suitcase out of the back, call out a last goodbye, and walk away. He has driven off before I reach the door.

My mother has put big pots of plants on the doorstep, and there is a window box outside my bedroom. All the lights are on, even in

my room. The door is unlocked, the air in the apartment warm
and moist. I find my mother in the kitchen, boiling up a packet of
chipped beef. She is in a new bathrobe, her hair wet from a shower.
The bathrobe is white with a striped sash tied tight to one side.
Her waist is tiny. There's an ashtray drying on the dishrack, though
my mother doesn't smoke.

She hugs me and she feels small in my arms. Her kiss on my
cheek is greasy. "How was it?"

The demolished rose garden, Elyse at the bottom of the pool,
Dad feeding between Mrs. Tabor's legs—it all blurs into a feeling
that seems to have no name. "I'm tired."

"Have you eaten?"

"Yes."

"Homework?"

"Tons."

"It's nearly eight-thirty."

"I know."

"Daley, you're going to have to—"

"I can't do homework over there."

"Then come home earlier."

"I can't."

"Then call me and I'll come get you."

"No!" The idea of my mother driving that car into the driveway of my father's house, where she lived for nineteen years, horri-
fies me.

She smooths out my forehead. "Don't make that face. You'll
get wrinkles."

I hand her the check and she unfolds it, then chucks it on the
counter.

"It's fifty less than he owes me." Her mouth presses into a
straight line.

She goes to her desk, writes a short note that begins *Gardiner*
—in her big round letters. When she is done, she rereads and un-
derlines several words, including the word *lawyer*. Then she slides
it into an envelope, puts a stamp on it, and shoves it into her purse
on a chair by the door. I don't need to know all the words now—I'll
hear all about it next weekend. Next weekend my father will be
waving it around like a flag.

"Come sit with me while I eat. Then you can start your homework."

We sit at the shiny dining room table. I hate chipped beef and
the smell of chipped beef. It looks like dog food mixed with phlegm.
Bulbs of steam rise from her plate but she doesn't blow on the food
and doesn't seem to get scalded as she eats. Her mood has shifted
since the check. My mood is the same—a burnt-out flatness that I
know bothers her. My answers to her questions are short and un-
imaginative. I don't want to be sitting there watching the chipped
beef go into her mouth but I don't want to do my homework or go
to sleep or watch TV. There's nothing I want to do.

"I saw *A Chorus Line* this weekend. I really want to take you."

"You saw it already? With who?"

"My friend Martin and his son."

Martin. There it was, just like my brother said.

"You said you'd take me."

"I want to. I just said that."

"No, you said you'd just seen it."

"And that I'd like to take you."

"But you already saw it. And plays are expensive. You're always
telling me that."

"Daley."

"I can't believe you saw it with somebody else's kid."

I sit back in the chair and cross my arms over my chest.

My mother laughs. "You're acting a little bit like a two-year-old right now."

Before I know it, the chipped beef smashes against the wall. My mother is still holding her fork and knife. Her voice is very very quiet. "Leave this room right now. I do not want to see you until morning. Any privileges you had are gone."

I stand up and start down the hallway.

"I swear, Daley Amory, you are like a wild animal every time you come home from your father's," she says, before I slam my door on her.

6

On the Wednesday night before Thanksgiving, Garvey comes home from college. A friend drops him off. I hear him shut a car door and shout something. Then he is there in our apartment for the first time, his long lanky body making everything—the sideboard, the desk, the walls—seem smaller. He is growing a sparse rust-colored beard, nothing like the hair on his head, which is thick and dirty blond. His eyes are small chips of blue in murky water. He smells like the sleeping bags in the shed on Myrtle Street. I breathe him in. I cannot get enough of it. I have missed him so much more than I knew. He has to peel me off of him to introduce himself to Pauline, my babysitter. He makes a point of shaking her hand, even though she's across the room and has to take off the oven mitt for the macaroni she's just about to take out of the oven.

"So you're taking care of the pipsqueak."

"We take care of each other." She smiles at me. I hear her accent—*each otha*—more distinctly with Garvey in the room. She comes every day after school until my mother gets home at seven-thirty, and we laugh a lot. At first I didn't understand why we couldn't have Nora. She'd moved in with her sister in Lynn and came sometimes to take me out to Friendly's and didn't seem to be working at all, but my mother thought I should have someone younger, and less expensive. Pauline is in tenth grade and her boobs are growing so fast they pop the buttons off her shirt. We're always finding buttons and cracking up. I see my brother taking all this in.

We eat the macaroni on the sofa. Garvey drills Pauline with questions: where does she live, what's that neighborhood like, does she have siblings, did her parents grow up here, has she done much traveling, where would she like to go most? Maybe we'll all take a trip there, to California, one day, he concludes.

And then Mom comes home and Pauline leaves.

"Wow," my brother says, smoothing down the back of his hair. "Va va voom."

"She's barely fifteen," my mother says.

"She's not going to be able to balance on two feet if she grows any bigger."

"She'll manage just fine." My mother hangs up her coat and gives my brother another hug. "Oh, it's so good to see you," she says through gritted teeth. She always grits her teeth when she's feeling affection.

"It's good to be here. Nice pad, Ma." He swings his head around. "You got some serious loot from the big house."

My mother eats the rest of my macaroni standing up. We're all still standing up. I'm not sure why.

"How's it going there?" she asks him.

"Oh, fair to middling."

"Yeah?" Meaning she wants to hear more.

"I've been in school so long."

"Garvey."

"I'm just saying. I was in boarding school for four years before this. Everyone else runs around like they've been let out of a cage, and I feel like it's just another cage. A less interesting cage, actually."

"Three and a half more years. That's all. Then it's over forever."

"Yeah." He slumps to the sofa and puts his boots up on the coffee table. Mom doesn't tell him to take them off. He pulls out a new pack of cigarettes, smashes both ends into his palm a couple of times, unwraps the cellophane, then slides one out and lights it. "Then I get to go out and find my perfect career that will swallow up the rest of my promising life." He blows out a long stream of smoke. "It all may be quite moot. I wasn't able to register this week for next semester's classes. Dad's a little late on the payments, it turns out."

My mother sits down on the couch beside him. "You're joking, right?"

"I am not joking."

"You need to talk to him about that. Tomorrow."

Garvey taps the ashes onto his jeans and rubs them in. My mother brings him an ashtray but he doesn't use it. "I don't need his money."

"Garvey, you need this degree."

"I can pay for it myself. Brian Foley pays his own way. He works in the library I think. I visited him a few weeks ago."

"UMass only costs three hundred dollars a year. Of course he can work it off. Harvard is several thousand."

"So I'll go to UMass. Harvard is a bunch of self-inflated morons. They all walk around in tuxes on the weekend. I'm not kidding. I met this bartender last weekend and he's starting a moving company, furniture and crap, and he asked me to do some jobs for him. Might have to miss a few classes, but it's good money."

"Please talk to your father."

"No."

"I'm worried now."

"I'm worried too."

My mother gets up and rinses off the plate in the kitchen. She takes her time. Eventually the dishwasher squeaks open and the plate is slotted in. I know there's nothing else for her to do in there but she stays in there, thinking.

I watch Garvey smoke.

"Dad and Mrs.—I mean *Catherine*—are married now," I say.

"I heard. A little Nassau combo platter: divorce, wedding, and a nice golden tan for the holidays."

"Frank's got your room."

Garvey snorts. "I'll have to show him my *Playboy* stash."

"He already found it."

"Really? Cagey bugger."

"He's weird. "

"With a mother like that."

"How's Heidi?"

"Who?"

I give him a look.

"She's got a new boyfriend. He's very dependable." He says the word *dependable* with nunlike primness, tilting his head, pursing his lips.

I laugh and that eggs him on.

"He shows up at precisely the right time, he says precisely the right things, and he always, always has a condom."

Frank has condoms. When we're really bored, Patrick and I sneak them out of his room and fill them with water and lob them at Elyse. She calls them greasy balloons and shrieks whenever she sees one.

"Do you have a new girlfriend?"

"Not really."

"What about Deena?"

"Who?" This time he really doesn't know who I'm talking about.

"That girl in your apartment in Somerville."

A grimace, as brief as a gust of wind, passes across his face. "I never had anything to do with her." He's a bad liar. He keeps talking to cover it up. "She's a very fucked-up young woman."

That's what she said about you, I want to say but I don't. I don't want to push him any lower than he already is.

"And you, my little hermitoid. What is going on in your sixth-grade world?"

I knew he'd ask this and I know just the kinds of thing he likes to hear so I prepared just the right story. "Funny you should ask," I say, warming up. He smiles and I continue. "There's this new boy, Kevin."

"Kevin what?"

"Kevin Mackerel."

"Mackerel? Like the fish?"

"I don't know. I think so."

"Oh, Kevin Mackerel," he begins to sing. "Is he a fish or a man? I can't tell and nobody can!"

My mother comes in then, all fired up with new reasons why Garvey has to stay in college and how she will talk to Al about how to proceed, and I never get to tell my story about how Kevin Mackerel got suspended for farting so much.

No way, my brother would have said.

Yes, way, I would have said, he did so. He just kept doing it really loudly and really stinkily and wouldn't stop. He got warnings, demerits, a note home but nothing stopped him. So now he's out of school until December first.

No way! I can hear him, his hands pulling at his hair, his face full of real laughter.

The next morning we get ready to go up to Dad and Catherine's. We'll have lunch there and dinner with Mom. I wear a black velvet dress. It has white lace cuffs and a white lace collar.

"Oh look, it's the first pilgrim!" Garvey says.

He's wearing the same jeans and a faded flannel shirt with a ripped pocket that flaps around. His hair is matted in the back. Because we're going to see Dad, I notice these things. So does my mother. "The shower's free," she says.

"Oh goodie," he says, and lights another cigarette.

We drive up in Mom's car. I know this is a mistake. We should have left earlier and walked.

My father comes out on the back porch. He's laughing and shaking his head.

"I thought," he begins, fake chuckling, waiting to make sure we're in earshot, "I thought your mother had decided to come for Thanksgiving dinner!"

They shake hands. I haven't seen them together since the beginning of last summer. I've never noticed their similarity before, the sloping backs, the narrow eyes.

"When d'you get here?"

"Me and a buddy drove up last night."

"Oh yeah?"

"You're looking good, Dad."

"Can't complain too much. Things good?"

"Yeah, things are good."

"Good."

I can't bear the fakeness and flee to find Patrick.

Frank is in the kitchen, fishing through a drawer in the kitchen.

"Hey," I say.

He grunts back, then, realizing my usefulness, calls out, "Where do you guys keep the tape around here?"

"I dunno." I keep moving. "Where do *you* keep it?"

Patrick and Elyse are watching the parade on TV from the recliners. Patrick moves over for me. His thumb is red and shiny with little indentations under the knuckle from his teeth. He's been sucking it, which he does when he watches TV and forgets people can see him.

A ten-story Snoopy floats down a crowded street.

I hate that parade, and get up.

I hear the screen door slam.

From the French windows in the living room, I see Garvey walking onto the tennis court. It's the first time he's seen it, seen the garden gone. I can't remember if I told him about it. The court's surface is unblemished, a deep dark green with bright white lines. He stands at the far service line facing me but he can't see me. He looks small. As I pass the stairs, I can hear Dad in the upstairs hallway, whispering loudly.

"It's a disgrace. Honestly. He's got on a filthy pair of jeans and an old shirt that smells like cat piss. And his hair." I know my father is waving his hands around his head. "It's a goddamn hornet's nest. You couldn't take him anywhere. 'Me and my buddy drove up last night.' Goes to Harvard and he can't even speak English. You couldn't take him to the club anymore. You couldn't. And she doesn't care. She let him leave the house like that. And then she lets him drive up here in the car I bought her! He has the nerve to bring that up here to my house!"

And then he's downstairs, at the bar, rattling in the ice bucket, cracking the paper on a new bottle of vodka. I go and stand beside him, watching him carry out the motions. On top of the vodka he pours a few drops of vermouth. He puts the tops back on the vodka and vermouth and then, with a small spoon, slides out four tiny onions. I put out my hand and he drops one into it. He puts the rest in his drink, which he stirs with a finger. He straightens the line of bottles, the line of glasses, wipes off the spoon and the counter with a paper towel. Only when he is sitting in his chair does he close his eyes and take his first sip. The clock above him says 11:35. The turkey is on the stove, pale and pimply. Catherine hasn't put it in the oven yet.

I sit beside him on the floor. At some point during the day, I have to tell my father that I'm going back to my mother's until Saturday morning, until Garvey leaves. "You have a good week at school?"

"Yeah," I say, stunned by the question, wishing I prepared for it. Then I realize I can tell my Kevin Mackerel story. This time I won't use his distracting name; I'll get right to the point. "A kid in my class got suspended for farting."

He's bent over his drink. He drinks and shakes his head. It seems like he hasn't really heard. On another day he might jerk up, eyes big and delighted, and say, "You've gotta be kidding me." Then I remember Patrick will have already told him.

"So who's coming for lunch?" I say.

"No one, thank God."

All my life we've had old Mrs. Waverly who had her voice box removed and buzzes out her words with the help of a little silver gadget that looks like an electric razor that she presses to her throat, Mr. Harris who owns the garden shop, and Cousin Morgan, Grindy's cousin who lost a leg and most of an arm in a war. They are all Mom's people and they'll never come to this house again.

My father lifts his lighter to his neck and speaks in Mrs. Waverly's robotic rhythm. "Hel/lo/Da/ley. Are/you/en/joy/ing/school/this/year?" My mother never found his imitations funny, even when he pretended to be Cousin Morgan insisting on passing the heavy gravy boat with his one hand and spilling it in my lap, which did happen one year. My mother's disapproval always made it hard not to laugh, but without it, it isn't as funny. Even my father isn't enjoying it. He starts to pull his arm out of his sleeve to do the gravy routine and then stops and looks at me like he's wondering where he is. Then he smiles and shakes his head. "Jesus Christ. Good riddance to all of them."

He goes back to the bar and I go into the dining room. It's set with Catherine's china, green and brown. I go to the sideboard my mother didn't take and open the top drawer. There they are, the place cards with the painted wooden fruit glued onto a corner and all the names in my mother's big handwriting: **Olivia** (Mrs. Waverly), **Donald** (Mr. Harris), **Cousin Morgan**. There is also **Gardiner**, **Meredith**, **Garvey**, and **Daley**. And way in the back are **Dad** (Grindy), **Mom** (Nonnie), **Judy** (my mother's sister), and **Ashley**,

Hannah, and Lindsey (Judy's daughters). I scoop up every place card and stuff them in my pockets. Then I go out to find Garvey.

He's still on the tennis court, with Frank. They're playing in bare feet. I'm not sure if Garvey has met Frank before. They aren't playing by the regular rules. The alleys are in and you get two extra points if you hit the other person with the ball. Four extra if you ace your serve. And you can serve from anywhere on the court, even right at the net, which Garvey is doing when I come down the old rose garden steps and stand at the green netting that goes around the whole thing. He whales on the ball and it nicks Frank in the shin before skidding off.

"Hit and ace!" Garvey says. "Six points."

They both crack up.

"Shit," Frank squeaks. He's bent over, his hands on his knees for support, laughing hard. I've never seen him laugh before.

I go around and sit on a lawn chair at the side of the court.

Garvey holds his racquet out to me. "Wanna sub in?"

I shake my head. I want him to be friends with Frank. If he's friends with Frank, maybe he'll come up here to Myrtle Street with me more often. I like having him here.

Frank serves the next one and Garvey returns it, a lob that Frank lets bounce as he prepares for an overhead slam. Garvey says, "Oh fuck," and bolts off the court, through the netting, and into the brown leaves beyond. Frank's slam bounces just inside the baseline, then flies up over the netting. To reach it, Garvey runs through leaves and brush and, with a yelp of delight, lobs it back. Frank is laughing too hard to finish the point.

It's the happiest game of tennis I've ever seen.

Patrick and Elyse come out and join me in the chairs. It gets colder and we have to run in for hats and mittens, though Frank and Garvey have unbuttoned their shirts.

After a long time, we are called in for Thanksgiving dinner.

Catherine is wearing a silky lavender shirt cinched over her short skirt by a gold chain belt. She hasn't done up very many buttons on the shirt and I can see the lace of her bra just beneath the four heavy necklaces on her freckled chest.

She doesn't bother with hellos or a Happy Thanksgiving to me or Garvey. She says, "I need plates, now" to me, and, "Will you open these fucking bottles of wine?" to Garvey. She's holding a carving knife and already talking with her eyes closed.

But Garvey, who often kills my mother's bad moods with kindness, isn't going to let her get away with that. "Don't I get to kiss the bride first?" he says, opening his arms.

Catherine puts the knife down hard on the counter but then gives up a small smile.

Even though there is only one less person than we normally have for Thanksgiving, it feels like a sparse gathering. My mother always said a prayer, but Catherine just starts cutting into her meat.

"Ahem." My father, from the other end of the table, looks at her in pretend sternness. "Aren't we forgetting something?"

"Oh, yes." She looks up at the ceiling. "Thanks for nothing, Lord. Next time you cook the goddamn turkey."

My father loves it. "You's a funny one," he says.

She kisses the air in his direction noisily.

He puts out two hands and squeezes, like he's squeezing her boobs.

Garvey raises one eyebrow at me from across the table, and I have to look down in my lap to keep from laughing.

"So." My father turns to Garvey. "Classes good?"

"Yup."

"What're you taking?" It seems less out of curiosity than to get Garvey to prove he's actually going to college.

"Calculus, Middle English, Psych, Anatomy."

"Anatomy? You find out where your dick is yet?"

"Jesus, Dad. You've got little kids here." He turns to Elyse who is finger painting with gravy on the table. "How old are you?"

Without stopping to look up, she says, "None of your beeswax."

"I'm just asking if you've found out where your dick is."

"I've got a pretty good idea," Garvey says, and then he seems to make a decision. He turns to Catherine. "What was Nassau like?"

She doesn't look at him either. "Hot."

"I have some friends who lived there for a couple years. They said there's a grotto out on the north side of the island with all these sea lions and then there's this funky bar where—"

She waves those things away. "We didn't see any of that stuff. We just stayed at the resort."

"They must have had some good-looking tennis courts down there."

Catherine nods.

Garvey pours himself another glass of wine. He's the only one drinking it. "What do you wear when you play tennis?" he asks her. "I mean, are women switching over to shorts or do they still have to wear skirts?"

"I like wearing skirts."

"You have more freedom of movement, don't you? Maybe that's why Billy Jean King beat Bobby Riggs."

"That was a setup," Catherine says.

"You think it was rigged?"

"No pun intended," I say. No one hears me.

"Of course it was rigged," my father says. "He could have beaten her with his left toe if he'd wanted to."

"So why didn't he?"

"Because he got a hell of a lot more money for losing."

"He let himself be a laughingstock for a couple of grand?"

"More than that."

"Where are you getting your information, Dad, from Don Finch?"

My father laughs in spite of himself. Everyone at the table does. Even Elyse knows Don Finch is the worst player at the club and the most hilarious to watch. There's a story that he once played a whole set without making contact with the ball once.

"You know who I saw at the club the other day? Gus Barlow."

"Gus Barlow," Garvey says. "Shit. How is he?" Gus was a classmate of Garvey's at Ashing Academy.

"He's good." I can tell my father is going somewhere with this. So can Garvey. "He's a good kid." My father puts down his fork and knife slowly. "You know, if you cleaned yourself up a bit we could go over there for a meal this weekend."

Garvey shakes his head. "My buffet days at the clubhouse are definitely over."

"Yeah? You're done with the club. Too good for the club now, I guess." He picks up his silverware again then points them at Garvey. "How does your mother feel about the way you look?"

"She hasn't mentioned it."

"Well I can tell you that when she lived in this house she would never have let you come to the Thanksgiving table looking like that. Never."

"I guess she's just lost her marbles."

"I think she has. I really do." His face is bright red.

"Well good for her," Catherine mumbles.

Garvey smiles at her. "Said the new wife, ambiguously."

Catherine laughs loudly.

"Garvey, I gotta show you something after dinner," Frank says.

"What?" Patrick asks.

"Shut up," Frank says.

"Is that jade?" my brother asks, touching the chunks of stone around Catherine's wrist.

"Jade and mother of pearl."

My father is glaring at her. She pulls her arm away.

Garvey and I do the dishes. There is no discussion about this. Everyone else brings their plates to the sink and walks away.

"Cinderella and Cinderello, the two stepchildren left in the scullery all alone." He feigns hunger and weariness, limply carrying the turkey platter to the counter. "Hey, I have a movie idea." He always has movie ideas. "Oh my God, it's going to make us millions. Okay, it's Thanksgiving night and this old man lives in a house all alone. His children came that afternoon with the meal but now they've all gone home to their families. He's been married three or four times but all his wives have left him and he's all alone on Thanksgiving night, all doped up on tryptophan but too depressed to sleep. And then he hears this noise outside. He goes out into his yard and there's this enormous turkey, the size of a house, gobbling at him. But the turkey has a human face, a gruesome one, like Mrs. Perth's face. You have her this year, right? I still have nightmares about her. And this turkey has all the man's wives tucked under its wings. They're all naked and they all have papers for him to sign because he screwed every single one of them out of his money."

Dad has come in to make a drink and is standing there, listening.

"Knock it off, Garvey," he says. "I don't want you corrupting her. She's an innocent little girl and she doesn't need a slob like you filling her head with bullshit."

"Look who's talking."

"I'll tell you something. Any bullshit either of you has gotten comes from your mother. Look at you. Just look at you. I tell you, I feel sorry for you with a mother like that. She left me a goddamn note right there." He points to the counter because the kitchen table isn't there to point to anymore. "Right there. Wouldn't even tell me to my face she was leaving." I think for a moment he's going to cry.

"She was scared you'd hit her."

"She was right about that. I would have hit her. Cowardly bitch."

Garvey laughs. My father joins him. My heart is racing and I scrub the scalloped sweet potato dish as hard as I can.

We leave as soon as the kitchen is clean. I mention to Dad that I'll be back up here Saturday morning and he just shrugs, like he couldn't care less, which is a lot better than getting yelled at.

We are late, very late, getting back to Mom's. I can see her trying not to let it bother her, but she's been cooking alone all day and now the dishes that she covered with tinfoil are cold and she sits down and picks up her fork without saying grace either.

"Where's Mrs. Waverly and Cousin Morgan?" Garvey asks.

"Oh, Mom," I remember the placecards in my dress pocket. "Look what I rescued!" I spill them onto the table. The wooden fruits clatter together.

She shakes her head at them. And then scoops them up and throws them all in the trash in the kitchen. "Sorry," she says to me, "but they give me the willies." And then she says to Garvey, "I thought it would be better to just have it be us this year. I'm not used to this electric oven and I didn't know what time to invite them for because I didn't know what time Catherine would be serving lunch up there and they never stick to a schedule anyway and I just thought it would be easier, but now I'm feeling so guilty. Who knows where they're eating. Probably at a restaurant. And they could have kept me company while I waited for you two." She looks sad, sadder than I've seen her since we moved here.

Garvey doesn't seem to notice. He puts his fingers to his Adam's apple. "You/didn't/want/to/hear/ Mrs./ Wa/ver/ly/com/plain/a/bout/ her/an/gi/na/this/year?"

"Stop it," she says harshly. "Stop that right now."

Garvey just laughs at her tone. I wish I could do that. "Oh my God, Mom, it's a scene up there. Catherine's walking around with her boobs falling out of her dress and they're both pounding down the martinis and her kids seem kind of shell-shocked. Frank is high as a kite and little what's-her-name is like a feral child. She's like Helen Keller." Garvey shuts his eyes and gropes around for my hand and when he finds it he moans and scribbles in my palm with his finger. Mom can't help laughing.

"You shouldn't let Daley spend too much time up there," he says.

I flail around blindly, too, but when I open my eyes no one is laughing.

They start talking about politics, about congressional seats and public funding. They can flip into this language I don't understand so quickly. When Garvey asks Mom about her boss, things get more interesting. Garvey has a way of sniffing out the real story. For three months, all I've known is that he is a lawyer named Paul Adler, and when you call his office you get a lady named Jean who is never pleased you are calling. I know that Mr. Adler is involved in politics, too, and that my mother often has to stay in town for fundraisers. But Garvey, in a matter of minutes, susses out that he is thirty-six, Harvard undergrad and law, unmarried, handsome, Jewish, and has a crush on my mother.

"I think you like this guy. I think you like him a lot more than Martin."

"Oh, Martin." My mother waves him off.

"You like your boss," he says in playground singsong.

"He's much younger than I am."

"Five years. And look at you. You look like a coed." It's true. Garvey has more wrinkles around his eyes than she does.

"It's all that grease she puts on her face at night," I say.

"Like a bug in amber," my brother says.

"He leaves me these little cryptic notes on my desk."

"I can just see him. Some poor kid in jail's life hangs in the balance, but he's busy at his desk composing the perfect little bon mot for you. Has he made a pass at you yet?"

"No."

"Oh c'mon. He hasn't even kissed you yet?"

"No. On the cheek."

"You're lying."

"I am lying." She bursts out with a huge long laugh. She is happy again, and relaxed, her hands dangling off the arms of the chair, her head off to one side. She keeps laughing, her mouth wide open, her front teeth slightly bent together but still white and pretty and young.

7

It turns out it's serious with this guy, Paul. Mom brings him home one Thursday night to meet me. He reminds me of a greyhound, lean and quick. He wears glasses. He notices everything.

"How do you like Ashing Academy Founded in 1903?" he asks when my mother has abandoned us to arrange the take-out on plates.

"You've done some research," I say.

He tips his head toward the corner of the room. "I saw it on your bookbag."

"I like it. I've never gone anywhere else so I don't have anything to compare it to." There's something about him that makes you sit up straight, makes you want to say things right.

He looks at me like he's really taking it in. "It's funny that way, isn't it? I've only worked for this one law firm, so I don't know any better either."

"Do you like it?" I've never asked a grown-up if they like what they do. I just assumed they all came home and complained about their work like my father did.

"I have a ball at work."

I must have given him a face without knowing it because he says he's serious; he loves his work. He tries to tug his pant cuff down closer to his shoe. He looks like he's a tall kid pretending to be a grown-up. Then he asks me if I feel cut off from the town, going to private school, and I tell him I didn't used to, but living down here has made me realize how few of the neighborhood kids I know. "Pauline, my babysitter, knows everyone," I say. "It's weird."

"It's not weird. It's to be expected."

I stand corrected, my math teacher says when someone finds a mistake on the board.

My mother puts the food on the table and calls us over.

"You are here," she says to Paul, patting the top of the chair she usually sits in.

"Couldn't I be over there?" he says, pointing to a side spot, next to the wall.

"No, no, you're the guest of honor," she says.

Paul sits but keeps looking up and flapping his hand above his head.

"What on earth are you doing?" my mother says, smiling, looking up to the ceiling, too.

"Just checking for swords hanging by hairs."

My mother bursts out laughing but I have no idea what he's talking about.

"They haven't taught you about Damocles yet?"

I shake my head.

In the fourth century B.C., he tells me, there was a terrible tyrant of Syracuse named Dionysius. He was brilliant in battle and mean as a snake to everyone around him. He liked to surround himself with intellectuals like Plato, but he also liked to toy with them. Paul leans back in his seat, as if he's telling a story about his own family. Dionysius once read some of his poetry to the famous poet Philoxenos, and when Philoxenos didn't like it much, Dionysius had him arrested and banished to the quarries. A couple of days later, he had the poet brought back to hear some more of his poetry. Once again he asked Philoxenos what he thought, and Philoxenos whimpered, "Take me back to the quarries."

We laugh, and Paul helps himself to the food my mother passes him.

"But why were you looking for a sword?" I say.

"Dionysius had a big court full of people and this fellow Damocles was the most obsequious courtier of all. He laughed when Dionysius laughed and hung on his every word—kind of like me with your mother."

"Ha," my mother says.

Dionysius got tired of it, Paul continues, and told Damocles he could wear his crown and sit in his seat and be king for a meal. Damocles was thrilled. But the crown was very heavy and he had to wait a long time for all the tasters to taste the king's food to make sure it wasn't poisoned, and then, in the middle of the meal, he leaned back and saw a double-edged sword just above him, pointing directly at the middle of his skull and hanging by one long horsehair. He begged to change places, but the king refused. He said he wanted Damocles to become closely acquainted with the fear that a great king lives with every minute when he is surrounded by his so-called friends. "I didn't bring any tasters with me tonight," Paul says, "but let's eat."

My mother has put food on my plate, noodles with crumbs all over it and some sort of soupy thing over rice.

"What is this?"

"It's Thai. You'll like it."

It smells very spicy. I don't like spices except oregano and basil in spaghetti sauce, but this is not bad. The crumbs in the noodles are crushed-up peanuts, and the sauce is sweet and creamy.

"Now, not to undermine your story," my mother says.

"Uh-oh, here we go," Paul says to me.

"But I do think you are conflating the two tyrannical Dionysiuses of Syracuse. Dionysius One banished the poet, and Dionysius Two hung the sword."

"She thinks I'm conflating," he whispers to me, then turns to my mother. "There was only one. You're thinking of Hiero One and Two."

My mother pats her lips primly with her napkin and Paul laughs. He was right—he does laugh at everything she does. Then she stands up and goes to the bookcases and pulls out our huge *Columbia Encyclopedia*. They flip through it together, giggling when a page tears slightly in their haste.

"Dionysius," Paul says loudly, then he looks at me. "One and Two."

He reminds me of a younger, more playful Grindy. "How on earth did you know that?" he asks her.

"My classics teacher at Miss Pratt's School for Girls wrote a book on Greek history. She branded every name and date on our hide."

After my mother puts the encyclopedia away, she asks about the Delaurio boy, but Paul puts up his hand and says, "We're not going to inflict our work on Daley."

We eat a little more and then he asks, "So who are your friends and enemies, Daley?"

Even my mother looks surprised by this one. I look across at her and she shrugs.

"'You shall judge of a man by his foes as well as by his friends,'" he explains to us.

"Who was that?" my mother asks.

"You promise not to correct me?"

"No."

"Joseph Conrad, I believe."

"Plausible," my mother says.

He bows his head briefly to her. And to me he says, "So tell me."

"I don't know. My best friend is Mallory. I've known her since nursery school."

"What do you like about her?"

There's something about the sound of his voice that pulls more words from me than I mean to give. "She's kind of unpredictable. I'll go over to her house to make chocolate chip cookies and we'll end up wearing wigs and pretending we have our own cooking show. And then we pee our pants because we're laughing so hard. Who is your best friend?"

He smiles. He wasn't expecting the question back at him. "That's a tricky one. There's Eddie, who was my Mallory growing up, but he lives in Chicago so I don't see him much. Here I have some good buddies from law school, and this new friend who appeared in my office last fall, but I probably can't tell you anything about her that you don't already know."

They smile at each other. It's weird. The whole thing is strange, but not awful. He has barely touched the glass of wine my mother poured him.

"Any other friends you want to mention?"

"Not really. There's Gina and Darcie, but I only call them when Mallory's busy."

"And there's Patrick," my mother says.

It's funny to hear her say Patrick's name. It reminds me that there was a day last spring when she took us to the Mug for donuts and Patrick asked my mother if he could drink the extra creamers beside her cup of coffee and the cream left a tiny crescent of white above his lip and my mother wiped it off for him with her napkin. He told me that afternoon that he thought my mother was the most beautiful mother he'd ever seen. He said she looked like a prettier Jackie Onassis. Now he doesn't dare say her name.

"And Patrick," I say. But that's weird now, too.

"And your enemies?" Paul says.

All I can think of is Catherine Tabor. But my mother wouldn't like me to say that. "With a family like mine, who needs enemies?"

"What'd she say?" my mother says, but Paul is laughing a loud hiccuppy laugh. I feel all warm inside, making him laugh like that. It's almost as good as when I can get my father going. But that's becoming harder and harder.

My mother serves dessert in the living room area. Paul takes a
seat on one side of the sofa and my mother folds her legs up beneath her on the other side so I sit on the middle cushion. I catch
them smiling at each other.

"What?" I say, but they won't tell me.

"No homework tonight?" my mother asks.

"I did it in study hall." The ice cream is coffee and I swirl it
around until it's soup. Paul has big shoes, dark brown leather with
laces, and thin socks that show the boniness of his ankles. He jiggles
his leg a bit, like Garvey. Everyone seems to have run out of things
to say.

When he stands to leave, Paul puts out his hand and we shake.
"You are everything your mother said you were, only more so."

"You too."

I don't know why he thinks I'm so funny, but it's nice.

My mother has a huge grin on her face when he says, "Adieu,
m'lady," and doffs a pretend hat.

"Not quite so fast," she says. "I'll walk you out."

They put on their coats and shut the door behind them. I race
to my room. The lights are off and I have a perfect view of the parking lot where they stop beside his car.

I know they're talking about me. He's pointing back toward
the door and she's laughing. I hope I've made a good impression.
They talk for a long time, leaning against the door of his car, looking down, looking up, looking at each other. He takes her hand
and then the other hand and when he tells her something she nods
and says something and they laugh at the same time. He bends
down and they kiss on the mouth, not for a long time, not any
longer than my last kiss with Neal. They end up in a long hug.
She pulls away to look at him and says something and I wonder if
she's telling him she feels like she's in a novel. I do, just watching
them.

8

"Oh my God, it's not possible," Catherine says. "Gardiner, look at this. She's got another one."

My father looks up from where he's spreading the large hotel towel on the chaise. "Oh Christ. What's that called, *Out to the Outhouse* by Willie Makit? *Overpopulation in China* by Wee Fuckem Young?"

I'd heard these jokes so many times. "*It's Not the End of the World* by Judy Blume."

"Blume," he says and shakes his head. "You're always reading the Jews. Just like your mother."

He has no clue about Paul yet.

"What's it about?" Catherine says.

"A kid whose parents get divorced."

She snorts. "What would you want to read about *that* for?"

She doesn't like all the reading I do. Neither does my father. They say it's rude. They make fun of the titles, the covers, and the way I chew on the skin of my lower lip when I get deep in a book.

But I have nothing else to do. We're in St. Thomas for spring vacation, and Patrick has made friends with the golf pro and now drives his own little cart, picking up elderly players at their cottages and driving them around the eighteen holes. He gets paid for this in snack bar tickets, so every afternoon when he gets off work we go have peanuts and papaya juice by the pool. Elyse has attached herself to another family for the ten days, a couple from Salt Lake City and their one-year-old son. Elyse loves babies. The mother from

Salt Lake sensed her usefulness immediately, and now Elyse spends her days under their cabana on the beach. No one knows where Frank goes. He leaves after breakfast and comes back before dinner with a secretive smirk and half-shut eyes that scare me.

Almost everything scares me these days. I have been on planes before, but this time I was terrified of the distance from earth, the smallness of the plane, and the flimsiness of its metal walls. When we actually landed, my gratitude didn't last long. There are lizards on the floor, red jellyfish at the shore, and shark fins farther out. I don't want to snorkel or water-ski or windsurf. And it isn't just the outside world I'm scared of. I'm scared of inside of me, too. On the second day I ran back to our cottage to go to the bathroom, and as I stood there on the tiles pulling down my suit, a feeling wrapped around my chest like a boa constrictor. The dead star feeling, out of nowhere. I struggled to breathe. I knew I was alone in the cottage and yet the bathroom felt crowded. My heart began to pound and made me so scared it pounded harder and harder until I thought there was no way my body could withstand the force of its beating. I'm just going to the bathroom, I kept telling myself, but my body felt something completely different, as if it were having a whole other invisible experience. Back on the beach, I felt weak and shivery and wrapped myself in a towel. I've been in the cottage alone since then, but at night the feeling edges in and I have a hard time falling asleep. Reading is the only thing that calms me down.

"You have your Jews," my father says to me later, when we are all showered from the beach, waiting to go to dinner, "and I have my magazines." He picks up the *Penthouse* he got Frank to buy at the airport.

"Read another letter, Gardiner," Patrick says.

"All right." My father flips through the pages. "*Dear Penthouse Forum,*" he begins. "*I never really believed these letters were written by real people, but since last Thursday night, I'm ready to believe anything.*"

"They always start like that. It's so fake," I say.

"Shhh," Patrick says

"Yes, Daley, shhh. This is serious literature." My father grins at me. He is in a good mood, with his drink at his elbow and the magazine in his hands. He reads about a girl who describes everything in her life as boring—her job, her boyfriend, her dog. My father thinks this is hilarious. "Even the fucking dog is boring!" She works in an office building in Chicago.

"Is she ever going to get to the *point*?" Elyse says, and everyone cracks up. It is cozy in our little cottage by the beach, sitting all of us together on the wicker furniture with big comfy cushions. My father continues to read.

One night she has to stay late to catch up on some work. She gets a little uneasy when the last person leaves, but then she waves her fear away. She knows she's being a baby. About an hour later she hears the elevator rise and her fear returns. She shuts off all the lights. The elevator stops on her floor and opens. She stops breathing. She thinks if she stays very still—she's in the corner, facing the wall—he won't notice her. She doesn't dare turn around. She thinks she hears something but she can't tell because her heart is beating so loudly—and then she feels hands on her neck. They are warm. *"For some reason I feel myself relax then. I know everything's going to be okay. His hands are so big. They slide down over my shoulders and around to my breasts. I'm wet instantly. I can hear him breathing and I smell cigarettes on his breath and I feel his stubble on my cheek but I never see him. He takes off all my clothes and pleasures me in every way imaginable and then, finally, he puts his long rod-hard cock inside me and—"*

"Gardiner, really, this is going too far," Catherine says. "Elyse is going to tell this to her class when she gets back."

"Elyse Tabor! Well, I never!" Patrick imitates the first grade teacher's constipated grimace.

We all laugh.

"Two more sentences," my father says. "*—and I feel him explode. And then he leaves the building. I never saw his face. I'll never know who he was.*"

The first morning in St. Thomas I went with my father to collect our passports at the front desk in the main building. Everyone else was still asleep. At home there was three feet of snow on the ground but now I was in bare feet and shorts. Our cottage was one of the farthest away, right on the water. We walked on the wide stone paths that connected everything at the resort, and, because it had rained a little before dawn, the stones were wet but warm. We watched a lizard chase another up a palm tree until we couldn't see them anymore.

"Your mother and I stayed in a place like this in Barbados," he said. It almost sounded like a fond memory. He never spoke about my mother in front of Catherine except to insult her. It was so much better when we were alone, but we were never alone. I pretended all the way to the front desk and back that we had come by ourselves to St. Thomas.

I have a crush on a blond boy I see at the pool in the afternoons. He's small and slender and wears long green swimming trunks with orange fish on them. He knows I like him. I can tell from the way he's always checking to see if I'm still watching him. He'll pretend to look beyond me, leave me off to the side of his gaze. When we first got there he was hanging out with two girls who looked a lot older than us, but they left after a few days and now he has no one.

"Stop looking at him. He's a total jerk," Patrick says. "Do you know what he did in the shop yesterday? He—"

"Shut up. I don't care."

We're finishing up our papaya juices. We're so badly sunburned that we sit at the edge of our chairs, careful to let our skin touch the least amount of chair as possible. We don't have sun lotion. We only have something called Hawaiian Tropic, which is coconut-smelling baby oil that promises to increase the sun's rays. We're obsessed with getting the deepest darkest tan possible. Elyse has had the worst reaction to the sun. Her skin has bubbled up on her arms and back, and the Salt Lake City family took her to the clinic in town where they wrapped gauze around her forearms, which had become infected. They bought her a long-sleeved shirt and sunblock and have hinted that we should be using those things, too. But we don't have blisters, just a good burgundy burn that will turn into a deep dark tan by the time we go back to school.

My father and Catherine appear behind the blond boy in their tennis whites.

"Let's go," my father says.

We pick up our racquets and loop around the pool.

"Ace 'em," the blond boy whispers to me.

I smile, relieved that my sunburn hides my blush.

The courts are clay. A black man in tennis whites is sweeping ours. The instruments are the same as at the club at home, a wide broom the size of a narrow hallway that you pull behind you like a cart, and a small round brush on rollers. We sit on the green bench and watch him drag the big broom in long dramatic curves across one side and then the other, then clean the lines with the small brush that makes a *scritch-scratch* noise as it passes us. The lines he cuts are crisp and perfect, which is not easy to do. I can't tell how old he is, in his teens or twenties or thirties, his hair cropped close, his thighs no thicker than his calves, and his legs and arms so long and so very black against the white of his clothes. I wish I could watch him do the other courts, but ours is ready and my father walks onto it with his big splayed feet, bouncing a ball off his racquet and scuffing it up immediately.

I think my father hopes, each time we step on the court together, that since our last match I have transformed myself into Chrissie Evert. I think he actually believes, despite years of witnessing the raw truth, that I possess that kind of talent and am stubbornly withholding it from him, deliberately making him suffer. He insists on getting me out on the court, even though it makes him miserable.

Garvey was the tennis player. His room, before Frank moved into it, was filled with trophies of little gold men getting ready to serve and Garvey's name on the plaques at the bottom. He played on the varsity team at St. Paul's his freshman and sophomore years and then quit. My father often refers to that moment as the greatest disappointment of his life.

So now there is just me, who's never done any better than the improvement prize in any sport.

"Daley and I will take you two on," my father says, to my relief. It's easier playing with him than against him.

We confer at the baseline. My father has that hopeful look on his face. "Catherine's wrist is hurting again. Play to her backhand. She barely has any strength in it. And Patrick—well, you can take on Patrick." Patrick is a very good tennis player. I've gotten about four games off of him in all the sets we've played, but my father hasn't forgotten them. "Okay, let's go get 'em." He pats my shoulder and gives me the three balls.

My practice serves go in.

"Look at that!" my father shouts. "Look at that!"

My real ones are abysmal. The first slaps the bottom of the net. The second hits the fence. My father comes down to the baseline.

"Stand right here. A little farther over. Good. Now," he stands behind me and lifts my racquet back for a serve, "try and snap your wrist at the top, like this." He takes my arm and slowly lifts it over my head, flicking my wrist at just the right moment. He smells like lime and cigarettes, his Caribbean smell.

I double-fault two more times.

My father comes back down to the baseline.

"If you'd just leave her alone, she'd be fine, Gardiner," Catherine says. "She just needs to warm up a little."

After that, I get one in. Patrick, startled that it has gone in, misses it entirely. My father high-fives me. I win the next point, too, by hitting down Catherine's backhand alley.

No matter what mood I begin with, I always have the same feeling playing tennis, a sort of claustrophobia despite the open space, fresh air, and wind in the trees, combined with a boredom bordering on despair. I keep looking at the clean lines and thinking about the black man in his white shorts. He has left glasses of ice water and a plate of sliced melon on our bench. For three sets a day I'm caged here, the white lines flashing in the heat, the sky too hot to be blue, and the sun searing our already burned skin.

My father never gives up. I don't think he feels anything but completely alive and exhilarated on the tennis court. He can't under- stand my mood, the stupor his ambitions for me puts me in. Even in the last game of the third set (0–6, 1–6, 0–5), he is still giving me tips, showing me the footwork involved in receiving an overhead lob. I watch him move at a backward diagonal, his lovely crisscrossed steps a dance I will never learn. I hit my best shot in the last point, a low crosscourt pass, but it falls just beyond the line.

"Out," Patrick yells, thrilled not to have won but for the match to be over.

"Bullshit!" my father yells back. "It was a perfect shot."

"Baloney, Gardiner," Catherine says.

He's too pissed to speak and threatens her with a finger as he marches over to their side. My father has a reverence for the rules of tennis, and is a gracious loser on those rare occasions when he does lose. But his desire for my one beautiful shot to be in is far greater than his abilities of perception.

The court is clay, however, and Patrick is pointing to the freshly made imprint, just outside the line.

"That's bullshit," my father says again, but weakly.

"I'm sorry, Dad."

He shakes his head as we walk off the court. "You just need to play more. Practice makes perfect."

But we have played every day for a week and I'm only getting worse.

I stand next to the blond boy that night at the salad bar.

"How's your game?" he asks, staring down into the cottage cheese

"I suck."

He smiles but does not look at me. "Beach afterwards?"

"Okay."

"Don't bring your boyfriend." He flicks his eyes at Patrick, three people ahead of us.

"He's my brother."

"Step," he corrects me. "Big difference, Daley."

He's found out my name and my family configuration. His power thrills me. I can barely eat. Things are tense at our table. Frank has not shown up.

"You play with fire, you're going to get burned," my father keeps saying. Even here he has his A-1 for his steaks. His nose has already started to bead up. Catherine isn't eating much either. She jerks her head up every time someone comes through the thatched archway into the restaurant. She drinks. This pleases my father.

"You's keeping up with me good tonight," he says, trying to pinch her tit discreetly. She flinches away. "Oh fuck that," he says under his breath.

Every night there is baked Alaska. The kitchen staff wheels it out and everyone is expected to stop eating and talking and watch it flame up.

"Oh for chrissake, don't clap for these monkeys," my father says.

There is dancing after dinner to a steel band. Usually my father and Catherine stay and dance while we go back to the cottage and watch TV, but tonight she doesn't want to.

"It's all right, my little pussy," my father croons at her, but she's just watching the doorway now.

"I know what you need," my father says, and does something to her under the table.

"Keep your fucking hands off me!" she says loudly. People look, even Elyse and her new family all the way across the room. Even the blond boy who hasn't glanced at me since the salad bar.

I tip my head to the beach. He nods. I get up then, leave Patrick, leave Catherine, leave my father and his purple sweaty face and yellow eyes and shaking hands and follow the blond boy to the sand.

The sun drops early at the equator. The sky is dark blue, no hint of a sunset left, just a cold pale line at the horizon. The sand is still warmer than the air. We walk down the beach away from the restaurant and all our cottages. We tell each other where we live. He's from Connecticut. When we get far enough away from the last old lady collecting shells, he pulls me down on the sand and starts kissing me. His kisses are hard and wet, purposeful, like he is trying to get something out of my mouth with his tongue. His saliva is all over me and makes my skin cold. I think of stopping him, then remember where I am, in St. Thomas, staying at that cottage that I don't want to go back to until all the fighting is over. So I refocus, try to remember Neal Caffrey's kisses and how floaty I felt afterward, and I try not to think about the *Penthouse* letter and the dead star feeling, and when all that fails I think once more that I should stop him and go home, but then I remember where I am again.

He puts his hand up the back of my shirt. "No bra," he whispers, his first words in a long time.

No breasts, I feel like saying, but he's about to find that out. His hand begins to travel around to the front. When it's just below my armpit, I reach up and pull it out. I stand up, the breeze blowing cold on my spit-soaked face.

"Prude," he calls as I begin walking toward the lights of the cottages. "Stuck-up prude!"

There is only one light on in our cottage. The bedrooms are dark, and the other lamp in the living room is broken, smashed to pieces on the floor. Patrick and Elyse are on opposite ends of the couch, crying.

"They're going to get a divorce!" Elyse wails when she sees me.

"No, they're not."

"I think they are," Patrick says, the skin around his eyes even redder than his sunburn.

"They just had a fight," I say.

"You weren't here. It wasn't a normal fight. She tried to strangle him."

"They were drunk. They won't even remember it tomorrow." I realize they don't understand about the drinking. They take the drunk behavior as seriously as the sober behavior. They don't get the problem at all. "They're alcoholics."

"What's that?" Elyse asks.

"It's when you can't stop drinking alcohol, like vodka and gin and all that stuff. The alcohol makes them behave like that. They can't help it. It's not really them talking."

"They're not alcoholics," Patrick says.

"Yes, they *are,* Patrick." My mother explained to me about my father's drinking this winter. She figured out that he was an alcoholic on their honeymoon, and it only got worse. She tried to leave him twice before, but he promised to change and did for a while, but then slipped back. She told me it was like a sickness, only the people who have it don't believe they're sick.

"Gardiner has a job and a house and he's the president of the tennis association at the club. He's not an *alcoholic*."

"Have you ever seen him sober at the end of the night?"

"Tons of times." He's lying. He can't bear to believe my father has a flaw. But he's crying. "That guy Murphy who sits in the corner of the sub shop. *He's* an alcoholic, Daley."

"I'm just saying that they drink a lot and they don't mean half of what they say to each other. It will all be forgotten tomorrow morning."

Elyse crawls into my lap and I stroke her arms and the bandages on her arms. Patrick sucks his thumb hard. I watch them both fall asleep, and after a while I carry Elyse into our room. I hear her fall back asleep immediately. I don't go to sleep for a long time. My heart is throbbing and I find myself worrying that they are right, that they are going to get a divorce. As much as Catherine annoys me, I don't want to be home alone with my father. I don't want to be the only one left for him to yell at.

When I wake up, Elyse is not in the bed beside me. I hear laughter in the kitchenette, the coffeepot gurgling. No divorce. I put on my bathing suit and a pair of shorts. Frank is on the couch, just waking up, and when he sees me he shakes his head and *tsk-tsks* me with his finger. Why would I be in trouble and not him? The chatter has stopped in the kitchenette. They're all there, my father,

Catherine, and Patrick, all standing in the narrow space between the fridge and the counter, and Elyse on a stool, eating her sugar-coated cereal. Catherine whispers something to her children and they leave the room. Even Frank slips out the sliding glass door.

My father and Catherine look at each other and sip their coffee. There is some charge in the air I can't identify. Maybe they are going to get a divorce. And they're telling me first, so I can break it to Patrick and Elyse. I'll be unemotional, I decide. I'll say that it's for the best.

"Daley," Catherine begins. The V in her bathrobe has widened, and I can see the long nipples of her breasts.

"Sit down," my father says to me, in a sudden guttural voice.

I move toward a counter stool.

"I said sit down."

"I am," I say, and my voice breaks. So much for unemotional.

"Daley, your father and I—"

My father breaks in. "I don't know who you think you are, but I will not have you come down here with all the lies your mother has fed you. I'm sorry." There is nothing sorry about him and the taut purple tendons running up his neck. "I'm sorry that you have to live with her, see her, listen to her, see those god-awful friends of hers. But if you start believing what she tells you, then you are an even bigger idiot than I thought."

"Do you really think we're alcoholics, Daley?"

I can't find my voice. The stool feels so small beneath me.

"Do you really think this"—she points to the water through the glass door—"is the lifestyle of alcoholics? Are we passed out every night on the floor? Do we have bottles in our closets? Are we asking for money on street corners?"

I answer no to each of her questions.

"So what's an alcoholic, in your opinion?"

"Someone who gets drunk all the time."

"Do we get drunk all the time? Are we drunk right now?"

"I don't know."

"It's eight o'clock in the morning and we're drinking coffee. Are we drunk right now?"

"No."

"Maybe *you're* drunk right now," my father says. "Maybe you were drunk last night when you had your little talk with Patrick and Elyse."

Catherine pats his leg to shush him.

"Maybe you and your fucking mother were drunk when you left my house with all my mother's goddamn jewelry. If I'm an alcoholic, she's a goddamn criminal." He makes like he's going to hit me and I almost want him to, want to have some mark my mother will see when I get back. But he just walks out of the cottage, muttering *fucking bitch* a few times and shaking his clenched hands around before careening down the path out of view.

Catherine finally notices that her boobs are hanging out of her robe and pulls it tighter. "We leave tomorrow, Daley. Could you just keep your trap shut until we drop you off at Water Street?"

The blond boy is at the pool, hanging his feet in at the deep end, talking to three sisters from Wisconsin who arrived yesterday. They all look at me as I go down the shallow end steps, then he says something and they all burst out laughing. I go under quickly. They are still laughing when I come back up. The youngest girl swims toward me.

"Is your name Prudence?" she asks, and the others behind her crack up again.

"Go to hell," I say, before I register how young she is, not much older than Elyse. Her eyes widen and fill with tears. She didn't know what she was asking, and I feel terrible.

I skip lunch and spend the afternoon in the cottage alone. I don't care if my heart starts to pound. I'm not scared of that anymore. I look at the phone and think about calling my mother at work, but there's the disapproving Jean to get past and I know I won't be able to speak anyway. I'll just cry when I hear her voice and she'll get worried that something is really wrong. Or I'll yell at her for telling me he was an alcoholic in the first place.

Frank leans in the doorway of my room, clucking. "Namin' the names."

"What?"

"Callin' spades spades."

He's wasted. I've seen him high, but not like this.

"Puttin' on the labels. Big white and red Campbell's soup labels. *Splat.* Right on the 'rents. You should have seen them wriggling under the pin. Fucking eels. Someday we'll cut off their heads and their tails and see if anything grows back." He undoes the button on his jeans and starts unzipping his fly and I'm just about to slam the door on him when he rolls around the doorjamb and heads for the bathroom.

In the taxi we watch the sun seep up over the water. It is still dark on the roads, but the water and the sky just above it are starting to glow. My father is up front, talking to the driver, who is a black man about his age. My father is turned toward him, fully awake. "Holy smokes, you can't beat that!" he's saying, and the driver is laughing. My father is wearing bright red cotton pants, a white oxford shirt, and blue blazer. His smell of Barbasol, Right Guard, and Old Spice fills the van. It is his morning smell, the smell that obliterates the A-1-cigarette-vodka smell of the night before. He is close-shaven, squeaky clean. We all admire him. We cannot help it.

The airport doesn't have walls, just a long red roof and palm trees on all sides. The driver unloads our bags onto a long cart. My father hands him a thick wad of money and the driver smiles and pats my father on the arm. My father pats him back and tells him to take care of himself and his family. The man cannot seem to take his eyes off my father and stands there by the side of his car long after my father has moved away.

Beneath the roof it is chaotic, with one check-in counter open and about fifty families trying to leave the island. We stand in the same place for a long time. We are hungry and it is starting to get hot. Our sunburns begin to throb beneath the stiff New England clothes we have not worn in thirteen days.

Patrick goes to sit on Frank's duffel bag and Frank swats him hard.

"Sit on your own fucking suitcase," he says.

Catherine's head snaps around and she fixes her meanest stare on Frank. "Chh," she says, spraying my arm with spit.

There are several boys my age in line but I do not look at them. I worry the blond boy is here somewhere or is about to arrive. I look down at my suitcase. It's my mother's old blue suitcase. I remember her taking it when she went on trips with my father, and then, when they returned, there would be presents nestled in it for me: an enameled ring from Venice, a cloth doll from Acapulco. I drape my parka over it, just as I did on the way down, hoping my father will not recognize it.

Another line opens up, then another, and we are through— our bags tagged and tossed down a chute—and sent to security. It's not like regular American security with one guy taking your ticket and asking you to step through the metal detector. Here there are many men in uniform with big gold badges and dogs on compli- cated leashes, dogs not panting in the heat but eyeing us seriously.

One of them twitches and the other two bristle in response. Their ears lift and their wet black noses flare and tremble. Then they are all barking at once, showing their long yellow teeth, straining on their leads, yanking the men who hold them across the brick paving to Frank. The dogs surround him. The rest of us watch from the other side of the metal detector. Frank and his duffel are taken out of line immediately and led away. The dogs follow, their barking drowning out all other sounds except one loud brief, "Mom!" before Frank is shoved around a corner and disappears.

Catherine stands with her hand over her mouth. On the loudspeaker our flight to Miami is announced.

"I'm getting on that fucking plane no matter what happens, you hear me?"

Catherine nods her head slowly.

"This is not my fault. I have nothing to do with this. Nothing." My father looks down the corridor and laughs his disgusted laugh. "Jesus Christmas. What kind of idiot would—"

"Shut up." Her voice scrapes viciously, like she learned it from my father.

"You," he says quietly, sifting through the pile of tickets he is holding with shaking fingers, "have a nice trip home." He hands her four tickets. "C'mon, Daley. I'm getting you out of here."

We follow the flow of people out across the tarmac, up the flight of metal stairs, and inside the small plane.

My father stops halfway down the small aisle and points to two seats on the right. "Here we go."

"You can have the window," I tell him.

"You take it." He is trying to be nice but he looks like he wants to lift me up and shove me in the seat.

I slip in and buckle up.

My father pushes the stewardess button next to the light above us, but she is busy directing traffic up front and doesn't come. He pulls down the tray even though he's not supposed to. He puts his hands on the tray and wipes it with his palms in wide sweeps. The backs of his hands are wide and brown, with veins bulging up, criss-crossed around the fine bones that connect to his fingers. I remember what it feels like to hold his hand, something I always did—crossing streets, walking through stores, driving in the car—but now never do. And then to my surprise he reaches down and takes my right hand in his. It is as warm and large as I remember.

"We's going to be okay," he says, and pushes the button again.

Nearly an hour later, after there has been an announcement about mechanical difficulties, after the stewardess has brought me a Coke and my father three tiny bottles, two of vodka, one of vermouth, Elyse comes running down the aisle.

"Gardie!" she says, and climbs carefully into my father's lap without knocking the tray with the bottles on it. I've never heard her call him that before—I've never heard anyone ever call him that.

"Hello, little peanut," he says, and pushes some hair back into her headband.

Catherine and Patrick appear at the front of the plane and look down the aisle nervously until they see us. Patrick's face relaxes immediately and he nudges his mother toward us. Despite all the sun she's gotten, her skin has gone sallow, dark gray beneath the eyes. She takes the seat across the aisle from my father but does not look at him. Elyse climbs off my father and takes the window seat next to her mother, and Catherine fusses with their seatbelts much longer than necessary. Patrick sits in front of me and I see his eye peering through the crack in the seat. I stick my finger in and touch his cheek. "Ow," he says and we laugh. And then Frank slumps into the seat beside Patrick, rattling everything on my father's tray. My father reaches out to steady the bottles, then lifts the plastic cup, still half full, and hands it to Catherine.

"I bet you could use this even more than me."

Catherine snorts a laugh and takes the drink. Then she reaches for my father's hand.

"Big pussy," she says.

"Little pussy," he says.

"What happened?" I whisper to Patrick when we are in the air.

"They couldn't find anything. They made him strip twice, they sent his clothes through this machine, the dogs were going wild, but they couldn't find a thing."

I peer through the crack at Frank. An unwashed, unbrushed clump of hair covers one eye. The other is shut. The skin of his face is blighted with zits and the scars from zits. His thin lips are bunched tight. Even in sleep, he looks like he's scheming something.

I've saved most of my last book for the two flights home. It's by Edith Wharton. Paul gave it to me for Christmas. He said it was just the beginning of the edification of Daley Amory. I'd had to sneak off and look up the word *edification*. When I get home from St. Thomas, my mother will tell me that Paul has asked her to marry him.

I pull out the book. When Catherine notices she elbows my father and points, and my father mutters, "Jesus, Mary, and Joseph— another goddamn book."

But I don't care. Archer has just sent the Countess Olenska the yellow roses, and my father and Catherine's world is already slipping away.

II

9

I didn't want a party, but Jonathan insisted.

"Just let people be happy for you," he said. And now he's created my favorite kind of evening: our closest friends, his homemade $3 spaghetti sauce, and a round of Oh Hell before dinner. It's June in Michigan. All the windows in the apartment are open. Bugs thrum and snap at the screens. There's wine, but not enough for anyone to get drunk.

At dinner we end up counting how many of us have lost a parent. Out of the seven of us, five parents are already dead. Dan's date, an earnest undergrad in shorts and a baseball cap, asks me how my mother died. Normally I just say she was hit by a car, but tonight—maybe because I'm leaving, maybe because she seems so young and doe-eyed—I tell her about the awful days that followed, how my father didn't even come to the funeral. I don't talk about my father much anymore, and I see him once a year at most, but I can feel a certain charge begin to run through me.

"He never called me or my brother to say he was sorry our mother had died," I tell her. "Never came by. Never wrote a note. We were at her place— a mile away from his house—for a week and we never heard from him. To this day he's never even *mentioned* her death to me."

"Maybe it's too painful for him." Her name is Janine, I think. A psych major.

"They split up when I was eleven. They hated each other."

"Still. Unresolved relationships can be the hardest to grieve."

I look at her hard because she should know this if she's going to be a shrink someday. "Some people are just assholes."

She looks ready to argue the point, but something behind me catches her eye and her expression is forced into a smile. It's Julie, coming into the room with a cake. Jonathan, behind her with three boxes of ice cream, starts singing, "Happy Berkeley to You," and everyone else catches on and I try to wave them silent but they just get louder. I'm not sure I'm done complaining about my father.

Julie sets a banana cake, my very favorite dessert, in front of me. She's decorated it with plastic palm trees and people on surfboards.

I hug her and she whispers, "I can't believe you're leaving me in this hellhole."

I laugh, because I'm not. She landed a job at the University of New Mexico and is moving to Albuquerque in two weeks.

Jonathan wraps his arms around me from behind, kissing the back of my neck as I cut the cake. "Can you make them all leave now?" he says in my ear. "We only have a few more hours together."

"This was your idea, Magoo." He is nearly a foot taller than me and I can feel him pressing against the base of my spine. "Get ahold of yourself."

We aren't going to be separated for long. He'll come out to California as soon as he finishes teaching the first summer session next week. I still can't quite believe he's coming with me. At the last minute Jonathan Fleury, who, as Dan likes to say, planned his bowel movements three years in advance, took the job at San Francisco State and turned down the one at Temple. Now it's up to me to screw the whole thing up.

"You're not going to screw it up," Julie said a few days ago.

"How are you so sure?"

"Because it's Jonathan. He won't let you. He'll be eight steps ahead of you."

"You're right. He will." It felt a little suffocating, actually, when she put it like that.

When everyone has a piece of cake, Dan lifts his glass in my direction. "Here's to Daley," he says, "who soundly rejected me five long years ago in the middle of our first date."

"Second," I say.

Dan lowers his wine. "What was the first?"

"Coffeehouse."

"Oh. Right." He raises the glass again, resumes his stentorian tone. "All because my car wouldn't start."

"Not because your car wouldn't start. Because you started pounding on the steering wheel and screaming *fuck fuck fuck* about fifty times."

"I was trying to impress you with my manly bestiality."

"Beastliness. Bestiality might have impressed me. Why is it that writers have such a lack of precision when it comes to the English language?"

"By the way, can you shut up? I'm actually leading up to saying something nice about you, so stop heckling me."

"It's so hard. You remind me too much of my brother."

"So you have said. Many times. Just what a rejected suitor wants to hear. Anyway, despite your strange and inexplicable impulses"— he looks over at Jonathan, who grins at me; Dan introduced us: by accident, he always insists—"you have been a comrade to me through dark times and light, and I will miss you more than I will ever let on."

Dan reaches across the table to hug me. His BO is as strong as always, and the grass smell of his hair brings back that first date when he kissed me in the middle of a conversation about Saul Bellow and my stomach spun for days at the memory—until the second date, when I had to get out of the broken-down car and walk away.

Julie clears her throat dramatically. Since Mallory, she's the closest thing I've had to a sister. We've shared an apartment for four years. Even the way she holds up her glass now, crooked, as if she doesn't care if it spills a little, is familiar to me. "I think we all know that Daley's name will soon be in textbooks, so this may be our last evening with her as a humble mortal. Anthropology professors at Berkeley rarely fade away."

"But they do get washed away," Dan said. Last year one of them jumped off the Golden Gate Bridge.

"She'll have Jonathan to hold her back." Julie looks down into her glass. The sentimental part is coming. "I just want to say how impossibly proud I am of you, Daley. You've been working toward this moment from the day I met you. And here it is." Her big smile rearranges everything else on her face. Even her hair shifts. She has the most amazing ability to reveal her emotions without embarrassment. She cried when I got the call from Berkeley about the job. I'd never seen anyone actually cry for joy in real life. And there Julie was, crying for mine. "I wish you, as my father used to say to me every night"—her smile twists suddenly and her voice frays—"the sun, the moon, and the stars. You deserve them all." I glance at Jonathan then. I can't help it. We have a joke about how often Julie mentions her father. But he won't meet my eye. He probably doesn't think we should enjoy an inside joke about Julie at this moment.

Nico says he will miss eavesdropping on my conferences. "You wouldn't believe the things her students tell her. It's like sharing an office with Sigmund Freud." He's not comfortable speaking to a group, even this small group around Jonathan's table. It makes me wonder how he gets through his lecture classes. "But the real testament to your character, Daley, is that you got the best job of all of us and nobody even resents you for it."

"I do," Jonathan and Dan say at the same time.

Kira says she wishes me the best but will not raise a glass because of the ritual's patriarchal roots. The concept of toasting, she explains, evolved from the custom of flavoring drinks with spiced toast, and when the toast ran out, she says, a woman's name would be called out to flavor the drink. "Yet another example of men attempting to consume women," she says. Dan pretends to slit his wrists with the cake knife, which he often does around Kira.

When it's Jonathan's turn, the room gets quiet. People tend to listen to Jonathan a little more closely. When I accused him once of having this effect, he said that white people in academia always have to pretend they're listening to the black man. He pulls a piece of paper out of his back pocket, glances at it in silence, then stuffs it back. He turns to me and speaks quietly. "I wrote down some things. I even had a quote by Bronislaw Malinowski for you." He laughs. "But what I really want to say is that I just feel so glad that, that somehow," he rubs his finger on the tablecloth, "you showed up in my life. I didn't expect that. As you know." He smiles. He tips his glass over to tap mine. "Here's to you and me and our unanticipated future." I'm surprised by the emotion in his voice. He's usually so controlled in public. I put my arm around his neck and he pulls me tight against him. I feel how fast his heart is beating and I think, briefly, the smallest pulse of a fear, that I am not worthy of that heart.

It's true that Dan introduced us by accident. Nadine Gordimer came to campus for a reading last fall, and there was a reception afterward at the chancellor's house. It was crowded, everyone hoping for a closer look at the writer, who was tucked away in some alcove at the back. Dan and I were at the buffet table when he saw a woman he was interested in across the room.

"We gotta get over there," he said, and yanked me smack into Jonathan. A few cubes of cheese from my plate bounced off his shirt.

"Oh, shit, she's leaving," Dan said, and since he knew Jonathan from a writing class, he introduced us.

I'd noticed him before, the lean body, short dreads, round glasses, angular face.

"You still writing?" Dan asked him.

"Just my dissertation."

"On what?" I asked.

"Hegel and Gramsci, supposedly."

"Not going well?"

"I'd rather be writing stories."

"You should," Dan said. "You were good. That story you wrote about the two boys and their dying uncle. I can still remember whole sentences of it."

We picked at the food. The room was hot. I told Jonathan I'd thought he was one of those precocious seniors who took graduate courses. He laughed and said he was thirty. I didn't believe him.

"Let me see your license," I said.

"I don't have one."

"What do you mean?" Dan asked. "It get taken away?"

"No, man," he said, irritated. "I grew up in the city. Never needed one."

"Shit. Really?"

"True. And my cousin just dropped off this truck she doesn't need at my apartment, and I can't even use it."

"You've gotta get taught," Dan said.

"I know it."

People were still squeezing in the front door. An old boyfriend was at the other end of the table, debating whether to come over. I needed to get out of there. "I'll teach you," I said, and handed him the keys to my Datsun.

It was late afternoon, the third week of September. The day had been warm, but now the sun was low and the trees on the chancellor's street shook out a cool breeze. In the car I helped him adjust the seat. He needed to put it all the way back. "I'm nervous," he said, before he turned the key in the ignition. I couldn't believe how beautiful he was. "I really don't want to crack up your car."

But he knew what he was doing. He just went very slowly. A line of cars grew behind us. I directed him out of town onto a back road, but still cars were behind us. He didn't seem to notice. Every time a car approached from the opposite direction he veered off onto the gravel shoulder and I shut my eyes. He slowly moved the car back onto the road after the line of cars had honked passed. He drove in a straight line. He didn't seem ready to make turns. Occasionally I'd offer up a tip I remembered from driver's ed, but mostly there was silence between us. And then, eleven miles out of town, he asked if I liked to sing.

Thursdays were the only afternoon we both had free. We met at the car and we drove and we sang. The first song, that first day, was "Maxwell's Silver Hammer." It took us the next three Thursdays to exhaust our repertoire of Beatles songs. Singing helped the driving. He went a little faster. Fewer cars trailed behind us. He began to argue with some of my driving suggestions. We came to a stop sign and I waited for him to slow, and when he didn't I screamed for him to stop but we sailed through it anyway. I called him Mr. Magoo after that. He retaliated, saying I reminded him of Tweety Bird.

"Yeah, well, I've been called worse cartoon characters."

"Like what?"

"My brother calls me Hermey."

I didn't think he'd get it but he said, within seconds, "The dentist?" and he looked at me. "I see that." He kept looking and laughing. "I definitely see that."

When we were through with the Beatles, he suggested Elton John.

"Which song of Elton's do you think crossed over to the black community?" he asked. It was the first time he'd mentioned his race. It felt strangely intimate, and I wanted to get it right.

"'Benny and the Jets,'" I said.

"Exactly," he said, with a little smile. "We had no idea what the hell it was about, but, man, we loved that song." Then he started pounding out the beat on the steering wheel.

"Watch the road, Magoo."

"You watch the road. I'm on drums." He made the intro noises and we sang, right on the same beat, "*Hey, kids.*" Then he sang "*walking in the ghetto*" while I sang "*talk about the weather,*" and we looked at each other and cracked up. Jonathan's smile felt like the full sun on my bare skin.

After Elton, he launched into "Thunder Road." And then we sang every Springsteen song we could think of, the fun ones like "Rosalita" and "Cadillac Ranch" and the mournful ones like "Independence Day" and "Nebraska." When we ran out of Bruce, we were driving through a small town surrounded by open fields and I started to sing "Little ditty 'bout Jack and Diane" without really realizing it, and he screamed "No!" and stopped the car in the middle of the road.

"Why?"

"That song is too fucking white."

"Every song we've sung so far is white."

"I know, but—"

"The Beatles and Springsteen are absolutely fine, but John Mellencamp is out?" I felt myself blushing for having made such a blunder. I worried that it had revealed everything to him: my father, Myrtle Street, Ashing—everything I'd worked so carefully to cleanse myself of.

He grinned. "I switch-hit, don't I? Shit, they talk about double consciousness, but I've got triple, quadruple—I've got origami consciousness. But I can't sing that song. People get lynched in towns like that."

I couldn't fake it when he wanted to sing songs by groups like Cameo and the Whispers. I didn't even know the choruses of those songs.

"This is tragic. Where'd you grow up, under a rock?"

"Pretty much."

We settled on Marvin Gaye.

He told me he grew up in Philadelphia with four brothers, that his mother was a nurse from Georgia, that his father had come to Philly from Trinidad as a boy and had died from a heart attack when Jonathan was fifteen, that his mother had never remarried, that he had a friend from college named Stella who did improv in comedy clubs. I pictured it: the wooden stage, the confident voice, the room erupting. I knew I couldn't compete with that.

I told him about my fieldwork in Mexico, twelve months in a village in the Sierra Juarez northeast of Oaxaca, and how the children I'd gone to study ran away from me for the first three months. When I did get close enough to observe their play, I found that the villain in many of their imagined stories, someone they called the See-through Demon, was me.

Once we passed an accident, a car on its side in a gully and three police cars and a fire truck along the shoulder. Jonathan drove slowly by.

"My mother was hit by a car," I said. It felt like something he should know.

"When?"

"Nine years ago. She died."

"Right away?"

"Yup."

I saw his hand flinch on the steering wheel, lift off, and plant right back down again, all in less than a second. It gave me hope, that tiny impulse to touch me that he'd checked.

Sometimes Jonathan would see an animal out of the corner of his eye and stop the car. A fox cutting across a field, a porcupine at the base of a tree. Once we saw a long wide V of Canada geese drop down into a small farm pond all at once, forcing up a great white fan of water. We rolled down the windows and heard all their honking and wing smacking. It was dusk. Jonathan kept binoculars in my glove compartment by then, so we took turns looking at their long dark necks and prim white chinstraps, laughing at how loud and rowdy they were at the start of their long road trip.

When we got back on the road, we passed a sign that said STRATHAM 2 MILES. "I've read about that place," he said. "It's the Knights' headquarters."

"The Knights?"

He looked to see if I was seriously asking. I was. "The Klan," he said. "Not the place you want to be stopped driving a white girl's car without a license." The road was empty and he made a wide U-turn.

Just a few miles out of Ann Arbor, and it was a different world for Jonathan.

We never did anything together after driving. We said goodbye on the street. In the car, while he watched the road, I watched him: his severe profile, the heavy ledge of his brow, the taut muscles of his jaw, and then when he turned unexpectedly, laughing at one of my nervous quips, that smile, his cheeks suddenly boyish. Sitting beside him in my car was becoming a form of torture.

"You've got to just kiss him yourself, Daley," Julie said. "Anyone can see that he's crazy about you." But she didn't know what she was talking about. We'd run into him once on campus, talked awkwardly, that was it.

I couldn't make the first move. I never had and I never would. She thought I was anachronistic. She proudly claimed that she made the first move in every serious relationship she'd ever had. Men are the tortoises of love, she often said. But my interest and attraction felt too strong. In the car I had to rein in everything: my hands, my questions, my fascination. Sometimes it felt like there was a part of me inside him that I ached to get to.

There was a general store on our route, the only store in a tiny town that we often passed through. One day in early December, he said he was thirsty and pulled into a parking spot. We'd never gotten out of the car during our drives before, not even for animal sightings. An old couple sat on stools behind the counter, and there were several men in the aisles, one lifting out a six-pack from the cooler, another at the magazine stand. Everybody seemed to be talking at once until they saw us and stopped. It reminded me of walking into the kitchen when my father and Catherine weren't expecting me. The same suspicious glares. Before I knew what I was doing I'd taken Jonathan's hand. It was the first time we'd touched, though I'd longed for weeks to put my hand on his thigh as he drove, longed to kiss the side of his long neck, had already imagined, I admit it, straddling him, my back against the steering wheel. It was such a relief to touch him, to feel him squeeze my hand with his. We picked out cookies and sodas and I let go reluctantly when we had to pay.

"You did not have to do that," he said when we walked to the car. "I didn't need your protection in there." He slammed the door.

I was stunned by his anger. I thought we'd get back in the car and laugh. I thought he might kiss me. My whole body was still straining toward his. I felt like he'd already touched me everywhere, the way his hand had felt in mine.

He started the car, put it in reverse without a word. I did not explain how to turn going backwards, and didn't need to. Before we went into the general store we'd been singing "O-o-h, child, things are gonna get easier," but now we drove back toward Ann Arbor in silence. I wanted *your* protection, I thought to myself. The man with the six-pack had scared me. But I didn't speak. I didn't know what was the truth. For the first time in my life I'd made the first move. My hand had gone out to his and he had taken it and now he was angry at me. I felt like a child. I wanted him to get out of my car so I could cry and cry. I watched the road signs. ANN ARBOR 12 MILES; ANN ARBOR 9 MILES. And then he turned down a road we'd never taken before. I hadn't seen a sign, didn't know how he knew it. It bumped along for over a mile, a dirt road with huge ruts and a rise of grass in the middle that scraped the bottom of my car. I thought maybe he was going to drop me off down here as a punishment, make me find my way back. His profile looked particularly harsh then, the jaw working, shifting. The road ended at a lake. The sun had gone behind the tall trees and the still water reflected the purple dusk plushly, like fabric. We stayed in the car and did not look at each other.

"You probably won't believe this," he said finally, staring straight ahead, "but I've never crossed the color line before. It just never seemed worth it somehow. I wasn't raised to believe that we're all the same deep down. My grandmother used to say to me and my brothers, Stay away from white girls. Stay away from them. She was from Vidalia, Georgia, and had a million stories from her childhood. They all ended the same. The black man ended up either dead or in jail. Where I grew up in Philadelphia, there weren't white people. Not in my neighborhood. Not on the streets, not at school, not in the shops. I knew they existed—I saw them on TV or if we got in my uncle's car and went somewhere—but I didn't think there were very many of them. I didn't understand what all the fuss was about white people. And then one day my uncle came by and took me and my cousin to a movie. I think we were six. He had some discount for a theater across town. We got there and there was a thick line of white people down the entire block and around the corner and down another block. All white. I didn't understand where they could have come from. I still remember the feeling in my chest, terrified, utterly terrified, but also something else, a little thrill or something, because the world was different from what I had thought." He was still looking straight at the lake, fingers looped around the steering wheel. I wanted to touch him again. "In there, holding your hand, I got that same feeling."

We reached for each other at the same time. Hands, then mouths, then our bodies pressing against each other. I could not stop tears from leaking out, so great was the relief of his touch and the end of his anger. I hoped he wouldn't notice but he did; he found them and licked them and apologized for yelling. I wasn't used to apologies. It brought on a few more tears.

I'd always paced things carefully with men, offered up my body piecemeal, resisted exploration of theirs until I felt certain the emotional connection was keeping pace with the physical. My mother had told me not to make love without love, but I had become a freakish air-traffic controller, determined to land the two, love and sex, at precisely the same time. It rarely worked. The orchestrating itself derailed things. With Jonathan I lost interest in control, lost the ability to control. And that first sex in the car by the lake was always with us, every time we made love afterward, and never once did I regret it.

I can't offer anyone a real goodbye at the end of the night. When people hug me, I insist I'll see them soon, I'll see them around. Julie squeezes me hard. This is the end of our life together. I took all my things out of our apartment this morning and crammed them into my car. There is only a little hole for me to squeeze into tomorrow and drive to California.

"I hate this," she says. "I hate that I'm not going to find all your dirty dishes in the sink tomorrow night."

"Please don't make me cry. If I start, I won't stop." But I feel numb, nowhere close to tears.

She kisses me on both cheeks and leaves them wet. She promises to visit in the fall. It doesn't feel real, my future, all that I have worked so hard to make happen. But the future always sits uneasily with me. I've never been able to really trust it. I've trained myself not to look forward to things very often. And I'm tired. I'm bone tired. Part of me just wants to curl up on a couch and sleep for a few years.

Dan is the last to leave. From his car he asks, "Can I use that bit about your father not going to the funeral?" He means in a story. "Please? I've already wrung my own childhood dry."

"Go ahead," I say, and then he is gone, just a hand out the car window, and then that is gone, too. He was my very first friend here.

Jonathan and I stack the dishes in the kitchen and lie on his bed in our clothes. It's how we've always done it, like teenagers, as if each night we spend together is our first. My old boyfriend David used to have to brush his teeth and change into a clean T-shirt and fresh underwear before he got near the bed, and liked me to do the same. I couldn't stand the sterile marriedness of it. I make sure I don't always sleep on the same side of Jonathan's bed when I stay over. I don't want ritual or routine in a relationship. Ever.

Jonathan traces a finger along my temple and around my ear. When he takes off his glasses you can see that he has little stripes of tawny gold in his dark brown eyes. "You were so funny when people were toasting you. You looked like they were giving you an enema."

"I hate watching people have to come up with nice things to say." I kiss his finger, the tender pink pad of it. "Thank you for the party."

"You're so welcome, my Daley bread."

We kiss hard, our hands reaching for bare skin. He lifts a breast out of my bra and into his mouth and my groin starts to ache. I wonder how long our desire will last. We've signed a year's lease in California. Will we still touch each other so hungrily after a year of living together?

He pulls me on top of him. I feel him hard beneath me under his jeans. I push against him lightly, then harder, feeling the rush, the swell, the want. "Everything on earth should be just this simple," I say. I take his earlobe in my teeth and feel him moan. "Tell me what it's like again," I whisper, still grinding against him, feeling the exact shape of him through our clothes.

It takes him a second to find his voice. "You know it's Paloma Street when you see the big fence covered in bright red flowers. And then five houses down you see a tree out in front. Enormous. Maybe a eucalyptus. Please take off your clothes."

"Tell me about the front door." He flew out to California last month and found the cottage for us.

"Yellow. It's yellow."

"And the little window in the door?"

"The color of pale green sea glass. Please."

I pull off my jeans, clumsily. I'm like a drunk when I'm horny, completely without fine motor skills. Jonathan scoots himself down and pushes my legs apart. He grins up at me, then slides a finger up inside me. I'm wet and swollen and it goes in easily. He pushes it in and slides it out and pushes it in again. Unable to wait, I press myself to his mouth, feel the warmth of his tongue on my clit and the finger drawing back and forth inside me. I can feel the orgasm now, assembling in the distance then moving swiftly in, opening up, opening me up, coming, coming closer, coming to split me down the middle.

But the sudden ring startles me. "Just the phone, tweety," he says without lifting his head.

Three and a half rings, then the machine catches it. The orgasm veers off. My brother comes on. "Jesus Christ, Daley. Where the fuck are you?" There's a panic in his voice I've never heard before.

"Don't," Jonathan says as I pull away from him. "Please don't."

But I'm already across the room, reaching for the receiver. "Garvey, what's wrong?"

"Oh fucking Christ. There you are."

"What's going on?"

"Oh my God. Dad. Dad is what's going on."

"Is he okay?" I feel that cool whiteness that happens just before you hear someone is dead.

Garvey starts laughing or crying, I'm not sure which. "No, he is not okay or I wouldn't have been leaving you so many goddamn messages."

I look at the machine. A red 5 flashes. "Please calm down and tell me—"

"You haven't been here. You have no idea what I've seen in the past—"

"Garvey, you are scaring the shit out of me. What's going on?"

"Catherine left him."

He's alive. That's all I care about. "When?"

"I don't know. Maybe a week ago."

I wait for the rest.

"He is a fucking *mess*."

I snort. "Tell me about it."

"No, Daley. He's totally lost his shit. He's threatening to kill all his dogs. And Hugh fired him. It was Hugh's wife who called me. He's drunk 'round the clock. He's unrecognizable."

"Unrecognizable would be Dad sober. Dad drunk is not at all foreign to me." All those years that I had to go up to Myrtle Street every weekend, every vacation, while Garvey showed up for Thanksgiving and Christmas dinners.

"Daley." His voice cracks. I haven't heard him like this since Mom died. "You gotta come here and help me out."

"What? No, Garvey. I'm driving to California tomorrow." He knows all about Berkeley. He calls us Malibu Smart Barbie and Black Marxist Ken.

"He's talked about offing himself."

"Oh, come on. He'd destroy every living thing on this planet before he'd kill himself."

"No, Daley, you have to believe me. I think he might hurt himself. I need some backup here."

"I'm not coming. Not right now. I have a job that's about to start in California."

"Stop saying *California* like it's so important. I'm in *Massachusetts* and I need your help with our *father*. Two, three days, that's all I'm asking. Just to kind of settle him down. You're good with him."

"Yeah, right."

"You are."

"I couldn't even get there tomorrow. I've got to send out this article I just finished and have lunch with my advisor and—"

"I know. You've very busy. Get here when you can. Just for a day or two."

"Goddammit, Garvey."

"Thank you," he says. "Jesus Christ, Daley, thank you."

Jonathan is sitting on the side of the bed, his head in his hands. I sit beside him. I have no clothes on.

"I have to, Jon. I have to. Garvey sounds really freaked out."

"He always sounds freaked out."

"Not like this. My stepmother has taken off and my father is falling apart."

"What can you do in two days to fix that? Nothing."

"I don't want blood on my hands. I don't want to hear that my father shot himself while I drove to California."

"That's just Garvey being hyperbolic."

"He needs my help."

"I don't think you've spoken to your father since I've known you."

"Probably not."

"But within seconds you've decided to fly off in the wrong direction to a man who's not even a part of your life."

"Garvey needs help."

"Are you going to tell your father you're moving in with a black man?"

"Not if there are any knives around."

He doesn't smile. "Don't do this. Don't go back there."

He's still trying to persuade me to head west when I squeeze into my car the next afternoon.

We're tired. We've argued in circles since last night. And now I'm doing it—I'm about to drive away in the wrong direction.

"Daley," he says. He squats beside the open car door and holds my hands. It's still the same feeling from the general store, every time our hands touch. "Please be careful." He, too, has an uneasy relationship with the future. We understand each other in that way.

"I'll be fine."

"Your father has a lot of power."

"You're confusing me with Julie. My father has no power over me. He wasn't even a father." I see he is scared for me, far more scared than I am. Clearly I've told him too much.

"He still has the power to hurt you."

"No, he doesn't. It's all scar tissue now."

"I'll be at the yellow door a week from Monday," he says, kissing me one last time.

"I'll see you through the sea glass window."

And then I start the Datsun and drive east.

10

You can't get to my father's house from the highway without passing the Water Street Apartments. I didn't mean to come here first. I meant to go straight to Dad's, but I find myself peering into my bedroom window. It's someone's home office now, with two computers, a fax machine, and a leather swivel chair. The posters of Robert Redford, Billy Jack, and the Fonz are gone. Paul would have taken them down when he moved out the summer after my mother died. I'm certain he's rolled them up neatly in tubes; he's saved everything for Garvey and me in storage somewhere.

My mother died instantly. People tried to comfort us with that. But to whom was that a comfort? To me? I would have liked to see her one last time, no matter how crushed her body was; I would have liked to say goodbye, even if she couldn't have heard me. Was it a comfort to her? Who would choose to die instantly, without a chance to process the transition? But then, I don't like to be startled. I don't like to be surprised. She and Paul had eaten dinner in Boston, he'd gone to get the car, she'd decided to cross Tremont to make it easier for him to pick her up, and a car had struck her. The driver had had a few drinks in him; my mother was prone to daydreaming. It's hard to say what really happened. No one claimed to have seen.

I walk around to the living room windows. The current tenants have a sofa where we had one, a large dining table where our small one was. I'd been in my dorm room when Paul called. I was a sophomore in college. My roommate was dating a hockey player who'd just gotten back from a game. His shoulder pads were leaning against the wall by the phone. Paul was crying. The inside of the pads were streaked with filth. *I just talked to her last night.* I think I told this to Paul many times. It might have been the only thing I said. I couldn't think of anything else. It was the only thing that made sense. Garvey came and got me a few hours later.

I often try to remember my mother's funeral. It was at the little Episcopalian church she used to take me to before she left my father. I can remember those Sundays: my blue velvet coat, the white gloves, and my mother's long prayers on her knees on needlepoint cushions. I don't think she went to church after she left him. I don't think she needed to. But I can't recall the funeral. I don't know what was said. All I remember about that day, that whole week, was my father's absence.

Garvey thought my expectations were ridiculous. "You're going to make yourself sick your whole life if you think he's ever going to behave like a father to you," he told me as we lay on the twin beds in my room after the funeral. "We're basically orphans now. Get used to it." But I could not.

I think I believed that with my mother dead the barrier between me and my father would fall magically away. I spent the second half of my sophomore year of college waiting for him to call me. I took a job that summer in a restaurant in Rhode Island and sent him my new number on a postcard, and he never called it. I didn't visit him before I went back to school. I spent Christmas with a friend's family. And then, spring break of my junior year, I took a bus to Boston and a train to Ashing and appeared at the kitchen door where he was feeding the dogs. "Well, well," he said. "You pregnant or broke or both?" I stayed the night. It was just the three of us. Catherine made a roast. As they got drunk, then drunker, I waited for them to slip and make a jab about my mother, the way they always did. I waited to catch them. I was going to make a scene. A huge hair-pulling scene. *For God's sake, she's dead. Can't you leave her alone now?*

But they never mentioned her. He hugged me goodbye at the train the next day. "You's a good kid for visiting," he said. I spent the rest of the break off campus, in a friend's empty apartment, alone, sobbing. I had held off the grief with anger towards my father, but now I was blindsided by it, terrified by the sudden gaping hole of my mother's absence. She was my ballast, my counterweight to the downward pull of Myrtle Street, and she was gone.

I take one last look at the apartment. My mother's toes used to snap when she walked barefoot. Alone in the bathroom she talked out loud and made herself laugh. I was unhappy when we lived here together. I ricocheted from this apartment to my father's house for seven years, until I went to college. I was never able to please either household. At my father's I was too bookish, too liberal, too much like my mother; at my mother's I was moody, mercurial, and underachieving in school. I'm sorry she can't know me now. *My daughter is a tenured professor at Berkeley,* she might have been able to say in a few years. She would have liked that. She would have liked Jonathan.

I continue on toward Myrtle Street. The BMW in the bank parking lot might be Catherine's. She'll go back to him. I feel sure of it. She just needs a few days to cool off. I cross the railroad tracks and head up the hill. The houses are larger on this side of town, big clapboard Capes and Colonials with wraparound porches and pots of daisies on the wide steps before their front doors. There are hammocks and swing sets and lacrosse goals in the long green yards. The harbor glitters behind them. I can smell the salt in the air. It's heavy, humid air. I need sleep. Garvey will have to let me have some when I get there.

I park next to Garvey's van. It's one of the small ones. He has his own moving company now, a fleet of six trucks with flying refrigerators painted all over them. The dogs go berserk at the sight of my car, the three of them, a tan one, a black one, and an auburn one, chasing it and then positioning themselves in front of the car door, their legs and chests motionless as statues, their mouths and throats furious at the foreign invasion. They make a ridiculous racket. The older I get, the more my father's dogs exhaust me.

"Calm down," I tell them coldly as they triple-team me all the way up the path. They are big dogs, retrievers of some kind. Something stirs on the porch. A little white and brown thing. A bunny? Then it bounds down the steps, or it tries to bound, but it ends up moving sideways, its hind legs stronger and braver than those in front. It runs right at me with no barking, then scrapes all its little paws at my jeans as if trying to climb straight up. The other dogs stop barking to watch.

"You're a little hairball," I say, laughing at its smashed-in face, its wet black nose. I scoop it up and it snorts a tiny spray at me. The tag on its collar says Maybelle. "Hello, little Maybelle," I say. And she buries her funny little face in my neck. I leave my suitcase on the lawn and carry the dog in instead.

I see them through the screen door. They are both on the floor, in that wide open space where the kitchen table used to be. My father is lying down, bleeding from somewhere on his face. Garvey is sitting up but bent over, rocking.

"Is he dead?" I hear myself scream. "Is he dead?" I don't know what I do with Maybelle. I'm on the floor between them, wiping the blood with my sleeve. It's coming from just below my father's eyebrow, not quickly. His skin is a green gray. "I think he's dead!"

"He's not dead," Garvey says quietly.

It's true. I can feel breath coming out his nostrils.

"I'm sorry I called you." He stands up slowly. It hurts him to straighten up. "He's not worth it. Just get in your car and go."

I don't move.

"I mean it, Daley. Leave. Go to California. I'm serious."

"He's unconscious and he's bleeding."

"He's fine. He's drunk and he has a scrape. C'mon, Daley. Get up and come with me."

"You did this. You hit him."

"All I did was defend myself. C'mon. We'll stop at Brigham's and I'll buy you a lime rickey." For the first time my brother looks old to me. Old and sad. He is growing jowly.

"You just had me drive sixteen hours in the wrong direction and now you want me to leave him passed out on the floor and drive away?"

"I said I was sorry. I was wrong, all right? Come with me. Now. Trust me on this one, Daley."

"I can't."

"Fuck it then. Suit yourself." He slides his old leather jacket off a doorknob. The screen door smacks behind him. "Call me when he's dead," he says, and starts down the steps.

"Garvey!" I want to run after him but I'm scared to leave my father. "You asshole!" I get up and scream through the screen at his back, moving away. "You fucking asshole! What am I supposed to do with him?"

"Walk away," he calls without turning.

I go back to my father on the floor. The van starts up, the dogs bark, and Garvey yells at them as they chase him and his goddamn flying refrigerators down the driveway.

Maybelle has taken to her leopard-print bed in the corner but jumps up when I get a rag out of the drawer. She follows me to the sink and back to my father.

As soon as I put the wet cloth on his forehead he comes to, or maybe he's been awake the whole time.

"Hello, elf."

"Dad, I'm taking you to the hospital."

"All right," he says. He sounds grateful, as if he's been waiting a long time for somebody to say those words.

*   *   *

I know the way to the hospital in Allencaster. Mallory and I were candy stripers there one summer. We take my father's car with automatic windows and seat levers. The steering wheel has a thick leather sheath. He falls asleep before we hit the highway. Every few minutes I poke him.

"Why do you keep doing that?" he says.

"Just checking on you."

"Don't check on me anymore." Unlike my brother, he seems not to have aged at all. He looks as I always remember him, tanned, taut, and bony. The knees beneath his khakis are the same knobs I've seen all my life. I find myself wanting to stare.

He smells of alcohol and I'm glad. The doctors will notice. Maybe they will suggest a treatment center. Maybe this is the proverbial rock bottom.

It's a small hospital with a small parking lot. We get a spot near the door. I help him out of the car and he walks slowly, more bent over than usual, one hand shielding his bad eye. I steady him, relieved when I see a wheelchair out in front of the door. I steer him toward it but he bats the idea away with his free hand and the word *pansy* and keeps walking.

After my father is admitted, I return to the desk and ask if I can see Dr. Perry Barns, who was his internist and occasional doubles partner when I was growing up. He comes quickly, short-limbed in his white tunic, one lone tuft of silver hair left on the top of his head. I barely know him; he is just a name I've heard on Myrtle Street all my life.

"Look at you!" he says from the doorway. People in the waiting room glance up at the unnecessary boom of his voice. He begins shaking his head. "You were this high." He puts a flat hand level to his kneecap

I stand and he gives me a hug and a moist kiss too close to my mouth.

"I'm sorry to bother you, Dr. Barns. It would just make me feel better if you'd take a look at him."

"At who?"

"At my father. I'm sorry. I thought they had explained—" I glance over at reception. The chair is empty.

"What's going on?" Like that, he switches from country club parent to doctor. I feel my body relax.

I tell him what I know, and he disappears through the swinging doors. I zone in and out of *The Price Is Right*.

When he comes back a few minutes later, he is smiling again. He sits next to me in a plastic chair and puts his hand on my leg. "You." He squeezes the skin of my thigh several times. "You are all grown up."

It would be one thing if I were recently grown up. But I am twenty-nine years old. "Could you tell me about my father?"

He pulls back his hand. "He's going to be okay. Honkey-donkey, as my daughter used to say." I never knew what a moron this guy was. "He'll be hitting those famous crosscourt volleys in just a few days."

"I'm concerned about his drinking."

"Drinking?"

"Since Catherine left, he's been on a bit of a tear."

"Your father has never been a binger."

I laugh. "You're right. More of a steady alcoholic."

He frowns. "Oh, now, alcoholic is a strong word. He likes his martinis, I'll grant you. But that's never been a *problem*."

I have a swirling slippery feeling in my stomach. I feel the small stool in St. Thomas beneath me. "You're right. I'm exaggerating. Please don't mention to him that I said that." I don't need my father's fury turned on me during the forty-eight hours I'll be in Ashing.

He smiles. "I won't." He puts his hand back on my leg and squeezes a few more times. "I promise."

My father is wrapped up in a lot of bandages, and in many more places than I thought he'd been hurt: both wrists, one ankle, his entire forehead, and around his chest. The wrist wraps look hasty and uneven and I wonder if he did it himself when the nurse left the cubicle. Once he has the bandages on he becomes even more frail, moving more slowly to the car than he did into the hospital.

When we get home I take him directly upstairs to his bed, hoping I can steal a little sleep as well. But as I'm leaving the room he says in a small voice, "Any lunch down there?"

At least I know what to make him: three hot dogs, no bun, and a sliced tomato slathered with mayonnaise. I've seen him eat that lunch my whole life. Tomatoes and hot dogs are the only edible things in the fridge. The other vegetables have blackened; the milk has gone sour. There is an explosion of dirty dishes in and around the sink. As far as I can tell, Garvey and my father ate everything with ketchup, which has now hardened into a scarlet shellac on every plate. I can't cook, can't even boil hot dogs, in such a filthy kitchen.

He looks at the clock when I come in with his tray, but he doesn't complain about how long it took me.

He sits up and puts the plate in his lap and says, "This is terrific." He picks up one of the pink-gray tubes of pig intestine, dips it in the mound of ketchup, and raises it to his open mouth. It makes a pop as it splits between his teeth.

"You have yours already?"

I realize I'm hovering.

"No, I—"

"Want some?" He pushes his plate toward me.

"No, I don't—" *eat meat,* I want to finish, but can anticipate the mockery too well. "Thanks anyway."

He confuses me. He disgusts and compels me. I don't want to stand and watch him eat three hot dogs (I had to use several different utensils to get them out of the package and in and out of the boiling water without having to touch them) and yet the sight of his fingers, the tip of a pencil embedded since kindergarten above the knuckle of his first finger, the long yellowing thumb steadying the plate, keeps me in place.

"Sit down. You're making me nervous." He says it in a bad New York accent. Noyvus. He points to the wooden chair in the corner. I pull it up to the bed.

He cleans the plate, then puts it on the bedside table. He lies back on his pillows.

"Dad, will you tell me what's been going on here?"

He closes his eyes and shakes his head. "You can't imagine what I've been through."

I wait.

His eyes flash open. "Do you know what that ungrateful asshole brother of yours said to me?"

"No, but let's start at the beginning. What happened with Catherine?"

He looks at me blankly for a moment, as if there's only room for one enemy at a time in his head. Then he smiles before shaking his head again, even more slowly this time. "Now there's a real beauty. There's a real little cunt for you."

"You had a big fight?"

"No we didn't have a big fight." He isn't one for narrative unless it has a punch line. "She just took off and I said good riddance."

"Were you home?" Did Catherine leave in the same way my mother had, on the sly, a note on the kitchen table? It seemed the only way.

"Yes. I was in the poolhouse. She drove right past me."

"What time of day was it?"

"About nine in the morning."

I figured she'd left in a drunken midnight rage, not on a sunny Saturday morning.

"She came crawling back, too, the next day. But I had a gun and told her to get off the property."

"A gun?"

"Damn right."

"A BB gun?" I try not to smile.

"If you aim it in the right place, that thing can do some damage."

"Dad, you and Catherine have been together a long time."

"Worst years of my life."

"Really?"

"Well, some of the worst."

"I'm going to talk to Catherine. I know you can work this—"

"If you do that—" he struggles to sit up and point a finger at me—"if you do that, if you go anywhere near her, I'll call the police. You can get out of this house right now if that's what your plan is. I want nothing, *nothing* to do with that woman, do you understand that?" His eyes are small and yellow.

"Yes," I say thinly. The walls of my stomach begin to buckle. I feel myself rise, put back the chair, lift his plate, and move quickly out of the room and down to the kitchen. Over my shoulder, as smoothly as I can, I tell him to have a nap.

It's been years since I've triggered my father's temper. I learned my way around it long ago. I do not bring up politics, history, literature, lawyers—especially Jewish lawyers—or any other subject that can be linked, however loosely, to my mother. I do not tease, and I receive teasing with a smile; I keep my thoughts and opinions to a bare minimum. I ask questions. I make myself useful. I do not discuss my interests, my relationships, or my goals. He and Catherine find me dull company, and tease me for that as well, but it is a small price to pay for peace.

It never occurred to me that he wouldn't want Catherine back. He'd wanted my mother back, or at least I thought he had. I have no Plan B.

I pick up the phone, the old one that's always been there, with the long cord and rotary dial. Jonathan answers before the second ring.

"It's just me."

"Hey, just you." His voice jiggles; he's flopped on the bed and smashed a pillow beneath his head. He's settling in for a long conversation. Suddenly I don't have that in me. "So how is he?"

"He's okay." It feels like too much to explain: Garvey, the hospital, the loss of Plan A. "I miss you. I want to be on Paloma Street with you."

"Nine and a half days. Here. I was just thinking of you. Listen to this. I've been reading *Go Tell It on the Mountain* again." There's a muffled scraping sound. "Okay, here it is."

It's a long quote and I try to concentrate, but the words just bounce off me.

"I like that," I say when he's done, but I don't have anything more to say about it. "There are these plates here. I remember coming back from my grandparents' that summer and seeing them in my kitchen: Catherine's good china. The kids ate off of plastic, but Dad and Catherine always used these plates. She didn't take them with her. She doesn't seem to have taken much of anything. That's probably a good sign, right?"

"You want her to come back?"

"It's my father's only hope, I think. He can't cope alone."

"How about some sort of housekeeper?"

"He doesn't like people he doesn't know."

"Did you really come from the loins of this man?"

"Please don't put it that way. How was class today?"

"Two more to go."

"They'll hand in their papers next week?" Once he got those papers and graded them, he could leave.

"Wednesday morning. You know, this Baldwin book probably means more to me than anything I've read in any philosophy class.

Narrative is the way to communicate ideas. Philosophy just tastes bad to most people unless you wrap it up in a good story." It's weird to hear his voice and the words *Baldwin* and *philosophy* and *narrative* coming through the same phone line we used to use for prank calls. *Is John Wall there? Are any Walls there? Then what's holding up your house?*

"I don't know," I say.

"You okay, Dales?"

"I should probably go check on him."

"You sure?"

I wish I hadn't called so soon. It's never a good idea to try and mix the world of my father with any other world. I'd learned that over and over. "I'll call you when I get on the road again."

"I love you," he says. It sounds dutiful. But I know that's the Doppler effect of being here in this house.

The minute I hang up I want to call back.

"Who was that?"

I flinch. He can really creep up on you when he wants to. "A friend of mine. She's moving to California, too." The impulse to lie is instinctive, like one of those desert cats hastily burying its kill in the sand.

He's changed into bright red pants. His hair is damp, combed neatly in ridges. "When do you have to go?"

"The day after tomorrow. I have a professorship at Berkeley that starts in ten days." I don't know if Garvey mentioned this to him.

He moves past me to the door where the dogs are scraping to be let out. They move in a runnel of fur through the opening he makes. He stays looking out the screen door. The little dog remains beside him. He nudges her with the toe of his topsider. "Well, we don't have a professorship, do we, Maybelle?"

He moves with sudden purpose to the bar. It's not yet 2 P.M. I've never tried to control my father's drinking, never suggested that he not have a drink when he wanted one. It would be like trying to separate a snake from a mouse.

It's all done with such precision: the ice into the monogrammed glass, the snap of the paper across the cap of a new bottle of Smirnoff's, the splash of vermouth, the tiny onions jiggled out so carefully. Then the pause, and then the sip, his eyes pulled shut by pleasure. I've never noticed what an act of love it all is.

Alcohol has never done anything for me. The first time I got drunk was with Mallory in eighth grade. My mother and Paul were out, and we mixed Grand Marnier with Hawaiian Punch. Mallory got giggly and I got sick. When my mother came home I was still bent over the toilet. She seemed more relieved than angry. "I think you're like me, honey," she said, rubbing my back. "You'll never be able to hold your liquor." She was right.

The afternoon, the evening, the night spreads out before us. Outside the sky is wide and blue; the sun beats on the grass, on the fur of the dogs on the back porch. Inside is cool and dark.

"Backgammon?" I say, slightly desperate.

"Sure."

We go into the den, to the cabinet where the games are kept. A hot cedar smell spills out. Backgammon is on the bottom, the fake leather case stuck to the wood. I have to give it a good tug. He takes his seat on the sofa and places his drink on the end table, a fluid gesture I have seen a million times. I pull around an armchair to face him, the game between us on the coffee table. The pieces are heavy, marbleized. The dice thud in their felt-lined cups. I haven't played a game with him since I was a very little girl.

We set up. There is no confusion about which side is home, my left, his right. He does not say, as Jonathan always does before any kind of game, *I am going to whup you silly*, just to up the tension. But I can tell by his breathing and the careful straight rows he makes that he is thinking about winning. I never think about winning at the beginning of a game. At the start I am always just thinking how happy I am to be playing a game, what a particular old pleasure it is, what a wonderful detour from regular life, regular conversation. My desire to win comes later, when I recognize that my delight has not put me in the lead. Then I become focused and anxious. If I lose, it feels like more than losing a game, and if I win, the elation is momentary—the other person's discouragement makes my own enjoyment impossible.

My first roll is a six and a five, lovers' leap. He tries to blockade my remaining man, but he doesn't get the rolls. I hit him several times on my way out. Soon I have trapped four of his men in my home.

When I win, he moans, falsetto, but he isn't angry. He's barely taken a sip from his drink. We set up the board again.

The dice are with me again. I double him after my third roll and he accepts.

"You're a little whippersnapper, aren't you?" he says. "You and your professorship. But I'm not as dumb as I look, you know." He gets double fives and knocks off two of my men. "I was pretty good at school once upon a time."

"Were you?"

"Don't sound so surprised."

"I'm not. I know you're smart. Maybe not really smart in backgammon." I come in on a four and a three, and bump off two of his men.

"You know what I loved in school?" he says.

"What?"

"Shakespeare."

"Shakespeare?"

"We had to memorize something from *Julius Caesar* once."

"A soliloquy?"

"I think so." It's his turn, but he doesn't roll. "*O conspiracy, sham'st thou to show thy dangerous brow by night, when evils are most free?"* His neck lengthens as he speaks, reddens, the Adam's apple sharp as ever, cutting its pale path. *"O, then by day where wilt thou find a cavern dark enough to mask thy monstrous visage?"*

"Wow, Dad. Good memory."

He looks at me like he used to look at Catherine sometimes, a defiant go fuck yourself look. And then he takes a long sip of his martini and the blush drains out of his face.

The next game he beats me. He gets up and makes another drink. He beats me again. He drinks faster when he is winning.

"I used to play this with my mother," he says.

I wait for more. It's rare for him to talk about his childhood.

"She used to send me to the kitchen to fetch the maid and she'd change the board around. She was a terrible cheater."

She was a terrible drunk, my mother told me.

"I'd say, 'Ring the bell for the maid.' There was a button under the carpet beside her chair, and all she had to do was step on it and it would ring in the kitchen. But she'd say 'The maid's going deaf.' There was no contradicting my mother. I learned that early enough."

"How? What would she do?"

"She'd put clothespins on my ears."

"What?"

"She'd put clothespins on my ears and I'd have to walk to school like that."

"Dad, c'mon."

"They hurt like hell, too."

"Oh my God, that's so twisted."

He laughed at the word. "She was twisted all right."

"Have you ever lived alone before?"

"Let's see. I had a single my senior year of college."

"And you ate in the dining hall?"

"I ate at my club."

"And your laundry was done for you?"

"Every Monday morning."

"Before I leave, I'm going to show you how to wash your own clothes and make a few meals."

"I know how to make steak and hot dogs. That's all I need to know."

"There's nothing you want to learn to cook?"

He thinks about it. "Hollandaise sauce. Catherine's was awful."

He wants my mother's recipe. He's saying he misses my mother's hollandaise. Even now, I thrill when I find a chink of light in the great wall between them.

When he comes back into the room with another drink, he says, "This is nice."

"What?"

"Playing backgammon."

"It *is* nice."

"I wish you could stay longer."

These are words I've never heard from him, simple words. *This is nice. I wish you could stay longer.*

"Me too." It feels true and then, after a few seconds, completely untrue. Two nights is all I can handle. And I know what he's doing, how he can put on the charm when he needs something from you.

I beat him the last game, backgammon him, and he laughs as I do it.

"You're a good player," he says, packing up the case.

Afterward I drag him up to the laundry room. It looks just the same, the ivory-colored machines, the hampers, the cabinet with the safe inside.

I explain the separation of lights, colors, and darks. There are enough of his tennis whites in there to make a small load, so I toss them in, measure out the powder detergent, read out the cleaning options, and pull the knob. Water rushes in and I shut the lid. We move to the dryer and I show him the dials. I scrape the lint tray clean. He says *Mm-hmm* and *Okay* at all the right times, but he isn't paying attention. He's behaving as if it's all hypothetical, like I'm preparing him for an emergency situation that will not actually come to pass.

He points to the old hair dryer standing on its wheels in the corner, a gunmetal-gray helmet my mother used to spend hours under, deaf to the world. I go over and touch the thick metal lip. I can see her foot bobbing, hear the pages of *Time* magazine snapping. I feel my ache for her grow and then freeze.—I can't miss my mother in front of my father. But she once stood here; we'd all once been a family in this house. It's like a story, a fairy tale, something told to me, not remembered. Once upon a time a beautiful lady lived with a handsome man in a big house near the sea. They had two lovely children, a boy and a girl. But the beautiful lady was not happy, and one day she took the little girl and all the jewelry and disappeared.

11

Since there is no space for groceries in my car, I take my father's to the market. Going down the hill into town, I get behind a Volvo whose bumper declares they'd rather be windsurfing. A Saab at the fish market says it would rather be skiing. I laugh as if Jonathan were beside me and had made a joke. Yeah, he'd say, where I grew up we put stickers on our asses that said I'D RATHER BE DRIVING A CAR. At the sight of my father's beige sedan, hands rise from steering wheels to wave and then surprised eyes peer in. They do not know me, but I know them: Mrs. Utley, chain-smoking in a green station wagon; Mrs. Braeburn, pursing her stiff lips in a navy Jeep; small Mrs. Wentworth leaning forward in a van, only her forehead visible; Mr. Timmons, who inexplicably retired in his early forties, parking his powder blue convertible outside the post office with the concentration of a leader of a small military operation.

After my mother died, I came to Ashing seldom and briefly. Two nights a year with my father and Catherine was enough. On the way, I'd think of all the people I wanted to see, old friends who might by chance be back visiting at the same time, friends of my mother's who'd written kind letters to me after she died. I'd plan to go to all the shops, poke my head in at the Mug and the penny candy store. I wanted to visit people because I missed them and because I knew it would be healthy to break up the intensity of seeing my father. But my father's house was not one you could flit in and out of. It sucked you in until it spat you out. It was seductively familiar, my father greeting me in the driveway, his scratchy voice animated, full of stories he'd seemed to save just for me. I rarely managed to time my visits with Patrick's.

After college he moved to Miami with a woman named Hill and her three children, and they didn't come north much. Frank ended up in New York City and Elyse in Wyoming, and I never saw them, either. So I'd sit with my father and Catherine the first night and wonder why I didn't come home more often. My father would get drunk, but he seemed happy, playful. That first night I never thought to go downtown to the bars like other people my age did when they came home to visit. I went to bed when he and Catherine did, and fell into a heavy sleep. But the show would always be over by the next afternoon. My father's good mood never lasted long. Catherine would have said something that pissed him off, or a neighbor would have come over uninvited, or someone from work would have called. His anger would ramp up, and by nighttime he was seething and muttering, while I just tried to dodge as many insults as I could. I never ended up seeing anyone else in Ashing. He made me forget my attachments to others; he made me reptilian. To go see other people meant they would see my scales.

But the circumstances are different now. The last time I was here my dissertation was over two thousand pages of notes in a milk crate in the back of my car and I'd just had a bad breakup. But I am beyond all that uncertainty now. Almost miraculously, I think as I walk up the slight incline of Goodale's parking lot to the glass doors, I have come back to Ashing whole.

It's been at least a decade since I've entered this store and seen Mrs. Goodale glance up in irritation, as if she needed another customer like she needed a hole in her head. I don't bear much resemblance to my child self: my hair has grown down my back, my skinny frame has filled out a bit, and the defensive grimace I wear in all the old photos is gone. I planned to be a spy in the aisles, listening for any talk of my father and Catherine, for where she might be and if there is any hope of her coming back. But Mrs. Goodale lifts her head and says, without a moment's pause, "Daley Amory, back from beyond the beyond."

It's a bit like being announced by a footman at the entryway of a ball. Her proclamation carries straight back to meats then ricochets across to frozen foods and dairy. Fortunately the store is nearly empty. There's only my sixth-grade teacher perusing the tomatoes, awful hard pale balls grouped in threes on green Styrofoam trays and wrapped in thick cellophane. Her scowl has deepened, though I think she's trying to smile at me now. I see she isn't as old as I once thought. She doesn't look more than sixty now. She didn't like me much. I had her the first year we lived on Water Street, the first year of my parents' divorce. She called me a sullen little girl in the report card that came home at Christmastime. Garvey taunted me about it. He even called me Sully for a while. When, at the end of that year, I got a perfect score on my math exam, she called it a fluke.

I slip into the narrow vegetable aisle and stand beside her, closer than I normally get to people, especially people I don't like. "Hello, Miss Perth." I'm not much taller than she is but I have on my favorite shoes, black lace-ups with a chunky heel, and feel like I'm towering over her.

She startles like a cat and steps back. "Oh, it's you," she says, not remembering my name. "Gardiner's sister."

That reminds me of another thing she said, a few weeks after school had started in the fall: "Well, you're nothing like your delightful brother, are you?"

"And what are you doing with yourself these days?" She says *these days* as if she doesn't approve of the expression but has forgotten how to better articulate the time frame.

I pause. I want to brag, prove to her that I was no fluke in the end, but I want to do it with humility.

"A bit at loose ends, it seems," she says.

"Not really." I laugh, but an explanation is frozen in my throat. Defending myself has never been one of my strengths.

"Daley?" A large woman in a navy dress hurries up to me from the back of the store. "God, it *is* you! You hot shit. Look at you in your shiny shoes!" She envelops me sideways, my shoulder disappearing between her enormous breasts. "I can't wait to tell Neal you're home." This is Mrs. Caffrey. Since I've been back I've forgotten to remember Neal Caffrey. Please don't, I think. Please don't mention my name to Neal.

"He's here, you know. I mean he lives here. He has a shop." She points back toward the middle of town. Neal Caffrey runs a shop in Ashing? He won all those subject prizes at graduation in eighth grade, and the big silver cup for excellence in scholarship, athletics, and citizenship. The Renaissance Cup. "He'd love to see you." She glances at my left ring finger, finds it bare, and gushes on. "I think the two of you would really hit it off."

"I'm only here for another day. I'm leaving for California on Sunday morning. I'm a professor at Berkeley." It's the first time I've ever said it like that, in the present tense. I speak loudly, but Miss Perth has turned the corner.

"Oh." Mrs. Caffrey looks gravely disappointed. She kicks an unpacked box of leeks on the floor. "He'll never meet anyone in this town. Everyone interesting leaves. Only the screwups hang around."

This is as much as I've ever spoken to Neal's mother. I remember her in the carpool line. She'd always be out of the car, leaning into someone else's window, then leaning back out, howling. She had that large person's jolliness and warmth. Neal didn't inherit that. By eighth grade he'd become more of a brooder. A popular brooder, though. He had his pick of girls. I never did speak to him after that summer. He didn't notice. He thought I was concave. That's what he told Stacy Miller in seventh grade, that I was so flat-chested I was concave. After eighth grade he went on to Exeter while I stayed at the academy.

Someone comes in the store behind us—I feel the short burst of warmer air—and bypasses the vegetable section. I recognize, just from the dimmest shape at the periphery of my vision, Catherine's long gait.

"So tell me what exactly you're a professor of, smarty pants," Mrs. Caffrey asks, her good humor returned to her.

"I have to run. I'm so sorry."

"Stop by Neal's shop on the way home! It's the one with the lighthouse on the sign."

I duck down the middle aisle where I saw Catherine go, but it's empty. At the back of the store, Brad Goodale is behind the meat counter, just where I left him in the early eighties. He's slicing up something for someone I don't recognize. In the last aisle there are two men my age, studying the yogurt. I rush past them to the front and see that one has his finger hooked in the other's belt loop. Despite my frenzy I smile, happy that change has come even to Ashing. I reach the register just in time to see the thick dark hair, more cropped than I remember, beyond the door, turning left into the parking lot. I think of chasing her but I don't think desperation will help my case. And I feel nothing but desperate at this moment.

"Guess she forgot her list," Mrs. Goodale says as she rings up Miss Perth's small batch of groceries.

I stare out the plate glass, breathing heavily, still struggling with indecision. I should go stop her before she leaves the parking lot. But is she, in the end, good for him? Wouldn't he be better off with someone more disciplined? But without *someone* he may simply self-destruct. I move to the door. And then I see her car, the little burgundy BMW, and on the back a new bumper sticker that says: I'D RATHER BE DIVORCED."

My father is watching the news in the den. It's strange to see him back in that room with his ashtray and his drink, as if he never left it for the sunroom and all those years with Catherine. A couch has replaced the recliners that replaced the couch my mother took to Water Street. The room looks almost back to normal, though the slipcovers are made of a nubby wool, something my mother wouldn't have chosen. He bends his head down to watch the television, his eyes straining up just beneath their hoods. A woman is discussing affirmative action on some courthouse steps. She speaks articulately, quickly, trying to get the most words into her few seconds of time on national TV.

"Why are black people always talking about black people?" my father says in his disgusting version of an African American accent, though the woman speaking has the regionless accent of a newscaster. "Have you noticed that?"

"Because in this country they are defined by their skin color, and they've had to fight for every basic right that we get automatically by being born white."

"Fight for their rights? This woman is fighting for inequality. This woman wants a black C student to be chosen over a straight-A student. She's fighting for their right to cheat."

My retort constructs itself swiftly. I've got a lot of ammo now on this question, yet none of my knowledge will help me win a fight with my father. He will cling to his position even when all reason fails him; he will cling to it as if it's his life and not his opinion that is in peril. He will get vicious and personal, and every negative thing he ever felt about me will pour out of his mouth. Ridding my father of his racist and anti-Semitic rhetoric would take a long time. It would be a whole reeducation. His prejudices are a stew of self-hatred, ignorance, and fear. If those feelings could be rooted out and examined somehow, maybe he wouldn't have to drink so much to squelch the pain of them.

"You don't have much of an answer to that, do you?"

Would Jonathan be horrified at my cowardice? Would he understand that to argue would be futile, would wound me deeply and do nothing to change him?

"I'm going to get dinner started." I can hear my mother in my tone with him. "Do you want me to call you when I'm ready to make the hollandaise?"

"The what?" Then he remembers. "Okay. Sure."

But when it's time, he slouches against the counter with his hands in his pockets, staring but unseeing as I whisk the egg yolks in a saucepan and add cubes of butter, one at a time.

"It's so easy, Dad. The only trick is to get the flame as low as possible and keep stirring. It'll curdle if it gets too hot. Here, you take the whisk." He takes it and, in a fairly good imitation of me, flicks the wire bulb through the thickening sauce. Hope swells in my chest. I have this idea that if he can make his own hollandaise he'll be okay. And if he can learn to make both hollandaise and wash his clothes, he won't need a wife at all.

At the table, A-1 sauce slathered over his rib eye, hollandaise over his asparagus, he is grateful. And very drunk. "You're a goddamn good cook, you know that?"

I sleep in Elyse's room, my old room. The rug is green, not yellow, the walls stripped of the daisy paper and replaced by a blue sponge wash. Out the windows are the same trees, though. Pine, beech, oak. One for each window. I get into bed and shut off the light. All my books are in the car. I have nothing to read to make me sleepy.

"Who we got here?" my father would say every time he came to say good night to me in this room. He'd yank Piglet up by the ear.

"No, not Piglet," I'd giggle.

He'd wind up and hit Piglet in the face with his fist. "Pow!" he'd say. "Right in the kisser." Piglet would go flying. Then he'd find all the rest of them scattered at the end of my bed and on the rocking chair and, one by one, speak kindly to them, wait for my false protests, then punch them across the room. I'd laugh and laugh.

*   *   *

In the morning I stand in the middle of the bathroom for a long time. It was here at the sink that my mother told me about her plan to leave my father. Eighteen years ago last week. I was wearing a white sleeveless nightgown. She was scared. I can see that now. Her lips were the color of her skin. Her eyes were filled, the brown trembling. She stood right there at the sink, holding her toothbrush, smelling the way she did in the morning, slightly sour. And now she is dead. Has been dead for years, though it doesn't seem that way to me. It seems like she is just off with Paul somewhere. In all my dreams she is away, just about to return. I am often on the way to the airport to pick her up, or on my way to Water Street to clean before she gets back, neither of which I ever did in real life.

Paul writes regularly, calls on my birthday, asks me to visit. I write back sporadically, rarely remember his birthday on time, and never visit when I come to Massachusetts to visit my father. I think I will, and then I don't. I wonder if he's on the Cape right now. He spends as much time as he can there, he wrote in his last letter. He and my mother rented a little house in Truro every summer, and last fall the owner sold it to him. The letter was filled with exclamation points, which was not his style, so I knew how excited he was about it.

Now I get back into Elyse's bed and wonder if I ever wrote back to congratulate him. I have no memory of it. It sets off a whole pageant in my mind of people I've let down or underappreciated. An old feeling, a weightless unease, creeps into my limbs. I need to shut my eyes and sleep it off, but I hear water rushing through the pipes for my father's shower. Morning is always the best time to be with him.

Today, though, he is sullen when he comes down, making his coffee without his usual songs or whistling, calling the dogs sharply to their bowls, opening the sports page and cursing some Red Sox player I've never heard of. He's even angry at his own foot, which he slips out of his moccasin twice to scratch. I notice he has a hole in the toe of his sock. It's unlike my father to wear anything torn.

"Look at that big toe poking out."

"I don't have one decent goddamn matching pair of socks."

"Well, let's get you some. Today."

"Really?" It's as if I've suggested cotton candy to a six-year-old.

"Sure. Is Piper's still around?"

"It sure is. I could use another pair of pants, too."

Maybelle bounces at the screen door. "Oh, I sees you," he says brightly, lovingly. "Here I am."

And there is Piper's, right where it's always been on the first floor of an old house with a big veranda. Through the window I can see the madras dinner jackets, the white canvas golf hats, and the belts with sailboats or trout or tennis racquets on them. I cringe at the sight of it all. But to my father there is nothing ridiculous and foppish about this style of dress, nothing fetishistic about having symbols of wealth, little ducks or martinis, sewn all over your pants. It is all he's ever known. This is what his whole world wears.

He pulls open the door of the shop and then stands aside to let me pass. But in the equally insulated world I have been in, men do not hold doors for women and, if they do, if they have just arrived from Pluto, women do not walk through them. I want to simply walk through the door he holds for me. Our outing has reversed his mood. I have less than twenty-four hours with him. The socks and pants he needs are only a few yards away and the smell of the store comes rushing at me, the sweet smell of new cotton clothes that brought me so much pleasure as a child. But I cannot do it.

I gesture playfully for him to go through first. He will not.

"C'mon, Dad. You're the one with the hole in your toe."

He laughs a disgusted laugh. "I am not going through a door held by a *girl*."

"Why not?"

He shakes his head. "Is this the kind of crap you get at your fancy schools? You learn to be rude to every person who shows the slightest bit of upbringing?"

I feel the fatigue of trying to communicate with him. Twenty more hours. I go through the goddamn door.

"Hello," a woman says to us from the back, where she's folding cable-knit sweaters. I can only see her dimly but I recognize the voice. My father veers right, into the men's section.

"Didn't I go to school with her?" I whisper.

"Her? No. She's twice your age."

"I think it's Brenda McPheney."

"Oh, Christ, that's not Brenda McPheney. Brenda McPheney was a skinny knockout of a girl."

"She had anorexia, that's why she was so skinny. She almost died senior year."

"Well, she looked a hell of a lot better with anorexia." He points to something over my shoulder. "Look at that. Isn't that great?" On a shelf was a shiny ceramic statue of a black Lab with supplicating eyes and a real leash hanging out of its mouth. "I love that." And he did. He stared at it like someone else might stare at a Van Gogh.

We pick out pairs of blue, gray, and black socks. We're going through the pants rack when my father looks over into the women's section, says, "Duck!" and pushes me down by the shoulders into a little nook.

"Jesus Christ," he whispers.

"Is it Catherine?"

"Christ, no. You can't buy muumuus in here. It's Tits Kelly. If she sees us, we'll never get out of here."

The wooden floorboards creak.

"Fuck. She's coming. Suck in your gut and don't breathe."

No one in town ever calls her anything else, except to her face, and I can't even remember what that name is. She's a terrible busybody and, as my father has said a million times, completely humorless. The ultimate condemnation.

Brenda McPheney comes over and asks her if she's looking for something special.

"Not really," she says, more of a sigh than words. Brenda goes back to her sweater folding. Mrs. Kelly cuts a long, low growling fart. Dad looks at me, delighted, making an O with his mouth and squeezing my finger to help him stay quiet. I laugh in silence, my stomach knotted in pain. We are bent over and mushed together to fit in this tiny hole in the wall. I don't know how it's possible she doesn't see us, but she takes her time choosing a man's shirt. Finally, she brings her selection to Brenda at the register.

"I wonder who she's buying that shirt for," my father says on the way home. "Husband Number Two left her last spring. You ever hear the story of little Davy Kelly and the two C-pluses?"

I have, but he's in such a good mood. "No."

"No?" He's thrilled. And he tells me about how in fourth grade little Davy Kelly brought home a report card with two C-pluses in math and social studies. Little Davy, according to his mother, never got anything but As. Then she found out that in both math and social studies, little Davy sat next to Ollie Samuels. So Mrs. Kelly marched over to the Samuelses' at dinnertime, stood in their kitchen, and demanded that Ollie tell her what he'd been doing to distract her son during math and social studies. Ollie told her he'd stopped talking to Davy long ago, when he realized Davy was paying Lucy Lothrop ten cents for her answers in English and only gave Ollie a nickel for his.

My father laughs like it's the first time he's heard it himself. It seems to me a story much older than Davy Kelly, a story my father might have heard on a radio show when he was little. It's just the kind of story he likes, about people getting their comeuppance. In my father's culture there is no room for self-righteousness or even earnestness. To take something seriously is to be a fool. It has to be all irony, disdain, and mockery. Passion is allowed only for athletics. Achievements off the court or playing field open the achiever up to ridicule. Achievement in any realm other than sports is a telltale sign of having taken something seriously.

I figure it is time to ask about work. "What happened with Hugh, Dad?"

"Fuck him."

"What happened?"

"That's over with. I've retired."

When we get home, there is a message on the machine in the kitchen. "Hey there, Gardiner, it's Patrick. I'll call another time. All right. Hope you're well." You can tell he was nervous. The message is breathy and full of lurches, not really Patrick's normal phone voice, which is, at least with me, as goofy as he was as a kid. It makes me miss him. I'll call him as soon as I get away from here.

"You should call him back."

"I'm not calling him back and you're not either, you hear me?"

"He adores you, Dad. You can't just drop him."

Watch me, his eyes say, glaring at mine.

He goes upstairs and changes into his new pants and blue socks with geese flying on them. I go to the bathroom off the den and stare for a long time at the framed black-and-white photographs on the wall, my father's team pictures from St. Paul's and Harvard, rows and rows, years and years, of white English-looking boys holding oars and footballs and tennis racquets. I have seen these so many

times I can quickly find my father in each one, his small nervous
face in the earlier ones, when he was only eleven and twelve, and
then his more mature, impatient expressions later on. Clearly no
one was encouraged to smile in photographs back then, so it is
impossible to say if he, or anyone, was happy.

He fixes himself a drink when he comes downstairs. It isn't
yet noon. We sit by the pool. I bring out tuna fish sandwiches,
and we play backgammon while we eat them. The sun beats down.
The pool glimmers and beckons. I'm not sure I still own a bathing
suit, and if I do it's buried in a garbage bag somewhere in my stuffed
car.

He makes trips to the poolhouse to refill his glass. I watch his
bowed spine, his splayed step, the need on the way in and the ful-
fillment on the way out, that first sip of a fresh drink, eyelids swoon-
ing shut, lips amphibious, reaching out and around the curve of the
glass, desperate to make contact with the alcohol. Sixteen more hours
until I can drive away from the sight of it.

The sun sears my back.

"Aren't you hot, Dad?"

"Not really."

"Maybe we should move under the tree."

"No."

He beats me.

"Have a swim," he says.

"Will you?"

"Nah. Not today."

"I guess I could just jump in in my clothes."

"Take 'em off. No one's looking."

He leans back in his chair and shuts his eyes.

I jump in in my shirt and shorts. The water is colder than I
ever remember it. Everything in my body withdraws, as if trying to
contract to a single point. By the time I reach the shallow end I can't

feel the skin on my legs. As I get out, the water rolls off them as if over rubber.

My father is laughing. "I thought you'd at least test it with your toe!"

"What'd you do, fill it with ice cubes?"

"Haven't turn on the heat yet." He wipes his eyes. "You should have seen your face. Priceless."

I flick water from my hair at him.

"Nice tits."

"Dad."

"Why do you wear such baggy clothes? You've got nothing to be ashamed of, believe me."

I can't find my voice.

My father rolls doubles and hoots.

"I would appreciate it," I begin, shakily, "if you would not speak of my body like that again."

"And I would appreciate it if you would just roll the dice. I was giving you a compliment."

Eventually he goes inside to take a nap. Fourteen more hours.

I call Jonathan from the poolhouse but only get the machine. I love the quick rumble of his voice. I feel like calling back just to hear the recording of it again. In a week we'll live in a cottage in California together. *Stop saying California like it's so important.* It is important. It is deeply important to me. What if one of us doesn't make it out there safely? I'm bad at trusting the future. It seems suddenly improbable that both of us will make it there alive. I have an urge to get in my car and outrun fate.

I get up off the floor of the poolhouse and go back out into the heat. I cross the grass to the tennis court. I reimagine the rose garden, the scrolled bushes, the faint blue paint of the fountain's basin, the smell of the black leaves when we cleaned it out the first nice day of spring. I see my mother in her kerchief and gardening gloves and me asking her as she sprays for aphids what a French kiss is. She wore bright cotton shifts, laughed loudly when Bob Wuzzy or Sylvie Salters was over, had so many convictions. And then in Paul she found a true partner, a fellow believer, and I would hear them on the couch late into the night talking about his cases, about the abuse of children and the rights of minorities, talking seriously, though laughter would always burst out unexpectedly. It didn't include me, and maybe that accounted for some of my sullenness with them, but it's still my idea of love, of harmony, that sound of them on the couch with all their beliefs and hopes and laughter.

I think I fall asleep in the grass. The next thing I hear is the snap of the screen door. I look up and my father is crossing the lawn again, showered, in another new pair of pants, drink in hand. Martini number five? Six?

"Ahhh," he says loudly, for my benefit, as he sits down. "I wonder what the poor people are doing today."

Twelve hours. Or I can leave at five in the morning, not six. Eleven more hours, then.

"I'm going to start cooking."

"It's barely six."

"Early supper tonight." Again like my mother, speaking cheerfully while fleeing the place he was, her words shot through with a lightness she did not feel but needed for protection.

I try to cook slowly. Lamb chops, mashed potatoes, lima beans. More foods of my childhood. I wonder what he'd do if I served him a tofu curry or *bi bim bap* and laugh out loud, imagining his overreaction. Occasionally I catch a glimpse of him through the window, sitting and staring at the pool. He makes his trips to the bar in the poolhouse; he switches from the chaise to a chair. The dogs follow him, resettle against his feet. When a neighborhood dog barks, all four of them lift their heads and tilt their ears, Maybelle rising to her feet. My father speaks to them. Settle down, fellas, settle down, he's saying.

Before I call him in, I drag the old glass-top table from the pantry back into the kitchen where it belongs. I set it with some old linens Catherine never used that I find in the dining room. They are perfectly pressed—my mother would have sent them to the dry cleaners—and smell of the pine of the sideboard drawer they have sat in for the past two decades. I remember the pattern, small white daisies on cornflower blue. The creases in the tablecloth stand firm no matter how many times I smooth it. The napkins are slightly frayed at the corners, but when I stand back everything looks as lovely as it used to be.

I don't know how he'll react. The table in this position is where my mother left her note before we left. But my father, when he comes in, seems not to notice at all. He is breathing in his heavy, drunk way. He puts his glass above the knife and sits in his old seat, the seat facing the stove, as if that intervening score of years never happened.

He eats the meat first. It disgusts me, the thin bone, the dead baby flesh, but I can't help watching him eat. I feel like I'm seven years old again. The sound of his breathing, the sweat on his brow and nose, the vodka and onions and tobacco create a sort of disorienting fog that obscures the present for long moments at a time.

"Dad, will you promise me right now you will take care of yourself?" I say, to shake off the spell.

"I will." He looks up from his plate. "This is good, by the way."

"And you'll make yourself vegetables?"

"Yup." He scoops three lima beans onto his fork unconvincingly

I want to ask him what on earth he plans to do with himself for the rest of his life. He's only sixty.

He eats a few bites of the mashed potato, pushes the lima beans around a bit, and sits back. I see how drunk he is then, just before he begins speaking. "And you'll take care of yourself, too, Daley?" I don't like the way he says my name. He says it like Catherine used to say it, Day-*lee*.

"I will."

"You'll go shut yourself up in another Commie college and get even more asinine ideas in your head about the way the world should be and how everyone who ever lived before you got it all wrong?"

"I guess so."

"Let me ask you something," he says, pointing his fork tines at my chest. "Let me ask you. Did they ever make you study the Second World War? Did they ever teach you about this country and what it did for the world? The sacrifices that were made to save all those goddamn people who now just want to stick it up our asses? I'll tell you what's fucked up. What's fucked up is everything that happened after 1955. That's what they should be teaching you. Everything—*everything*—they are teaching you is a crock of shit, and you people are all so far gone you don't even know it. You don't have a clue."

He leans forward and hoists himself up. He takes a few steps to the bar and then realizes he didn't bring his glass and comes back for it. I see how it will be when I leave, and an image of him on the floor of his bathroom comes to me.

Ten hours. I can do this. I can say something. "Dad, I'm worried you're going to drink yourself to death."

He slams the glass on the counter of the bar. "You know what, Day-*lee*. Just go off to college—again. For the third decade. Spend your whole life in college. Don't grow up. And take all your faux concern for me with you."

"It's not faux, Dad." I'm surprised he has that word in his vocabulary.

"Yeah, well," he mutters, going through his rites at the bar and returning with an exceptionally full glass, "you know why I drink? You know why? I drink because of people like you, people who think they are so perfect, who think they have all the ans—"

"I do not think I am perfect. By any means."

"Good, because you are not perfect. You're a disaster. You're an embarrassment. You and your brother." He puts his hands on his head as if they can stop his thoughts of us. And then he looks right at me with his yellow eyes. "You two are everything I'm ashamed of."

I put down my knife and fork. I'm done taking this shit. "And you *should* be ashamed. You should be dying of shame. Because your two children didn't get a father. They got a monster. They got a drunk, ignorant bigot who poisoned them with pure *bile*." My argument begins to form itself. I have so much proof. I'm going to shove all my memories in his face.

He laughs. No, he doesn't laugh, but there is no word for the noise my father makes when he is surprised and furious at the same time. "You know something. You turned out worse than your mother, you little bitch."

The mention of my mother, his first since she died nine years ago, slits my vocal cords clean through. All I can do is get myself out of the room and up the stairs.

I cry on my bed with the despair of a child. I keep telling myself to get up and drive away. But I can't. I feel pinned down by the weight of all the years and insults. I can hear him downstairs, doing the dishes, letting the dogs out, letting them back in. It's a normal night for him. A quart of vodka, a vicious argument. He probably feels damn good, like he's just played two sets of tennis. I worry he might even try to say good night to me, so I hoist myself up long enough to lock the bedroom door. The feel of the lock in my fingers is so familiar to me. It's a little silver macaroni-shaped thing with a deep solid *thunk* when the thick tongue falls into place. I can practically feel my mother on the other side of the door, pleading with me to come down and say hello to Cousin Grace who's come up from Westport. But I don't want to. I've just gotten out the big wicker picnic basket of Barbies and their camper from the closet and am settling in for the afternoon. I do not want to have tea with Cousin Grace.

Back on the bed, I think of Paul and how respectful and patient he always was with me, how he did edify me after all, and how now I'm certain I didn't write him back after he bought the house. I'm the closest thing to a child he ever had. I cry for him and how his grief at losing my mother was too much for me at the time, and how we couldn't help each other and how it was easier for me to just close the door on him and all his evocations of her, my mother, who loved me but did not protect me, who let me go off every weekend for years and years to my father's even though I returned a wild animal and she never asked why.

12

If I sleep, my dreams are a continuation of my thoughts and my thoughts are like muscles, flexing and twitching inadvertently and repetitively, squeezing but never quite hard enough. I feel certain, as one does in bed in the dark, that if I can line up the right sequence of thoughts I can solve the problem of my father, the problem of me and my father in the same room. My mind circles. But at some point through the thin lids of my eyes I begin to feel the slightest lifting of the night from the sky, and then I'm liberated from the cell of these useless thoughts, and I see eucalyptus trees, a narrow road, and a yellow door with a pale green window. My heart begins to pound. I'm free again. The little hollow of the driver's seat is waiting for me. The radio works. Jonathan had it fixed for me last week. I'll stop at Howard Johnson's for breakfast. I'll sit in the booth my mother and I sat in on the way to Lake Chigham. As I pack up my few things and make the bed neat and tight, just as she taught me, I'm aware of how mercurial my emotions are, how last night my mother felt lost to me in a terrifyingly permanent way, and today she feels close by. Death is like that. Death is mercurial, too.

The hallway is dark, the air moist. I smell the cedar balls in the old chest as I pass it. If I go down the front stairs I'll see my father, who always leaves his door ajar. But the back stairs are a straight shot to the kitchen and out the door. These steps are steep and I take them slowly, the wallpaper with its relief of ivy and berries beneath my fingers as I descend, the worn steps full of old smells, and then the humming refrigerator at the bottom, the little wedge of space between it and the wall I used to fit in neatly, so warm in winter. The big dogs are downstairs for some reason. They leap to their feet when they see me.

"Don't get up, fellas," I whisper, giddy. "Please."

They try to block my path. For the first time since I've been here, they seem to think I'm in charge. They seem to think I should be feeding them, and they push their noses into my thighs.

The table is clean, cleared of dishes, the blue cloth still on it with just a few grease spots from the lamb. In his careful, slanted boarding-school script my father has written: *The pills should do the trick. Goodbye, Daley.*

There are neurologists who postulate that we have not one but as many as eight brains tucked in our heads. At that moment I'm proof of it. Some of my brains are trying to misinterpret his words. Pills for the dogs? Antidepressants he didn't tell me about? And some of my brains just want me to keep moving. He's lying, one says. It's a trick, says another. But one brain knows that my father and Catherine have a medicine cabinet full of painkillers and sleeping pills.

I find him on his bed in his clothes on top of the covers. He's breathing but I can't wake him. I'm still not sure it isn't a trick, but I pick up the phone.

I press 911, then wonder if it's 411, then wonder which one I actually pressed. But a woman is on the line, asking me what happened and quickly with sirens there are people in the house and a stretcher and my father's eyes open but he can't tell them what he took or how much. There's no trace of anything by his bed and none of the many prescription bottles in his bathroom are completely empty.

They pump his stomach. Seven Bayer aspirin.

A psychologist comes to talk to me in the waiting area. He has the eyebrows of a surprised cartoon character, thick diagonal charcoal smudges.

"He's very lucky," he says quietly.

"Don't I know it. Another twenty and he could have irritated his stomach."

The man's eyebrows invert and become quite stern. "This was a serious cry for help, young lady," he says, though he can't be more than five years older than me. "People cross a line when they take pills, no matter their efficacy. Your father might very well have believed seven aspirin *would* do the trick. And the statistics are that he will make another attempt and it will be more dramatic. He will need to be monitored closely."

"I am leaving for California today. I won't be monitoring anything."

"They told me you were his daughter."

"I am."

"Your father has attempted suicide."

"He drinks on a temperate day six or seven strong martinis. In my opinion he has been trying to commit suicide most days for the past thirty or forty years." I feel so still and cold inside. I feel like I could rip this man's lungs out if I tried, and you can hear it in my voice. Goddamn my fucking father for doing this now.

He scrawls something at the bottom of the white page on his clipboard and rubs his face.

"I specifically asked if there was alcohol abuse because of the blood tests I saw, and his doctor assured me absolutely not."

"His doctor is one of his oldest drinking buddies. Not a reliable narrator."

He nods, makes crosshatches in the top corner of his sheet of paper. "Are you familiar with the term *intervention?*"

I laugh. Hard. "Let's see. His second wife just left him, his son claims never to want to see him alive again, his parents are dead, he has no siblings, and his friends should all be in rehab themselves. That would leave me and him in a room. I'd have a better chance in the Coliseum with a bunch of lions."

"There's no one who could support you in this?"

"This is not a man who can change."

"Anyone can change, given the right tools."

"I challenge you to this one. You take him on and call me when he's all fixed."

"California can wait a week or so. Your father needs you."

"California cannot wait a week or so. I am a full-time professor and my job starts a week from Wednesday."

"Where?"

"Berkeley."

"Nice." He puts down his pen. He is suddenly seeing me as a compatriot. I am in his league now. And I am a woman, I see him also realize. "What department are you in?"

"Anthropology. I'm going to go in and say goodbye to my father now."

I move down the hallway, blue under the fluorescent lighting. I feel stiff. *You're worse than your mother, you little bitch.* Seven aspirin, for fuck's sake. He had everyone jumping around for seven aspirin. I hope he's asleep.

But he is not. He lies there with the sheets tucked up to his chin, his eyes wide and staring at the door before I come through it. I stand several feet from the bed, keep my hands in my pockets.

"I'm not doing so well, elf." He bunches the sheet up in his fists. His face turns a raw red and he begins to cry. "I'm not doing well at all."

I really don't know where he should begin. The man needs so much. I squeeze the car keys in my pocket. I have to go. This is a sick man. This is a sick man whose problems I cannot remedy.

"I'm not doing well at all," he whimpers again.

"You're not, Dad. You need help."

"I do need help."

"But not my help."

"Yes, I need your help."

"No, you need professional help. You're sick."

"I'm just . . . I'm just . . . I don't know what I am." The crying turns to sobs. His chest pumps up and down and his mouth opens crookedly. His teeth are yellow and gray.

"Dad, let's get you some doctors who can help you."

"What can doctors do? Perry? Perry can't help me."

"Not Perry. You need to go somewhere where people are going to take care of you and help you get better."

"Where?"

"Some beautiful place. Maybe Colorado or Arizona."

"No."

"Maybe nearby. Vermont."

"You're talking about that place Buzz Shipley went to."

"Maybe someplace like that."

"That guy came back a fairy. He went in a perfectly nice guy and came out a fairy."

"You need to stop drinking. You won't be able to see anything clearly before you do." I wait for him to lash out.

"Okay," he says quietly. "But I won't go anywhere."

"Dad, you can't do it on your own. No one can. A program is the best way. You go away and you get a lot of support and therapy."

"Therapy? You mean a shrink?"

"Someone who can help you figure out—"

"No shrink. No way. That stays on your medical record for the rest of your life. It ruins people. Remember that wing nut McGovern picked for vice president? Never. I will not give her the satisfaction."

"What do you mean?"

"I won't have anyone talking about me the way they talked about Buzz."

"No one's going to talk—"

"Oh yes they will. You don't know how this town talks."

"We can say you're coming to California with me. No one will have to know."

"I'm staying in my house. If I leave she'll come and take everything from me. Everything."

"What about AA?" Julie's uncle is in AA. He hasn't had a drink in over twelve years. "I bet there are meetings nearby. Will you do that?"

He nods.

"Every day?"

"Yes," he says.

"Dad, I know you're not going to do this."

"I am. I need to. I know I need to." He is not convincing.

"I'll leave and you'll just go back to your old patterns."

"So stay and watch me."

"I can't."

A nurse comes in. She pads across the room like a child pretending to be a nurse. Her hands move efficiently, though, changing the IV bag, making a ripping sound with Velcro, sealing everything back up.

"Let me show you how the bed works, Mr. Amory." She taps the blue and red buttons on a remote with a long fingernail. "This will sit you up and this will make you lie back down. Would you like to sit up a bit now with your daughter?"

"Yes, thank you. Ah, that's much better. Thank you."

"You're welcome, Mr. Amory."

"You'll come back before one and show me how the tube works, right? The Sox are in Cleveland this afternoon."

"Oh I know just where they are. And Clemens's ankle's worse, and they'll probably start Ryan, Lord help us all."

"Oh, c'mon. Six-point-five's not good enough for you?"

"Not by a long shot."

My father laughs. She pulls the door shut and then he looks back at me and seems to remember he's supposed to be suicidally depressed.

"I know you need to go. I'm proud of you. I really am. I know this is no way to show it but I am, Daley."

"Thanks."

"You know what I keep thinking about is that time we went to get your mother a painting in Wellesley. Do you remember that day?"

"No."

"You weren't more than four or five. We snuck out of the house early so we didn't have to tell her where we were going. You'd gotten yourself dressed in a little pink dress and you'd put some sort of bow in your hair all crooked, and we went to a gallery where there was this painting of the swan boats that your mother liked and we walked in, and the man there said hello and you lifted your dress up all the way and you weren't wearing anything underneath. You should have seen the man's face!

"You know, the saddest day in my life was the day your mother drove off. Saddest day of my life. I never thought she'd do something like that. And take you with her. Take you away from me. I know it was tough on you, but it was tough on me, too. My daughter was gone. I kind of went off the track then, you know. I shouldn't have hooked up with Catherine so quickly. It wasn't right. It was never right. She wanted me to be someone else. They always want you to be someone else. Even you want me to be someone else."

"No, Dad. I want you to get sober and then see what things look like from there." It's slightly hallucinatory, the whole idea of him being sober, becoming self-aware.

"Oh Jesus, you sound like that girl Garvey brought home one time. What was her name? Lynnette? Lianne?"

I don't supply the name, Lizette. I don't say anything.

"I'd go crazy if I had to see things any more closely. Ever since Catherine my brain has been gnawing on itself."

I know that feeling. "And you drink to stop feeling that way?"

"Oh Christ, I suppose so. If I stop with the booze, I just don't want to turn into a guy like Bob Wuzzy. Remember him with his diet sodas? Jesus Christ."

I can't help smiling. "You won't become anyone else, Dad."

He looks out the window. I study the fine crosshatching near his eyes, the thin straight ridge of his nose. "I know you're right," he says without looking at me. "I know you are." His hands are folded neatly in his lap, like a sad little boy in church. "But you'll go and I'll go home and it won't feel like you're right anymore."

At least he knows himself this much. I have to be on campus on July ninth, ten days from now, to start an urban kinship project. I can skip the stops to see friends in Madison and Boulder. I can drive straight through, taking catnaps along the way.

"I'll make you a deal. I'll stay for six more days. You go to AA every day. You have one drop of alcohol and I'm gone. On top of that, you will not make racist jokes or objectifying remarks about my body. Plus you will not be allowed to insult me or my mother, or anyone else for that matter. Deal?" I put out my hand.

He unthreads his fingers and clasps my hand tightly. "Deal."

"You're going to be miserable."

He gives me a thin smile. "I know it."

13

We take a cab back to Ashing. It turns out my father coached the driver's son in Little League three years in a row, a team called the Acorns.

"You remember that coach for the Pirates, big guy, big paunch?" he says to my father, looking at him intensely through the rearview mirror.

"The one who always ate the peanuts?"

"The very one."

"He was a real beauty."

"Prison. Five to ten."

"Jesus. For what?"

"Nearly killed his girlfriend."

"Jesus." My father looks out the window a moment. We're off the highway, going past Shining Saddles. Little girls in hard hats, no longer velvet-covered, more like helmets, are posting in a ring. He turns back to the mirror. "You remember that game against the Astros?"

"When we were down by seven?"

"And that little scrawny kid, never hit the ball in his life, Barry something—"

"Barry Corning."

"That's it, Barry Corning; he popped one right out there over the fence. You couldn't wipe the grin off his face for the rest of the season." My father rubs his hands on his pants, one of his happy gestures. "He was a good kid."

*   *   *

The dogs, hungry, distraught at the disruption of their routine, circle my father even closer than normal as he comes through the door. He presses down their heads, speaks gently to them, gives them each a long rub, then squats in the middle of the kitchen to receive all their licks and nudges. Finally he gets up and goes to the pantry for their cans, and they leap and shake in excitement, their nails skittering to keep their bodies pressed to him as he moves.

My bag is still near the table, where I dropped it that morning. I look out at my stuffed car in the driveway. I don't understand why I'm not in it. The dogs receive their food, and their collars begin to clank loudly against their blue ceramic bowls as they jerk down their smelly clumps of brown.

My father stands against the counter with the can opener in his hand, looking at me. He looks older now, as if the years have just descended on him, as if for the first time I am seeing him not as the forty-year-old man of my youth but as the sixty-year-old man he really is. The skin beneath his eyes is dark gray, while the rest is green-gray. His eyes are bloodshot.

"Thank you, Daley. Thank you for being here."

"You're welcome, Dad."

I see him glance at the clock. It's late afternoon and he wants a drink. I cross the room to the bar. I take two bottles at a time, by their necks, to the sink. My heart is pounding, my body tensing itself, preparing for violence. But he does not strike. The can opener does not come smashing into my head as I pour all the alcohol—first the vodka, then the vermouth, then the gin, the bourbon, the scotch, and the rum—down the drain.

I make us grilled cheese sandwiches for dinner, the first time I've fixed him something I can eat, too. Afterwards, while my father watches the second of the Red Sox's doubleheaders, I make some calls and locate the head of the region's AA chapter, a man named Keith who tells me the times and locations of nearby meetings.

Then I call Jonathan.

"Hey there." His voice is rich and happy. "How far have you got?"

He thinks I'm calling from a pay phone. He's entirely certain I have been on the highway all day.

"I'm still in Ashing."

"Very funny."

"My father tried to commit suicide."

"What?"

"We're home now, but he's a little shaky. I think it was more a gesture than anything else." I listen to the silence, then say, "I have to stay for a few more days."

"You've got to get yourself across the entire continent in your car."

"I know. I'll make it. But I think you'll beat me out there. I'm sorry."

"No."

"I promised I'd stay for six more days, just to—"

"Six more days? You don't *have* six more days. You have to be there on the *ninth*."

"I know that. I'll drive straight through."

"You can't arrive having not slept for three days. I'm coming right now and airlifting you out of there."

"No, Jonathan."

"I think you've lost your grasp on reality."

"He promised to stop drinking."

"Of course he did."

"He admitted it was a problem." Didn't he? "He's never done that before."

"You are living on a big pink cloud."

The AA meetings in Ashing are held in the rectory of the Congregational Church every evening at seven. I drive my father there the next night. I need to see him walk through the door. I need to make sure he stays there the whole hour. He's quiet in the car as we go down the hill and through town, and the silence in the car at this time of night reminds me of the Sunday evenings when he drove me from Myrtle Street to Water Street. I pull right up to the stone path.

"This is going to be good, Dad."

He nods and gets out of the car. He takes his long splayfooted strides up the path, a handsome well-groomed man in his light blue cotton pants and navy blazer. His hair is still damp from his shower, combed down neatly. I glance at my watch, and when I look up I see him glancing at his. Two minutes to seven. I wonder if he'll wait out the two minutes, but when he gets to the door of the rectory, he doesn't pause. He pushes down the brass handle and disappears. Other people come after that. A man in a T-shirt and work pants stops outside the door to finish a cigarette. Two elderly ladies come up and speak to him and then he holds the door for them and they all go in. A woman with long stringy hair comes running up five minutes late. She fixes her sandal strap while holding onto the door and then swings through.

It's only then that I realize what an absurd amount of faith I've put into this idea of AA. Where did it come from? Linda Blair and that Afterschool Special? Bob Wuzzy? Julie's uncle? I'm not sure, but it now feels like I've always believed that if I could just get my father through the door of an AA meeting, all would be well. But when I imagine how it must be in there, a small room with a stained carpet and the smell of old coffee grounds, metal chairs, and a motley group in a circle speaking of their *feelings*, I see what a complete disaster it's going to be. I can hear Garvey laughing at me already.

I brace myself for him to come sprinting out of the building. I stare at the green door, the institutional handle, the black mat on the granite stoop. I wonder if there is another exit, if my father is already halfway home. The sky dims. Streetlights come on. A few teenagers walk by, look sidelong into the car, speak loudly. Mallory's old piano teacher, no longer young but still brilliantly blonde with her excellent posture that we used to imitate, passes by with a limping greyhound. At 8:09 the green door swings open and a cluster of eight or ten people emerge, my father among them. Several of them shake my father's hand. He nods goodbye to the group of them.

"Okay, let's go," he says before he's all the way in the car.

I decide not to ask him about it and he volunteers nothing.

I fix him a steak and french fries for dinner. I make myself a salad with avocados and put some on his plate, though I know he won't touch it. He is at his place at that table without a drink by his plate. It's dinnertime and my father is not drunk.

"Good steak. You get it from Brad?"

"Brad wasn't there. It was Will behind the counter."

Usually any mention of Will Goodale, the third of the Goodale sons, is enough to launch him into a tirade. Will is a crook, a pig; they shouldn't let him within twenty yards of the place. He is going to singlehandedly sink the business that his father started in 1933. Old Mr. Goodale. They don't come any better than him. There was a gentleman. Always wore a coat and tie to work, every day. He didn't deserve a slob like Will for a son.

But all he says is "Huh," and returns to his steak.

I want to say encouraging things, but to make a fuss might be the wrong move.

Over his ice cream and chocolate sauce he says, "I think I'll go over to the club tomorrow and hit a few balls." He looks up. There is a terrible amount of despair in his face. "Do you want to come?"

"I'm sorry, Dad." How am I going to say this without starting a fight? "I can't go to the club."

"Sure you can. I know you're not a member, but you're under the roof."

I take in a breath. I try to speak as gently as possible. "I can't support an institution that chooses its members based on their skin color, religion, and bank accounts."

"All right."

All the fight has gone out of him.

He does the dishes and goes to bed.

The next night I drive him back to the church. The woman with the stringy hair is outside smoking. My father says something that makes her smile and then goes inside. I watch her lean against the wall and blow smoke up into the trees until the library clock across the street says five past seven and she goes in, too.

I get out of the car and stand on the sidewalk. I have no idea what to do with myself. After my mother died, I started studying. I'd never really studied before, never *applied* myself, as my report cards in high school always suggested I do. But I worked hard my last two years in college to get into Michigan's graduate program in anthropology, and I worked much harder there, my sights on Berkeley from the start. For so very long, my life has been about deadlines, weeks at a time indoors, nights without sleep, reading, writing, and typing. I have been a slave to professors, to students, to the computer room, to syllabi, and then to my dissertation, a behemoth at five hundred and eighty-six pages called "Spirited Play: Zapotec Children's Understanding of Life and Death." When I was finishing it in the spring I didn't see anyone for twenty straight days. I stayed in the apartment of a friend who'd gone to Nagasaki for her fieldwork on the *hibakusha,* the "explosion-affected people." I stocked up on rice and beans and water and chained myself to the desk. I slept in the chair, head on a book, for a few hours at a time. When I ran out of toilet paper I used a sponge, which I scalded with hot water afterward. I had only the vaguest sense that that was disgusting. At the time it felt efficient. When I was done and had defended it, Jonathan took me to the Upper Peninsula for a long weekend, but talking was difficult, and everything in the natural world seemed to be moving at an alarming velocity. The wind felt so heavy against my body, the new leaves whipping around so fast. I had a sense that some force was at work, not a neutral force but an angry, aggressive force that made me afraid of the physical world. Jonathan expected me to relax, to luxuriate, but I didn't know how to anymore. I felt as detached and remote from my life as I had when I came back from my fieldwork in Mexico. He was patient and took me on long walks in the woods and across sandbars, and I did slowly, slowly, let down, but within a few weeks I was back on deadline, with three articles to revise for publication and a hundred final undergraduate essays to grade.

Since then I've often thought proudly back to those twenty days of pure mind-life. Jonathan and Julie refer to that time as the lockdown, and I freely admit I became a freak, but I liked it. There is a part of me that could live in my head quite happily, a part of me that longs to return there, that doesn't need or want the body. But now on the sidewalk in Ashing, removed from any intellectual demands and thrown back into my child mind, which senses only the visceral—the smells of my father, low tide, wet dog, and the sounds of seagulls and church bells and station wagons—I feel the need to let my mind wander. Does it know how to wander anymore? Do I know how to think without a book or a notebook or a computer screen? I think of Wordsworth and Coleridge and their walks through the chalk hills. I suppose a walk would be a good start.

The sun has dropped behind the library and the sky has gone lilac white, waiting for night. Most people are home, fixing dinner. The library is closed, Goodale's too. Only the gas station is open; a man in a loosened tie is filling up his Audi, his gaze unnecessarily fixed on the task. The sub shop has lights on, teenagers in the booths. Then there is a row of dark storefronts, places and awnings that didn't used to exist: a kitchen store, a pizza parlor, a fancy stationery shop. There is only one light at the end of the street near the railroad tracks. As I get closer I see it is a small wooden sign lit by a bulb above it. LIGHTHOUSE BOOKS.

Concave. The creep.

His store is tiny, not much bigger than a walk-in closet. All the walls are shelves; a freestanding bookcase runs down the center. Books, new and used, are squeezed in tight, their spines carefully aligned with the edges of the shelves. More books are stuffed in horizontally above them, and even though it's all neatly done it has the chaotic feel of a professor's office. There seems to be no cash register, no counter, and no owner.

My educated adult self pleads with the adolescent to step out of the shop. Proving to a jerk that you have finally developed breasts—not huge ones, by any means, but proportional—is a stupid reason to be in a bookstore. But then my eye catches on a Penelope Fitzgerald novel and what looks like a new Alice Munro collection, and soon I'm squatting on the floor, trying to find *Independent People,* which Jonathan is always urging me to read; it's there, and so is *Song of Solomon,* which Julie worships and I haven't read yet. Then I see that there's actually an anthropology section all on its own, not combined with sociology or general science, and there are both volumes of Lévi-Strauss's *Structural Anthropology* and *The Collected Letters of Franz Boaz.* They are not the rarest of finds, but I specialized so early in Zapotec children that I didn't get a very broad base in my own field. There's even Ruth Benedict's *Patterns of Culture,* my first bible, which I lent to someone once and never got back. I have a tall stack of books in my arms when Neal steps through the door. I completely forgot about him.

"Sorry about that. I meant to leave a note," he says, not looking, putting a sub wrapped in tinfoil on a little card table in the far corner. "You finding everything okay?"

He has his back to me. I assent with the slightest murmur.

His voice is exactly the same. Why are voices so distinct, so recognizable, when all they are are vibrations against two reeds in the throat? It's understandable that there can be a few billion variations of the face, given all the variables, but the voice? Neal's is smooth, like skates on fresh ice. It hasn't deepened much, though he has grown tall. And there is his hair, the same brown curls Miss Perth used to tease him about. She called him Shirley Temple when he was bad, which he sometimes was. Shirley Temple, go sit on your stool, she used to say without turning from the blackboard. I have eyes in the back of my head, Shirley Temple. In second and third grades we had red math workbooks and we used to race each other to finish one and get the next. We were paired together, pitted against each other. In those lower grades we were sent out of our classroom and into the next grade up for English. In fifth grade we were captains of opposing spelling teams. And then my parents divorced and my grades slipped and Neal's never did.

He was small and narrow, almost scrawny, when he was younger, with square teeth too big for his face, but now he is long and broad, shirttails hanging out, an overgrown prep-school kid. I know the type and avoided them in college, those guys who never quite adjust to the world that isn't boarding school, who can't believe their angelic faces, long bangs, athletic achievements, loose-limbed walk, cow eyes, and quick sardonic responses are no longer enough to impress every teacher or get every girl. They have a knack for sniffing me out, those disillusioned preppies, sensing my background despite all I have done to disguise it, and I run from them as fast as I can. Boys like that turn into men like my father.

I keep my back to him, moving toward poetry at the back. I hear him sink into a cane chair, prop up a book in front of him, unwrap the sub.

"I'm ready to settle up," I say, after I hear the foil crumple and drop into a trash can.

His head jerks up from his book. I suppose my voice hasn't changed either. "Jesus. I thought my mother was delusional. *Daley Amory's in town, Neal. That go-getter is a professor at Stanford.*" He does a pitch-perfect imitation of his mother. But I don't like being used as a prod. I didn't realize she had a cruel streak. She seemed glad to have him home, proud of his store. The brief performance leaves me at loss.

"Berkeley, not Stanford," I say, finally. And then, looking around, "This is a great store."

"Yeah, well, I think I should call it Between the Idea and the Reality Falls the Shadow, but maybe everything is like that." He clears a spot on the card table. "Here, put those down here."

I slide my stack of books onto the table, nudging off a receipt pad. I bend to pick it up, noticing that the last person has bought *The Pickwick Papers* for $3.95.

"Your dad okay?" he asks as he writes down my books, his tone already apologizing for the question. How much has he heard? What does the town know?

"Yeah, I think he is." I want to tell him that my father is at his second AA meeting, that he dresses for them like he's going to a cocktail party, and who knows who is in there or what they talk about. I want to ask him if he has known anyone who has gone to that meeting in town and if it really might work—no, I don't want to hear any stories of failure. "How are your parents?"

"They're all right. They endure."

His mother was such a presence that I barely remember his dad. A beige windbreaker is all that comes to mind.

I don't know what to say after that. I watch him write, the handwriting familiar, bunched.

"Congratulations on the job at Berkeley," he says, handing me my books, the receipt stuck in the middle of the one on top. "That can't have been easy to get."

I smile more than I should. "Thanks." That job is my talisman against all this. "Take care of yourself, Neal."

I look back before stepping off the stoop, but he's putting the cash box back on the floor.

I head back toward the church. "Well, that was awkward," I say to the empty sidewalk. "Not sure he even noticed the boobs."

And then I hear it, the sound of heavy pieces of metal knocking against one another. I'm flooded with an old feeling, a delicious anticipation. It's coming from behind me, across the tracks. I turn and, sure enough, the trucks and trailers have just arrived. The true sight and sound of summer in Ashing: the carnival is being set up.

I wish I could go watch like I used to with Patrick and Mallory, straddling our bikes outside the fence, sometimes for hours at a time, mesmerized by all the trailers and what came off of them, the enormous limbs of rides like the Scrambler and the Salt 'n' Pepper Shaker, the horses for the merry-go-round on their poles, the big crowns of lights and mirrors, upholstered seats, little boats and planes. Once a boy about our age brought us some fried dough from his family's stand a day before the carnival actually opened. We devoured it and asked him questions about his life, if he got to ride for free, what was his favorite ride, his favorite food, his favorite town. "Not this one," he said. "Rich towns like this keep all their pennies up their asses." We laughed hard and a couple of other boys came over, but that caught the attention of a big guy attaching the fake balcony to the haunted house. "Hey," he called down to us, "don't harass the kids. They got work to do." *Rich towns like these, Pennies up their asses,* and *Don't harass the kids* all became refrains for us for years.

I sit on the bench outside the library until the clock strikes eight, then I cross the street and wait in the car until my father comes out. I recognize hardly any of them from the night before, but again they all make a point of saying goodbye to my father.

"All righty then," he says when he gets in. "Home again, home again, jiggety jig."

"How was it?' I think I can risk it, given his good mood.

"Good." He looks at the door of the rectory.

I can't tell if he's faking it all for me.

"Not too much God?" This is one of the things I've been worried about. My father hates God almost as much as he hates Democrats.

"No." He's still looking out the window, away from me. "To each his own."

To each his own? I think of quoting this to Garvey and have to clench in a laugh.

The light is out at Lighthouse Books.

"I walked down here while you were in your meeting. To the bookstore."

"Oh yeah? Never been in there. Nice place?"

"Small, but good books."

"That poor kid."

"What do you mean?"

He shakes his head. "With a mother like that."

"I like his mother."

"Yeah, well, let me advise you right now, stay away from her. She's got a big screw loose in her head."

We pull into the driveway, and I realize I forgot to check the sign in the park that tells the day the carnival will open. I hope it's before I have to leave.

I have Dad cook his own pork chop and show him how to poke holes in the potato before baking it.

We eat by the pool. The dogs swim. When we're done, I ask him how he feels.

"Good," he says, in his new preemptive way.

I can tell he doesn't feel good. His right leg bounces incessantly, like Garvey's, his eyes flit from thing to thing, and his skin is gray, not the purple gray it gets after many drinks but a pale ash. He smokes one cigarette after another, their tips trembling. I got a book out of the library to help me understand what he might be feeling, but all I learned was that each body reacts differently to the sudden absence of alcohol.

"I know it has to be really hard right now."

He jiggles his leg. Many times he looks at me like he is going to say something and stops. Finally he says, "I'll tell you what. I need you to sweeten the deal. I do this for you, and you come to the club with me on Saturday morning, just to hit a few balls."

"First of all, you are not doing this for me. You are doing this for you. And second, we made our deal. I stay for six more days, and you don't drink."

"If I make it to Saturday, will you come? I can't miss another week."

I point to the court in his backyard. "We can play right there."

"I like playing at the club. I like clay."

"Dad, I haven't played tennis since I was sixteen."

"Please?" He needs me in case Catherine is there. He needs someone beside him when all eyes are on him. "Please, elf?"

It won't kill me to be for an hour the daughter my father has always wanted. I can give him that memory before I leave. But the idea of going up the long private drive to the white columns of the brick clubhouse is almost enough to make me wish my father won't hold up his end of the bargain.

14

But he does. After probably more than forty years of vigorous daily drinking, my father goes six days and six nights without alcohol. On the phone Jonathan suggests that he could have a stash somewhere. But I know the difference between my father drunk and my father sober. I know the sated smugness of the early drinks, the agitation that turns to wrath of the next few, and the slack yellow-eyed hollowness at the very end. I've also cased the joint. I've rummaged through his closets and cars, through the basement, attic, shed, and garage. Nothing. And I stay up late, hours after he does, hearing only the heavy, steady throttle of his snore.

On Friday night, after his meeting, he takes me to the Mainsail for dinner. It's the only fancy restaurant in Ashing, with a dining room that overlooks the harbor. The entrance is a dock that rises up from the parking lot and makes everyone's footsteps ring out. I wear a blue dress, wrinkled from days in my hot car. My father is nervous and cups his hands tight as he walks.

"Well, hello to you," he say to the wooden statue of a boy holding a net with a wood fish in it. "That's probably a six-pounder you got there."

He's worried Catherine will be here, but I've reassured him that she knows this is his restaurant, his territory, and she won't dare. I hope I'm right.

Harold, the bald obsequious manager who has been stationed at the podium in the entryway all my life, bows to us. "Good evening, Mr. Amory. Good evening, miss."

"Oh for chrissake, Harold, it's Daley."

He bows again. "Good evening, Miss Amory."

"Ms., if you wouldn't mind."

My father lets out a small groan.

"Oh, did you get married?"

"No, but please, just call me Daley."

"I will do that," he says, lifting two long leather binders out of the holder on the side of his podium, his lips tightly pinched, clearly displeased by how unsmoothly this interaction has gone.

"Daley," my father says when we slide into our chairs beside the enormous window, "please don't go around trying to paint this town Commie red. Someone calling you *miss* is not trying to harm you in any way."

"I don't care if they're not trying. It does harm me."

"Why?"

"Because the terms Miss and Mrs. are like branding cattle. No one needs to know I'm unmarried."

"Yes, they do. People want to know these things."

"There's this tribe in New Guinea where the available women are given a suffix to their name that literally means *tight vulva* and the taken women are given a suffix that means *floppy vulva*. Should we do that, more to the point?"

"You are making me sick to my stomach, for chrissakes." But he is amused. He is having fun.

"Here you are, Mr. Amory." Harold drops a vodka martini on the rocks with two onions and an olive beside my father's right hand. "And what can I bring your lovely daughter?"

I can feel the vibration of my father's jiggling leg on the wooden floor beneath us. I can feel the attraction between him and the martini, and his restraint, everything it takes to not get that martini down his gullet and into his blood system. He lifts it up and hands it back to Harold. "Sorry about that, sir. She's keeping me clean tonight."

Harold glances at me—*haven't you made enough trouble already?*—and then sympathetically back at my father. "Excuse me, Mr. Amory. I shouldn't have presumed."

I watch over my father's shoulder as Harold goes back to the bar with the drink. I can't remember the bartender's name but I know he has a tattoo of a submarine on his upper arm and a roll of crystal mint Lifesavers in his pocket. His head jerks up toward us when Harold speaks. He shakes his head, then dumps the drink in the sink.

My father doesn't need to look at the menu. He always orders the filet mignon with béarnaise sauce. I hurry to figure out what I can eat. All the writing is in big slanted script. I worked in a restaurant like this in college, waited on people just like my father, with their regular drinks, their regular cow parts.

There is vichyssoise, but when I ask Harold if it has chicken stock he returns from the kitchen quite pleased to tell me that indeed it does. My father shakes his head. He apologizes to Harold when I order a plate of steamed rice and french-cut green beans.

"To each his own, Dad."

Across the harbor, the Ferris wheel begins to turn. Its red and blue lights smear slowly into huge purple rings. It's the first night of the carnival.

"Oh, Christ," my father says, briefly eyeing the door. "They won't leave me alone," he whines, though his face betrays nothing. I wonder who it is but he'll be furious if I turn around to look. "Here they come," he whimpers, and then he glances up, feigns convincing surprise, and leaps to his feet to shake the man's hand firmly and kiss the woman on the cheek. I know them, her squat forehead and his puffed-out chest. I kiss them both as they marvel at how long it has been and what a lovely girl I've become, and my father shoots me a look because he knows how I feel about being called a *girl* at the age of twenty-nine. I ask them about their kids, hoping to jog my memory. Carly was in Woods Hole, Scott was working for Schwabb, and Hatch was in Colorado "doing who knows what," the woman says, laughing.

"There's always one of those," the man says with a phlegmy chuckle.

"I'm two for two," my father says. I think he's forgotten for a moment that he isn't out with Catherine.

"Hardly." The woman covers up for him. "I heard this one got herself a fancy job out west somewhere."

I remember their names, Ben and Barbara Bridgeton. Their children went to Ashing Academy with us, but none of them were in Garvey's or my grade. My father coached at least one of the sons.

"What is your area of expertise, Daley?" Mrs. Bridgeton asks.

"Oh, Jesus. Don't ask," my father says.

"Post-Contact Zapotec, the children in particular, and how, if they survive, they process the high infant and pre-school mortality rates."

I see Mr. Bridgeton shoot a look at Harold, who trots right over with their drinks.

"Okay, Margaret Mead," my father says. "Let them sit down."

"How long are you here for, dear?" Mrs. Bridgeton squeezes my hand.

"Until Sunday."

"We'll take good care of him once you're gone. Not to worry."

Harold leads them to their table and my father and I sit back down. "One more minute and you were going to start in on the floppy vulvas, weren't you? And I should have warned you not to tell her when you were leaving."

"Why?"

"They were coming over every night after Catherine left. Quiches, soups, some sort of goulash. I had to toss it all down the pig. Even the dogs wouldn't touch it."

"But that's so nice of them to be thinking of you."

"About the only ones, too. That bitch has told so many lies about me. All over town."

I have to get him off the topic of Catherine. "Did you coach Scott or Hatch?"

"Both. Six years of that woman yak-yak-yaking. Remember I got her that Assistant Manager cap and she wore it all summer? She didn't even get the joke."

Our salads come. Iceburg lettuce, mealy tomatoes, and one skin-less slice of cucumber with creamy Italian slathered over it. The Main-sail is its own time capsule. But I know better than to make fun of it.

My father pokes his fork into it once and then sets the salad aside.

"So what happens? You drive out there and they have a place for you to live?"

"I found a place. A little cottage." It's so silly, what rises inside me, a swell of warmth, of good feeling, a flood of endorphins—all because my father is asking me a question about my life.

"Near the school?"

"Five or six blocks." I want to tell him about the eucalyptus tree out front and the color of the door but I know I'll lose him. I have to sound blasé, as if it doesn't mean much to me.

"Expensive?"

"No, it's pretty reasonable, for California." It's actually a great deal, four-fifty a month. "Probably pretty beat up."

"You haven't seen it yet?"

"No. I had a friend out there take a look at it for me."

"And this job of yours, how long does it go for?"

"I hope it's permanent, if I get tenure."

"And how do you make sure you get that?'

"I don't know." But of course I know. I just have to get the right tone with him, not too cocky, not too flaky. "I'll have to publish steadily, get consistently good student evaluations, make nice-nice with all my coworkers, and lead at least one team in fieldwork somewhere."

He watches Harold's tray as it passes, scotch and sodas for the people behind us. "You got it all figured out, don't you?"

Too cocky.

I coach myself to stay upbeat, not react. The man wants a drink. Of course he's going to be irritable.

"No, I don't. But I like having a goal. Something to move toward." Too transparently preachy. He'll know I've shifted the conversation to him. My insides weaken, wait for the cut.

But he nods. "Good to have your eye on something."

I'm grateful when Harold arrives to remove the salad plates and replace them with the filet mignon and the steamed vegetables. I've had enough of talking with my father about my life.

Later that night, when he starts snoring, I call Jonathan.

"Six days and six nights," I boast.

"And tomorrow morning you're driving away."

"Sunday morning."

"You said Saturday."

"No, it was always Sunday." Wasn't it? "I never really believed he'd be able to do it. But he trudges down the little walkway to his meeting and he comes out again all spry and bolstered up."

"Sunday at the crack of dawn."

"Stop worrying."

"You're getting sucked in. I can hear it in your voice."

"I'm not sucked in."

"I think we should go camping at Crater Lake next weekend."

"Aren't we going to want to unpack a little?"

"I got this guidebook. You should see the pictures. I'm not sure I can wait."

*   *   *

The next morning, I call Garvey.

"Hmmm," he answers after a lot of rings. I've woken him up.

"I know you don't want to hear about Dad but—"

"You're right."

"Garvey, he's quit drinking."

A huge muffled laugh.

"He has. Six days and six nights."

"Oh, Hermey, you gullible titmouse."

"I've combed the place, believe me. There's nothing hidden. He's doing it. He goes to AA every night at the Congregational Church."

Another huge laugh. "I don't believe you."

"I drive him there. I watch him walk in. He gets all dressed up in his summer pants and blazer."

"And I'm sure he walks right out the back door."

"No, Garvey, I see him come out. He's chatting with people, shaking hands."

"He might be doing this for you for a few days, but the man can't change his ways now."

"He can if he has help. Couldn't you come here for a few days next week after I'm gone? Just to help him along a bit."

"Fuck no. Daley, you don't get it. God, for all your education you really don't have much smarts." He said *smaats,* Boston accent, just the way Dad would.

"Oh, shit, it's nearly ten. He's calling me. Please think about it, Garve."

"I won't. Where are you going?"

"Just out with Dad."

"Hmmm. Ten A.M. on a Saturday morning in July. Could it possibly be to the Ashing Tennis and Sail Club?"

"I lost a bet."

"I want a photo."

"I have to go."

"You'll have to wear one of those little pleated skirts."

"I have some white running shorts."

"How quickly we forget. You're over eighteen and you have to wear a skirt."

"That was in 1972."

"But it's 1952 in Ashing. And it always will be."

He is right. I have to have sneakers, a skirt, and a shirt with a collar. My father takes me to the pro shop and a woman my father calls H puts me in a dressing room with saloon doors and keeps sticking her bony sunfried arm in and out until I've chosen a skirt with navy stripes and its matching polo shirt. Then she fits me into some very cushiony tennis sneakers.

"Hey, hey," my father says when I come out. He hands me a brand new racquet. Before I can protest, H has put my hair in a high ponytail. They both beam at me. In the mirror across the room, I look eleven again.

My father makes a point of saying hello to everyone we pass on the way to court five, of introducing me with much more enthusiasm than normal. "Look at my Daley, all grown up," he says to several people.

Look at Daley, fucking out of her mind.

I want a father who doesn't get drunk. He wants a daughter to take to the club. It's a deal with the devil for both of us.

He hits a few soft ones to me at first, perfectly placed so that all I have to do is swing. The first few go way out, and the next few into the net, but my father shows me how to follow through on the stroke, finishing with my weight moving forward, and my next shots are decent ones.

"Holy smokes," my father says, reaching the ball easily. "I've got to stay on my toes today."

It feels great to move with my body, think with my body. I haven't exercised in months. I copy his movements. My focus is pure. I feel my father's desire for me to play well but it doesn't disable me like it used to. For the first time I can fully appreciate what a beautiful player he is. No matter where I place the ball he is there in a few steps, having anticipated its direction as soon as it leaves my racquet. His strokes are fluid, graceful, deceptively strong. There is nothing that looks like effort in his game. He sweats more eating a steak.

I can't explain why I'm suddenly okay at tennis. Maybe I was never as awful as I thought. All I know is that it is pleasurable. I like the feel of the clay beneath my new leather sneakers and the pale mark the ball leaves when it lands in front of me and the moment when the ball has crested from the bounce and has just started to drop and I strike it with my racquet in just the right place. The racquet has a huge head and is surprisingly reliable. I even like the skirt and all its pleats that swing as I run. I'm an imposter, an interloper, in a deeply familiar environment. I'm here but soon I will be far away. This is my own dirty secret. Everyone I know would be disgusted with me. I smile at that thought.

"You could be a damn good player, Daley. You know that?" My father says when we take a break at the water dispenser between the two courts.

We sip from paper cones, and I feel the cold water hit my stomach.

Then he says, "I can feel the difference."

"What do you mean?"

"Without the cocktails."

It's the first benefit he's mentioned.

We play two sets. He beats me 6–3, 6–4. I know he has the ability to beat me 6–0 left-handed if he wanted. I kept thinking I could tire him out by hitting them to one side and then the other, but he returned them all—it never even looked like he was running.

Afterward we sit on the bench beside the court.

"I thought you had me that first set, when it was deuce and you fired that winner down the line."

I have no idea what he's talking about. I can't remember individual points once a game is over. The whole thing fuses quickly together.

"By the end of the summer you'll be beating me," he says.

"Dad."

He smiles and shakes his head. "For a minute there I thought you were sixteen years old."

For a minute there, I almost wish I were.

That afternoon, while my father is napping, I call Julie and confess where I've been.

"I know this sounds weird but I think there is something kind of powerful about wearing a tennis skirt," I say.

"Oh, God, Daley," Julie says. "Get out of there."

"You sound like Jonathan."

"You're not going to tell him where you were."

"Not over the phone. When I get out there and he's calmed down. I really think the skirt helped me play better, though. It's a uniform, and all uniforms are about power."

"Or denigration."

"I did refuse to eat at the clubhouse."

"At least you have a shred of sanity left."

"Tell me what you see out your window." She just got to Albuquerque.

"Dirt."

"Dirt?"

"Dry, yellowish dirt. I keep walking around my neighborhood thinking, What is going to become of me?"

"What *are* you going to do until school starts?"

"Work on my syllabus. Read. Eat. And other things I haven't done for seven years. I talked to my father today. He told me to set aside that long weekend in October. He says he's sending me a plane ticket, but it's a mystery as usual."

I can see now that my old irritation about Julie and her father was the pain of envy. They are very close, capable of talking on the phone for two hours at a time, desultory conversations that can go from toothpaste brands to Simone Weil. She can call him at night and he will never be drunk. He's a doctor, a radiologist, and he has a doctor's smug confidence. I've always been half infatuated, half repulsed by him. The first time he met me, he told Julie I was a diamond in the rough. We laughed at the image, but secretly I puzzled over it for a long time, wondering exactly what on the outside was so rough, and where exactly the diamond was.

"I hope it's to California. You can be our first houseguests."

"If you promise to wear your new uniform."

"Of course. I'm sure I'll be playing in a ladies' league by then."

That night, my father pulls out a piece of paper from one blazer pocket and his reading glasses from the other. "I heard this tonight at the meeting. *Thank you is all you need to say to get God's attention.* I thought that was pretty good." He looks embarrassed, then laughs when he sees that my eyes have filled.

I lie in bed Sunday morning after the alarm goes off. I can hear the opener slicing through the dogs' cans, the spoon whacking against the bowls, the dogs' frenzy as my father carries the bowls to their place against the wall, the silence as they eat and my father returns to his coffee and paper, and then the smack of the screen door when they are done and need to go out. My father yells something at one of them. I'm relieved by the sound, the regular impatient tone. There will be no drama this time. I keep urging myself up, then rolling into another even comfier position. I was hot during the night and my blanket is at my feet, but now I pull it back over me. It looks cloudy and cold outside. I feel like sleeping all morning. I haven't packed my clothes yet. They are in a heap on the floor.

I put on jeans I haven't worn since Michigan. They remind me of winter there, of the big black boots I used to wear with them, of Jonathan and the orgasm he once gave me with just his thumb on the outside of these jeans. My stomach does a slow backflip. I need to get to him. I put the tennis outfit at the back of a drawer in the bureau. I pack the sneakers. I shove the books I got from Neal's store into the sides of the bag and zip. Halfway down the stairs I realize I've left my toothbrush by the sink, but I keep moving. There will be plenty of toothbrushes on the road to California. I love a road trip. I can get at least as far as Indiana by midnight.

"Morning," I say, my bag knocking through the doorway.

"Well, if it isn't Little Orphan Annie," my father says, lowering his paper. Then he gets up and takes the bag from me. "Christ, what'd you do, steal the silver on the way out?" He puts it by the door. "Coffee?"

Nearly every morning he's offered me coffee and I've always said no. I like feeling a little sleepy at the start of the day, and he drinks instant. "Sure," I say. "Thanks."

He gets down a cup and saucer, white with pale pink flowers. They rattle so loudly together he carries them in separate hands to the stove.

I wish I'd said no to the coffee. I need to get out before he blows up or collapses.

"What are you going to do today?"

"Beats me. Perry hurt his ankle again so tennis is canceled. I need to vacuum the pool. I never showed you the new vacuum."

"The meeting's at one today. You know that, right? Because it's Sunday."

"Yup," he says, heading toward the door where the dogs are scratching to come back in.

They go directly to their places surrounding his chair.

I wait for him to tell me that at one he'll be pouring his first martini.

"I can call you every night, see how it's going."

"You don't need to do that. We'll be fine here." He pats the gray dog's head, and the others lift their heads hopefully. "Don't spend too much time inside. It's not good for you. Get out and see the sun. Play a little tennis. You got your racquet? You didn't get it, did you? You take that with you. Early birthday present."

"Belated, actually. My birthday was two weeks ago."

"All right then."

"This is a real opportunity for you, Dad."

His eyes are looking straight ahead, unfocused. He nods. "Today is the first day of the rest of your life."

I've spent so many years swallowing my feelings for my father, constructing a glib false self that sloughs off his jabs, evades questions, conceals facts that would displease him, that now I have a hard time finding the truth in his presence.

"You have been so strong this week. I know you can keep going." Ninety meetings in ninety days is what they say. If you can make it that far, a return to drinking is much less likely. "Ninety in ninety. Do you feel like you can do it?" They also say, of course, one day at a time. Maybe I should shut up.

"Everyone leaves me." He says it so quietly it takes me a second to understand what he's said. It's less than a whisper, as if it has just emanated up through him, despite his efforts to quell it.

Everything is silent after that. Even the dogs' collars, a steady white noise in my father's house, are still.

I put my hand on top of his, the raised veins pulsing hard against my palm. "I'll call you every night." And then I add, awkwardly, it has been so very long: "I love you, Dad."

He nods and lets out a long breath.

The dogs chase my car down the driveway, then turn back to my father, who is still standing there, his hands in his pockets, in the shadow of the garage. He isn't yelling at them as he usually does. When they reach him, he puts his hands on their heads and then turns toward the house. The slope of his back disappears behind the trees.

People are already walking up the hill to the beach, even though it's only nine-thirty on an overcast day. The Ferris wheel is motionless. A big banner announces the carnival will open up again at noon. I have missed my chance. Kids are already circling the area on bikes, waiting. Lighthouse Books has a CLOSED sign dangling from its doorknob. The Congregational Church's doors are flung open, the organ playing. The Bridgetons will probably ask my father over for cocktails this week. On Water Street the shades are down in the front windows of our old apartment. I turn up Middle Street, toward the highway. The green signs appear, the regular white paint replaced now by a reflective silver. Route 4 North and Route 4 South. I'll take Route 4 South to 95 to 90, fork off to 80 in Ohio, and take 80 all the way to Berkeley. My father will not go to another AA meeting. I pass the Route 4 North on-ramp, put on my blinker for the next, but go straight under the overpass toward the town dump. Beyond the dump, in what used to be woods, a new subdivision has gone up. I turn into the long, newly asphalted drive and follow its smooth perfect circle past the freshly built houses, then turn back on Middle Street, back toward town.

He is standing at the pool when I pull up. There's a thick cord that runs from the poolhouse right into the water. I walk across the grass. At the bottom of the pool is a little white box moving all by itself, sucking up all the dirt in a straight line. When it hits the side it turns and goes in a different direction. It is only when I am standing right beside him that he lifts his eyes.

"You know who the Sox are playing at one, don't you?" he says.

"The Yankees?"

"But you're going to make me go to that meeting."

"Yup."

"Shit."

Then we watch the new vacuum make its clean random tracks across the bottom of the pool.

15

I call the chair of the anthropology department that afternoon. I've rehearsed a few phrases in my head, but once the phone begins to ring I forget them. A teenager answers eagerly. I didn't imagine Oliver Raskin with a family. He's out in the field for years at a time, has written over twenty books. This young voice gives me hope that as a family man, Dr. Raskin will understand my situation. The phone is dropped on a table and more than a few minutes later he picks up an extension.

"Please forgive me for calling you at home on Sunday, Oliver."

"Not at all." He speaks from a small silent room. "I'm sure you have questions, Daley. Fire away."

"I am not able to come to California right now."

"The project doesn't start until Wednesday. I thought that was clear."

"It is clear. I can't get there by then. My father is sick."

"I'm sorry, Daley." I can't tell if he means he's sorry about my father or sorry that my father's sickness doesn't change anything. "What's the matter with him?"

"It's complicated."

"I'm listening."

I'm not sure why I thought he might understand. I can tell by his breathing he won't.

"He's going through a rough—"

"Is he *dying*, Daley? Because for you not to be here on the ninth of July he would have to be dying."

"I worry that he will die if I don't stay."

"If you stay, he won't die. If you leave, he will die." I can hear him take a sip of something. "Are you a god, Daley?" I wonder if he's drunk. "You signed a contract, if you will remember, in which you agreed to begin your research here in a few days. You may have ten more, if you think you can work your magic in that time."

"I'm going to need more than that."

"How many more?"

Ninety in ninety. "Three months."

Silence. Another sip. More silence. "In other words, you've called to resign."

"It's a family emergency. I'd hoped I could have some sort of deferment."

"This is not like applying to college. This is not a custom design situation. This is one of the most coveted positions in the country. We considered over a hundred applicants. We flew five candidates out here. The selection process took up the whole year."

"I understand that."

"Are you really my next suicide, Daley?"

I don't want to work with this man. He's a prick. "No, I'm not, Oliver. I guess I'm your first defection."

The phone rings during dinner. My father answers.

"Yup, she's right here," he says, holding the phone out to me. But there is only the dial tone.

I put the phone back on its cradle.

"What happened there?" my father says.

"We got disconnected, I guess." I'm trying to keep my voice steady.

"That your boyfriend?"

I nod.

I can't eat what's on my plate. I have no way to call Jonathan back. He's already on the road by now. I'm not sure talking would help anyway.

The next morning my father is in a coat and tie. "I'm going to go in and meet with Howard this morning."

"Howard Gifford?" The name of his divorce lawyer brings back pains in my stomach.

My father nods. "I want to get this thing moving."

"If that's what you're sure you want."

"Christ yes."

After he leaves I unload the dishwasher. I carry the stack of plates into the pantry where Catherine kept them and stop in the middle of the room. I don't have to put them there anymore. She isn't coming back. Everything—silverware, napkins, glasses, salad plates, cereal bowls—can go back where they belong. As I work, I catch myself in conversations with Oliver Raskin or Jonathan or some amalgam of the two, trying to convince them that I have no choice but to stay here for a little while, that it is my duty not just as a daughter but as a human being.

When everything is back in place, I dig out the leashes in the coat closet and clip them on the dogs. They don't know how to behave on leashes; my father only uses them for trips to the vet. As we make our way down the driveway, they weave themselves into tight tangles over and over, little Maybelle practically dangling off the ground.

"You guys are pathetic," I say to them when we reach the street, and honestly their heads seem to lower in shame. "This is what we need to do. Sadie, you need to walk out that way, to my right; Oscar, way out to my left; Yaz, in front, and Maybelle, I'm attaching you to my waist like this." I thread the small handle of her leash through my belt loop. "And now we walk." We take up the whole sidewalk and the grass on both sides. Anytime Oscar looks interested in Sadie's grass I tell him to cut it out and keep his eyes ahead. They obey me. Yaz, the biggest of all of them, pulls us all forward like a sled dog.

We pass the Vance sisters' old driveway, filled with bright plastic tricycles and trucks, an enormous garage where the chaotic garden used to be, then take the shortcut, down Lotus Lane to the sandy path, ignoring the new NO TRESPASSING signs. I am having some trouble breathing properly. It feels like there's a baseball in my lungs, taking up most of the room. I can really only half believe that I had that conversation with Dr. Raskin, and only half believing is shocking enough. The dogs, hearing the waves, smelling the smells, strain hard on their leashes. When we reach the boardwalk, the sea suddenly below us, I unhook them all and the two big dogs take off down the weathered wooden steps. They sprint to the water in a spray of fine white sand. Maybelle stays by my feet, taking each deep step down with brave caution.

Warm air rises from the sand and cold air comes off the water. Gulls screech and waves swell and break in gorgeous white diagonals all the way down the beach. Farther out the water is pale and glossy or a rumpled deep blue, depending on how the wind is touching it. Seeing the Atlantic is always like seeing an old love: a familiar ache, a tremendous pull, and a deep sadness. It's so vast, so muscular, so devastatingly beautiful. Jonathan and I have never seen any ocean together. We were waiting for California. Our cottage is 2.4 miles from a beach. He clocked it when he was out there.

The big dogs stay in the shallows, barking at the waves as they grow and retreating when they shoot to shore. I take off my shoes. The wind flaps my T-shirt and shorts. I try to take in deep breaths.

There is a smattering of people down the beach near the main entrance, setting up their umbrellas, spreading out their towels. But down here there is only me, the dogs, and an old couple in coats, walking toward the rocks. I wonder if my father will have lunch in Boston with Howard Gifford. The dogs see the old couple and begin to run toward them. They will go to Locke-Ober's and Howard will order a drink. When I call the dogs, my voice is thin and they don't hear me.

Back at the house I sit at my father's desk with a blank sheet of paper—it wasn't easy to find one that didn't have his name and address embossed on it—and a ballpoint pen. I have to write Jonathan, and I have to get the letter in the mail this afternoon so that it arrives in California when he does. I want to tell him that I need a little more time here, less than three months. And then we can go to Crater Lake. Maybe we both can apply for jobs in Philadelphia for next year. I can see him in his truck, the truck he couldn't drive when I first met him, heading toward a job he didn't even want. He wanted to get back to Philly. That had been his plan.

But nothing about me was in Jonathan's plan. And he always has a plan. It's the way he copes with fear. The way I cope is to never have expectations, so I'm not disappointed. Even with Berkeley I never let myself get attached to the idea. I wanted it, but I didn't expect it. Maybe that's why I can let it go now. I never really believed it was mine. And with Jonathan, too, I held back, until he called me on it.

"I want to have a relationship with you."

I laughed. We were both naked. "I think we are having a relationship."

"But these things need to be said. I think you don't think I'm serious. Or maybe you're not serious. What are your intentions toward me?'

I laughed again.

"I'm serious, Daley. What are they?"

"My intentions? You act like I'm angling to marry you or something."

"Are you?"

"No."

He was quiet.

"Aren't you relieved?"

"No. I'm not interested in being glib."

"I'm not being glib."

"I'm not sure any of this is meaningful to you." He put his hand on my chestbone. "You're all sealed up in there."

It was true. I loved him so much, and I was desperate to hide the extent of it. But slowly, he cracked me open. He pulled out all my feelings and made me talk about them. He had the ability to articulate emotions that most people simply feel as a clump in the belly. Carefully, patiently, he built a strong platform for us, and I came to trust that I could put the whole of my weight on it. It's because I am standing on that platform that I am able to help my father now.

I stare at the page. It all feels so raw and wordless and unbelievable. He is driving west and I am not there. I am not going to open the door. I have broken my promise. I put my head on the paper, and soon the page is wet and buckled. I toss it in the trash and go up to my room.

On my bed I think back to our last night together, before Garvey called, lying with him, his finger slipping up into my underwear. He is on me, heavy, hard, his lips on mine. I want to fuck you, I whisper, and he pushes in and I come quickly. Too quickly. I lie there for a minute, sadness pooling, and then I take it slower, and come deeper. I can feel it spread everywhere this time, beneath my toenails, across my scalp. I feel close to him, lying here. I don't want to stop and feel the distance between us again. I start moving my fingers again in the syrupy wetness until I hear hard knocking on the kitchen door.

I zip up my pants and smooth down my hair in back. My limbs feel loose but strong as I go down the stairs.

It's Barbara Bridgeton. She frowns at the sight of me through the screen door.

"Have I woken you?"

No, but you did interrupt my third orgasm. "I was just cleaning."

I let her in, and fortunately the kitchen is spotless from all my rearranging.

She swoops her laserlike gaze over everything and then puts a stack of Tupperware on the counter. "I made three meals for your father, but maybe he doesn't need them now. Is he out?"

"He's gone into Boston."

"By himself?"

"Yes."

She pinches her lips together. She wants to know why he's gone to Boston. She looks unhappily at her meals on our counter. "I thought it was Sunday you'd be leaving."

"I did too. But I'm going to stay longer."

"Can you?"

"I can."

"Maybe I should just take all that food home then. I've got both Scott and Carly coming this week."

"By all means. We've got plenty. In fact, I'm trying to encourage Dad to learn to cook." I sense her objection and hurry on. "But thank you. He is so grateful for everything you've done for him."

"Well, he's an old dear friend."

Once the Tupperware is back in her arms she doesn't look so pleased about it. I wonder if I should have just accepted it graciously.

"Well, you're a good daughter," she says, as if to convince us both. "Your dad needs his family right now, and at least he has you. I'm sorry Garvey wasn't able to do the same. If ever a father loved his son." She puts the Tupperware back on the counter and shakes her head. "If ever a father was proud of his son. You know they won the father-son tournament six years in a row. I'll never understand what happened to that boy. And he had the lead in the eighth-grade play. What was it that year?"

"*Bye Bye Birdie*."

"That's right. You probably don't remember it."

Of course I do, and I remember my father prancing around afterward, singing "Put on a Happy Face " effeminately, making a mockery of the whole play in a few minutes.

"And he was always on the honor roll, which is more than I can say for two out of three of mine, though most of those smart kids turned into druggies and are a misery to their parents, so you never know. That Lukie Whitbeck, you remember him, with all the hair? I think he got every award in Scott's class. Everyone thought he was so wonderful, but he had a mean streak; I had to talk to his parents more than once about it. He was in jail last year, not for long, but still. Well, I'm so pleased you're here, Daley." She smiles broadly. She seems to have perked herself up by that dip and spit into the past. "You're a good daughter." And she kisses me on the cheek, takes her food, and leaves.

My father comes home at three and falls asleep on the couch. When his snoring reaches full volume, I bend over him and smell his breath. Hamburger, fries, and ketchup is all I get. At six-thirty I wake him for his meeting.

"Losers of the world unite," he says as he hobbles upstairs to shower.

I cleaned out the Datsun that afternoon, brought a few bags to my room, and put the rest in the shed. He groans when he gets in and exaggerates the lack of head and legroom by scrunching up into a little egg. The smell of his Old Spice fills the small space.

"You don't have to keep driving me," he says.

"I like to." I want to get to the point where I trust him to get to the church every night at seven, but that will take time. Sometimes he is so sad and quiet on the way I feel certain that if I weren't there he'd pull into Shea's, the liquor store, and down a quart of vodka in the car, or head to the Utleys or the Bridgetons, who were sure to be having cocktails on their patios.

After I let him out at the church, I walk to the carnival. The fried dough is calling me. I have nothing due, nothing to research, no deadline. My mind keeps moving to that list and finding it empty. Over and over. Each time my body grows a little lighter.

It's hard to recognize the park when the carnival is planted in it. All the structures—the swing set and slide, the baseball diamond, the gazebo—are swallowed by it. As a kid I had a hard time holding the two concepts in my head at once, and if on occasion I did notice that it was the baseball bleachers people were sitting on to eat red foot-long hot dogs before going on the roller coaster beside them, it was like discovering an artifact from another lifetime, the way they discover the Statue of Liberty at the end of *Planet of the Apes*.

I pay the six-dollar entry fee and go in. They've put down hay to protect the grass. It used to be free to wander around the carnival, and no one ever cared about the grass. It always grew back. Ashing is starting to be self-conscious that way, with its new matching awnings above the storefronts and the renaming of certain streets I read about in the paper. Snelling Street is now Coral Avenue. And Pope's Road has become Bayview Lane. But the music at the carnival is the same as always, "Sweet Caroline" and "Mandy" and "My Eyes Adored You." I can see Jonathan rolling his eyes, but he'd be singing along with me anyway. He'd know all the words. It's packed, full of kids and teenagers and brand-new families, the parents my age, the children in little pouches and strollers. Again I feel like an interloper, a spy on my own past.

I go directly to the fried dough window. The woman hands me an enormous slab with pools of oil on top, and I shake the plastic tub of cinnamon sugar over it until it's a deep, dark brown. I mean to find a bench and eat it slowly, but it's so good I polish it off right there next to the condiments. After I buy a small book of tickets I go in search of the Tilt-a-Whirl. It's right where it always was, to the left of the Ferris wheel, its hooded blue and white cars just coming to a slow undulating stop on their circular tracks. Mallory, Patrick, and I probably took this ride together over a hundred times. I always sat in the middle because Mallory and Patrick were heavier and could make the car spin faster by leaning to each side. Mallory screamed shrilly in my ear and Patrick kept his mouth shut, making little ghostlike moans every now and then. Just the sound of my feet on the thin metal steps after I give over my tickets brings whole summers back to me. The seats are still smooth red leather, the bar that comes down over your knees the same scallop shape. I have the same rush of anticipation as the man pulls the lever, and the belt that all the cars are on begins to move. I sit on one side of the car to make it spin more. Soon I'm being flung in circles so fast my brain gives up trying to ground itself, and I am left with that rush of abandon that is one small part fear and the rest sheer ecstasy. I hear myself shrieking along with other shriekers. There are moments on the Tilt-a-Whirl when you can raise your head and look briefly around before you are sent into another vortex. At one point I look up and see Neal Caffrey on a bench watching me. The next time he is gone. When the ride ends I stumble along its edge to give the operator more tickets and go back to my red seat. While I am spinning it's impossible to think about Jonathan or Oliver Raskin or the cottage with the yellow door.

When I get off, I only have twenty minutes left. I want to ride the Scrambler, the Salt 'n' Pepper Shaker, and the Ferris wheel. I can't decide which, so first I get some more fried dough. This time I shake out the cinnamon sugar and the powdered sugar until it is tick-gray. Delicious. Then I get in line for the Ferris wheel, which is on a long ramp leading up to its base. Two little girls and their mother are ahead of me. The girls are trying to decide which color compartment they hope to get. The compartments are round, with a column in the middle that holds up a matching metal umbrella. The girls are hopping with the same mix of sugar and excitement that I feel. I wish I could ride with them, and am almost on the brink of asking when Neal taps my foot.

He's on the ground below. "Hey." He looks like he's forgotten the rest of what he was going to say.

The girls and their mother get into a green compartment. One of the girls is crying. She wanted blue.

I look at the long line behind me. "Are you trying to cut?"

"I don't know. Maybe."

"Well, you'd better hurry," I say, and he hoists himself up by the metal railing and threads his body through the bars.

Our basket arrives. It's blue and the little girl is howling above us. I give the man enough tickets for both of us then we crouch down to fit beneath the rim of the umbrella and sit on opposite sides of the circular compartment. The man drops a bolt through three rings on the door. We rise up a few feet and stop. I have no earthly idea what to say to Neal Caffrey. And really, I don't want to talk. I want to go up high and look down at the town and out across the pale water.

"Oh Jeez," Neal says as our basket rises again, much higher. It stops close to the top and swings a bit. "Oh shit."

"Don't tell me the winner of the Renaissance Cup is scared of heights. Look how gorgeous it is from up here." I turn to see the harbor spreading wider and wider below us as we ascend, and then the open ocean beyond, dotted with islands, and the beginning of night lying flat against the horizon.

"Please don't do that. Please don't move around." He is leaning forward, gripping the circular bar.

"You mean like this?" I shift my weight the slightest bit, a little forward, a little back.

"Please don't," he whimpers.

I'm a little shocked by what a baby he is.

We move and stop again, right at the very top. All the color is gone from Neal's face, and his eyes are clenched shut.

"It's beautiful up here. The harbor is full of boats and the water is so still."

We begin to move again, dropping down.

"Okay," he says, exhaling. "Okay."

"Do you want to get out?'

"No. I'll get used to it."

"Are you sure? They let kids off all the time if they start freaking out."

"No. I can do this."

We circle down and around several times. He keeps his eyes closed. He says he's sorry a few times. He tries to smile. I can still see the boy in him if I squish up his features, darken his freckles, thicken the hair slightly. When he smiles I see the same square teeth, the gap between the front ones gone. He must have had braces sometime after eighth grade.

Very carefully he leans back in his seat. "I thought you were leaving. I thought you were already gone."

"Yeah, well. Maybe Berkeley is a little overrated after all."

"Unlike fried dough and the Tilt-a-Whirl." He smiles and I see his teeth again, and the gap, even though it's been closed up.

"Exactly."

"Seriously, Daley. What happened?" He is squinting, peering out at me through tiny slits.

"Seriously, the chair of the department won't give me an extension. I had to be there Wednesday or not at all."

"I thought your father was doing okay."

"He is. But he needs help getting where he needs to go."

He doesn't say anything. I can't tell what he's thinking or what he knows about my father. There's probably a lot I don't know.

"How long have you been living here?" I ask.

He shakes his head. "A long time."

"How long?"

"Nearly ten years."

"Jesus." I thought he was going to say one or two. Ten years means he dropped out of college. I don't do a very good job disguising my horror.

He laughs. "I know. I'm Ashing's own George Willard."

We read *Winesburg, Ohio* in eighth grade. I'm smiling, but his eyes are sealed tight now. "So aren't you going to tell me to get out while I can and follow my dreams?" I say.

"No, I hate advice," he says, then adds, "Live your life. There. That's my advice."

"Are you living your life?"

"No."

I laugh. "You didn't have to think very hard for that answer."

Our compartment stops and swings. Neal groans. People down below are being let off. We will be one of the last.

"I wrote an essay about you in graduate school." There is something about his eyes being shut that makes me able to speak my thoughts.

"What?"

"You called my chest concave, and I wrote that that moment was my initiation into the world of the male gaze."

"I never called you concave." He sounds like he knows exactly what I'm talking about.

"Not to my face. But Stacy told me."

"I didn't. That's not what I said."

"Well, I got an A on the essay."

Our compartment stops suddenly at the base of the wheel and the man slides open the bolt and swings the little door wide. "Great ride," Neal says to the man.

We head back toward town. The way he walks beside me, a sort of long bounce, reminds me of his performance in *The King and I*. *There are times I almost think I am not sure of what I absolutely know,* I can hear him sing. I laugh out loud.

"What?"

His eyes seem abnormally large now that they are open, and I laugh again.

"Jesus, what?"

"Nothing. Or, rather, too many things."

"I think I liked it better with my eyes closed."

"Why?"

"I feel like every time you look at me you're asking, *Why are you here? Why are you here?*"

"I'm not. Honestly, I was just thinking about what a good King of Siam you were. That's all."

"Same thing."

When we reach his shop he pulls out keys from his pocket.

"You're going back to work?"

"I live here. Up top." He points to a few dark windows on the second floor.

"I thought you lived with your parents."

"I'm pathetic, but not that pathetic."

I worry for a moment that he'll ask me up, but he says good night and disappears into the dark store. A few seconds later a light goes on above, though I can only see the ceiling from where I'm standing. He doesn't come to the window. I'm not sure why I thought he would. I start walking again. When I pass the sub shop, three teenage girls are coming out, still drinking their sodas.

"C'mon," the first one says, tugging the next one by the sleeve.

"No!" she says jerking her arm away. "I told you it's not true."

"C'mon. He lives right down there. We'll go ask him and find out."

"No!" she shrieks as the other begins to run down the sidewalk. The third girl is doubled over laughing. But she is all talk, the first one, and when she gets to Neal's door she only pretends to knock. Eventually the other two drag her toward the carnival.

My father is outside the church, smoking a cigarette with the man in work pants from the first night. This man looks a little like Garvey, the way he holds his cigarette backward, pinches it between thumb and forefinger, the lit end hidden by his palm. I wave and get in the car. Next to him, my father looks old, his hair no longer sprinkled with gray but an even silver. His stoop is more pronounced, his neck angling away from the back collar of his blazer, leaving a gap. His sidewalk conversation is always jocular; he speaks to people, men and women, as if they are about to go out onto a field. Take it easy, he always says upon leave-taking, take it easy, says the man who has never taken it easy. But right now with this guy my father is listening, nodding gravely, looking up over the top of the library across the street and then saying something serious. They speak for a few minutes after their cigarettes have been pressed out on the walkway, and then they pat each other on the arm and separate.

My father gets in the car and lets out a long breath.

I start the engine and pull out into the street.

"I tell you, no one's got it easy, that's for sure."

I look at him. There is pain on his face, pain for someone else. My father is feeling compassion.

The dashboard starts beeping.

"What the fuck is that?"

"It wants you to put on your seatbelt, Dad."

"Oh for fuck's sake. Is it going to tell me when to piss, too?"

He leans toward me to snap in the buckle—it's tricky, you have to go in at just the right angle. He groans, then gets it, then says, "What's that smell?"

"I don't know." The Datsun is old and has lots of smells.

"Food or candy or something."

"Fried dough?"

"Disgusting. You're eating that crap before dinner?"

"Two fat slabs of it."

"Just like your mother," he says. He's right. I'd forgotten that. It's just like her.

We pass Neal's lit windows, then the carnival. The Ferris wheel makes its big turns. A feeling is pooling inside me, flooding my chest and up into my throat and down the backs of my calves. It's a minute or so before I recognize it. Happiness.

16

My father *plings* across the linoleum in his golf spikes. He can't find his five-iron.

"That goddamn Frank musta swiped it."

He goes to look in the mudroom again.

"That kid was never any good. I don't care what kind of snazzy job he has now or how many zeros he gets in his paycheck. He stole my fucking golf club!" He clenches his fists. His face is bright red. The dogs dance around him, misunderstanding his excitement.

I know I've seen the striped rubber handle of a golf club somewhere. Then I remember. "It's in the poolhouse."

"What?" he says, but he's remembering it, too.

He marches across the grass and returns with it. I can tell he wishes he hadn't found it. It makes him madder. "Now I'm late. Now I'm really late." But in fact he'll still be early to the club. Tee off isn't till nine.

When the dogs have returned from chasing his car down the driveway, they clamber around me while I unload the dishwasher, waiting for our walk. Just as I'm about to fasten on their leashes, the front doorbell rings. The dogs jerk away from me, howling and scrambling as fast as they can toward the sound, barking even louder once they get there. No one but the mailman ever comes to the front door, and he rarely has reason to knock. The dogs are going crazy. It's someone very unfamiliar to them. Neal Caffrey? I go to the door.

But it's not Neal through the windows. It's Jonathan.

For him to be standing right here now, he's been driving since he hung up the phone yesterday morning. He's wearing one of his better shirts, the striped one he defended his dissertation in. I quickly drag the dogs by their collars back into the kitchen and shut them in, then run back to yank the sticky front door open.

I am ashamed about the barking, ashamed that he looks different to me here on the front terrace of this house. "You've gone in the wrong direction, Mr. Magoo." It comes out funny, like I have a frog in my throat, because I'm already crying.

"I know it," he says, and he wraps his arms around me. He smells like coffee and Doritos and, when I press my nose into the side of his neck, our life in Michigan. I try not to shake.

When I trust my voice, I say, "I can't believe you're here."

"I called from Des Moines, kept going as far as Omaha, and turned around."

I feel weak, as if I haven't eaten for a while, though I just had cereal. I don't want to let go. I don't want to have to say anything more. I kiss him and he kisses back. I feel him growing hard against me and I press into him, but he pulls back. And then he drops his arms and we are separate again.

I'm still holding the dogs' leashes. He stares at them in my hand. His eyes are red and his mouth doesn't seem to be able to hold a shape. I've never seen him not in full possession of himself.

"Come in." I step toward the door.

He shakes his head.

"My father's not here."

"I'm not afraid of him. Do you think I'm afraid of him?"

"No." I feel very small, very young. I want to say something that will return him to me. I flail for the first thing that comes to mind. "I saw this raccoon the other day. It had knocked over our trash can, torn into the bag, and was sitting on top of the barrel eating a piece of Swiss cheese, just holding it in two hands like a newspaper and nibbling at the top."

He smiles at my effort. He takes both my hands. He's about to say something serious, then changes his mind. "What's an elk? I might have seen an elk. Right beside the highway. In the median strip. It had these antlers." He drops my hands and spreads out his arms. There are huge round sweat stains under each one. "They went out to here. It was absurd. I don't know why he didn't just fall over."

I try to laugh.

"You need to come with me now."

"Jon."

He looks up at the house, which seems its largest from this spot on the front terrace, fanning out with rows of old windows and shutters on both sides and up three stories, and then the dormer windows on a very tiny fourth floor that's just storage but makes it seem absurdly tall. "I don't understand one thing that has happened in the last two weeks."

"I need to stay a little bit longer."

"No, you don't. You need to leave now."

"I can't be the next person who gives up on him."

"You would not be giving up on him. Daley, you're his grown daughter. He knows you need to live your life."

"He'd feel abandoned. And he's already come so far. He likes AA. He likes those meetings."

"Why are we talking about AA? What does AA have to do with our life? Daley—" He steps away and presses his lips between his teeth.

"He won't go if I leave. I know he won't."

"Then he's not really doing it for himself, is he?"

"Not yet, not entirely. But he will, when he gets stronger."

"How can he grow stronger when you're here letting him be weak? That's not how people grow stronger. He needs to do it on his own."

"He needs something to lean on right now. I'm like a splint for his broken leg."

"At what cost, Daley? The splint eventually goes in the trash. Has it occurred to you that your mother and your stepmother tried for years and years to be splints, too?"

"But they wanted more from him than I do."

"Oh, Daley, you want so much more than they ever did. You want the daddy you never got. You want him to make your whole childhood okay."

"This isn't about me. It's about him."

"I know it doesn't look like it's about you. You've got it nicely cloaked in a gesture of great sacrifice."

"Jon, *we* would be stronger if I had a better relationship with my father."

"This is what I mean."

"I'm just saying it has its advantages."

"Daley." He takes me by both shoulders. His eyes are bloodshot and sad. "You *can't* stay here. Everything is at stake for you. Don't you get that? You lose this job and—"

"And I lose a job. That's all. I will be a person who lost a job." Across the street Mr. Emery has come out of his house and is standing in his driveway looking at us. Jonathan doesn't notice. I shake off his grip on my shoulders. "I have this window of time, right here, right now, to help my father. It's the only window I'll ever get. And I'm the only one who can do it."

"It must feel good to play God."

Why do people keep saying this? "He has been sober for eleven days."

"I know a lot of people I could try and save, and it would be futile for me to try. You know that."

"This is my *father,* Jonathan."

"Why was having a father never important to you until right now, right when we're about to move in together?"

"Please don't make this about us. It's not about us."

"What the hell is it about then? A week ago it was you and me and California, and now it's this creepy town and a house built by the goddamn pilgrims and the bigot in residence." He moves toward the steps, to his truck parked in the semicircle below. And then comes back. "Have you already called Oliver Raskin?"

"Yes."

"And this is fine with him?"

"No."

"What do you mean?"

"He's giving the position to someone else."

Somehow this is the thing that makes it real for him. I watch his eyes fill up. "Why are you sabotaging your life like this?"

Julie cried for my joy, and now he is crying for my loss. But I feel very little. All these words feel like mashed-up cardboard in my mouth. Mr. Emery, I see, has gone back inside.

He pinches the tears off the bridge of his nose and shakes his head. Then he laughs. "I can't fucking believe this."

"Jonathan." He is on the other side of the terrace now. "Nothing has changed. I want to be with you. I want a life with you."

"Not enough. You don't want it enough."

Can he not understand that this is not my *choice*? Wouldn't he do the same in my position? "What is wrong with you?" Anger snakes its way up. I don't care what Mr. Emery hears. "Why can't you get this? Why can't you see that I don't *want* to do this but that I *have* to do it? Yes, we had a plan. And now I've changed the plan slightly. Why can't you adjust to that?"

"Slightly? You have not changed the plan slightly." His voice is deep and bare. "You said you were going to work at Berkeley. I turned down Temple to be with you. And then instead of going to California, you came here. For two days, you said. And then you said, six days more. And now you've given up the job. Why should I trust that you will *ever* come to California?"

"I will, Jon."

"I don't believe you. You know, you can poke fun at me and my plans, but I have no options. If I want to eat, if I want a roof over my head, if someday I want to support a family, I *have* to have a plan. But there are no real consequences to your choices. Because you can just set a match to everything and your daddy will pay the bills. Grad school wasn't just pretend for me."

I've been on my own for eight years. I had a smaller stipend at Michigan than Jonathan. We were impoverished together. And now he's twisting it all around. "You know what? Fuck you."

"Fuck you, too." I've never seen his mouth so tight, so mean.

He turns and drops down the stairs. Such a base ending. No better than an exchange between my father and Catherine.

I hear the truck start up, old and loud, and then the tires in the white gravel, and then silence as he reaches the pavement and is gone.

My father comes home from golf well after lunch. For a moment I think he is drunk. For a moment I see a mirage, a flashback to his drinking face, a slackness around the mouth, guilt in the yellow eyes. But as he gets closer and lifts his eyes and catches me watching from the kitchen, he changes back.

"We took no prisoners," he says when he comes in. Then he looks at me closely. "What's wrong?"

"Nothing."

"You sure?"

"Yeah. Just tired."

"Tell you what. Let's go out to eat tonight. Anyplace you want."

17

July passes.

In the mornings, if he doesn't have a tennis or golf date, my father is full of industry around the house. He mows the grass on his tractor, cleans the pool and gives it its chemicals, or weeds the vegetable garden and goes to the dump. He likes to putter, to play with his tools in the garage, to walk back and forth from house to garage to shed to poolhouse with a purpose I can't always discern. Occasionally he sits at his desk in the den with his reading glasses on and pays bills. He seems not to miss work in the least. I try to appear industrious too, though I am tired of industry. There is a thick caul of inertia around me. I walk the dogs to the beach, around to Littleneck Point, downtown to Neal's store. I have begun an essay for lay readers about poverty and community in the Sierra Juarez, but I can't find my bearings. I can't get past the second page.

If I'm not careful, my father will have us on the tennis court most afternoons, so I have to come up with alternative activities. At the beginning of August, when my father has a yellow thirty-days-sober chip in his pocket, we drive a half-hour north to the Hook's Island ferry, which is a glorified raft with flaking green railings and a few benches. Neither of us have ever been to Hook's. We stand at the stern and my father looks out at the water, at the small white wake and the lobster pots and the handful of Whalers and sailboats moored close to shore, at the gulls who are squawking and diving into the same churning patch of water. The temperature drops as we pull farther from land. The ocean lies in strips of color: pale lavender, powder blue, cobalt, navy. My father looks but he does not comment on its beauty. It may be the first time he's seen the open ocean all summer.

"My mother rented a house on an island one summer," he says. "Reminds me of this."

"I thought you always went to Boothbay."

"That was after she married Hayes. He had that house in Maine."

"Where was the island?"

"I'm not sure. Duck Island, I think it was called. Or Buck Island. I was only five or six."

"Just you and her?"

"And Nora."

The ferry jerks suddenly and we turn to the bow and the island is right there, all beach at its edges, a hillock in the middle. There are no houses. The whole thing is a wildlife reserve. The boat slides into its slot. The August heat returns.

The tourists hoist their backpacks and wait for the ferryman to unhook the chain. We let a family go ahead of us, a squat man, a willowy wife, two kids with mountain bikes. They smile at us. I can see they recognize that I am a daughter on a picnic with her father. I feel a small swell of pride. I smile back.

The best beach, said the woman who sold us our ferry tickets, is on the other side of the island, and we follow the path she told us about through the woods. It is dim and cool, the ground sandy.

"We played a game with a white handkerchief," my father says. "It rained a lot. There was a little box for kindling by the fireplace and I hid the handkerchief there every time. Every time. Because it made my mother laugh. I think it was in Canada," he says.

Prince Edward Island? Campobello? But I don't want to waste a question on place. I stay silent. I wonder if what they speak about in AA is making him look back. I don't pry about his meetings; I don't know if he has a sponsor or if he is doing the steps.

"Nora got sick and stayed in bed. And my mother had to play with me."

Through the break in the trees I can see the crests of the dunes, overlapping, blown to sharp peaks by the wind.

"All my life I heard about how smart my mother was, how she won some big prize at Smith and wrote articles about her travels in Egypt for *The New York Times* even before she'd graduated. But you know what I saw most of the time? A woman sitting in a chair staring at nothing. Even before my father died. Maybe you'd hear her complain that the steak was overdone or her glass had spots or that I was making too much noise. But that was about it."

"She sounds angry."

"She *was* angry. Why? She had a comfortable life. Her parents left her plenty to live on."

"Maybe she didn't want a comfortable life. Maybe she wanted a challenging life. You'd shoot yourself if you had to be a smart woman in Dover, Massachusetts in 1930."

We climb up between two high dunes. The ocean is darker over here, facing directly east, the waves more dramatic. I have read that at sea level the horizon is always only three and half miles away, but right now this seems impossible. I am stunned by the great empty blue enormity of it. After we'd had sex in my car that first time, Jonathan and I sat on the small gravel beach and debated why large bodies of water are so alluring. I said it was all about color, and he said it was space. No one could pave it or build on it or sell anything on it. It's just a huge relief for our eyes, he said. But for me it's something more. The water always seems to be saying something to me, urging something from me, though I never know exactly what it is.

"Why do you always do that?"

"Do what?"

"Do what you just did with my mother."

"What did I do with her?"

"Make it all be about her being a woman. It's like what happened to that kid in Garvey's class, David Stevens. You remember him? You probably wouldn't. He wasn't there long. Came in fifth grade, and then in seventh he cheated on a test and was given a warning. Next test, cheated again, and got kicked out. Parents made a huge deal about it, said it was because he was Jewish. No one knew he was Jewish! His name was Stevens, for chrissake. But for them, that was the reason. That poor kid never had to take responsibility for what he had done."

I have a vague memory that there is more to the story, that there were two boys cheating and the other one had just been suspended, not expelled. But I don't want to argue about the politics of Ashing Academy. "So you want me to just say, *Wow, your mother was a basket case,* and not look at why she might have been unhappy?"

"Don Finch's mother was an appellate court judge. Shep Holliston's was a doctor."

"They were the exceptions."

"So be an exception. Life's not fair. It isn't fair for you and it's not fair for me. But if you say her life was awful because she was born a rich woman in the early twentieth century, I'm not going to shed any tears. Your generation seems to think men forced women to marry and shoved them in the kitchen. Let me tell you it wasn't like that. We were the ones being railroaded into marriage."

"Oh, come on, Dad."

"It's true. If you wanted to have sex with a decent girl."

"From a good family."

"Nothing wrong with that."

"A girl you could take to the club."

We've slid down the dunes and now walk along the beach, looking for a good spot.

"Listen, I don't like all the whining your generation gets into." He laughs. "Like that black woman last year who testified against the judge."

"Anita Hill."

"Anita Hill. What a beauty. Here she had an opportunity to see one of her own become a justice of the Supreme Court, and she threw herself down on the tracks. She comes out of nowhere to destroy him. First of all, do you really think an important fellow like that, a guy who had been working towards something like this his whole life, is really going to talk about a pubic hair on a can of Coke? And supposing he did, what would you do?"

"I have no idea."

"I hope, I just hope, that you would get back to work."

"Dad, Anita Hill didn't come out of nowhere. When judges are nominated to the Supreme Court, they need references just like the rest of us, people who have worked with them and can answer questions about their character. So she told them what she knew. You could tell she didn't enjoy it. But she had the courage to speak up and tell the committee that he consistently used his power over her to abuse her and oppress her with a barrage of pornographic language."

"Sticks and stones."

"Words are just as damaging, Dad."

"People shoot the shit at work. If women can't handle it, they should stay home."

"Sorry. We're not going to be herded from the workplace anymore. Women have been kept at home as slaves long enough."

"That all sounds pretty, but are you a slave? Are your hands bound?"

"Not—"

"Just answer my question. Are you in chains right now?"

"No."

"Do you have the right to free speech, to vote for the candidate of your choice, to pursue the career you want? Did you have trouble excelling in school because you were a woman? Did you get passed over for that professorship because you were a woman?"

"No, we've made progress but—"

"All right then." He stops walking. "What's in that picnic basket?"

We eat everything I've packed: chicken sandwiches, potato chips, watermelon slices.

"I tell you, Daley. Everyone's always talking these days about advantages and privileges. Well, it only gets you so far. You know who's had all the advantages and privileges I can think of?"

I know, but I shake my head.

"Garvey. He's had 'em all. Good schools, good breeding, good everything, and look at him."

"I don't want to talk about Garvey."

"All I'm saying is that the guy will be lucky to get into the Rotary Club someday."

"There's absolutely nothing wrong with Garvey and I think you know that. It's too bad you had such a specific idea of who he should be."

My father sits on his towel, tall pointy knees up near his shoulders, pouring sand onto a piece of cellophane. A family nearby has gone swimming and the gulls are pecking at their open box of saltines. "You know," he says, "when Garvey was in the fourth form, he won a prize for a short story. Your mother and I went to this big event and all the runners-up read their stories and then Garvey gets up there last. His tie is crooked, his shirt untucked, and he reads the most boring godawful thing you've ever heard in your life about these people going to a cocktail party. Somebody passed around a flask of gin and thank God for that."

"What happened in the story?"

"Nothing! I couldn't understand for the life of me how it won first prize."

"What did Mom think?"

"Oh, Garvey was the Christ child to her. He could do no wrong."

I smile. She would have understood that the story had been a satire.

"Did you like St. Paul's, Dad, when you were there?"

"Yeah, it was all right. Except for the religion. Chapel every five minutes."

"Do you see any of your friends from there?"

"No. They all went to New York or someplace. I was in touch for a while with my tennis coach, who was also my history teacher, though I didn't do so well in his classes. He was a friend, young guy at the time. But then I saw him in Boston once and that was it."

"What do you mean?" I picture a sexual advance, a hand placed on my father's thigh.

"He called me up and told me to meet him at a fancy French restaurant and when the check came he just let me pay. A hundred bucks for two people, which was a hell of a lot of money then. He calls me, chooses the restaurant, and then has me pay for the whole thing. I never spoke to him again. He was a good guy, though. Great player. But that whole thing was a setup."

I can feel how open he is. It's like I could ask him anything. "Did your mother drink?"

He nods. "Even though Nora was sick that week on the island, every night she had to get up and help my mother to bed."

"Do you think it started when your father died?"

"No idea. But it didn't improve when she married Hayes, that's for sure."

"Was he a drinker, too?"

"I think so. But with him it was harder to tell. He was a big guy. I was a little pipsqueak next to him."

"Did he ever hit you?"

"No, he never hit me." I notice a slight emphasis on *me*.

"Your mother?"

"I think so."

"Oh, Dad."

"Yeah. Well," he says, pushing the cellophane down deep and smothering it with sand. "They're all dead now. Good riddance."

He lies down then, tips his face away from the sun, and very soon his hand twitches twice and he is asleep. I walk down to the water. The sand is loose and cold and a wave breaks and rushes at my ankles, then pulls away hard, sucking the sand beneath everything but the very center of my feet. The outdoors always brings Jonathan so much closer. He'd stand here with me and feel the sand get sucked away, feel the thin line beneath each foot you were left balancing on. I can feel his fingers on my arm as I start to walk back to the towel. Wait, he's saying, one more time. Why didn't I take him to Ruby Beach? Why didn't we go right there? I'd had the dogs' leashes in my hand. We could have watched the dogs sprint down to the water in their clouds of sand. We would have said different things there. We never would have been so cruel to each other. When I think of our exchange of fuck-yous I feel like someone is lighting my stomach on fire.

I read *The Gate of Angels* on my towel. I dab sunblock on my father's nose when it begins turning red, and he barely wakes up, just murmurs a thank-you and drifts off again. Eventually I put my book down and try to rest, too.

But I can't. Resting and sleeping have become harder since Jonathan was here. My mind churns. It wants to pore over what happened on the terrace, and then it wants to go back. It wants to relive everything, as if in the process it can change the ending. Now we're on his bed, the first time I ever spent the night at his place. We've been touching and talking for hours. It's 3 A.M. and he's lying against me sideways, his head on my stomach, the backs of his fingers running along the inside of my arm. He's telling me about Wicker Street.

"I was surprised the first time someone referred to my building as 'the project on Wicker Street.' Projects were something else. The projects weren't where *we* lived." When he entered fourth grade he had to go to a white school they were trying to integrate thirty minutes away. To get inside the school from the bus, they had to walk through a thin space between two lines of white parents hollering at them to go home. "We would have liked to go home, let me tell you." Their parents told them to keep their heads down and keep walking. They put their fists in their pockets. "There's a photo of it my mother cut out of the newspaper. If you look really closely you can see the outline of my friend Jeff's middle finger flipping them all the bird." Once they got into the school they were fine. It was the parents who gave them the most trouble. His first white friend was a boy named Henry. Henry had a cat, and whenever they went to Henry's house this cat would be curled up on the couch and Henry would give it a stroke and then Jonathan would give it a stroke and it would leap five feet in the air.

The worst thing he could be called by one of his older brothers, he told me, was white. "They'd see me playing with my friends and they'd say we played white. This brown pair of shoes my mother bought me was white. The way I took off my shirt was white. And then my mother would knock me upside the head and say I was acting like a nigger."

When his mother got her nursing license, they moved into their own house. They had a backyard with one tree. "I remember sitting alone in the evening on the grass one of the first nights we lived in that house and looking up at that tree, just a slender little tree with smooth bark, and I got this feeling about the tree, that I liked it and it liked me. And it occurred to me that the tree didn't care if I was black or white. Really, honestly, didn't care. It didn't matter to the tree. And for a few seconds I kind of felt like I was floating. I think that's the first time and maybe the last time I felt free, truly free."

"From being black?" I asked.

"From being anything but what I really was."

*   *   *

"Get away, you fucker. Get the fuck away!" My father is swatting at a seagull. It has hopped out of reach but is still looking intently at the corner of plastic wrap sticking out of the sand. "Oh for God's sake, take it." But when he throws it, the seagull isn't interested. "I don't know what you want, then. I can't help you." He sits up. "Let's get out of here."

I think we can make the four o'clock ferry, but we hear it pull out while we're still in the woods.

"Jesus H. Christ," my father says, his fists clenched tight.

"It'll come right back. They leave every half-hour."

He looks at me as if I've arranged it all on purpose. He's a little boy who's woken up from his nap in a terrible mood.

"Take a few deep breaths, Dad."

"And you take a long walk off a short pier. Christ, I need a drink."

"Very funny." But I see he wasn't joking. He'd forgotten. I watch the rage pour into his face.

"You know what, Daley?" Day-*lee*.

Before he can tell me what, I say, "I don't want to hear it. Just keep it to yourself. You're in a shitty mood and I'm in a shitty mood so let's just get on the ferry and go home."

"I'm not going to that goddamn meeting tonight."

I've been waiting for this. I've even rehearsed my calm response. "Okay."

"I am so sick of those people and their problems. I don't have anything in common with them. Nothing."

"Except that you want a drink."

At quarter of seven that night he calls up to my room. When I come down into the kitchen he's showered and dressed and standing by the door.

18

When I was little my father loved to surprise people. It was not uncommon for him to go upstairs during a dinner party and come down in a Marie Antoinette wig and my mother's underwear. Once he gave us all presents on *his* birthday. At Christmas there was always something unexpected: a kitten, a drum set, a new car in the driveway. But if the surprise was revealed prematurely, look out. Garvey never received the Ping-Pong table he found in the shed two days before his birthday, and my father never spoke to Mr. Timmons again after he told my mother to have a good time in Hawaii—which was to be a surprise for their fifteenth wedding anniversary. Apart from their abrupt departures, neither my mother nor Catherine had been much for creating surprises themselves, and I doubted his unhappy mother or even Nora, who was kind but not playful, had done much in the way of the unexpected for him. So I decide to throw my father a surprise party on the twenty-ninth of August, which is both his birthday and his sixtieth day of sobriety.

I stop by Neal's to ask if he knows any caterers. He gives me the number of someone named Philomena. His shop is empty so we sit on the stoop. The town is fogged in this morning, the air so wet and briny it's hard to inhale, as if salt and seaweed have been ground up into it. Even without the sun, it's already hot. Neal is wearing shorts, which look funny on him and he seems to know it. He keeps covering his pale knees with his hands. His hair has curled into ringlets around his ears.

"How do you know her?"

It would be just like Neal to have a girlfriend named Philomena.

"She's an old friend of the Dead Girl."

"Who?"

He looks down at his hands. "A girl I used to know."

"But she's not really dead."

"No."

"Bad breakup?"

He nods. I wait to see if he'll say anything more about it.

"You ever had your heart smashed to pieces?" he asks.

"Yes."

"I mean *really* broken. Everybody walks around saying they've had their heart broken, but they mean they went out on two dates and they really liked the guy and he never called back. Or they're like my brother, who went out with this truly awful girl for two years and all he did was complain and make fun of her and then she slept with someone else and he said his heart was broken in two. And then he had a new girlfriend by Tuesday. I'm not talking about that kind."

"You're talking about waking up every morning feeling like someone has beaten you up and you can't quite take a regular breath."

Neal shuts his eyes. "Yes."

We sit there. Cars goes by. There's a copy of Simone de Beauvoir's *Second Sex* in the window now. I read it last winter for the first time. One morning I was reading it on Jonathan's couch while he vacuumed. He was much neater than I was. I've never owned a vacuum cleaner. "I'm the third sex," he said as he went by. "But ain't nobody written a book about me yet."

"What happened?" Neal asks.

"I lost the job and the guy. No deferments for either."

"He'll come around."

"I don't think he will. I would have heard from him by now." I still jump every time the phone rings, still feel hopeful when the mail arrives. I've called information, but there's no listing for him on Paloma Street or anywhere else in the Bay Area.

"What's his name?"

"Jonathan." It hurts to say the syllables. I need to get off the subject. "And your Dead Girl?"

He shakes his head. "I don't say it anymore."

"What happened?"

"Too long a story."

"I've got time."

"I don't."

"Just give me a detail."

"Started freshman year of college and ended six years later in a Pottery Barn at the Chestut Hill Mall."

I lean back against the doorjamb. "C'mon. A few more."

"Don't do that. Don't get all settled in for a good yarn. Girls are always like that, always trying to leech everything out of you."

"No, *girls* are not always like that. *Women*—those are people of the female sex eighteen and over—aren't either. I happen to be interested because I am a behavioral anthropologist. Or was. What happened at the Pottery Barn?"

"She was going to move in with me. Here." He points upstairs. "I wouldn't pay for half the bed we were buying. I had the money; I just thought it should be clean—she buys the bed, I buy the couch. Just in case. And she turned it into this whole big thing about trust and commitment."

"Which it sounds like it was."

"Yeah. I've had a few years to replay the scene about ten thousand times. It was."

"Where is she now?"

"I'm not sure. Vermont, maybe. Your turn. Tell me something about Jonathan."

I wish I hadn't told him his name. It feels like I've given him a gun with bullets.

He leans back on his elbows.

"Don't get comfy."

He laughs. "Just go."

But there is no story yet. It's just a tight searing knot.

"Hey, it's okay," he says, giving me the slightest shoulder nudge.

A woman and her daughter come up the steps with a long summer reading list. "We're a little late, but she reads fast," she says, handing the sheet of paper to Neal.

"Ashing Academy," he says, waving it at me.

"Renaissance Cup, 1978," I say to them, pointing at Neal who's heading inside.

"Really?" the mother says, impressed.

He points back at me. "You do that again and you will be banned from this store." And then he is all business, gathering the books for them, and I rouse the dogs from their naps and we go home.

I mail invitations to my father's closest friends, the ones who have not sided with Catherine, the ones he speaks of more or less fondly. I buy tiki torches and hide them in Neal's storage room. In the thrift shop I run into the bohemian woman who is often late to the meetings, and she tells me her name is Patricia and that she's enjoyed getting to know my father, so I invite her, too.

If I could make my father deaf for two weeks I would. I am terrified someone will slip and mention the party. When we are downtown together, I feel quite ready to lunge at the throat of anyone I suspect is about to blurt out the secret. Every time he comes home from the hardware store or the dump or a meeting, I wait for him to tell me he does not want a fucking surprise party. And when finally, very casually, I ask what he might like to do on his birthday, he says, "Nothing. I hate birthdays."

I reassure him that we'll have a quiet dinner at home with the dogs. And when the night comes I tell him I want to make a special meal and ask him to drive himself to his meeting. It's the first time I haven't accompanied him, but it feels fine. It feels like it's time. As soon as he's gone, Philomena and her team arrive and we begin quickly setting up tables and chairs on the lawn beside the poolhouse. Mrs. Bridgeton comes early with several big pots of hydrangeas that she puts around the pool, and helps me arrange the flowers and candles for the tables.

"I remember you in a fuzzy pink bathrobe passing out hors d'oeuvres at all the parties your mother used to have. You were such a precious little thing. And now here you are, throwing a grown-up party all by yourself."

The pale blue hydrangeas look beautiful. It's exactly what my mother would have done.

Neal has volunteered to waylay my father outside the church. I told him to ask my father if he'd seen Billy Hatcher, the Red Sox outfielder, steal home a few weeks ago. That conversation will last a good half-hour. My father cannot stop reliving the moment.

At seven-thirty my father's old friends begin appearing around the pool. I asked them to park well beyond our driveway so they come on foot. They come in summer attire, cotton prints in bright colors. They are a clean, well-groomed generation. They smell of flowers and spices and booze. I warned them in the invitation that no alcohol would be served, so they've come well lubricated.

Mrs. Keck takes hold of my hands and won't let go. She is much more frail than I remember her. "This is a wonderful thing you're doing for your dad." Her head wobbles. Parkinson's. She looks around at the tables covered in white cloths, the delphinium in jars and the torches lit and flashing in the dusk. "A very wonderful thing."

And then the phone rings in the poolhouse. It can mean only one thing. Neal didn't find my father outside the church. He is AWOL. I pick it up.

"The eagle has flown." I can tell he's smiling. And then he hangs up.

I am scared. I've lost most of the feeling in my hands. My father's car turns up the driveway. I can see it through the tree trunks, slowing as he makes the turn and sees the pool and the tables and the torches. He comes to a full stop before the poolhouse. His window is down.

"What the hell are you people doing here?"

"Surprise!" everyone says in unison, though I never suggested anything of the sort.

"Jesus Christ," he says, and drives on into the garage.

When he comes across the lawn, people call surprise again and he shakes his head. People go to greet him. His face is red. I can't tell if his smile is fake or real. One of Philomena's helpers approaches him with a plate of smoked salmon on crackers and he takes one and nods his thanks.

"Where's Daley?" he says with his mouth full. "Daley, get over here!" But he is coming over to me, pointing a finger. "You do all this? You plan all this?"

I nod.

"But when I left you said—"

"I know. It's a surprise party, Dad. I had to lie a little."

"But none of this was here. And who are those people in aprons?"

"Caterers."

"Caterers." He says the word like he hasn't been to thousands of catered parties in his lifetime. "Jesus Christ." He turns around and looks at the tables set with china. One of the servers is filling the water glasses. "Everyone's staying for dinner?"

I tell him they are. "Prime rib," I say, because I know he wants to know.

"Just like Sunday nights at the club."

He seems a little in shock. People come up and speak to him, and he is buffeted around on the grass. He makes responses, but all the while he is looking around like he's never seen the place before. My mother had plenty of parties like this, fundraisers for so many different candidates and causes.

"Let me get you a club soda, Dad. Then we can eat."

We've set up a table with juices and sparkling water near the diving board. It's too far away and not many have found it. The glasses are still spread out neatly, the bottles full. I have no idea what my father is feeling, so I have no idea what to feel myself. I pour the soda and feel scared to turn back around.

"Boy, you were right about Billy Hatcher. He had *a lot* to say."

It's still strange to hear Neal's voice again. I don't understand why it's soothing to hear a remnant from my past when my past was not soothing.

I smile and watch my father over his shoulder.

"You can relax now," Neal says. "You did it."

"I don't know if he's enjoying himself."

"It doesn't matter. You did something kind for him. You can't control his response to it."

"I guess you're right."

"Now have a cranberry fizz." He hands me a cup and knocks his own against it. "Cheers." I wonder if Neal is a drinker, if he gets plastered every night upstairs in his little apartment by himself. I wonder if he, too, had something before he came.

Not surprisingly, I've had my share of alcoholic boyfriends. The last was a Brit who hid his addiction well for a while and then, when I was safely smitten, flaunted it like something he was vastly proud of. He was sharp and sexy and always horny, no matter how much he'd put away. I had fast, intense orgasms when he was drunk. And then he hit me, at a party. It wasn't a hard blow and didn't even leave the proof of a bruise on my face. After that I learned how to spot even the very sly ones. Dan was one, and I figured it out before I saw him drink anything at all, knew it the minute he started pounding on the steering wheel. Jonathan and I liked the taste of red wine, but neither of us enjoyed the feeling of being drunk or even buzzed, and an open bottle could hang around his apartment for weeks. Drinking was something neither of us remembered to do very often.

"I need to give this to him. And there's Patricia." I pour another cranberry soda and take one to my father and one to Patricia at the edge of the lawn. Thinking she'll need to be introduced I lead her toward the party, but she seems to know nearly everyone.

I feel like my mother, greeting, kissing, directing the servers, integrating the guests. Now and then I sense Jonathan watching me, angry, cynical, shaking his head and muttering, *And so another Ashing socialite is born.* Or maybe it's Garvey. Jonathan would just be shaking his head, still in shock. *You gave up me and Berkeley for this?* In California it is still afternoon. Whoever has my job has already begun the fall semester. The urban kinship project is well under way. But with the last of my own money I have thrown a catered party in the suburbs.

"When I left the house she was making a nice dinner for two!" I hear my father say. "She got me good, I tell you. She got me good."

I manage to get everyone seated at a table, and the servers come immediately with salads. My father and I sit with the Bridgetons, the Utleys, Neal, and Patricia.

The sky has gone quickly black. The five tables are close together on the lawn, a candle on each that lights our plates and faces but nothing beyond. It feels very intimate, exactly what I imagined. For the first few moments it is quiet. No one is drunk. No one is squawking. Everyone seems to be taking it all in, as I am.

Mr. Gormley at the table next to us breaks the silence. "Well, we haven't been to such a classy event at this address in years. Usually you go over to Gardiner's for drinks and you end up on the roof wearing a hula hoop!"

"It ain't over till the fat lady sings," my father says.

The main course arrives. I check my father's plate: a thick slice of prime rib, very rare, bathed in jus, very few vegetables, exactly how I asked Philomena to prepare his plate.

"Hey, hey," he says looking down at it. Then he looks at me. "You are something, you know that."

"No, *you* are something, Dad."

"Yeah, something awful."

"No, Gardiner," Barbara Bridgeton says. She is on his other side, patting his hand. I see Patricia lift her head. "You are very special to all of us."

"Hear, hear!" Mr. Utley says, raising his plastic cup of soda water. Mile High Mr. Utley, Garvey and I used to call him, because he's at least six-five.

"How's that shop of yours doing?" Mr. Bridgeton asks Neal.

"Let's just say I don't think my gross profit will outdo IBM *this* quarter."

Mr. Bridgeton, who works for IBM, looks momentarily confused, then laughs. "If you've got anything in that store as good as *Shogun,* I'll come and get it tomorrow."

"I remember reading that the author had been a prisoner of war in Japan," Patricia says. She is mothlike, thin and slightly translucent. "And that he was treated very badly and nearly starved to death."

"Is that right?" my father says. I wonder what they know about each other. Like my father, she goes to the meeting every night.

"But then he wrote this sensitive portrait of that country, which in the end made the English look like the barbarians."

"Huh," my father says.

They recommend in AA that if you're single you do not get into a romantic relationship until you are sober a year. It seems like good advice. I hope Patricia will still be around by then. I like her, and I think she likes my father, though he seems entirely oblivious.

"I've never had a better prime rib," he says, putting down his fork, vegetables untouched.

After the cake is served I stand and tap my glass.

"As many of you know, my father is a man of surprises. All my life he has surprised me with gifts, live animals, lectures, highly inappropriate jokes—" People laugh. "But nothing has surprised me more than his strength and determination these last two months. I couldn't be more proud of him. Or more thankful. I love you, Dad."

There is applause as I kiss his cheek and he hugs me and says something I can't hear.

People start chanting "Speech, speech," and my father who, despite his desire for attention, dreads all forms of public speaking, stands up.

"Well, you all outsmarted me, that's for sure. Ben telling me he was going fishing with his son this weekend, and then Neal there pretending that he hadn't seen Billy Hatcher steal home when he was actually *at the game,* the lucky bastard. So thank you all for showing up here tonight. I need to raise a glass to my daughter now because she did all this for me. She has given up so much for me—" The next word comes out as a squeak and he shakes his head and their are tears in the cracks of his skin around his eyes. He raises his cranberry soda and then sits down quickly and his napkin shakes in his fingers as he lifts it to wipe his face.

I pat his leg. He takes my hand and holds it tight. If Jonathan hadn't thrown that party for me in June, I wouldn't have given this night to my father. I wish he knew how grateful I am.

After dinner I change the music in the poolhouse to Glenn Miller, and when I come out people are already dancing in the grass and along the edge of the pool. Eventually nearly everyone gets up and bounces around. Only a couple of my father's old friends, men who need a few drinks in order to dance, sit on lawn chairs and watch. My father, who has never needed even music to dance, spins me around. I see Neal dancing with Patricia, Mike dancing with Mrs. Keck, William with Philomena. Every time I look I see a different combination of people. When I'm dancing with Mr. Utley, Dad cuts in on Mr. Keck for Patricia. He spins her. Then he runs into the poolhouse and comes out with a lifesaver ring around his waist. The music turns slow and my father takes her hand in one of his and puts his other in the hollow of her back. Mr. Utley does the same with me. He is so tall my arms are reaching straight up, as if I'm climbing a ladder.

"I've never seen your father quite like this, Daley. You're a good influence on him."

Particia looks uncomfortable now. She is leaning away from him, and when the song ends she leaves the dancing area. She goes directly to her purse, shoulders it, and heads for her car.

I catch up with her before she reaches the driveway. "I'm sorry, Patricia. Did my father say something that offended you?"

"No, no. That's not it. I'm just not feeling very well."

"Please tell me."

"I don't want to."

"Please. I need to know what he said to you."

She looks down at the keys in her hand. She just wants to leave. "He's drinking, Daley."

"No, he's not."

"I'm sorry."

"I know my father when he's been drinking. I know exactly what that's like."

"I'm so sorry."

I let her disappear into the darkness beyond the torches. I walk slowly back to the party. My father is dancing with Philomena, perhaps even more ridiculously than he danced with Patricia, still in the white ring, strutting like a chicken, a snorkel in his mouth like a rose. I see how she could have thought he was drunk. So much of him is still a child. But he isn't drunk. He's just himself, and he's happy.

"Now *that* was a party," my father says as we sit on the porch steps afterward while the dogs take their last pees before bed.

"What did you think when you pulled in?"

"Fire. I thought there was a fire."

"The torches."

"And all the people. I swear I saw some of them carrying buckets."

I laugh.

"You probably don't remember, but your mother used to have these kinds of parties, just like this: round tables, white tablecloths, waitresses. But they were never for me. It was always for some Democrat. She never even wanted me there. I hope she's watching right now. I hope she saw what you did for me tonight."

"How did you hear that she died, Dad?"

"We were playing paddle at the Chapmans'. Herbie Parker told me just as we were walking onto the court."

I see the Chapmans' paddle tennis court in the woods behind their house, the heavy stumpy paddle racquets, my father's head bent to listen. I need my father to talk about her death. The party has brought her back for me too, all night long.

"And what did you feel?"

"Oh, God, I think I probably felt everything in the book. I didn't play very well that day. I remember that."

"And then what'd you do?"

"Went home. Catherine already knew. It was a shock. She was the first one of us to go."

"Did you ever think about how I was feeling? Or Garvey?" This is hard. Everything in me starts quivering. "Because you never called or came by."

"I guess I just couldn't acknowledge it."

"What? Her death?"

"No." He looks down at his hands on his knees. "Your attachment to her."

"Because it felt like a betrayal?"

"Something like that."

"I wish it didn't always have to be a competition."

"Me too." He puts his arm around me and kisses my forehead. It reminds me of Grindy. "I'm sorry, Daley."

He's never said that, not once, ever, for anything.

The dogs rustle around in the woods. It's close to two in the morning. I feel heavy and tired.

My father stands up and the dogs come racing up the steps. "Well, I've had a lot of surprises in my life," he says. "Most of them bad. But this was a good one." He puts out his hand and pulls me up. "You's a real keeper, you know that?"

He is steady on his feet. He smells like prime rib. Patricia was wrong. He is perfectly sober.

19

I can't help calling Garvey the next day.

"Don't tell me," he says. "You've met a venture capitalist from Marblehead and the wedding's next Saturday at the Episcopal Church."

"He's doing well, Garve. Day sixty-one."

"It's creepy the way you count the days like that."

"It works."

"It's all going to end in tears. Remember how Mom used to say that whenever we were having fun? *It's all going to end in tears.*"

I ask him how plans for the new branch in Hartford are going and he says he's been interviewing "cuties" for the office manager position.

"You've heard of sexual harassment laws, right?"

"I'm not going to harass them. I'll leave them alone afterward. Seriously, I did meet someone. This doctor who was moving out of her place, getting a divorce. We have a little sizzle going on. She's having a party Saturday night."

"You going?"

"I might, if I'm not too tired."

He had a bad breakup a few years ago and now claims love is not worth the ugly ending.

"Come visit us."

He laughs. "Not a chance."

"What'd he say to you that morning, Garvey?"

"Nothing new."

"He was in a lot of pain then."

"And now with your magical anthropology PhD wand, you've erased it all."

"What if he's still not drinking at Thanksgiving. Will you come for that?"

"No."

And then, that same morning, I get a phone call. My father hands me the phone and my heart is racing but the voice is female. It's Mallory.

"I hear you're throwing big parties," she says.

"Only for people sixty and over," I say. "Where are you?"

"Here, but we're leaving this afternoon. Can you meet me at Baker's Cove in an hour?"

I hitch up the dogs and grab the little bag with my notebook in it. It's where I keep notes for a letter to Jonathan. I have fifteen pages of them already, fragments with no structure, like a bad freshman essay. I don't know where to send it, if I ever manage to write it. I don't know where he is. He terminated the lease on the cottage. The landlord sent me back the first and last months' rent but not the security deposit. And when I called the philosophy department at SFSU, the receptionist had never heard of him. She was new, she said, but there was no one on the faculty with the last name Fleury.

It's high tide so the cove isn't too smelly. I climb out over the rocks to a little pool of water with its own tiny beach. The dogs find shade behind me and I sit for a long time with the notebook open, writing nothing.

I hear a thud, and a child's pail with a white braided handle appears on the top of one of the rocks. And then a little girl, not more than six, crawls up, sees me, and sits down abruptly. She has inch-long pigtails just behind each ear. She scoots down the rock, her bucket bumping behind her. When she reaches sand, she drops the bucket and goes right to the water. The pool is no deeper than her knees. She wades in then stands still, bent over, hands on chubby thighs. She is wearing only the bottom of a red bikini with white bows on either side. She remains completely still until her hand shoots into the water and stirs up a cloud on the bottom and then quickly carries something with thrashing claws to the bucket.

"Gracie! My God. I asked you to wait on the rocks until I caught up."

I only need to see the long O's of her knees above me on the rocks to recognize Mallory. She climbs down carefully, a baby in a plaid pouch on her chest, beach bags in both arms.

"Which ones you got," I say, "your mom's Larks or your dad's Winstons?"

She lets out one of her big laughs, deeper now. "Can you be-lieve what delinquents we were? That one is starting to read now so I'm thinking I have to throw out all my old diaries so she doesn't get any ideas. I was just telling her this morning about how we used to argue about whose dog was better."

I hug her sideways, not wanting to squish the baby, who is so small and sound asleep. In grade school Mallory towered over me and was the kind of girl people called "big-boned." But now she feels small in my arms, with bones no bigger than mine. Her hair is shorter, but her face is just the same.

"Mine was," I call to Gracie. "Hers was boring."

"That's exactly what you said! I was so mad I didn't speak to you for days. Her white dog was always filthy, Gracie."

"Gray. The dog was a gray dog."

"He needed a bath."

"You've reproduced."

She laughs again. She has a great laugh, like it comes all the way up from her feet. "I'm a factory. I've got a two-year-old boy back with my mother." She scrunches up her face. "The challenging middle child."

We laugh because that's what Mallory is.

"I cannot believe it." I'm about to add that I didn't know she'd gotten married but then I have a flash of a memory of an invitation that most likely arrived after being forwarded a few times and right in the middle of some crisis: an overdue paper, 200 exams to be graded. Had I even responded? I can't remember. Is it possible that I didn't even RSVP to Mallory's wedding? A small parade of wedding invitations flashes by: Ginny, Stacy, Pauline. I'm not sure I responded to any of them, certainly never sent a gift. It made no sense to me, why people wanted to get married.

She glances over at where I've been sitting in the sand with the notebook. "Can we join you?" she asks, and then she sees the dogs panting in the shade behind us. "What's this? *More* dirty dogs?"

"You be nice. You're a role model now."

"God help us." She spreads out two enormous beach towels and erects a little tent for the baby when it wakes up. She attaches a toy to its ceiling. "He blisses out on this hanging chicken thing." From her cooler, she offers me a selection of juices in small bright boxes and a box of animal crackers.

"Those are mine!" Gracie calls as she drops what looks like a small lobster in the pail. "But you can have them."

"She's pretty fearless, isn't she?"

"She's obsessed with crustaceans. Whenever we come to Ashing we spend all our time at the water's edge."

"How far away are you?" On the phone she said she lives in New Hampshire now.

"About an hour and a quarter. We're near Nashua."

Nashua. It was the kind of name we would have made fun of when we were kids, the kind of place whose racetrack was advertised on channel 56. *Nashua*, we would have said in our pretend

Boston nasal accents. *Naaashua, New Hampsha.* I expected Mallory
to be living somewhere glamorous.

"The rumors are flying around town about you." She laughs
hard. "I even heard you were dating Neal Caffrey."

"No dates, but he *is* my only friend here."

"So you really are living in Ashing?"

"My father had a bit of a breakdown when Catherine left."

"I heard she left. In June, right? Just like your mom."

"Spring with him must be hell, I guess."

Gracie howls and Mallory leaps up. Something pinched her
finger. Mallory holds the baby's head as she bends over Gracie in
the water, but the baby wakes up anyway. By the time she returns
to the towel he's red and bleating and kicking. She unfastens a series
of snaps and pulls out from the cup of her bathing suit an enormous veined udder with a wide brown center and an inch-long
nipple which the child seizes in his mouth, sucking the skin up into
pleats around his pumping lips. Jesus.

"I was always a little scared of your dad," she says, then asks if
I remember the time we missed the train and he and Catherine came
to get us in Allencaster. I didn't. She says she has a long diary entry
about it, how I calmly told them there was a mistake in the schedule but they didn't believe us. "I cried when they kept yelling at us,
but you were so cool and controlled and never cracked."

"I don't remember that at all."

"Really? I swear, once you have kids—Gracie!" She jumps up
again, baby still attached and sucking, and sprints to the water. She
splashes in and plunges her left arm to the bottom while the right
keeps the baby in position, and hauls up Gracie, whose face has
momentarily lost its confidence.

"Breathe," Mallory shouts, and whacks her on the back. And I
watch as the color comes back into the child's face. Then she looks
down at the sandy bottom and up at her mother and bursts into

tears. "It's all right. You're fine." Mallory tries to wipe her wet hair out of her eyes but Gracie swats her away.

"I almost had an eel and you scared it away!"

Mallory smiles. "There are no eels here, honey. There's never been an eel." Which makes Gracie even more furious.

When Mallory comes back I want to compliment her on her patience but I feel like that might be insulting Gracie. The baby's meal has gone on uninterrupted. His legs and most of the blue pouch are soaking wet but his eyes press tighter shut each time he sucks.

"You're thinking, and that's not even the complicated child."

I laugh.

"She has no interest in learning how to swim. And she wants to be in the water all day long."

I'm curious to know what she'd been about to say about having kids. "So, you've been reading your old diaries recently?"

"Yeah, I have. It's funny—" she winces, then yanks her nipple out of the baby's mouth. It doesn't look easy. The skin stretches an inch before he releases it. He wails as she lifts him up and out of the wet pouch, and he keeps wailing until she slides him in the tent with the hanging chicken and he stops short. "He starts to bite when he's done. Drives me crazy." She pushes her boob back in her suit. I see the long nipple fold in half to fit. Mallory got breasts before me, like everyone else, but they had been normal, not these pale raw tubers. She doesn't seem to remember, again, what she was about to say.

We watch Gracie dredge the bottom of the pool with both hands, occasionally taking in water and croaking it out. She has elements of Mallory at that age, the straight dark-blonde hair, the strong thighs, but her square slightly squished face is someone else's. Her focus, her fixation on a thing, is from her mother, too. And yet that seems to be gone from Mallory now. She can't follow through on a thought. Her snacks are neatly packed, though. She brings out thinly sliced apples laid carefully in a plastic container with a lime green top. Gracie grabs a few and then hurries back to the water.

"Plumber's butt," Mallory says, and Gracie pulls up the droopy back of her suit. "Remember the hours we spent in your mother's closet? All her fancy clothes. And that wall of shoes! Oh, she was like a real live princess to me."

The words are familiar. She was at the funeral, I'm remembering now. I sobbed in her arms. And she sobbed too. And then I didn't see her again until this moment.

Gracie totters slowly toward us with her bucket. Water sloshes at the sides. "I'm thirsty and hungry and thirsty," she says. She puts the bucket down and takes a little box of juice from her mother. She puts the straw in her mouth and it turns purple. She sucks it all down without stopping, her breathing growing louder and her belly pushing out, then hands the shrunken box back to her mother. "More," she gasps. But the baby has started fussing in the tent and Mallory is on her knees changing his diaper.

I reach in the bag for another juice box.

"Say thank you, Gracie," Mallory says without looking. She's lifting the baby up by his feet with one hand like a plucked chicken.

"Thanks," Gracie says and hands me back the box half full.

I offer her some crackers but she shakes her head.

"Wanna see my collection?"

I get up and peer into her bucket. Snails, crayfish, starfish, and crabs are piled on top of each other. The crabs are fighting, two against one. I ask her what she'll do with them, and she says she'll put them all back. She asks if I'll help her.

"I'll carry the bucket," she says, and lugs it back to the edge of the water. The little white bows on her red bikini have come untied. "Don't drop them all out together. You need to find the right spot for each one." She wades in. "Here. Here's a good spot for a crab."

She wants me to reach in the pail and get one.

"You're going to have to pull them apart first."

"Easier said than done," I say.

"I know!" Her laugh is just like Mallory's. I feel like I'm playing with Mallory again, only I've grown up and she hasn't yet.

I stick my hand in the cold water and grab one by the sides of its body and shake but they all stay stuck together.

"Here," she says, and her little fingers go in and all the crabs shoot apart. I don't even know how she did it.

We place each crab in different parts of the pool.

"Off you go," she says quietly each time. We watch them float to the bottom, then scramble furiously beneath the sand to hide.

Before she puts the snails back, she puts one hole-side-up in her palm. "Did you know they come out of their shells when you hum to them?"

"What?'

"It's true. Watch carefully."

She hums one note over and over but the hole stays dark. Then she hums the first few bars of "Edelweiss" and a little bit of water seeps out and then a brown tube inches out of the shell like a periscope.

Up on the beach, Mallory is putting the baby back in his carrier. They have to go. "I'll call you when we come down again. Will you still be here?"

"Maybe."

Gracie is swinging her empty bucket around in a wide circle. "Will you come here tomorrow, Daley?"

"I will, but I don't think I'll see you."

"I know. I'll be in my home. But will you come say hi to everyone for me? You don't have to take them out of the water. You can just wave."

"I can do that."

"Thanks."

I stroke the little patch of fine hairs on the baby's head. They are light and soft as milkweed. And the skull beneath feels spongy, like it hasn't hardened all the way yet. I stand on the rocks and watch them move slowly around the cove, Mallory's shoulders weighed down by the beach bags, the tent, and the cooler, and Gracie skipping through the water, and Mallory telling her she is going too deep. I should have offered to help them back home. I never learned the baby's name, or how old he is. My chest is burning for all three of them.

In my notebook I write: *Mallory. Gracie. Baby with fat legs kicking in his pouch. I want that. I do want that, J.*

He gave me a blue silk robe for my birthday. We were on his bed, and he'd brought me breakfast and a wrapped box.

"My first choice of outfit is this, of course." He pulled the sheet all the way off me and kissed my bare belly. "But short of that, here you go."

I opened it. He knew it was my favorite color, and my favorite fabric. I slid my arms through the sleeves and tied the sash. It was scandalously short.

"Now you are one sexy white girl."

"Woman."

"Sorry, but if I'm using the modifier white, it's got to be girl. When I say white woman it makes me think of Edith Bunker or Maude."

"I learned about menopause from Maude," I said. "I'd never heard of it before." Jonathan was one of the few boyfriends I'd had who'd watched as much TV in the seventies as I had.

"Please, please let's not talk about white women in menopause."

"Another twenty years and that's me."

"Really? Only twenty? We better get going."

I shook my head.

"You don't want babies?"

I'd never been asked by a guy about babies before. I'd never *wanted* to be asked about babies. It was like being asked if I wanted a polar bear.

He undid the sash of my new robe and traced his finger along a hip. "You've got some good baby-making hips."

"Yeah, right."

"You really don't want kids?"

"Not anytime soon," I said finally.

"Ever?

"I don't know."

"Two years, four years?"

"I'm not really a long-range planner."

"Just tell me. When are you going to have your white babies?"

"Oh, so that's what this is about."

"What?

"My *white* babies."

"I didn't say that."

"You did. You said, When are you going to have your white babies?"

He grinned. "I didn't mean to say that."

"It's all very loaded, this topic."

"Everything's going to be with us. Black and white *is* loaded."

"I mean the whole *baby* thing. I don't know if you're trying to tease out some maternal desire in me and then get freaked out by it. Or if you're insinuating that I'm nonmaternal. Or if you're testing to see if I'm averse to having a brown baby come out of my white vagina."

He raised his eyebrows with his eyes shut. "Okay, easy now, Miss A, B, and C. We don't need to be quite so *graphic* at this moment. Or suspicious. I think I've made it clear that this is a big serious deal to me. I had to rewire my mind to go out with a white girl."

"Woman."

"*Maude*. So I want to know if said girl-woman wants babies. Because I do. I want kids, and it's not *complicated* for me to say it."

"So many things are less complicated for a guy to say."

"True."

"I need think about it. Maybe you can ask me again in California."

"All right."

"Don't forget."

"Won't."

I can't sleep. I keep seeing Gracie, her small fat hands, her untied bows. She's like an infatuation, a song you can't shake.

I get up and put my clothes back on. My father sounds like someone heaving up a chicken bone when he snores. It's so loud in the hallway, loud enough that the dogs in his room don't hear me pass by. I get into my car and drive. I drive past the lobster shack, over the tracks, past Neal's, which is dark upstairs and down, and through town. There is a cluster of Fords and Chevys outside Mel's Tavern, and a few sporty foreign cars outside the Captain's Table. Town and gown, the way it has always been in Ashing. I pass the apartment on Water Street and wave. There are lights on behind the curtains in my mother's room. I sometimes slept in her bed when we first moved in there and I couldn't fall asleep. I'd watch how she rocked herself to sleep, one hand around her waist, the other around her neck, a close embrace, the rocking short and shallow, a little rowboat. And then I'm on the highway. There are only trucks. I turn off when I see Howard Johnson's orange roof.

As I cross the parking lot there is a great clamor above me. I look up and a long thin slanting V of birds is moving just above the restaurant's cupola, talking all at once. Canada geese. Jonathan and

I taking turns with the binoculars. They pass directly over me, their voices raucous, deep and certain, excited for the trip. The sound is still thundering in my chest long after they've flown behind the trees.

Inside the Howard Johnson's, a few people are at the counter, ordering ice cream. The older woman at the register glances up and tells me to sit anywhere I like. She wears the orange and turquoise sailor cap pinned to her hair. I take the booth at the back on the right. This is where we sat. We ordered fried clams and a club sandwich. She wore her kerchief and her nervous smile. We had my bike and eight-tracks and the television in the car.

A waitress comes and takes my menu and brings me french fries and a garden salad. Four cops come through the door. The woman behind the counter greets them easily. The people getting ice cream give them more room than they need. They drink their coffees standing up. Their walkie-talkies beep and hiss at the same time. And then one of them puts his cup on the counter and walks over to my table.

I panic. Registration? Inspection sticker? Unpaid fine? I hate cops, hate being stopped by them, can never be natural or easy around them like the waitresses are. I have no idea how people charm their way out of a ticket. I can never be anything but sullen and humiliated when a cop appears at my car window.

"Daley?"

I manage to raise my head and nod.

He laughs at my guilt, my deep blush. "You don't have any idea who I am, do you?"

It never occurred to me that I could know him personally, an armed, barrel-chested, meaty-faced man in full uniform. There were two Ashing cops when I was little: the rangy one who looked a little like Gilligan and dated the girl at the Mug, and the red-headed one who came to the house whenever the alarm system was set off accidentally. This guy is neither. He is amused by my complete bewilderment.

"Jason Mullens," he says finally. "Patrick's buddy."

"Damn." While I remained in school, other people were going out and growing up and getting real jobs and wearing uniforms, for chrissake. "I cannot believe I know a cop."

He laughs again, and I stand and give him a hug. He is very hard and bumpy with his oblong chest and badge and buttons and buckles. I am used to slender, unshaven, underexercised men in flannel shirts. It's like being introduced to a different species.

He slides into the seat across from mine and puts his thick fore-arms on the table. My waitress brings him a coffee cup and fills it.

"Thanks, Amy," he says quietly, as if he is aware that he's a cliché, like something out of the *Andy Griffith Show,* but can't help his good manners.

"I'm stunned. You became a cop. I am sitting here across from a cop." It is so preposterous that wily little Jason Mullens has grown up into this that I feel completely comfortable, as if it isn't really happening. "Why on earth are you a cop?"

"It's kind of a long story." He glances over at his buddies. They're talking to an older couple, their backs to us. "I was planning to be a lawyer but then my dad's friend got me this job in a law firm for a summer during college and I watched these guys spend their time trying to get around the law for their clients. It really bugged me." He looks down at his hands; then he looks up, surprised that I'm wait-ing for him to say more. "I realized I wanted to uphold the law, not try to bend it."

"But you were such a rule-breaking hellion."

He lifts his eyes to the ceiling, smiling. "Especially at your house." His perfectly shaven cheeks are round and shiny.

"How is Patrick? I've been wanting to get in touch with him, but—" I don't know how to finish.

"Yeah, I heard about your dad and Catherine. I'm sorry. Patrick was here a couple of weeks ago, helping her move into her new place."

I heard she'd rented a carriage house north of town. But Patrick was here in Ashing and I didn't see him? Why hadn't I called him months ago?

"I didn't see him either," he says, seeing my disappointment. "I was away that weekend."

One of the other policemen is at the door, the other two already on the sidewalk outside. Jason holds up a finger and the last cop gives him an indulgent smile.

I can't believe he actually thinks Jason is trying to hit on me.

Then Jason says, "I'm off at midnight. You wanna do something?"

"At midnight?"

"Mel's is open until two."

So we meet at Mel's. I wait in my car until I see him pull up. He looks even broader in civilian clothes. He smells clean, his thick hair damp and combed straight down. Everyone knows him at the bar. He introduces me around. I watch Jason joust and parry reluctantly with the crowd. He's in his element but he worries about me. He tries to include me. He doesn't understand that it feels good to hold a beer bottle in a bar with people my age who are all a little too buzzed to care what I'm saying. It's been so long since I've had any alcohol that the beer takes full effect and pulls me away from myself just a little. Normally I don't like the feeling, but right now it's a relief. People crowd around Jason. Someone offers him a shot and he looks at me and turns it down. Someone says something quietly to him and he laughs until his face gets red. "I'll explain that one later," he says to me. Like Garvey, Jason has changed socioeconomic groups, and I'm interested in this. I hope we'll stay till closing, but instead of ordering another round he steers me out the door.

We go to his apartment, the second floor of a house on South Street. It smells like a gym. He runs around picking up the balled-up clothes and dirty glasses. He opens the windows and turns on a fan and hands me a beer. We sit on a red velour couch and he pulls

off his shirt as if wearing it was causing him pain. It is truly a rippling torso, wide and deep, with very little hair and tiny tight nipples,
tapering down into a narrow taut stomach with a deep clean belly
button. He takes my hand and lays it on his chest and I cannot pull
away. I have to know how it all feels. My fingers trace the skin across
his chest, pausing at the dip in the center, then moving to the far
side and over to his right arm which he is not flexing but is solid as
steel, wrapped in veins. And then I am kissing his hard warm stomach, pressing my tongue in the taut belly button, and he is hard
immediately and sighing and I feel his lips on my neck before he
lifts me in one quick motion right on top of him and we kiss, hard,
our teeth knocking, and then I hear Jonathan, slightly bemused,
taking everything in, the gun he surely has in the house, the uniforms, the absurdly inflated pale chest, saying, "What do you think
you are doing, tweet?" Jonathan, tracing my hip with his beautiful
finger, talking about babies. I stop kissing and rest my head on his
shoulder.

"I'm sorry, Jason. I'm so sorry."

His hands are moving all over me. "It's okay."

On one vacation, when I was in high school, I had a room right
next to my father and Catherine, separated by a very thin wall. "So
now you don't want it," I heard him say to her in the middle of the
night. "I thought you wanted it, but now you don't want it."

A vast heaviness weighs down my body.

"Really, it's okay, Daley."

He helps me find my shirt and shoes.

"It's my fault," he says when I'm at the door. "I took it too fast.
I misinterpreted the signals." It sounds like a line from some educa-
tional video on sexual communication. "I always had a little thing
for you." He's lying now, poor guy. No one had a thing for me back
then, not even a little one. He tries to hold my face in his hand to
gauge my distress, but I turn and get out the door.

20

I didn't have a boyfriend until college. Before that, the only time I can remember even the possibility of one was when Patrick came home from boarding school one weekend with a friend, After dinner that first night, Patrick asked me if I liked Cole. I said I thought so. He told me that Cole liked me, then teased me about how fast my face turned red. I waited for something to happen, but it never did, even though I liked him more and more. He was very funny and smart, quick but not mean. The three of us played Ping-Pong, saw a movie, went to the Peking Garden. I laughed at Cole's jokes and he laughed at mine, but nothing else happened. They took the train back to school on Sunday. The next time Patrick came home I asked him, jokingly, trying to hide the hours I'd agonized over it, what had made Cole change his mind about me, and Patrick looked at me oddly.

"It's like you don't get it," he said.

"Get what?"

"After I told you he liked you, everything you did said stay away."

I was stung and stunned by this. *Stay away.* I somehow said *stay away* with my outside while my inside was yelling *come here.*

"I cannot believe you made out with a cop. You really do have a thing for uniforms," Julie says.

"Please don't tell anyone." I mean Jonathan. If she is in touch with him. Which is a question I never ask. It's better for me not to know.

"So what are you doing on the Thursday before Columbus Day weekend?" she says.

"Not much. No, actually," I say, pretending to look at a calendar, "it's a very hectic day. The dogs are going in to have their toenails clipped."

"I cannot get there too soon."

"What?"

"My father's birthday present. A night in New York to celebrate my grandparents' fifty-fifth wedding anniversary, then a trip up the New England coast. Give me directions to your house."

"Whoever that was put a smile on your face," my father says.

"My friend Julie. She and her father are coming here next Thursday."

"To stay with us?"

"No, just for lunch. I think we should take them to the Lobster Shack."

"What's this *we* shit?"

"Oh, Dad, please join us. I want you to meet her. She's my very best friend."

"Is she your vewy vewy bestest fwiend? Bester than me and Maybelle?"

"It's a three-way tie," I say, rubbing Maybelle's little head.

"Where're they from?"

"Brooklyn. But he lives in San Francisco now and she lives in Albuquerque."

"San Francisco. He a fag?"

"Dad."

"I'm just wondering."

"He's had three wives."

"Jesus."

I don't bother to remind him that he is not far behind.

"What's he do?"

"He's a doctor." I didn't want to tell him that, either. He doesn't like being around strangers with successful careers. At least I was careful not to say Jewish psychiatrist.

On Thursday he is cranky all morning. The tractor isn't working properly. The new guy at the hardware store is useless. He screams at the dogs. I see him glance at the clock, like he used to, waiting for it to be drinking hour. I think he does it to get a rise out of me, but I don't react.

And then they are here, Julie leaping out of the car even before her father cuts the engine, dodging the dogs up the path, reaching me at the bottom of the porch stairs. She's cut her hair straight across at the jawline. She told me but I forgot. She's wearing new clothes. She looks different, older. She's a full professor now. It's disorienting, seeing her here in my yard. She is Michigan and card games and all-nighters and Jonathan on the floor with us because we never did get a kitchen table, all of us eating his $3 spaghetti. Her hug is tight. There are so many things I can't have back.

"This town is so cute! I'm not sure I ever knew it was on the water, I mean *right* on the water. I always pictured it so gloomy and sinister. And this house is enormous. It's like a B & B."

Her father comes up the walkway, tucking in the back of his shirt. "I'm starting to understand why even Berkeley might have paled in comparison." He kisses me on the cheek.

"It wasn't really a choice of geography, per se." I hear the sudden peevishness in my voice and soften it. "Thank you for making the detour for me."

"Hardly a detour. You were always part of the plan," he says.

I haven't seen Julie's father in a couple of years. He looks the same, a medium-sized man with a full head of silver hair he wears cropped square, a grown-out buzz cut. I wonder if he remembers the diamond-in-the-rough comment and what he will say after this visit. There's always the expectation on Julie's part that we will get along instantly. But it has always hurt a little to be around them.

My father comes out on the porch. I lead them up to meet him.

"You found us," he says, and puts out his hand. "Gardiner Amory."

"Alex Kellerman."

There's always tremendous subtext when two men of their generation shake hands. It's always a power grab. I watch my father accentuate his height advantage while Alex stands with his thick legs too far apart, as if he might need to crouch and spring.

"And this is Julie, Dad."

My father's shoulders soften and he bends his elbow as he takes her hand. "Great to meet you. I know Daley misses you a lot. Her housemate now isn't much fun."

I've never in my adult life introduced my father to anyone.

Alex peers in the house. He wants to have a look around, as I would in his place. But I only have a few hours with Julie and do not want to spend it in the New England WASP Museum. I suggest a walk on the beach and then lunch in town. Alex asks if he could use the restroom.

I walk him through the pantry and dining room to the bathroom off the den.

"The light's a little tricky," I say, punching the round black cylinder hard.

"Whoa," he says, noticing the team photographs. At the feet of the boys in the front row was always the same black board with white letters and numbers identifying the team and the date. 1940–1949 were the years accounted for at St. Paul's, and I knew that wouldn't slip Julie's father's notice. Two great-uncles of Julie's had died at Treblinka while my father was at a fancy boarding school.

"Which one is your dad?" he asks, tapping the glass of the Football Thirds, 1941.

I put my finger on the smallest boy in front, looking warily ahead but not at the camera.

"He looks scared, doesn't he? Imagine having been shipped away from your mother at such a young age. Hey, here he looks about twelve and already on varsity," he says, tapping another picture.

"He was always good at tennis."

"He's half the size of his teammates."

"He was really small, and then he shot up. Look." I point to a photograph on the other side of the bathroom, near the sink. In it my father is on the far right, his hair darker and his face much narrower, holding one of the oars, the tallest man on the team. He looks as if he has better things to do than stand around having his photograph taken by some moron.

"It's a real slice of history, isn't it?" he says.

"One privileged sliver of it, I suppose." All the St. Paul's boys stare at me, fresh cut grass on their cleats. Then I remember Alex wants to go to the bathroom and I quickly leave him to it.

On the porch, my father and Julie seem to be talking about pool vacuums. He's making an effort with her. He's facing her directly, not looking off somewhere like he often does with people, and bending toward her to make sure he hears her response. He asks if she's made some friends in Albuquerque yet, and she says she thought in a warmer climate people would be more approachable, but the people in her apartment building are always rushing downstairs with mountain bikes on their shoulders, no time to chat.

"You'll have to get yourself a mountain bike, I guess," my father says.

"Yup. Right about when hell freezes over."

My father laughs. Julie, I see now, is the kind of woman my father would call a real pistol.

⁕ ⁕ ⁕

We get in their rental car, the men in front.

"So here we are with our fathers," I say quietly.

"Just another regular day," Julie says.

We look at the backs of their heads and laugh.

I point out the Vance sisters' driveway.

"The ones who called each other mother and father," Julie says, as if it's from a book she read a long time ago.

I show her Mallory's parents' house, and then, quietly, Patrick's old house. The beach lot is full so we park in the driveway of a summer house that has been empty for years. All the green shutters have been pulled closed.

"It's like the Ramsays' house," Alex says, getting out of the car.

"'Will you fade?'" Julie says. "'Will you perish?'"

"'We remain!'" Alex bellows.

My father flashes me a look: *They're not playing with a full deck, are they?*

The ocean is across the street, booming with waves. Alex stops before stepping onto the sand. "Magnificent."

Julie and I take off our sandals and let the fathers go ahead of us.

"So who's the guy with the mountain bike?" I ask.

"What?"

"The guy who won't talk to you."

She crosses her arms. The wind is blowing her short hair into a short funnel. "Damn. How'd you know?"

"I've never heard you complain about people not being *approachable*." Julie could make friends with a barnacle.

"He lives in the apartment above me. Alone. But I haven't been able to speak to him."

"What?"

"I know, it's weird. I just get all—bashful."

I laugh into the wind. "We need to track this. This is a first. He's bringing out your tortoise side."

"It's so good to see you." She slips her arm through mine, and I squeeze her to me. "I'm trying to get a sense of your days here."

"My father marked his ninetieth day in AA two weeks ago. It's a big deal."

"I was talking about *your* days," she says, but the men have stopped to wait for us so I don't have to answer. What could I tell her? That in three and half months I'd written less than three pages of a nonacademic article?

"I love the proportions of this beach."

"The proportions, Pop?"

He shrugs. He likes to be teased by her. "Some beaches are too long and skinny, some you have to walk a mile to the water. This one is just right."

"The Platonic ideal of beach?"

"Exactly. And see that island out there, slightly off center? There always has to be something asymmetrical within the concept of perfection. Like Julie's nose."

"Daddy!" she says, covering it. It bends slightly to the right.

He wraps his arm around her and kisses her on the forehead. "Asymmetrical perfection, my love. Nothing more, nothing less."

My father and I walk back to the car behind them.

"Nice guy," my father says. "Did you know he was a shrink?"

"I did."

"He told me a story about a guy who came to see him for a few years. Passionate fly fisherman. He'd bring his box of flies to every appointment, and that's what they'd do: go through each fly, what it caught, what time of the year you could use it. The guy can't ever say why he's there, can't answer that question. Two years go by, and one day the guy holds up a fly and says, 'This is the fly my son tied the day before he died.' Christ, that's a story, isn't it?"

At lunch we all order lobsters, except my father, who ribs Alex for wearing his bib.

"This is a decent shirt," Alex says.

"I just hope we don't see anyone I know."

"You can tell them I'm your retarded cousin from Akron."

"Daddy!"

"Excuse me, Jules. So how'd you end up here in Ashing, Gardiner?"

"My wife told me we were moving out of Boston, and the next thing I knew the vans were at the door."

Alex laughs. "It's like that with women, isn't it? They know what they want."

"And what they don't want," my father says, looking down at his paper plate.

I ask whom they're visiting in Maine, and Alex tells us about his friend from med school who has set up clinics in war-torn areas. They're lucky to be catching him in the country. He describes his own visit to the clinic in Guatemala and the experience of using a translator for therapy, how he was able to be much more aware of the person's emotions as they were speaking to him because of the delay in meaning. Julie and I have many questions for him, about the conditions and the civil war, and his answers just stir up more questions. My father eats his hot dogs and nods and says, "Is that right?" several times, but he's not listening. He has a hard time re-laxing. His leg jiggles continuously beside me. He's like a boy in school waiting for the bell to ring, or, if you look closely, like an animal who's not certain there's not a predator nearby.

After plates are cleared and fingers cleaned with lemon-scented wipes, Alex gets out a small set of watercolor tubes and a small black notebook with thick pages. He looks over my shoulder at the harbor and hastily dabs paint onto a page. My father insists on paying the bill.

He and I sit in the back on the way home to Myrtle Street. The maples along both sides of the road are old and flourishing, impossibly tall, their leaves just starting to turn. My father rubs his thumb on a seam of his pants.

I invite them in, but Alex says they have to be in Wiscasset by five. It's Julie's turn to go to the bathroom, so I take her in the house and wait for her in the kitchen while our fathers talk in the yard.

When she comes out she says, "I thought if I came here and saw you it would all make sense, what you decided."

"And that didn't happen?"

"That man is doing just fine. You don't need to be here, Daley."

"He puts on a good act. And he *is* getting better. He's growing."

"I'm worried you're waiting for something from him that he can't ever give you. And if that's not it, I just hope you understand that your life and your growth is every bit as important as his."

I can't bear another parting lecture at the door. "You need to think of me now as a sort of Charlotte Brontë figure, the unmarried daughter of the town vicar."

"Please don't say that, even in jest. I don't know why you've thrown everything away." She looks like she's about to cry.

"Tell me you wouldn't drop everything to be with your father if he needed you."

"He wouldn't *let* me."

"If your father broke his back and couldn't get out of bed, you'd be right there for him."

"He wouldn't let me stay. It would break his heart if I lost something I'd worked for my whole adult life because of him."

"Your father must have a lot of people he could lean on, but my father has no one but me right now. I'm it."

"I understand that it's important to you to believe that."

"Spare me the therapy-speak. I am fixing something with my father that got destroyed when I was eleven years old. What job title could ever compare to that?"

"I'm not talking about the job, Daley. You can get another job. I'm talking about Jonathan. You two are what all the rest of us are looking for."

"Don't idealize us. It was a flawed relationship, obviously, if he couldn't understand my decision."

"*I* can't understand your decision. No one understands what you've done."

"But you are still speaking to me. Jonathan has disappeared."

"I think for some reason you're scared of what you have with Jonathan."

"He's gone, Julie. It's over. Use the past tense."

"No."

"Do you know where he is?"

"No."

"You really haven't heard from him?" My heart is slamming now.

"No."

I realize I was counting on her to tell me today where he's gone and how he's doing. The big fist of pain shifts and forces up a few tears. She puts her arms around me and makes it burn even more. She's leaving and Jonathan is really gone.

"Let's make you a plan," she says softly. "How much longer do you think you'll stay here?"

"I don't know how long he'll need me."

"Then you've got to decide how long you want to be needed."

Alex calls from the porch. He's worried about traffic.

"I'll call you tonight," she says.

I wipe my eyes and walk her to the car. My father says goodbye, telling them to stop by whenever they're in the Northeast again. He looks spent. I know he'll go right up for a nap after they drive away.

I hug them both. Alex hands me a watercolor. It's not of the harbor as I expected, but of me and Julie with her shorn hair. We're leaning in, talking. There's little I recognize in his rendering of me, but he's captured Julie's mouth and her perfectly imperfect nose with only a few brushstrokes.

That night, after AA and supper, we watch the Red Sox play Cleveland. My father is pissed at Clemens, pissed at the announcers. He thinks they talk too much. At the seventh-inning stretch, he takes his glass in for more soda. He lets the dogs out and then back in. He returns, and when the players are back on the field, he watches in silence, his breathing heavy. Mo Vaughn makes a double play, and he says, "Now that's how you do it." There is something slightly self-satisfied in his voice that makes me turn. He meets my eye, raises his eyebrows slightly. He's been on his best behavior all day, and he hasn't said a mocking thing about Julie or her father since they left. But honestly, I don't know anymore if he is fucking with me.

21

By November, Neal is still my lone friend in Ashing, but I only see him when I go to his shop. The rest of his life is a mystery to me.

"Are you really as reclusive as you seem?" I ask him.

"Pretty much."

"Were you always?"

"Not so much." He's particularly preoccupied today, watching the cars through the door, fidgeting with a pen cap. The skin under his eyes looks bruised. I'm probably not looking so well myself. The cold has brought on doubt and fear. I cannot seem to make a plan. The dead star feeling has taken hold. It makes everything feel struck, as if my whole body is a big bell that won't stop ringing. I sleep less and less. I roam the house at night. I look for hidden bottles. I am ashamed of my lack of trust in my father, when I always thought the problem between us was his lack of trust in me. I write more fragments in my Jonathan notebook. My heartbeat is too fast and too heavy. What will become of me? At times it seems there is only a paper-thin wall between me and permanent full-blown panic. Neal calms me. If I described how I felt I know he would say he feels that way too.

"I heard you had a drink with Jason Mullens."

I laugh. "Two months ago."

"You gonna go out with him again?"

"No."

"Has he called?"

"He's left a couple of messages. He keeps calling himself Officer Mullens on the machine. My father must think there's a warrant out for my arrest."

Neal pretends to laugh. Then he stands up and says he has to go. He's going to close the shop for a lunch break.

Two days later I'm in Goodale's parking lot, loading groceries into the car, when a station wagon pulls up next to me, a bright red French armoire strapped to its roof.

Neal's mother, who usually drives a Volkswagen Fox since she gave up the Pinto, leaps out. "Isn't it just divine?" she says, and hugs me hard. There is an awful stench to her, pungent, animal. "Isn't it to die for?"

I give the armoire the attention she requires. I stroke its unpainted feet, marvel at its size. I can't picture such an enormous and loud piece of furniture in their small house on July Street. "Wow," I say.

"It has about a thousand shelves on the sides. It is crucial to getting things organized *chez moi.*" There is something extra-intense about the way she is looking at me, as if I am just about to reveal a great secret. She's got the wrong person. I've been cleaning bathrooms all morning. I have very little to impart.

"It's been the most amazing day. I'm not sure I've ever had a day like it, Daley. I discovered something. Something about stockings."

"Stockings?"

"It's really a miracle. And no one ever talks about it. I don't think anyone else knows. You can just piss. Did you know that? You can piss in your pantyhose and it doesn't leak. It just sort of evaporates. I've been doing it all week. Nobody can tell! But I've got to get home now. I promised Neal I wouldn't go out and I did, and now he's going to be furious with me." She looks delighted by the idea. "You know he won the Renaissance Cup, don't you?"

"I do know that." I smile. "I remind him of that more than he'd like."

"Oh, he is such a *pill,* isn't he? You have no idea until you have a son what they put you through. But they're better than a husband, that's for sure. My husband just disappeared. *Poof.* Gone."

"Really?"

"He does this on occasion. Huge drama queen. 'I just can't abide this and that' sort of thing. You know that store almost didn't take my check, for crying out loud. They are a bunch of asses on sticks. Filthy French mongrels." She looks at me as if I've just appeared. "Oh, Daley, it is so good to have you back home." She pulls me to her again and, now that I know what the smell is, it's worse. "We need your youth and beauty and inspiration in this tired old town." She is hollering in my ear. "See?" she says, pulling away, looking at the ground between her feet. "I did it again and nothing came out."

After she leaves, I drive straight to Neal's. The shop is closed and he doesn't answer his upstairs bell. I wonder if he is out trying to find her. This is what my father meant when he said Neal has not had it easy. I go back in the afternoon and he still isn't there. I leave a note. The next day I leave another. The shop is closed every day that week. Neal's upstairs lights are never on. I wonder how bad it gets and how it ends.

Now that the evenings are shorter, my father goes to bed earlier. The first night Neal comes over it's just past nine and my father is already asleep. He taps on the back door quietly. At first I think it's the wind, and the door isn't shut all the way. But there is Neal's face, bending to fit in one of the panes of glass.

"I see you, Shirley Temple," I say, before I open the door. I'm surprised by how relieved I am to see him.

"Hey," he says softly, his voice gutting out. He has his hands in his pockets.

I step onto the porch to hug him and he falls into me. His breaths are deep but not smooth.

"I'm so sorry," I say.

"She told me she saw you. I work so hard to keep her away from town when she's like that."

"Where is she now?"

"McLean's. She always ends up there. They pump her back up with lithium and give her a good talking to about taking it regularly even when she feels she doesn't need it, *especially* when she feels she doesn't need it. And then they send her home." He doesn't lift his head from my shoulder. I touch his hair, too gently for him to notice. "My dad couldn't handle it. He's never been able to handle it. Her mania ignites some sort of terror in him. Now I just tell him to get out, and I call him when it's over. I don't know how she was when you saw her, but she can get viciously angry. It's crazy. And then she can become a puddle of syrupy sickness, on and on about how you are the most sacred, the most perfect being ever to be put on earth. I remember once when I was little she tried to convince me that I was Jesus Christ. I was so scared. I didn't want to be Jesus. I didn't want all those holes in my body."

I hold him tight.

After his breathing has smoothed out, I ask him if he wants to come in for some tea.

"I've been inside for so many days. Do you mind if we stay out here?"

I get a jacket and we go over to the lawn chairs by the pool. The pool is covered now by a taut green sheath, but we haven't put the chairs in the shed yet.

Neal sits in one of the recliners and pulls me down with him. We lie sideways, his chest against my back, his breath in my hair. It feels so good to be held.

"Is this okay?" he asks.

"Yes."

"I hate seeing her strapped down. I don't care what she says. I can tune that out. But the look on her face. And her body all cinched up."

"How often does it happen?"

"The longest she's gone between episodes is two and half years. But normally it's a shorter cycle."

"I had no idea."

"People have been discreet. It's a good town in that way."

"And this was happening when we were in school together?"

"All my life. They used to pack me off to my aunt's in Maryland for the summer."

"Every summer?"

"The bad ones."

He comes most nights after that, tapping at the windowpane, lying with me on a lawn chair in the dark. When the nights grow colder he brings a blanket. We look up at the autumn stars and can only name a few. We spoon, and sometimes we push against each other slightly, but we never kiss.

His mother comes home from McLean's and he opens his shop back up. "No one even noticed I was closed," he says.

We talk, but it's more like thinking aloud. I'm often not sure what I've actually said. On clear nights the stars pierce a million holes in the darkness. Jonathan said once that the stars made him feel powerful.

"That's weird," Neal says. "They make me feel minuscule."

"Me, too. Maybe it's an Ashing thing."

"Do they make you think of God?"

"No."

"You don't believe in God?"

"If there is a God, we haven't been introduced yet." I stare at the dark vault above, the little pinpricks of light that are really balls of fire, many bigger than the earth. All these things we're meant to believe. "Stars just make me think of death." I tell him about the first time I had the dead star feeling. I don't say I have it now, that it seems to have set up camp in my chest.

He says he likes the theory that the universe expands and then contracts, over and over, that your life comes around again, every sixty billion years or so.

Another night I ask him, "Are you writing a novel that begins freshman year of college and ends at a Pottery Barn?"

He doesn't answer and I start laughing.

"I hate you." He squeezes me harder. "I hate being a cliché."

He has three different jackets, his brother's old leather one, a brown canvas one, and a red-and-black wool lumberjack one. The lumberjack one is an extra large. He wraps it around me and buttons me in, my back against his chest. Sometimes I see him during the day on the street in that jacket and I smile.

"Is she like your mom?"

"Who?"

"The Dead Girl."

"No. Yes. I mean she's not cuckoo crazy, but she has a lot of energy."

"My mother always thought it was important to be bubbly."

"I like bubbly. But it has to come with some gravitas."

"And the Dead Girl has gravitas?"

"Being dead helps."

"Tell me her name."

"No."

I make guesses: Megan, Susan, Leslie. He says no to all of them. "Good. I hate the name Leslie. No, that's not true. I hate the name Lesslie. Lezlie's fine. But if you ever call a Lesslie Lezlie look out. It's spelled the same so how are you going to know?"

He takes his hand off my stomach and puts it over my mouth. "Her name's not Leslie."

"Molly?" I say, through his hands.

"Nope. No more guesses. You've used up your weekly ration."

The next night he says, "I didn't say you were concave. I said I wouldn't *care* if you were concave. Which you weren't. And certainly aren't now."

"Now he notices," I say.

And then there is the night we hear the geese, just a few, not even in a V. They are flying too low and at first they make no sound. And then I hear it, a thin frail cry and then another one, more dire, starving maybe.

"They're too late," Neal says. "They're not going to make it." And then says, "Hey, hey," but I can't stop crying for those geese.

One night when I'm buttoned into his red and black jacket he asks, "What would happen if you rolled over and faced me?"

"I don't know."

"I don't know either." The smoke of his breath drifts past my ear up toward the stars.

Then he doesn't come for three nights in a row. I stop by his shop. It's only four-thirty but it's nearly dark. Streetlights and headlights are all on. It's cold enough to snow. I'm wearing my old Michigan parka. I got it at the secondhand shop for ten dollars. It's orange and slightly misshapen, and Jonathan called me the UFO when I wore it.

Neal is with a customer when I push open the door, their backs to me, looking up at a shelf near the ceiling. They turn at the same time. Neal grins at me, apologetic, grateful, happy. The woman's cheeks are flushed. There is a suitcase near Neal's desk.

"The Dead Girl," I say, before I can stop myself.

"The Dead Girl," he says.

"*What?*" she says, wheeling around. She is lovely, of course, with round brown eyes and a wry smile.

"I'm Daley." I put out my hand.

"You really call me that?" she says to him.

"What's your real name?"

"Don't tell her!" Neal says, but too late.

"Anne."

"Anne?" I look at him. I could have gotten Anne.

He shrugs.

"It's an awful name," she says. "I hate it."

"Not as bad as Lesssslie, though." He looks straight at me, seeing if I understand how it is. I do. I always have.

"Not half as bad," I say.

22

And then it's Thanksgiving. Cold, overcast, the way I always remember Thanksgiving in New England to be. Despite weekly urgings, I couldn't get Garvey to come. I did get him to talk to Dad. It was a brief conversation, stiff but benign. Maybe, Garvey told me, he would come for Christmas.

My father has his meeting at one that day, and then we go to the Bridgetons for lunch.

They live north of town, down a long wooded road. All the leaves are gone from the trees. Every one. When we're almost there, my father says they talked about Grace today.

"Grace?" I don't know who Grace is.

The car stops. The road has ended at the ocean and the Bridgetons' house. "Patricia said that grace is accepting love, that we all spend so much more time resisting love than just taking love. It's funny, isn't it, to think of rejecting love. What a stupid thing to do. But I guess we do it all the time."

"I guess we do." I am very flat. I hate Thanksgiving.

"Yeah. Well." He opens the car door. "Let's eat some turkey."

The Bridgetons have their own rocky beach below the green clapboard house. I might have said I'd never been here before, until I stand on their lawn looking down at the rocks and remember climbing on them with an older blond boy, falling down and scraping my knees. Through a window I see the mudroom with a sink in it where my mother washed my cuts and put on Band-Aids.

My father and I cooked and baked that morning: green beans, garlic mashed potatoes, and an apple pie. He can now make five different main courses, and he does his own laundry. We walk around to the front of the house with our platters of food. My father insisted I dress up a bit, so I'm wearing my interview outfit, a beige suit and boots with heels.

Carly Bridgeton opens the door.

"Uncle Gardiner!" she says, and gives my father a big hug. Carly is his goddaughter. I forgot that. She's the oldest of the Bridgetons' children, well in her thirties, but the quilted vest and knee socks she's wearing take twenty years off her.

"Hey there, little peanut," he says.

"Look at you," she says. "You look great, Uncle G."

And he does. His skin is a tawny pink, and his eyes clear and alert. He's gained a little weight. He looks fit and strong and a good deal younger than sixty-one.

"You remember Daley."

"Of course I do." She hugs me, too. "We made cootie catchers together, remember?" But I don't. Her narrow nose and big freckles are not familiar to me exactly, but if I saw her on a street in a big city, I would think I knew her. She looks like a lot of people I grew up with.

Carly takes our coats and leads us into the living room. On the pink chintz sofas are the two Bridgeton boys, both in coat and tie, pouring handfuls of Chex mix into their mouths. They stand when they see us, wiping their salty hands on their pants before shaking. I can't remember which one is the one who is doing "who knows what" in Colorado. They both seem to be what Ashing Academy followed by a New England boarding school and a small liberal arts college conspire to produce: clean-cut, self-deprecating, socially agile men. Together we identify who was just a year older than Garvey (Scott) and who was just a year younger (Hatch), who had been on

Dad's undefeated Little League team three years in a row (Hatch), and who remembered Garvey winning the declamation contest with Kipling's "Gunga Din" (all of us).

Mr. Bridgeton comes in the room then, lurching, his right foot in a blue cast, the toe of his white sock poking out. On this little patch of sock, someone has drawn a smiley face. A scotch and soda rattles in his hand.

"Holy Christ!" my father yells. "What happened to you?"

"Oh, just a little run-in with a moose."

The boys laugh and Hatch fetches a doorstop at the other end of the room. It's a brick covered in needlepoint, the head of a moose stitched in brown and beige on the top.

"Ouch," I say.

"Tripped right over the goddamn thing in broad daylight. Never saw it coming." Mr. Bridgeton is looking above our heads and smiling helplessly. He is clearly enjoying his painkillers.

I hear the pulse of a food processor and excuse myself to help Mrs. Bridgeton.

"Don't go in there unarmed!" Hatch says.

Scott offers me the cheese knife.

The kitchen is small, the pea green color of so many Ashing kitchens in the fifties. Mrs. Bridgeton is putting pecans on top of mashed sweet potatoes carefully smoothed into a fluted pie dish. She has a cocktail on the table, too, nearly drained.

"It smells good in here," I say. It does. It smells like our kitchen did when my mother was making the Thanksgiving meal.

"Oh, Daley, I'm glad you're here." She kisses me on the cheek. Her own cheek is warm and smells like baby powder. "And look at you!" I can see her struggle for a way to compliment the severe colorless outfit.

"My father made me wear it," I say, to let her off the hook.

"He did? Well, you look lovely." Her voice grows quiet. "How is he?"

I reach into the bag of pecans and begin another circle inside the one she is finishing. "He's doing really well. This week he started coaching basketball with this youth group. He loves it." Kenny, who I recently discovered is my father's sponsor, told him about the opening.

"I just wish Hugh would take him back."

"I don't think he'd want to go back to an office. He enjoys this much more." He told me a few nights ago that coaching was what he'd always wanted to do full-time, but it wasn't considered a respectable choice of profession. "Screw respectable, Dad. Follow your passion," I said.

"Well, he's wonderful with children," Mrs. Bridgeton says. "We all know that."

"My mother used to make this."

"I know she did. I gave her the recipe." She reaches in the bag for more pecans. "She and I were friends, you know, before she got involved with the Democrats and all the rest." She says the word Democrats the way my father does, as if they are a cult that whisks away decent people.

"And then you slather it with brown sugar and broil it?"

"You bake it and then at the very end you broil it."

"My mother sometimes burned it."

"It's easy to burn. It goes from brown to black very quickly."

"Thank you for having us here. It's nice."

"Holidays are hard alone."

He's not alone. I want to say. I'm not alone. I wish she were capable of appreciating his progress.

"Who's in here?"

My father ducks to come through the low doorway.

Mrs. Bridgeton brushes back her hair and smoothes down her green dress.

"Just us Thanksgiving elves," she says.

My father is handsome in his charcoal suit, crisp white shirt, and tie with the blue and green fish on it. "Look at this feast." He eyes the vegetables in bowls, the golden turkey lit up in the oven.

"Same meal I've been making for thirty-nine years," she says, wiping her hands on a dishcloth.

"If it ain't broke," my father says absently, looking out the window at the gray water. I know he wants to drink with the rest of them in the living room. I can feel it as if the craving were in my own body. I want to hold his hand and tell him it will pass. Be strong, I'd tell him. The holidays are the hardest.

"I bought a little bottle of bubbly to have with dessert. Can you have just a few drops, Gardiner?"

I feel like she's just soaked me in ice water. I hold back. It is not easy.

My father shakes his head. "Nope. I'll stick with my seltzer."

I smile at him but he doesn't look at me.

"Daley," she says, handing me a silver water pitcher, "would you mind filling up the water glasses in the dining room? We'll be ready to eat soon."

In the dining room there are big bowls of orange and green gourds and place cards in the shape of turkey tails. I'm seated on Mr. Bridgeton's right and Scott's left. My father is down at the other end of the table, next to Mrs. Bridgeton. Everyone around him has a highball glass full of alcohol. Why were we here among people who could not see his struggle, who probably didn't even believe it was a disease? I feel I've failed him, failed to find him an alternative set of friends, another way of living.

Eventually we all take our places and pile our plates with food. Scott and I ask each other polite questions. On the other side of the table, Hatch and my father reminisce about the Pirates. Mrs. Bridgeton indicates with her napkin and the word *gooseberry* that Mr. Bridgeton has some gravy on his cheek. They all drink steadily but no one seems particularly drunk. No one gets angry. No one's personality changes. They tease but they don't snipe. They seem genuinely glad to be together. When I ask how often they all see each other, Hatch says not enough, but it turns out that none of them have ever missed a Thanksgiving or a Christmas, and they spend at least two weeks together every summer at their cabin in the Berkshires and another ten days in the Bahamas in March.

Afterward we all, minus Mr. Bridgeton and his bad foot, take a walk down to the water. The tide is out on the small beach, the sand a wet dark gray. You can see more islands from their point than you can from Ruby Beach. Hatch names them for me. The others have a rock-skimming contest. Scott leans back and flicks one across the shallows.

"That's a beauty!" my father calls out as Scott's stone bounces across the skin of gray water. "Nine."

Hatch tells me about the software start-up he's been working for in Boulder. I have no idea what he's talking about. "What about you? How long are you planning to live here?"

"Not much longer." I feel defensive and tired. "Maybe through the holidays." Is this true? My future is the exact color of the ocean.

Mrs. Bridgeton picks up a stone and throws it badly, though it manages to skip twice before sinking.

"Not bad," my father says gently. "You'll get another try in a minute."

Mrs. Bridgeton is flushed and smiling.

On the way home we see Jason Mullens standing at the window of a cruiser, talking to the driver. He looks up when our car passes and his hand shoots up in a wave.

"You going out with that guy?"

"No."

"Why's he looking at you like that then? And leaving messages."

"Oh, it was stupid. I had a drink with him one night."

"You had a *drink* with him one night? When was that?"

"Last summer."

"You snuck out?'

"I didn't *sneak* out, Dad. I couldn't sleep and I ran into him and we went to Mel's."

"To Mel's. He's a real class act."

"He's a good guy."

"Oh yeah? You going to marry a cop?"

"I'm not interested in Jason."

"Who else have you had drinks with? You've got me going to meetings every damn night and you're out boozing it up all over town."

"One night, Dad. One beer."

We turn down Myrtle Street. It is such a grim afternoon. I have to think of something to lighten our mood. We can't go back to the house feeling like this.

"You better watch out yourself," I say. "I think Barbara Bridgeton is getting a little crush on you."

"What? No," he says. I've amused him. "Now you've really lost your marbles."

"You better watch it, is all I'm saying, or you'll be eating a hell of a lot of quiche and casseroles."

The next day I call Mrs. Bridgeton to thank her.

"Well, it was wonderful to have you both here. Perhaps we can start a tradition."

"Next year, our house," I say. Am I joking? I'm not even sure. "I think it was good for us to be with your family. Dad's in great spirits today." I can see him out the window. He woke up full of energy, vowing to fix the garage door and rake up the last of the leaves, two things he's been putting off for weeks.

"I'm pleased to hear that, Daley."

I feel suddenly close to her, hearing the sincerity in her voice. I think of the meals she brought over at the beginning and the hydrangeas for his party. A lot of women in Ashing ask about my father in passing, but Mrs. Bridgeton really cares about him. She might not understand about alcoholism, but she does want to help. I feel the need to apologize for my resistance to her.

"Thank you. Thank you for everything."

"Well, we're right here when you need us. We've known your dad for a long time. I knew him before your mother did."

"I didn't know that."

"He was Ben's roommate's doubles partner. He had a number of different girls, you know. And then he brought your mother to the Harvest Dance, and that was it. You never saw him with anyone else after that."

"What was he like back then?"

"Just like he is now. Kind, sweet, honorable. I hope you find a man just like him someday soon, Daley."

Over the weekend it snows. The snow blankets the cover of the pool and lies in raised, even stripes on top of the plastic bands of the lawn chair.

Neal has gone to Vermont with Anne.

My father comes home from coaching on Monday with a large ziplock bag of cookies.

"Where'd you score those?" I ask.

"Barbara gave them to me."

"Where'd you run into her?"

"I stopped by their house on my way home."

Wednesday he's got a coconut angel food cake. Thursday a shepherd's pie. I haven't seen shepherd's pie since grade school: underlayer of overcooked hamburger, overlayer of mashed potatoes, sprinkle of paprika.

On Friday my father stands with another dish in his arms and tells me that he and Barbara Bridgeton are going to be married.

I burst out laughing. "What are you talking about?"

"I asked her and she said yes."

"Dad, she's already married. And so are you, technically."

"She's leaving him." He looks at his watch. "She's telling him tonight."

"Dad. You can't break up a family like that."

"She loves me. She told me. She wants to be married to me."

"Ben Bridgeton is one of your oldest friends."

"She's not happy with him. I can't help that." He puts the dish down and pinches the cellophane tighter along the edges. "That's not my fault."

"Remember in AA they say you shouldn't get into a relationship for at least a year?"

"AA says a lot of things. Barbara doesn't think I ever had a real drinking problem, not like the rest of them."

I feel the blood leave my hands and legs. I try to keep my voice steady. "And what do you think?"

"I don't know what I think. I don't think I've been able to think for myself for a long time."

My throat and chest start buzzing. The kitchen feels very small. "Because of me?"

"There's just been a lot of noise. Everyone talking at me. Talking talking talking." There is a look on his face that I recognize from the early years with Catherine, a sort of predatory flush. He'd had

sex with Barbara Bridgeton that afternoon. And then, like a good
boy, he'd asked her to marry him. "And what does any of it matter
to you?" he says. "You're leaving after the holidays, aren't you?"

Is that what started all this?

"Do you want me to?"

He doesn't answer.

"I just said that to Hatch because it was something to say. You
need to get to your meeting. It's late."

He looks at his watch again. "Barbara's going to call."

"I think you should talk to Kenny, Dad. That's what a sponsor's
for."

"Fuck Kenny," he says, but he drives down to the church.

Barbara doesn't call. We eat a silent dinner. I go to my room
and hear him yelling at the Patriots. "Don't listen to those ass wipes!"
And then, "You moron! You fucking butterfingers!" and finally, "Yes,
yes, there you go, *yes*!" He stays up and watches the entire game
and then the news.

At eleven-thirty the phone rings. He gets it before the second
ring. He snaps off the TV but I can't hear anything. I get out of bed
and move slowly to the top of the stairs.

"It's all right. It's all right. Sweetie, it's going to be all right."

After a long silence, he says, "I do. You know I do. I always
will. We's gonna be okay, you and me."

The next day Barbara Bridgeton arrives with two baby-blue
hardshell suitcases. My father drags them upstairs while I make
us some tea. Barbara stands near the dishwasher, her coat still on.
I do everything slowly, to delay the moment when I have to turn
and face her.

"I know how strange this must be for you, Daley," she says to
my back, "but I've loved him—I've loved your whole family—for as
long as I can remember." Her voice breaks, and I hear her drop into

a chair. "Please be on our side. Someone needs to be on our side." The sound of her weeping is awful. I think of Thanksgiving and her boys in coats and ties and the brick covered in needlepoint. It had been their thirty-sixth Thanksgiving in that house, Scott told me.

"Have you talked to your children about all this?"

She nods. Her crying quickens.

"They're having a hard time with it?"

She nods again more vigorously. "Scott hung up on me. Hatch and Carly listened, but they think I'm being rash."

"You are both being very rash."

"We're not teenagers. We know what we want."

"My father does not know what he wants. You have to understand this. He has a lot of work ahead of him."

"I don't want him to do any work. He's perfect the way he is."

"I know to outsiders he appears that way but—"

"I'm hardly an outsider, Daley."

Somehow he has hidden vast swaths of his personality from people who do not live with him. We hear him cross the dining room, enter the pantry. She wipes her face and stands up.

He hugs her and she starts crying again and he tells her he has cleaned out a bureau in his room for her. I slip out of the room.

Barbara insists on making dinner that night. She says she needs something to do with herself. There is a tenderloin in the fridge, but she has me go down to Goodale's for cubes of lamb and some heavy cream. It's clear she doesn't want to go herself. Word has probably already gotten out about where she's shacking up. She is right. I can tell by the way Mrs. Goodale greets me, her voice a bit louder, with just a hint of mischief in it.

When I get home with the groceries, they are upstairs again. They already took what Barbara called a siesta after lunch. I take the dogs for a walk to the beach. It's freezing. I don't like sand and snow mixed together. It seems unnatural. I don't let the dogs off their leashes; they'll try to swim. They strain toward the water. We are the only beings in sight.

If I move out now, my father will stop going to AA. It won't last with Barbara. They'll have their fling and she'll return to her good solid family. I need to stay right here and hold his place so he won't have to start all over again after she leaves him.

When he puts on his coat for the meeting that night, Barbara asks, "Why is it held at seven? Why right at dinnertime?"

I wait for my father to tell her that he never eats before eight, but he doesn't. He just shrugs.

"Maybe it's because that's when people really want a drink," I say.

"I see," she says with a pout.

When he comes home she wants to know if anyone she knows was there.

"That's the anonymous part," I say.

My father separates the lamb from the sauce, eats a few bites, then says he's full.

He leans back in his chair and looks at me. "You don't wear your hair back like that very often, do you?"

"No."

"That's a good thing. You've got some big ears."

This is the first criticism of me he's made in a long time. It burns a little, but I don't let him see that. "I'm pretty sure I know where I got them."

"Oh, you do, do you?"

"Garvey's got them too. We measured once. Whose do you think were the bigger, Garvey's or mine?"

"Yours."

"Nope. Garvey by three-eighths of an inch."

He gets up and rustles around in a kitchen drawer. "Here we go." He holds up a ruler to my left ear "Two and three quarters."

I do the same to his. "Three and one-eighth."

He raises his arms straight up. "The biggest ears in the world!"

"Don't I get a chance to compete?" Barbara asks.

We look at her ears. They're tiny.

"Nah," we say at the same time, and laugh.

The next morning Barbara wants to help me unload the dishwasher. Dad is outside shoveling out the cars. I tell her to sit and finish her coffee, but she wants to know where everything goes. I don't want to show her. I don't want her tell me it would be better to have the mugs closer to the coffeepot. But she doesn't. She holds up a plate with pink flowers and a gold rim and tells me it was the breakfast china my father's mother gave my parents for their wedding.

"I remember your mother opening up the boxes of it at the shower." And then she puts the plate on the counter. "I wish you wouldn't focus on your father's flaws, Daley."

"What?"

"It's not good for his self-esteem."

"Are you talking about his ears?"

"Yes, that's one thing."

"I think it's great to be able to laugh at your own small irregularities."

"He has beautiful ears. And so do you. If you really want to help your dad, build him up, don't knock him down."

For the first three nights, my father doesn't watch sports after dinner. But on the fourth night the Patriots are in some important game and he asks her if she wouldn't mind if he watched a little.

"Of course not," she says, and goes to fetch her needlepoint. My father is trying so hard to watch passively, without leaping to his feet and hurling expletives at the screen, that his hands twitch.

The phone rings. My heart does its usual throb. I've never quite given up hope that Jonathan will call. I reach it on the third ring.

"I'd like to speak to my wife, Daley."

I look at Mrs. Bridgeton. She has the needle between her lips as she untangles a small knot within the small squares. The rounds of pink in her cheeks made me suspect that the phone made her heart pound, too. She's a fine actress, though.

"Barbara," I say, and watch her force a delay, then look up. "It's for you."

She stands and places her needlepoint in the hollow where her body has been beside my father. He watches her and she moves toward the little study where the phone is. I hand her the phone and shut the door on my way out.

My father's fists are balled tight during the next play. After all the men on the field have fallen into another enormous pile, a commercial comes on.

"I'm going to have to get the number changed, you know," he says. "He can't be calling here."

"Dad, you have to let them speak to each other."

"No, she's made her choice."

"He must be pretty devastated right now. And if it leads to divorce, then everything will go smoother if they're communicating well."

"*If* it leads to divorce? She's divorcing him, Daley. I think that's pretty obvious."

"You have to let her make her own decisions. You can't force it."

"You think she's going to go back to him? Is that what you think?"

"I have no idea what she'll do. But forty years of marriage shouldn't be underestimated."

When another commercial comes on, I say, "Don't get derailed by this, Dad. Hold on and think about what you really want."

"I know what I want. I know exactly what I want. And you need to butt the hell out."

He clenches his furious face back on the game. Barbara opens the door and I go quickly into the kitchen and jangle the dogs' leashes. They come scrambling in.

I hear my father blow. "You are not serious!" At first I think he's hollering at a ref, but then I hear Mrs. Bridgeton murmuring something and my father screams back, "I don't care if he's turning a hundred and five!"

Before I can get the last leash hooked on a collar, Mrs. Bridgeton comes running in, wailing, "He's my baby boy!" And then her body breaks into sobs.

I wait for them to subside. I really don't want to be her confidante, and the dogs are scraping the door with their nails.

"I'm sorry, Daley."

I hand her a paper towel.

"We have had Hatch's thirty-fifth birthday party planned since last January," she says. "We're having this Boston band he loves come play, and some of his oldest friends are flying in, one even from Germany. Ben was just calling to see if I'd given the final numbers to the caterer. That's all he wanted. But your father doesn't believe me and he doesn't want me to go to the party." She breaks down again, her small frame trembling in slow motion.

"Of course you should go to the party. He'll come around in the morning." But I wasn't sure about that. "He'll come around to it eventually."

"I don't want to do anything to ruin what we have."

What do they have? What could they possibly have built in five days? "You won't." I touch the white wool of her sweater. "You won't."

*   *   *

For the rest of the week there's no more mention—in front of me, anyway—of the birthday party.

On Saturday my father's team has a game in Allencaster. He won't be back until six, he tells me.

At four, Barbara comes down in a navy blue dress and navy blue pumps. Above her left breast she has fastened a pin in the shape of a teddy bear. The gold plate has rubbed off of its feet and face. "Hatch gave this to me for Christmas when he was five years old. His father let him pick out anything in the store, and this is what he picked." Her eyes fill and she speaks loudly, as if to stop the tears. "That was thirty years ago. Oh, Daley, I hope I'm doing the right thing."

"What did Dad say before he left this afternoon?"

"He didn't say anything."

"Did you tell him you were going?"

"I was afraid to." Worry settles over her.

"I'll explain it to him. You go."

She smiles uneasily. "Thank you, Daley. I won't stay long. Just through dinner. Then I'll leave the ball like Cinderella."

Her analogy makes me even more certain she won't want to come back.

When my father comes home he's keyed up. His team won by twenty-six points. "You should have seen the last play. Unbelievable. Those kids were on fire today." He looks around. "Barbara out getting dinner?"

I can't tell if he's faking it.

"It's Hatch's birthday."

"What?" But it's not a question. I always thought he had to be drunk to speak with such pure bile.

"Dad, she has a family."

He sticks a finger, the one with the pencil lead stuck in the knuckle, out at me. "She knows exactly how I felt about this. Don't defend her."

"All right," I say. It's her battle, not mine. Better she learn earlier, rather than later, the kind of sacrifices my father requires.

He goes to his meeting and then eats dinner in front of the game. It was supposed to snow tonight but it's raining instead, a hard cold rain that pelts against the windows in the den. I go to bed early, hoping to sleep through the night.

I wake up past midnight to banging and go out into the hallway. All the lights are out, my father's bedroom door ajar, like it used to be before Barbara moved in. I can't hear him snoring. The banging is coming from the kitchen. I go down the back stairs quietly, keeping all the lights off.

Barbara is on the porch, both hands pounding against the panes of the back door.

"Daley!" I hear her cry out in relief. "Daley." She rests her forehead on the glass.

I haven't made it halfway across the kitchen to her when I hear my father hiss, "You let her in and I put you both out."

I can just barely make out the outline of him in his pajama bottoms, fists clenched, hovering in the doorway of the pantry where she can't see him.

"Jesus Christ, Dad," I say, and keep moving. Barbara is pressed against the door, crying, the teddy bear brooch clanking against the glass. Behind her are her two hardshell suitcases, getting soaked in the rain. My father must have put them out there before he locked the door.

I reach the doorknob. It is cold. Mrs. Bridgeton moans, "Oh, Daley," and I start to turn it and she screams and then my grip is not enough. I am smashed against the wall: head, shoulder, hip. And then I'm on the floor. My whole left side aches, the shoulder wrenched. There's no one through the glass of the door anymore. It's possible I've been unconscious.

I notice my father, crouched beside me. "You okay there?"

I nod.

"You sure?"

I nod again.

He helps me upstairs. He pulls down the covers so I can get into bed. He sits beside me, near my knees. My ear is throbbing. My shoulder is on fire. I don't want him to know this. I can smell his humid metallic nighttime smell from childhood. I can smell it now, the exact same smell, coming off of him like a steam.

He pats my thigh through the covers. "Well, we dodged that bullet," he says.

"Good night, Dad," I say evenly. It's important to give the impression of calm.

He doesn't move. He strokes my thigh. I shut my eyes and, after a few minutes, make my breathing heavier. He gets up then and goes down the hallway to his room.

I wait. I keep waiting. Physical pain is a relief at this point. It blots out everything else. His first snores are weak and uneven. Soon they even out to the steady thrum you can hear all over the house.

It doesn't take long to put all my stuff in garbage bags. It hurts and I have to carry them one at a time with my left arm to the car, but it's all done in half an hour.

Barbara's suitcases are still on the porch, but her car is gone.

I pass through the kitchen with my last bag. I look at the kitchen table. I have no note for him.

III

23

My daughter is speaking in an English accent, which means she is either a queen or the head of an orphanage.

"You must try to look people in the eye when they speak to you," she says imperiously to her little brother. "They only mean well." She has heard that from me, the encouragement to make eye contact. It's like listening in on their dreams; tiny fragments of their lives are stitched carefully into the story.

"Not witches. Green-faced witches don't mean well," Jeremy says. It's been a few years, but he still hasn't recovered from seeing *The Wizard of Oz* at his grandmother's house.

"Not always. But people do."

"Yes."

"M'lady," she whispers.

"Yes, m'lady."

They clatter through the kitchen solemnly, Lena wearing my high-heeled sandals and black wool skirt as a cape, Jeremy with an elaborate duct tape belt and a walking stick from the yard. I'm not allowed to acknowledge them.

The phone rings, and a formal voice asks for Daley Amory.

"Speaking." I wait for the sales pitch. But there is a long pause instead.

"It's Hatch. Hatch Bridgeton." He says his name like it is a small joke between us.

"Oh." My father must be dead.

The children, sensitive to my tones of voice, stop their game.

"Your dad had a stroke. A big one. They can't stabilize him."

I got an invitation to Hatch's wedding and, six years later, a group email about his divorce. I sent my regrets and a ceramic bowl for the wedding, and a short but I hoped sympathetic reply to the email. Other than that, I've had no contact with him in all the years that we've been stepbrother and sister.

"Are you there now?" I ask.

"I am. But I'm flying home tomorrow. I've been here a week and things are falling apart at work."

"A week?"

I can feel him struggle for a way to explain the seven days between my father's stroke and this phone call. But I know he's just been following instructions. "I left a message for Garvey, too. They don't think he'll make it through the weekend."

"I'm not sure," I say.

"I understand. Scott and Carly are sitting this one out, too."

In my mind, Carly and Scott are still skipping stones on their beach in Ashing on Thanksgiving Day. But life has lurched on for them, as it has for us all.

In the fifteen years since I last saw my father, I have spoken to him once. It was the night the Red Sox won the Series and broke the curse. I knew he'd be up. I didn't think about it. I just dialed the number. Barbara answered and I surprised her. She didn't know what tone to use with me. She told me to hang on and covered the phone. I could hear him refuse, and Barbara insist. I felt her try to seal the holes of the phone's receiver more securely, heard his voice rising and snapping, and then a sudden, "Hello there," fake, and drunk as hell.

"I won't keep you on long, Dad. I'm just calling because of the Red Sox. I couldn't help thinking of you."

"What? Oh, yeah. Wasn't that something?" He kept his voice flat. He wasn't going to celebrate with me, not even for a second. "Listen, I gotta go."

"All right."

"Yup," he said, and hung up.

Barbara is waiting for me at the hospital in Allencaster, which is fancier now: revolving doors and a glass-domed lobby with an enormous information desk. She is smaller, crumpled. There are black hollows around her eyes, as if the sockets are receding to the back of her head. Her squat forehead is even more foreshortened, the wrinkles thick and deep. I don't know if this transformation has occurred over the last fifteen years with my father or just in the past sleepless week.

"Oh, Daley, I'm so glad you've come." She is tiny in my arms. She tries to say more but her chest shudders, like my children just before they throw up.

"It's okay. It's going to be okay." I stroke the coarse hair at the back of her head.

We don't always like our children, Daley, but we do always love them, she wrote me after she married my father. She hoped I would come visit them. She'd redone the kitchen. When I didn't answer that card, or the next, or the next, she wrote a fiercer one. I'd always been a rude and spoiled child, she said. She vividly remembered seeing me at a Christmas pageant when I was five or six and complimenting me on my pretty velvet dress and I turned away with my nose in the air. Julie told me to stop reading the cards. They always had a little tender flower on the front, or a baby animal. She begged me to burn them unopened. I lived with her then, in New Mexico. She saw the pain they brought on, the time it took me to recover from one. It wasn't Barbara's attacks on my character that hurt; it was the passing references to my father, the portrait of his life with her that she unwittingly depicted for me. He'd gone back to work for Hugh. He wasn't coaching the "derelicts" at the youth center anymore. They'd been to a party and he'd had everyone in stitches when he snuck upstairs and came down in a kimono and slashes of eyeliner.

"How is he today?" I ask her, as if we are just picking up from yesterday.

"They've stabilized his heart rate. They still can't get his blood pressure down and he was very agitated last night. But they took off his restraints this morning, so that's good."

"Restraints?"

"He wasn't being cooperative with the nurses."

"I thought he was unconscious," I say, trying to hide my uneasy surprise.

"He's in and out."

"Is he talking?" Hatch told me he couldn't speak. I wouldn't have come if I thought he could say something to me.

"No. Nothing coherent. Just babble."

I follow her down hallways. The walls are hung with harbor and beach scenes. She stops at a pair of double doors and puts her palm under a dispenser on the wall. I do the same. Antibacterial lotion squirts out automatically. I rub it over my hands as we go through the doors. The lotion is cold then evaporates. The whole place smells of it. There is a bank of desks and opposite them a row of cubicles. Most of the curtains are open. In the first one is a black man with wires attached all over his bare chest by round adhesives that are not his skin color. In the second a white woman is sitting up, opening her mouth for Jell-O that a nurse feeds her. TVs are blaring: news, sitcoms, the Animal Channel. Two nurses are typing at computers. There is the smell of old cooked eggs. I am aware of everything, as if each pore of my skin is a receptor, waiting for the sign of my father. He is there, in the third cubicle. I feel like I am floating slightly, carrying less than my whole self. I follow Barbara's coat toward his bed. He is a long log under the covers with arms and a head sticking out. The arms are covered in wide black bruises with green centers. Everywhere else his skin is gray and loose. It hangs off his neck like fabric, and the features of his face, always pronounced and angular, are exaggerated now like a bad caricature. His straight bony nose has a bend in it, and his big ears now have enormous earlobes to match, with a crease in the middle, as if they have just been unfolded. His hair has gone past white to yellow, though his eyebrows are a bright silver, as wiry and abundant as they have always been. A tube is attached to the cartilage between his nostrils but he is breathing through his mouth loudly. At the opening of his hospital gown I can see wires attached to his chest too, the healthy peach of the adhesives no more able to match his gray skin than his neighbor's. His hands at the ends of the bruised arms lie on either side of him, healthier looking than the rest of him, both curled slightly but not closed, as if holding things: a tennis racquet, a drink.

There is nothing more familiar to me than those brown veined hands.

There are two chairs, one beside his head and the other beside his feet. Barbara points me to the one at his head. I sit without taking off my coat or scarf. Barbara removes hers and lays them on the other chair, straightens her blouse, and faces my father from the foot of the bed.

"It's Daley, Gardiner." She speaks loudly, almost angrily if you cannot see how hard she's trying not to cry. "Your daughter's come to see you."

His eyes flash open. I don't expect them. I feel my body flinch backwards. He scans the room with his yellow eyes, their color and shape and wariness unchanged by time or sickness, before settling on me. I smile as if for a camera. Friend or foe, those eyes seem to be asking.

"Hey there," I say, my throat dry.

Friend, he decides. The wariness recedes slightly. And fear floods his face as he sees the machines behind me and realizes he is not in his bed at home.

"You're going to be okay," I say quietly.

His head moves back and forth slowly.

I touch the metal bar at the side of his bed. "Yes, you are."

His head moves in quicker jerks. He lifts his arm with the tubes coming out. His first finger tries to separate from the others and touch the mattress.

"No, Dad, you're not going down."

His eyes widen, as if he's surprised to be understood, and he nods.

"You're going up. You're going to pull out of this."

He shuts his eyes. His hand twitches. And then he moans. "Ay ay ow." Way way down. To hell, he means.

"No, Dad, you're not going to hell."

"Daley!" Barbara says.

My father grunts. His eyes stay shut. His mouth opens and he begins to snore.

"What on earth was that about?" She is not pleased.

"He *can* talk."

"It's just babble. He's certainly not talking about hell, for God's sake." She is irritated, questioning already her decision to have had Hatch call me.

My head is pulled back to my father. I need to keep watching him. It feels unnatural to look at or listen to Barbara when he is in the room. I put my hands back on the metal railing and lean in. At the clink of my ring against the bar, his eyes open again right on me. My pulse quickens. I am scared, too.

"Hi, Dad." It feels strange to say the word Dad again.

"Leh ma tehsumm." Let me tell you something.

I bend down. "Tell me."

I feel Barbara watching.

His face is a maze of thin lines in every direction. Drool spills down one side of his chin. His mouth closes then opens slowly. "Espays. Airna seva dray hee." This place. They're not serving drinks here. "Godagedashekango." We gotta get the check and go.

"What's he saying?"

"Gogehalmury." Go get Hal Murry.

"Hal Murry?" I ask Barbara.

"What?"

"He wants me to go get Hal Murry. Is that his doctor?"

"God, no. Hal Murry. He wouldn't have mentioned *him*."

I wait for her to realize the improbability of me coming up with the name Hal Murry on my own.

"He's the new manager at the Mainsail. Your father can't stand him."

"Is paysino goo."

"Dad, this place *is* good for you right now. While you get better."

He jerks his head. "Inahn goo shay."

"You're not in good shape now, but you will be. You're on the upswing." I'm not sure this is true. I have come, after all, to say goodbye. But he was supposed to be unconscious and dying. He doesn't seem to be dying now.

"Na. Na. Dow." He tries to point his finger again and winces.

"Gardiner, don't try to move. Stay still." Barbara turns toward the nurses' station. "I'm going to go find somebody. He's agitated again."

He watches Barbara speaking and then, when she leaves, bunches his eyebrow hairs together. Who the hell is that? he is asking.

"Barbara," I say quietly

"Wha she doo hee?"

"She's your wife, Dad."

"Ma wife? Ahm mar to Barba *Bidgeta*?"

"Shhh, Dad, she'll hear you," I say playfully, and his mouth curls up on one side.

"Is na posseb."

Barbara comes back with a nurse who checks all his tubes and the machines they are attached to. There seem to be many liquids going in to him. One bag is sucked nearly empty. She produces a full one from her pocket and replaces it.

"You want to sit up a bit more, Mr. Amory?" she asks. She is a large woman, my age, with deep brown skin and a southwestern accent. Texas, maybe. How has she ended up here in this strange corner of the country?

"Uh-huh."

She pushes a button on the side of the bed for a few seconds, and the bed goes up but my father sinks down. So she hoists him up easily and he hollers out, right in her ear.

"No screaming, you big baby," she says. "You're going to damage my eardrum and I'm going to have to sue your you-know-what."

"I'll sue you first," my father says, but the nurse can't understand him.

"That's his favorite," Barbara says when she leaves. "He's very good with her. Gardiner, can you see this necklace I'm wearing?"

"Ya."

"Do you remember giving it to me?"

"Na."

"You gave it to me after you got out of the hospital the last time. Do you remember why?"

"Na."

"Because you said I took such good care of you."

My father nods, then looks at me hard. I know what he's saying. I can hear him clear as a bell: Yeah, she took such good care of me, look where I am now, with tubes up my nose and out my ass.

*   *   *

I drove straight from Myrtle Street to Julie's that night, with a torn
rotator cuff and three sprained ribs. I washed down Tylenol with
coffee and got there in thirty-six hours. She took me to the hospital
and then back to her apartment. We can find some humor in it
now—the wounded bird I was, my months on her couch, my tears
in public places. And Michael, the unapproachable mountain bike
man, tells it from his perspective, how he was just summoning the
nerve to ask out the introverted professor ("one of my many, many
misperceptions," he'll say) when suddenly below him there was
talking and crying every night. He assumed her girlfriend had moved
in, and it took us a while to correct this impression. I took a job
leading tours through Chaco Canyon and Mesa Verde and other sites
of the Ancestral Puebloans. I walked through those villages built
into the cliffs, trying to re-create for my audiences—groups of retir-
ees, schoolchildren, and teachers—a sense of the real lives that were
once lived there. I often overheard a pitying remark about how different life was for them, how basic their needs, how narrow their
world. But the more I climbed through the carefully laid-out houses
and imagined the families who once ate and slept in them, the more
I felt how little the difference, how simple our real needs still are:
food, water, shelter, kindness. I loved trying to make that world
come back alive for people, especially for the kids, whose imagi-
nations were still so open. When it was time for Michael to move
in with Julie, I moved a block away. For four years my social life
was Julie and Michael, just as Julie's had once been me and
Jonathan. Occasionally they asked someone else over for dinner,
a colleague of theirs, but it never took, not for any of us. We had
our rhythm. A new person always threw us off. Julie says that when
she told me they were getting married, I looked like someone who
was trying to be cheerful while my leg was being sawed off. I just

couldn't understand why they wanted to ruin a great relationship with marriage.

I used to sit at my computer and stare at Jonathan's address online:

1129 Trowbridge Avenue
Philadelphia, PA 19104

There he was. He was there. He'd made it home again. I had his phone number, too, but when I thought of calling, all I could imagine was him straining to get off the phone. Julie wanted to invite him to the wedding but I couldn't risk having to meet a girlfriend or a wife, see photos of a little baby. But then, without telling her, I put an invitation in the mail. I knew where she kept the RSVP cards people sent back; he never responded.

Julie and her father argued about the ceremony. Alex disapproved of the bridesmaids, the poetry, and homemade vows. He took a sudden interest in Orthodox rituals. He wanted her to circle the chuppah seven times and to enter it alone with her face fully covered. He wanted the rabbi to read the traditional wedding contract in Aramaic. She said it would take forty-five minutes and was nothing but a pre-nup, all about how many cows Michael would have to pay to divorce her. At least, Alex insisted, Michael would smash a glass as a warning against excessive joy. "I *want* excessive joy!" I heard her scream at him.

She got married in the small garden of the house she and Michael had just bought. The guests filled the seats outside as I helped her dress, slipping the satin buttons through their holes, threading flowers through her hair.

We stood side by side, me in a dark blue silk dress, she in white tulle.

"My dissertation was called 'Women and Rites: The Misogyny of Custom,'" she said. "How can I explain this white dress to my students?"

"They'll never have to know."

Then she looked at me closely. "You look so beautiful, Daley." She said this as if it were an important day for me, and not her.

I shook my head. "You're the beautiful one. You are stunning, Jules." And she was. She was glowing with excessive joy. But I still didn't understand why she wanted to be married.

And then her father called up to us. It was time.

I didn't see him right away. He was sitting behind the big hats of Julie's aunts, and I was under a frilly chuppah. Alex was in front, beaming, teary, all the tension between them already forgotten. And then one aunt leaned over to say something to another, and there he was. My shock broke his nervous face into a wide grin, and that sun hit my face after years in the shade. I couldn't help the tears. While her cousin read an Emily Dickinson poem, Julie squeezed my hand and whispered, "You see, there were *many* good reasons for me to get married."

After the ceremony we met in the middle of the garden and held each other for a long time without a word, our bodies slotted together in the same way. Everything—his smell, his skin, his thudding heart, his breath on my neck—was what I knew, familiar as a season. So this is what happens to me next, I thought, and I finally understood what my mother had meant about falling in love. It was the surprise, the recognition that everything had been moving in this direction without your ever realizing it.

"I didn't think you'd come," I said.

He pulled out four invitations from his jacket pocket. "How could I not?"

Despite what I'd said, Julie had sent one anyway. And Michael had sent one before that. And so, it turned out, had Alex. All these people, looking out for me.

"I knew this would happen," he said in my ear. I wanted his mouth to stay there, right there. There wasn't anything else left in the world to want but this.

"What?"

He slipped his hand between us to rub his chest. "All these *feelings*."

"You don't sound so pleased."

"You know I like a little more control over myself than this."

I did know that. There were so many things I suddenly knew.

We got married in that spot in Julie and Michael's garden a few years later. Jonathan's mother and brothers, Garvey and Paul, were our only other guests. I never knew before that moment that you can feel love, like a slight wind, when it's strong enough. You can do this, they all seemed to be saying. This is where you can put your love safely.

After I hung up with Hatch, I stood in the door of Jonathan's study.

"My father is in the ICU."

"What happened?"

"Stroke."

He came and put his arms around me.

"They think he's going to die." I laid my cheek on his collarbone. I didn't feel sad because my father was in the hospital. I felt sad for his entire life.

"What are you thinking?" he asked, after a while.

"I don't know. I couldn't go alone. I'd need you there." This is what had happened to me in eleven years. I'd learned to need him, to lean on him, which is separate from love.

I could feel him taking that in. "Then I think we should go. All of us," he said. "We'll find a hotel with a pool. The kids will love it."

"Really?" We were saving for a trip to visit his father's relatives in Trinidad.

"We have to allow for emergencies."

"I don't know, Jon. I don't know if I can do it."

"He's unconscious, right? You'll be able to say whatever you need to say to him without rebuttal."

"I'm not sure I have anything to say."

"Then you can say goodbye. You didn't get that chance with your mom."

And he didn't get it with his dad. "But it's so complicated."

"Of course it is."

"I don't think I'd regret not going." I'd have to take personal days at work; the kids would miss school.

"But there's a chance you will be glad you went, an outcome that has a far greater value than nonregret."

"Said the philosopher."

"I knew that PhD would come in handy someday."

Neither of us ever became professors. I teach middle school social studies—ancient civilizations and world history. I like those grades, sixth through ninth, my students still open, willing to reveal their curiosity and imagination and humor to me, willing to allow me mine. Jonathan works part-time for his brother building houses, and writes fiction. He and Dan were nominated for, and lost, the same prize last year, but it's his first novel that gets the most attention. I see paperback copies of it around school in the fall because a colleague of mine teaches it in the high school. It's based on the year after he left the terrace on Myrtle Street and roamed the country in his truck, working when he needed cash, moving on when he'd made enough, his careful plans destroyed. He was as itinerant and broke as his father when he first came here from Trinidad, and his life was threatened more than once. It's a hard book for me to read.

We decided to drive up to Massachusetts the next morning.

*   *   *

Barbara and I eat lunch in the cafeteria. She thanks me for coming. Her crumpled face crumples even more. "I know it means so much to him, Daley."

"I'm not sure he has any idea who I am, but I'm glad I'm here."

"He knows. He's missed you."

I don't know that I believe her, but I've missed him too. We missed each other. We aimed and we missed.

In the afternoon my father dozes, loud and rattling. They are short naps, sometimes only a few minutes long. And then his eyes open. They move to the TV first, then to me and Barbara, then to the nurses' station where all the action is, doctors picking up and dropping off paperwork, people tapping things into computers.

"Okay, then, you *do* that," his favorite nurse says into the phone. My father imitates her without opening his mouth. He catches her inflection perfectly. He is like a parrot with its beak shut. Barbara takes out her needlepoint and urges me to read my book or get some magazines from the waiting area, but I don't want distraction.

Visitors pass by on their way to see patients farther in, and again on their way out. They appear briefly, cross our six-foot stage from curtain to curtain, and are gone. A tall young woman in a cape and long black hair passes by. She looks a bit like Catherine did, years ago. My father's head snaps toward me, eyes wide. I laugh. He tries to speak but it's just a long croak, a hopeful croak, almost like he wants to say hello to her.

"I don't think that was her. But it looked like her, didn't it?"

He nods, still looking at the place she disappeared from.

"Who looked like who?" Barbara asks.

I decide not to answer.

He dozes off. Fifteen minutes later he wakes up and says, very clearly, that Chad Utley came to visit that morning.

"Oh, Gardiner, no, he didn't," Barbara says. "Chad Utley is dead."

My father looks at me. "Deh?"

I shrug. I'm sorry to hear this. Mile High Mr. Utley. He was always kind to me. But I don't think my father needs to be reminded of his death right now.

"We went to the funeral," she says.

My father takes the news hard. He stares at his hands. They're folded on his belly. Barbara and I are at cross-purposes. She needs him to meet her in the present, and I am happy for him to remain deep in the past.

His mouth slackens and he falls asleep again.

"You know, Daley," Barbara says quietly, "your father lost a lot of friends by marrying me. They all sided with Ben against us. It was very unpleasant. We were alone. Totally alone. Hatch was about the only person who would visit. And Virginia Utley was the worst of them all. But when Chad died, your father was the first one over to her house that afternoon. And she has never stopped thanking him for it. I know you two have had your difficulties, but I don't think you have any idea what a good man he is."

I can see her assembling another vignette, so I ask about her needlepoint.

"It's the ship your father and I took to France when we were first married. It was honestly the most romantic trip. We danced every night. They had a wonderful band."

"What kind of music did they play?" I have to speak loudly. My father is making a racket in his sleep.

"Oh, all stuff before your time. Our song was 'It's Like Reaching for the Moon.' They played it every night, the last song. Out on the deck. Beneath all the stars."

"I don't know it."

"You don't? It's lovely."

"How does it go?"

You never know, from someone's speaking voice, if they will be able to sing or not. Barbara has never had a mellifluous way of talking, but she sings beautifully, surprisingly low and rich.

It's like reaching for the moon,
It's like reaching for the sun,
It's like reaching for the stars—
Reaching for you.

At first she sings down to her needlepoint, but soon she lifts her face to me. I do not hide my pleasure from her. Then she looks at my father and she stops short. "Oh, sweetie, oh, sweetie, don't do that." She leaps up and goes to the other side of the bed to wipe the tears from my father's face with her hand, but her own fall on them both. She holds my father's hands. "That was our song, wasn't it?"

My father nods. His face is red and wet.

"It's strange," I say to Jonathan that night in the hotel room. "They've had a life together. I always thought it was such a desperate act, but I think he grew to really love her. And she has many stories in which he's the hero."

"How was she to you?"

"Very kind, appreciative that I came."

"I'm glad."

We're on the big bed in our hotel room. Lena and Jeremy are on the floor in front of the TV, hair wet from swimming, surfing the two hundred and eighty channels. I've got an eye on the screen, unsure what might flash on next.

Jonathan tips my face toward him with a finger, away from the TV. "It's okay," he says. My overprotectiveness is something we struggle with.

"My father is so entirely himself, that's the weird thing. You can strip someone of so much, but he's still there. Just the way his hands rest on the mattress."

"It must be hard to see him like that."

"I know it should be. But it feels so much safer with him in that bed. I never thought he could be felled."

"I didn't really either," Jonathan says.

"Thank you," I whisper, and kiss the hollow below his ear. "Thank you for being here with me." I feel the defenselessness of my love for him, an utter vulnerability, all my guards down and gone.

It took me several years to agree to marriage. Julie listened to all my fears and said, "You seem to think that once you get married your love for each other is going to start draining out like it's in a bucket with a leak, like you get this one tank of gas and can't stop for more. You aren't allowing for the possibility that love doesn't always start dying, that it can actually grow." I thought she was delusionally optimistic.

"You're gooey," Jonathan says. It's Lena's word for when she feels all floppy with affection.

"I am."

"Stop hugging!" Jeremy says, his head popping up at the foot of the bed. And when we don't move away from each other, he climbs up and tries to pry us apart. But he can't budge us.

I have no memory of ever seeing my parents touch. I suppose it is a luxury, his aversion to our affection with each other. I hope someday he will see it differently.

Lena clicks on CNN. The primaries don't start for four more months, but they're playing clips of Hillary Clinton and Barack

Obama campaigning in different parts of Iowa, as if the caucuses were next week. Jonathan and I look on, but we don't have our usual argument about them.

"Is your father going to die?" Lena asks after we shut out the light and lie, all four of us, in the king-sized bed. They have no name for him. He is my father, but not their anything.

"I don't know what's going to happen."

"Are we going to come with you to the hospital tomorrow?" Lena asks.

"Briefly. Daddy will bring you over mid-morning, and if your grandfather is stable you can say hello."

"Hello and goodbye," Jeremy says. Death hangs lightly on a six-year-old. Then he thinks more about this. "Do you like your dad?" It's new to them, me having a dad. They've always known that my father lives in Massachusetts and that I haven't seen him since long before they were born. But he was never real to them until now.

I don't know how to explain it all to them. "Yes, I like my dad." I try to think of why, because that's what they'll ask next. "He is so familiar to me."

"Yeah, because he's your dad," Jeremy says.

"That's right."

But he wants more. "Why is Granny the only grandparent we see?"

"Because Daddy's dad is dead," Lena says. "Mom's mom is dead, and Mom's dad is dying. That's why."

"But he wasn't always dying."

I assumed that once I had children I would get in touch with my father. I thought it would feel important to me for them to know their grandfather. But in fact it was just the opposite. "Here come the little pickaninnies," I could hear him say under his breath as we approached the house. It wasn't just the possibility that they would overhear a racial slur, or see him drunk and raging. When I became a parent, even moments I had once thought of as tender went rancid: ridiculing Mr. Rogers, pummeling my stuffed animals at night. Once, when the kids were younger, our neighbor, Maya, who was eleven, came over to bake cookies with us. She had a rope bracelet around her wrist, the first hint of breasts beneath her T-shirt. I realized that she was the age I'd been when my parents divorced, and Lena was Elyse's age. They were both just little girls. My throat squeezed shut and I had to rasp out my instructions. "Why are you talking so funny, Mommy?" Lena asked. Once the cookies were in the oven I went into the bathroom and pressed a washcloth to my face. I had been a little girl, too, with a rope bracelet and breast buds and a father who was reading us *Penthouse* at night.

The next morning my father is back in restraints. He has had a rough night, hollering and thrashing. A nurse is walking around in a neck brace, and I fear he's responsible.

Barbara is nearly done with the sea in her square of needlepoint. All she has left is the red hull of the ship. My father is sleeping. He has worn himself out.

A new nurse fiddles with a machine. She changes his IV, then pokes his finger for a drop of blood. He wakes up screaming.

"All right, drama king, settle down," she says. "You want those restraints off?"

My father nods with pleading eyes.

"You gonna behave yourself?"

He nods again.

With routine dexterity she unfastens and removes the stiff bands of cloth. "You're sort of smooshed down at the bottom." She turns to us. "Wanna help me get him up?"

She and Barbara each take an armpit and I am told to push his
feet. My father is alarmed.

"Na," he says. "Na!"

"You have to help us now, Mr. Gardiner," the nurse says. She
pulls up the bottom of the covers to his knees. "Now, your daughter is going to have her hands right here on your feet and you are
going to push with your legs."

It is strange to be called a daughter. I put my hands on his bare
feet. They are all bone, every toenail long and gray and bumpy. His
calves are nearly as thin as Lena's and the same shape, doubly familiar to me.

"Push. Push," Barbara and the nurse say to him. "Push!"

As soon as his torso is lifted from the bed, he starts to wail.
"Bacafumee," he says. I don't know what he means. "Bacafumee."
It's the first time I can't understand him.

"What's he saying, Daley?" Barbara asks.

"*Bacafumee*!" His face is squinched and red.

We get him a few inches higher in the bed. He is covered in
sweat. Be careful of me, he was saying. I think of his drunk mother
staring at the wall. Isn't that really all we've been saying to each other,
generation after generation: *Be careful of me*? I am trying so hard to
be careful with my children. I look at my father. He's still whimper-
ing a little. I'm sorry, I say silently. I'm sorry we couldn't be more
careful of each other.

Afterwards, he sleeps again. I try to read, pretend to read, but
mostly I watch him. I find him as intriguing as a painting. His body
tells me a long story that I have, in the past fifteen years, nearly forgotten.

My phone dings.

"They're here," I say to Barbara, after I read the text.

We meet them outside the double doors to the ICU. They're
putting on the antibacterial lotion, Jeremy smelling his palms and
then his sister's.

Jonathan puts out his hand to Barbara but she ignores it, steps right past and flings her arms around him, as if she'd never written in her last missive, after a conversation with Neal's mother who'd seen us at Neal and Anne's wedding, that I didn't need to date a black man to get my father's attention. That time I did write back and never heard from her again.

"Thank you so much," she whispers. I watch his arms go around her soft pink sweater. Somehow she understands that without Jonathan I would not be here, and she is grateful for his forgiveness. She bends down to greet the kids. They don't know what to make of this hobbit face and the tears that slip along the wrinkles in her cheeks. "You two have come a long way. They have yummy pies in the cafeteria. Do you have a favorite kind of pie?"

They look up at me to answer.

I put my hand on Lena's head. "Strawberry rhubarb or pecan," I say, then move to Jeremy, "and blueberry."

"Or apple. Or cherry in a pinch," he adds. He is wearing a baseball cap backwards. *In a pinch.* My eyes fill.

Barbara smiles for the first time. "I think they have nearly all of those." She looks at me and Jonathan. "May I take them down there while you two go in first?"

I'm not expecting this. I'm not ready to trust her with my children. My mind spins for an excuse. But before I have one, Jonathan says, "Sure," and the kids bounce with pleasure. Pie at ten in the morning!

Jonathan and I go through the ICU doors alone. The man in the first cubicle raises his eyes briefly at Jonathan, thinking for a moment he has a visitor. Jonathan catches this and lifts up his hand to the man.

My father's eyes are open. He looks at my husband for the first time.

"Good morning," Jonathan says. Like our children, he has no name for my father. There is a guardedness to his face, a thin shield only I can see. He's had his own tortured relationship with this man. He's wrestled with him through me, with the wraith of my father that's still inside me.

My father nods, makes a small sound, does not take his eyes off of Jonathan. He doesn't appear scared, as he did when he was being lifted earlier, and he doesn't appear angry or surprised. If anything, it's a childlike curiosity I see in my father's eyes. What's going to happen next? he seems to be saying. And he seems to think Jonathan has the answer.

"Dad, this is my husband, Jonathan."

Without looking at me my father nods. I know that, is what he means. His right arm twitches. "Ow do?"

"I'm fine, thanks," Jonathan says. "How are you feeling today?"

"Ahm in pre gu shay." I'm in pretty good shape. "Pre gu shay."

"That's good. You'll be out of here soon, then."

My father looks slightly to either side of Jonathan, seeing where he is. "Oh," he says. "Ya."

"They treating you well?"

"Oh, sur. Isa gu play."

Jonathan takes something out of his coat pocket. "I wasn't sure if I would be able to see you, so I got this just in case." It is a card, a greeting card. On the front are puppies sleeping in a basket. Jonathan holds it up so my father can see it. I have no idea where this card came from.

My father makes a soft moan of pleasure.

"'If you get lots of rest,'" Jonathan reads, then opens the card. From a microchip in the paper comes the sound of many puppies yelping. "'You'll be howling good in no time!'"

My father loves this. For the first time I see him lift both his bruised arms. He takes the card in his hand and shuts it and opens it for the barking and shuts it and opens it again. He looks up at Jonathan. "Ah lie tha," he says.

"I'm glad."

He points to Jonathan. "Av doe?"

"No dogs," Jonathan says. This is because of me. "Two kids, but no dogs."

"Ki? Wa they?"

"They're eating pie with Barbara," I say.

He looked confused. "Who Barbra?"

"Barbara Bridgeton. Your wife."

"Ma wie!" He says and he laughs and then winces and grabs his stomach and then laughs again. He points at me. "Daley's funny," he says, clear as a bell.

The sound of my name startles me, shatters my illusion that I have been a generic figure, an everydaughter, in the room. And then, before I can respond, he is asleep with his mouth open, making his gagging sound.

Jonathan takes my hand and pulls me closer. We've been standing unnecessarily apart from each other. We laugh about it without saying a word.

A cart rattles by outside the cubicle. My father doesn't wake up. We sit in the chairs.

"Every time he falls asleep," I say quietly, "I worry that my reprieve is over, that he'll wake up and remember he hates me."

Then I hear the kids in the corridor, their small steps, their attempts at whispering.

Barbara pulls back the curtain. "They told me I could sneak them in, just for a few minutes, since he's been so calm today. I've got to go down to the pharmacy in the basement anyway. These children are so *polite*." She smiles at them. Would she have said that if they were white? "See you in a little bit." She closes the curtain, closes us in with my father.

My father's eyes open and my heart races. What if now is the moment he remembers everything? What if now, with my two children right here, is the moment his memory returns and he hollers, *What the fuck are you people doing here?* I wish the restraints were still on him.

He makes a small noise, not unhappy. Lena waves to him. He makes another sound, more high-pitched and affectionate. *Hello there*, he's saying, not fake but real, a sound he might use on the dogs when he came home in the evening and they bounded around him at the door.

I gently urge the kids forward a few feet. I keep close behind them. Jonathan stays at the foot of the bed, equally vigilant. I don't know if my father remembers meeting him, fifteen minutes ago. "This is Lena, and this is Jeremy, Dad. Our children."

He stares at Lena hard. She has her hair pulled back in a polka-dot cloth headband. She looks a little like my mother in her kerchief. She has my narrow face but Jonathan's smile. She is making eye contact. Then his head swivels quick as an owl's to Jeremy, who leans back heavy against me. He's wearing a Sixers T-shirt and my father says something about it that I can't understand, but when I ask him to say it again he shakes his head. He tries to lift his hand but it doesn't move very far. He looks back up at them apologetically.

Lena reaches down and touches his fingers. "It's nice to meet you."

"It's nice to meet you," Jeremy repeats.

"Ni to mit too," my father manages. His eyes move from one to the other.

If my father notices the color of their skin—Lena's a milky fawn, Jeremy's a more concentrated brown—he doesn't let on. He feels around for the card Jonathan has given him. It takes him a little bit but he grasps it and holds up the photo of the puppies in a basket.

"Ooooh," my children coo at the same time.

My father nods happily. And then he opens the card and Lena and Jeremy burst out laughing at the sound.

One side of my father's mouth flinches up high. He breathes heavily through his nose.

"Oo itl ragal." Two little rascals.

He is looking at my children.

"Did he say something about *The Little Rascals?*" Jonathan whispers as I walk with them to the lobby.

I laugh. I feel light. "Not the show. He just meant they were two little cutie-pies."

"He isn't mean, Mom," Jeremy says. "Why have we never seen him before?"

Both my children watch me carefully. Was I wrong to have withheld him from them? Perhaps my father would have loved them, perhaps he would have been kind and generous with them. I could see him on the court with them, showing them how to hit a backhand. I could see them easily imitating his grace.

I don't know what to tell them. I want to be fair: to him, to them, to myself.

"Some people you just have to love from afar," Jonathan says.

I kiss them goodbye in the lobby. They are going to Ashing for lunch. In Lena's pocket is a map I drew this morning of the town, of Myrtle Street, Water Street, Ruby Beach, the sub shop, and the penny candy store. Lighthouse Books no longer exists. It is a cell phone store now, Neal told me in his last email. Jonathan will show them the front terrace on Myrtle Street, where he stood asking me to come with him to California. They know this story. They love to hear it, love the thrill of thinking about how we almost didn't become a family. I can listen to Jonathan tell it, the way he exaggerates the size of the house, the barking of the dogs, and the leashes in my hand, and laugh. But when I am alone I can remember the years of pain, the hollowness of my life after that moment, and it aches for a while, as if that time never ended, as if it never turned into a funny story that we tell our children.

I get a sandwich in the cafeteria and go back up to the ICU. The woman next door is wheeled away to a different wing. She is sitting up, holding a jar of flowers. Her two sons, old men themselves, walk on either side of her gurney. My father sleeps, loudly, mouth open, ropes of white spit shaking and breaking and forming again after a swallow. Barbara leaves to run some errands, and I am alone with him for the first time. I watch him as if he were an event of some kind. The lines on his face have dug deep: laugh lines, scowl lines, squinting lines. On his forehead they are perfectly horizontal and vertical, etched in squares, a tennis net across his brow. His hands twitch in his dreams. They are surprisingly smooth, not creased and buckled like his face, the veins raised, more green than purple, the most pronounced where they cross the bone in the middle, the pencil lead still blue beneath the skin of his knuckle.

A beeping comes from one of the machines and his favorite nurse comes in. She lasers his wristband, checks his IV, punches a button to stop the beeping. He looks up at her with devotion.

"Are you thirsty, Mr. Amory?"

He nods and she opens a drawer and peels the plastic wrapper off something that looks like a lollipop, swabs his mouth with it, and tosses it into the trash. It is a small moist sponge. He looks at her gratefully.

"They're right here." She pats the drawer. "You can do that anytime for him."

She flicks a switch on the side of his bed, and his head comes up almost to sitting. She opens another drawer and pulls out two small pillows which she slips under each of his arms. He looks much more comfortable than he's looked all day. I thank her. I'm not sure she hears me.

"Pretty green eyes," she says to me on her way out. "Just like your dad's."

I wait for him to drift to sleep but he doesn't. He is more up-right now than I've seen him, his arms resting on the pillows as if he held a drink in one and a cigarette in the other, as if he were lying on a chaise by the pool thinking about a dip and saying, "I wonder what the poor people are doing today." He stares straight ahead, puffing up his cheeks, then blowing out the air, watching his nurse through the opening key a report into a computer and laugh at something a doctor behind her is saying. Did my father ever have a conscience? Did he ever wake up in the dark and think: I have treated some people badly; I have been selfish; I have caused pain? Or did he truly never develop to that extent? Was he only ever capable of feeling his own needs, his own pain? Was there any way to have had a good relationship with him?

He turns to me and groans. "Ow," he says. "Ow ow." He points to his stomach. "Desomfinfissdowdere." There's something fishy down there.

"There is, Dad. It's a catheter."

"Ow!" he says, more loudly, and puts his hands down in the covers. He lets out a terrible wail.

"Don't touch it, Dad. It needs to be there."

He brings his hands out but he glares at me. He balls his fists together and spits out something. "Sick of it," I think he says. "Sick of it," he says again.

"I know it's uncomfortable, Dad."

He glares. No, you don't; you don't know the half of it, he is saying to me.

There he is. There is the man I know. "Try to relax. Let's think of pleasant things." I wonder what would be pleasant to him now, apart from a martini. "Let's imagine you're back at home on a summer day."

He glowers. He starts muttering so fast I can't understand him. He is pissed. He is yelling at everyone, but he can't get his voice to go much above a whisper. I can make out a few swears, but not much more. He is looking down at his own fists. I feel how distant I am from all his emotion now, how little any of it is connected to me. I'm glad my kids aren't here to hear him.

"Go to sleep, Dad," I say finally. "You need rest."

He turns and notices me again. There are tears leaking out of his eyes. I get up and wipe them, then open the drawer with the sponge lollipops. I peel off a wrapper and put it on his tongue. He closes his mouth around it and sighs. When he opens again, I pull it out, put it in the trash, and sit down in my chair beside him.

His hand knocks against the metal bar. "Wiya ju ho ma ha?"

I put my hand over the bar and onto his. It is cold. I squeeze and he squeezes back. I keep my hand in his for the rest of the afternoon.

That night, around three in the morning, I wake up crying. I cry on my stomach, the tears spreading on the bottom hotel sheet. I shake the bed, but no one wakes up.

Barbara calls at six. They've discovered a large clot in his lungs. They won't let her in to see him.

"We're coming over," I tell her, and we hurry to dress.

We meet in the cafeteria. I let the kids have pie with their breakfast. Barbara insists on paying. Her hands shake as she tries to pick out the change from her wallet.

We take a table in the far corner. And then Lena and Jeremy gasp. I look up to see what gruesome bombing in Iraq or Afghanistan they have seen on one of the screens hanging from the

ceiling, but they are not looking at the televisions. They are looking at a man in the middle of the cafeteria smooshing his face
with his hands for their benefit. They are looking at their Uncle
Garvey.

They run across the room and leap on him, hike up him like
a tree, and he pretends to try and swing them off. They are still
hanging from his back as he hugs Barbara, who is crying, and then
Jonathan, and then me, also crying. He smells like his van: chicken
and cigarettes.

"They won't let me in to see him," he says.

"They're intubating him," I say.

"Jesus. What does that mean?"

"There's not enough oxygen in his blood because of a clot, and
they have to put in a breathing tube and then try to get his blood to
thin."

Garvey nods, breathing in. He is nervous. He thought he'd see
Dad this morning. Now he has to wait. Now it might be too late.

"How are you holding up?" he says to Barbara.

"Having all you kids here is the silver lining." Her voice breaks.
I think about that Thanksgiving, about how she'd held a family together for nearly forty years and then broke it for my father. Family
is important to her. And we are my father's family.

"Let's go get you some pie," I say, steering him back toward
the food.

"Someone's lost her fiery roar," he says, once we are out of
earshot. He has gotten his fair share of cards, too.

"I know."

"What's going on with Dad? Is he going to croak before we can
get another good swipe at each other?"

"I don't know. It seemed like he was doing better. He was alert
and talking."

"How'd that go?"

"Good. He's sort of circa 1980, so that makes things easier between us."

"You're kidding."

"He thinks I'm joking when I tell him he's married to Barbara Bridgeton."

Garvey laughs.

"Hatch told me he was unconscious, and then I get here and he opens his eyes and starts talking to me. Sometimes they have to strap him down because he's taken out a few nurses. They're all walking around with neck braces and bandages."

"Jesus Christ."

"It's a little trippy." It feels so good that Garvey is here and I can exaggerate everything.

"Is he about to die? Is the doctor going to come find us and pat our backs and tell us they did all they could?"

"I don't know."

My father dying still doesn't seem possible to me. It never has. Seeing him in a hospital bed seems like a violation of natural law. And now, with Garvey here, he's turned back into a caricature, fodder for jokes, not someone who is our father and is about to die. We don't know how to be serious about that.

Garvey looks toward the parking lot. "I don't really want to be here for that."

We pay and head back toward the table. "Kids look good," he says. "Lena's shot up three feet. They're not mad you dragged them up here for the macabre deathbed scene?" He throws his head back, raises and tightens all the tendons in his neck, and rattles quietly, so Barbara can't hear, "*Don't let them take me!* He's not exactly going to go gently, is he? Jeremy looks darker than he did last Christmas. He got some serious African genes, didn't he? Very Masai. Lucky bastard. Shit. No sickly pouffy-haired portraits of him by a fucking fountain looking like Lord Fauntleroy."

"How's Baby D?" Lena asks when we reach them.

Baby D is my namesake. Garvey pulls out a new photo. She's a very large two-year-old and Garvey likes to take Paul Bunyan-like photos of her. In this one she is lifting up the back end of one of his moving vans.

"How does she do that?" Jeremy asks.

"She's a strong little girl," he says, and winks at Lena.

"We have a giganormous TV in our hotel room!" Jeremy says.

"Cable?"

"Two hundred and eighty-six channels!"

"They don't get much TV at home," I explain to Barbara. "So it's a big deal."

She nods but she's not listening to us.

"There's a TV right there," Garvey says, pointing up. The screen is split three ways, with John McCain getting into a black SUV, Hillary making a speech to a huge crowd, and Obama springing up the metal steps of his airplane with the big O sunrise on it. "I guess I don't have to ask who you guys are for."

I wait for Jonathan to react. He lets Garvey get away with a lot, but this assumption is a particular vexation of his.

"We're one of those families they interview on local news shows, split right down the middle," he says.

"Daley's always had that dyke side," Garvey says. "I should have warned you."

"Could you watch your mouth, please?" I tell him, a perpetual refrain when he's around. "And I'm the Obama supporter, thank you very much."

"You're for *Hillary*?" Garvey asks Jonathan.

Jonathan is used to this. He has condensed his response. "He can't win. She can. She has the party behind her and she knows how to play hardball."

"They did find in medical examinations that she has one more testicle than he does," Garvey says. Lena and Jeremy are perplexed. I need to carry earplugs. "I don't know, man," he continues, serious now. "I think you're underestimating him. This guy knows how to play the game."

"But in the game, the real game, there's no room for a man of color."

"Have you seen the crowds he draws?"

"Hillary is beating him fifty to twenty in the polls."

"Not for long."

"If he wins the nomination, we'll get to see how deeply racist this country really is. The guy doesn't have a prayer."

"He's going to be our next president."

"And then everyone can dust off their hands and forget about the black poverty rate and that one in nine young black men are in prison. We'll be *post-racial*. Have you heard that one yet?"

"Man, and I thought *I* was cynical," Garvey says. "I bet your mother doesn't share your sentiments." He and Jonathan's mother have become good friends over all the holidays we've spent together.

Jonathan laughs. "No, she does not. My mother is the biggest pie-in-the-sky dreamer there is. She's walking door-to-door with her Obama pamphlets right now, I'm sure."

"Our mother used to do that," Garvey said. "Remember all the rallies she dragged us to?"

I shake my head. Garvey often remembers me into his youth, but most of the time I was home with Nora.

"I'd vote for Obama," Barbara says.

Garvey pats her hand. "I think you need to lay off the hard stuff in the morning, Barbara."

"I like him. I like his smile."

"Well, he's got the white vote at this table," Garvey says. "It's the black vote that's going to be the bitch."

At quarter of twelve we move over into the ICU waiting room. Jeremy brought a deck of cards, and Jonathan and Garvey play War with him and Lena on the floor. Garvey introduces all sorts of new rules and strategies, allowing for alliances, pacts, spies, and explosives. They make a great deal of noise with all the bombing and the laughing, but we have the place to ourselves. I sit on a flowered couch with Barbara, and when I notice she is crying I pat her arm.

At one-fifteen the doctor comes out. They have gotten his blood oxygen saturation levels up a little bit. He's still sedated, but we can go in, two at a time, briefly.

Barbara urges Garvey and me in first. "He'll want to see you. He'll want to know you're both here." Will he? Or are we all just pretending, playing the parts we're supposed to play?

He's in the same room. His bed has been lowered flat, which makes him look more seriously ill. There's a tube now coming out of the side of his mouth, taped to his cheek, and a thinner one coming out of his nose. He's asleep, not rattling anymore. The machine breathes for him, *pshhhh, click, pshhhh, click*. Garvey stops halfway to the bed.

"Shit." He looks back at me.

"I know," I say.

I let him have my chair. He sits tentatively and does not lean forward. He watches my father, his father, for a long time. It is strange to have all our DNA in the same room: our big ears, our bony knees, our brittle defensive humor. And our father lying there, the gash in his children's heart.

Garvey opens his mouth to say something, then stands up. "I can't do this, Daley. I don't know why I'm in this room."

"Sit down. It will come to you."

"I doubt it." But he sits.

We both watch his mechanical breaths.

Garvey starts laughing. "Do you remember Libby Moffet?"

I see a chunky teenager doing a swan dive. "Who used to babysit for the Tabors?"

"Yes, her. I was home one time and went up to see Dad and Catherine but they were out and she was babysitting Elyse."

"I don't remember that."

"You weren't there. You were at camp."

"I never went to camp."

"Then you must have been down at Goodale's snorting coke with the stockboy. So they come home, Libby and I have fallen asleep after having sex in their bed, and Dad is ripshit. He wants to fight me. And I tell him he's too drunk and I'll come back the next morning for a fair fight. So I come back the next day, right at eight like we said, and Dad's just sitting there on the top step of the back porch. He's got tears in his eyes." Garvey has told me this story before, I realize now, but I let him continue. "It was the morning Gus Barlow shot himself. Remember that? Dad had just heard. He made me promise I'd never do anything that stupid."

He never told me that part, about the promise.

"Keeping that promise hasn't always been easy, to be honest with you. He really looks like crap, doesn't he? He looks like he's aged fifty years since I last saw him. How old is he? Are you sure this is our father?" He pretends to stand to get a nurse.

"He's seventy-six."

"He looks ninety-six."

"Hard living."

"Yeah, it was rough, all those days at the Ashing Tennis and Sail, all those nights of martinis on the rocks and filet mignon."

"I think he doesn't have much of an infrastructure, with all that alcohol."

"Maybe you're right."

"Maybe we should tell him our best memory of him and then say goodbye."

He laughs and shakes his head and wipes his face with both hands slowly. "All right. You go first."

I thought I would tell the story about running around the pool naked with him. I've never been able to erase the joy and flight and love from that moment, no matter how hard I try. It was a memory I clung to for so long after my parents divorced. But instead I say, "I liked holding your hand yesterday, Dad."

Garvey waits for me to say more and when I don't, he laughs. "Huh. That's an awfully recent memory." He turns to my father. "I like the way you just let go of that drool down your chin, Dad. It was very beautiful and truthful to me."

"Shut up and go."

"I'm going to tell you my memory now, Dad. Are you listening? When I was a wee lad of six and seven and eight, you used to drive me to peewee hockey. Remember that? Practices were at five in the morning, five mornings a week. You didn't play hockey, didn't even like hockey much. But you'd wake me up at four-fifteen and we'd make the drive all the way to the rink in Burnham. We'd stop at Dunkin' Donuts and you'd get a black coffee and I'd get a hot chocolate and the rest of the way we'd polish off a few crullers each. It was always freezing cold, and the heat in the station wagon wouldn't kick in till we were nearly there. We talked and I have no clue what we said, and then we'd pull into the parking lot and I'd go in one door and you'd go in another and I'd be on the ice for an hour and a half and you'd be in the stands stomping your feet and breathing in your hands to stay warm. You'd have to work a full day after that at a job we all knew you hated and I never became much of a hockey player, but you never complained. You complained about a hell of a lot of other things, but never about that."

I put my hand on Garvey's back and he leans his chin on Dad's metal railing and doesn't say anything more for a long time.

*   *   *

We drive back home that evening. My father is transferred out of the ICU five days later, spends eight more days in the hospital, and then is moved to a rehabilitation center in Lynn. *Lynn, Lynn, the city of sin,* my father would say, if he could remember it, *you never come out the way you went in.* In June he is able to move back to his house in Ashing.

I suppose it happens often enough. People rush to someone's death-bed and then they don't die. Life, sometimes amazingly, lurches on.

My father's memory never comes back in full. He seems only to have a loose handle on the present. It feels like a play, like one of my children's make-believe stories, the last months of his life, in which I call him and his voice lights up and before I can ask how he is, he asks me how I'm doing and how the kids are, calling them by name. Sometimes he doesn't remember we live in Philadelphia, but he always asks if we've gotten a dog yet. We do finally get one, a thick-haired, big-headed puppy, and this pleases him. He is always kind to me on the phone, but occasionally he lifts his mouth away from the receiver and uses his scraped voice to hurl a string of swears at someone, Barbara or the nurse they've hired to help him get around. Barbara says he gets frustrated that he can't do the things he used to do. She says this as if it's new, this quick, vulgar temper. She would like me to visit, but I prefer the polite phone calls.

The last of our conversations is on election night. Jonathan and I stay home to watch the returns. He doesn't want to watch the results with anyone else. His mother is having a "victory party" across town, but he thinks it's tempting fate and refuses to go. I've never known him to be superstitious, but in the days leading up to November fourth, everything to him is unlucky, inauspicious. Since Iowa, we have both devoted our time to the Obama cam-paign, making calls at night, dragging our children door-to-door on weekends. He has had to eat all his words. Garvey has made sure of that.

When the first results come in and Virginia and Indiana look like they are going for McCain, Jonathan threatens to shut off the TV.

"You see? You see? It's all been a naive fantasy that this guy could win in this country!"

Lena and Jeremy tell him to sit down and hush up. I hold his hand. I pray. I have started praying, short little flares of petition and gratitude. It's hard not to believe in something when your heart gets stuffed full. And then they go, one by one: Pennsylvania, Ohio, Florida, all for Obama. When he is declared the next president of the United States, we all leap up at the same time, as if someone has yanked us up, and fall into each other, arms tangled, and for that moment we are one organism, whole, bound in awe. I can barely believe this is our world. Jonathan holds me hard, long after the kids have let go, his body shaking, and even Jeremy doesn't try to pry us apart. "It feels so good," he moans. We are still crying, and I send up a flare of deepest thanks. I hold my husband. I feel so close to him, a part of him, and yet I feel, too, how separate our experience of this moment really is. I have become closer, and more apart, from him, from Lena and Jeremy, on this night.

The phone rings a few minutes later. I figure it's Jonathan's mother or one of his brothers, or Garvey, or Julie and Michael.

"You up?" His speech is better, as if he has just two marbles in his mouth instead of ten.

"We are definitely up."

"Jonathan there?"

"Right here."

"Kids too?"

"Yup."

"Good. They should be."

"It's late."

"Nearly eleven-thirty. I gotta get some sleep for chrissake. You stay out of trouble, okay?"

"You too, Dad."

"I can't get into trouble anymore."

"That's probably a good thing."

"That Jeremy. You tell him he could be president one day."

"Or Lena."

He laughs. "Or Lena. Christ. Isn't that something."

"It *is* something, Dad. It really is."

Three days later it's Barbara who calls. Another stroke.

He was quiet when he went, she says. He didn't make a sound.